THE SCARLET LETTER

---

by Nathaniel Hawthorne

A Longman Annotated Edition

Gert Coleman, Editor
Middlesex County College

PEARSON
Longman

New York San Francisco Boston
London Toronto Sydney Tokyo Singapore Madrid
Mexico City Munich Paris Cape Town Hong Kong Montreal

Acquisitions Editor: Kate Edwards
Series Editor: Yvonne Collioud Sisko
Marketing Manager: Thomas DeMarco
Production Manager: Denise Phillip
Text Design: Jonathan Lippincott
Project Coordination and Electronic Page Makeup: TexTech International
Illustrations: Adam Bridgewater
Cover Design Manager: Wendy Ann Fredericks
Cover Photo: © The Everett Collection, Inc.
Senior Manufacturing Buyer: Dennis J. Para
Printer and Binder: R. R. Donnelley & Sons / Harrisonburg
Cover Printer: R. R. Donnelley & Sons / Harrisonburg

Library of Congress Cataloging-in-Publication Data

Hawthorne, Nathaniel, 1804–1864.
    The scarlet letter / by Nathaniel Hawthorne; Gert Coleman, editor; illustrations
by Adam Bridgewater.—A Longman annotated ed.
      p. cm.
    Includes index.
    ISBN-13: 978-0-205-53252-0
    ISBN-10:   0-205-53252-7
      1. Boston (Mass.)—History—Colonial period, ca. 1600–1775—Fiction.
    2. Triangles (Interpersonal relations)—Fiction.   3. Illegitimate children—
    Fiction.   4. Women immigrants—Fiction.   5. Married women—Fiction.
    6. Puritans—Fiction.   7. Adultery—Fiction.   8. Revenge—Fiction.
    9. Clergy—Fiction.   I. Coleman, Gert.   II. Title.
    PS1868.A2C 2008
    813'.3—dc22   2007025577

Please visit us at www.ablongman.com

ISBN-13: 978-0-205-53252-0
ISBN-10:   0-205-53252-7

1 2 3 4 5 6 7 8 9 10—DOH—10 09 08 07

To my loving and supportive family—
Peter, Lorraine, and Ian Coleman

CONTENTS

FOREWORD

I hope that you and your students enjoy reading *The Scarlet Letter* as much as I have enjoyed discovering, rediscovering, and working with the novel. The richness of the novel speaks for itself. While the archaic language may seem strange at first, you will soon get used to its patterns and cadence as Hawthorne takes you back to Puritan New England in the mid-seventeenth century for a tale of obsession, revenge, and redemption.

High on content and pedagogy, this edition offers many options and ideas for discussion, group work, and writing projects while reinforcing reading comprehension skills. Every sentence, every phrase, every word is most carefully and purposely weighed to ensure maximum productivity in teacher- and student-friendly materials.

As coordinator of basic reading instruction, I introduced literature as a very successful component of our syllabus. The reading faculty began a tradition of sharing lessons and pedagogy to engage developmental readers and give options to new and seasoned faculty members. I wish to express much gratitude to my wonderful colleagues: Lucille Alfieri, Jim Bernarducci, Leah Ghiradella, Evelyn Honey, Kristen Honey, Andrew Kistulentz, Georgiana Planko, Renee Price, Ellen Shur, Helena Swanicke, and Shirley Wachtel.

Special thanks go to colleague, friend, and mentor, Yvonne Sisko, author of *Looking at Literature* and several other texts, for her encouragement and support all these years and, in particular, for this project. I also deeply thank my writing circle—Gail Wood Miller, Louise McCallum, and Michaele Basciano—for their encouragement and friendship.

And, much gratitude, of course, goes to my husband Peter, daughter Lorraine, and son Ian, who asked good questions, proofread when I needed it, and waited for their turns on the computer. I sincerely appreciate their love, encouragement, humor, and support. Special thanks also to illustrator Adam Bridgewater for his fine illustrations.

Gert Coleman

PREFACE

To the Student

It seems that human beings have always loved a good story. In fact, anthropologists tell us that storytelling has been used to teach rules and ideas for millenia. This book will take you on an adventure as you read a full-length novel.

However, the Longman Annotated Edition of Hawthorne's *The Scarlet Letter* is designed to do more than simply take you on an adventure. Each chapter is surrounded with exercises that will help you better understand each chapter and the novel as a whole. First, the book begins with an Author's Biography that introduces you to the author and gives you information that is helpful in reading the novel. Then, each chapter includes:

- **Vocabulary Exercises**—Vocabulary exercises help you define the words you need to know for each chapter, before you even read it.
- **Questions**—Questions help guide you through each chapter.
- **Journal**—After reading, you can record and organize your thoughts in a journal.
- **Follow-up Questions**—You can demonstrate what you have learned in follow-up questions.
- **Discussion Questions**—You can offer your opinions here.
- **Writing Ideas**—At specific places in the book, there are writing ideas to help guide your writing.

To understand better how this book works, turn to the Sample Lesson on page 1 and work your way through it. You'll find that you will be actively participating in this book, which will make understanding and appreciating the novel easier and more rewarding for you.

Welcome to the novel! Read this book, study it, and—most of all—enjoy it.

To the Teacher

The greatest assets of this series are its participatory lessons and the many options these lessons offer you. Certainly, the novel is the core of this book, but the pedagogical materials that surround every chapter, every chapter group, and even conclude the novel require the students to actively participate in the book from beginning to end. Simultaneously, these materials offer you multiple choices of administratively efficient diagnostic and assessment tools. Each chapter is a self-contained lesson, and all the chapters, chapter groups, and end materials are consistently formatted, thereby offering students clear expectations and offering you multiple options.

Sample Lesson

This book begins with an applied **Sample Lesson.** The Sample Lesson can be used in class, or it can be assigned as homework. Written in simple and accessible language, this introductory lesson walks students through basic narrative components, using Kate Chopin's short story "Ripe Figs" as an example. This lesson, as well as all lessons, opens with Pre-Reading Vocabulary—Context, and Pre-Reading Vocabulary—Structural Attack to help students define important words used in each chapter before they read the chapter. Then Pre-Reading Questions are posed to add purpose for the students.

While reading "Ripe Figs," students learn notation strategies that they can then apply to each chapter. With the story completed, students move on to the Journal exercises, which are comprehensive and participatory studies of the story. The Sample Lesson explains the tasks in each Journal section, offers sample answers to get students started, and introduces relevant literary terminology.

With the Journal completed, students now have an active, working understanding of "Ripe Figs." They can then move on to the three sets of Follow-up Questions. These questions consistently use multiple assessment formats: (1) multiple-choice questions objectively assessing comprehension, (2) significant quotations subjectively assessing comprehension, and (3) essay questions subjectively assessing comprehension. Discussion Questions encourage debate and can be discussed or written. Each chapter group ends with Writing suggestions. In the Sample Lesson, students are introduced to pre-writing and outlining strategies. At the end of each chapter group, students will find multiple writing prompts.

I suggest that you work through the Sample Lesson in class, for it is here that you will find the dynamics and possibilities of this book encapsulated.

Pedagogical Structure

Each chapter in the novel is set amid carefully designed teaching materials and, because the format is consistent, you will be able to find material easily. These materials were discussed generally in the overview of the Sample Lesson above, but here we look at the materials more closely.

Pre-Reading Materials Each chapter begins with pre-reading materials. The pre-reading materials prepare students for reading while offering you insights into their vocabulary mastery and study habits.

Pre-Reading Vocabulary—Context presents words that are crucial to understanding the chapter. These words have been chosen to make the reading accessible to students and may or may not be the most sophisticated words in the chapter. These are, very simply, the words students will need to know to understand the chapter.

Pre-Reading Vocabulary—Structural Attack offers structural analysis exercises. These words have been chosen not for their sophistication, but because they help students apply structural analysis skills. Thus, before students start the chapter, they have defined at least 20 words in context and 10 to 30 words by structural analysis. The need for distracting glossed words and marginal definitions is thereby eliminated because students are well prepared by the pre-reading vocabulary to attack the chapter.

Third, **Pre-Reading Questions** offer food for thought as students enter each chapter.

The Novel

This is the full and accepted text for this novel. No words or sentences have been shortened or simplified. This is the real thing. The only changes concern offensive words, which have been very carefully weighed and elided or removed.

Journal

After students have read and annotated the chapter, the **Journal** then draws them into active reflection and participation.

- **MLA Works Cited**—Students record the novel in MLA Works Cited entry format, using the generic model provided.
- **Main Character(s)**—Students separate, describe, and defend the character(s) they have selected as main character(s) (applying and reinforcing the separation of main ideas from supporting details).
- **Supporting Characters**—Students separate, describe, and defend the characters they have selected as supporting characters (applying and reinforcing the separation of main ideas from supporting details).
- **Setting**—Students describe the setting and any relevant prop(s) (applying and reinforcing inference skills).
- **Sequence**—Students outline the chapter's events in order (applying and reinforcing the separation of major ideas from minor details, sequencing skills, and outlining skills).
- **Plot**—Students summarize the chapter's events in no more than five sentences (applying and reinforcing the separation of main ideas from supporting details and summarizing skills).
- **Conflicts**—Students identify and explain the relevant conflicts (applying and reinforcing inference and judgment skills).
- **Significant Quotations**—Students explain the importance of selected quotations that are central to the chapter (applying and reinforcing inference and judgment skills).
- **Recap**—Students reflect upon and summarize the novel's progression of events (applying and reinforcing summarizing and synthesizing skills).

- **Foreshadowing, irony, or symbolism**—There may be a section to discuss foreshadowing, irony, or symbolism. Students explain foreshadowing, irony, or symbolism as relevant (applying and reinforcing inference and judgment skills).

The Journal is a comprehensive cognitive workout for students. In the Journal, students reflect on the chapter, sort out the details, and organize the chapter's components while applying and/or reinforcing the many skills noted above. You can collect any and all of the Journal components you assign. The wealth of diagnostic information in the Journal will enable you to spot misunderstandings, illogical thinking, and so forth, that may compromise comprehension. Requiring a completed Journal for classroom participation also assures you that students are prepared to discuss the chapter.

Follow-up Questions

The Journal is followed by three follow-up question formats. The **Follow-up Questions** are designed for individual assessment, but can also be used for small-group or class discussion. All of these questions are intended to measure comprehension; they purposely avoid literary controversy.

- **Short Questions** offers multiple-choice questions.
- **Significant Quotations** ask students to explain the importance of quotations that are always central to the chapter and usually are different from the quotations in the Journal.
- **2 Comprehension Essay Questions** provides two essay prompts.

The Follow-up Questions offer you multiple, efficient assessment options. You may decide to use some questions for discussion or some for testing. If you are trying to establish standardization, the Short Questions are applicable for standardization, measuring comprehension efficiently by presenting at least six questions with three choices each.

Discussion Questions

Each chapter provides two thought-provoking questions. Unlike the Follow-up Questions, **Discussion Questions** encourage reflection, personal opinion, and/or literary debate. Again, you may choose to have students discuss these or to have students write their answers.

Writing Prompts

Each chapter group concludes with options for **Writing**. Here, at least two prompts for personal writing are included. Then, under **Further Writing**, you will find prompts for more advanced, research-oriented writing. These prompts may be literary (compare and contrast this character with another character in this book, with another character in another work, and so forth) or topical research suggestions.

Parts of the Book

Each chapter has a full complement of pedagogical materials, from pre-materials through discussion questions. However, in order to offer you even more options, chapters are also organized into chapter groups that include the full complement of all post-materials, including the writing prompts. Finally, the book ends with culminating post-materials that apply to the novel as a whole.

First, this offers you logistical options. Because the novel's chapters may not fit well into your quarter, trimester, or semester, you have many options. You may choose to assign the novel chapter by chapter. You may choose to assign the first chapters individually and then assign the remainder of the novel in chapter groups. You may choose to assign given chapters individually and then other chapters in groups. Or you may choose to assign the novel as a whole. Thus, the wealth of pedagogical materials here offers you multiple options in adapting this book to meet your logistical needs.

Second, the comprehensive pedagogical materials offer you many teaching options. You may assign all the pedagogy surrounding each chapter, or you may assign just the pre-material for each chapter and combine this with the post-material for each chapter group, or any other combinations therein. You may assign discussion questions for writing, and writing questions for discussion. You may assign journal exercises for individual work or for group work. The rich and comprehensive materials in this book make this book highly adaptable and, therein, offer you multiple options.

We hope you enjoy using this book as much as we have enjoyed producing it. Other title in the Longman Annotated Edition series include Bram Stoker's *Dracula*, Mary Shelley's *Frankenstein*, Stephen Crane's *The Red Badge of Courage*, and Agatha Christie's *The Secret Adversary*. Please note that natural complements to this series are the stories offered in the books in the Longman Literature for College Readers Series. These books include *American 24-Karat Gold*, which is a collection of 24 classic American short stories; *A World of Short Stories*, which is a collection of 18 short stories from around the world; *Looking at Literature*, which is a collection of 12 short stories, a play, and a novel; and *Sterling Stories*, which is a collection 12 highly accessible short stories.

Yvonne Collioud Sisko

A SAMPLE LESSON

Ripe Figs
by
Kate Chopin

The best way to learn how to use something is to do just that—to use it. This Sample Lesson presents a very short work, "Ripe Figs" by Kate Chopin, to demonstrate how this book works. This Sample Lesson presents all the materials that surround each chapter. Generally, each chapter starts with pre-reading activities that are designed to make your reading easier, and ends with a journal, follow-up questions, and discussion questions that are designed to improve your understanding. Then, chapter groups end with a more expansive journal, follow-up questions, discussion questions, and writing assignments, all again designed to improve your understanding. This Sample Lesson also introduces the elements of a narrative—elements that you will be using throughout this book.

Let's begin.

RIPE FIGS

KATE CHOPIN

PRE-READING VOCABULARY
CONTEXT

Use context clues to define these words before reading. Use a dictionary as needed.

> The words that are critical for your understanding of the chapter are presented at the beginning of each chapter. These are not necessarily the most difficult words. Rather, they are words that you will need to know to understand the chapter more easily.
>
> The **Pre-reading Vocabulary—Context** exercises present words in sentences. You should try to define each word by using the **context clues** in the sentence. Note that the first eight words have been defined as examples for you. Look at question 1. The word here is "fig," and the clues let you know that this is something "small" and "purple" that grows "on a tree" and is "delicious." Since "delicious" implies it is something to eat and since fruit grows on a tree, we can define a "fig" as "a small, purple fruit that grows on a tree." Using this same strategy, check the meanings of the next seven words. Then use the clues and define the remaining words.

1. The small, purple *figs* grow on a tree and are delicious. *Fig* means <u>a small, purple fruit that grows on a tree</u>.

2. Some may say "mom" or "mama" for "mother," while the French may say "*mère*" or "*maman*." *Mère* or *maman* means <u>a name for "mother"</u>.

3. The campers rowed their boat slowly through the reeds along the side of the *bayou*. *Bayou* means <u>a slow moving body of water</u>.

4. The children licked the long *sugar cane* they found in the field. *Sugar cane* means <u>a stick-like food</u>.

5. The elderly person's fingers seemed to cross each other in *gnarled* knots from old age and arthritis. *Gnarled* means <u>knotted or crisscrossed</u>.

6. Ted is so *patient*; he doesn't mind if Laura takes two hours to do her hair. *Patient* means <u>willing to wait</u>.

7. There is a stone *statue* of a little boy in the middle of the garden. *Statue* means <u>a carved or sculpted figure</u>.

8. The tiny *humming-bird's* wings moved so quickly that you could not see them. *Humming-bird* means <u>a small bird with rapidly moving wings</u>.

9. José was *disconsolate* after he lost the championship game. *Disconsolate* means _____.

10. Kings and queens usually walk in a very upright and *stately* manner. *Stately* means _____.

11. Furniture is often first covered in a simple *muslin* under the fine *fabric* to protect the fabric. *Muslin* means _____.

12. The haze of color often drawn around a saint's head is called a halo or *aureole*. *Aureole* means _____.

13. In spite of all the upset and confusion, Luis stayed cool and *placid*. *Placid* means _____.

14. The bride's dishes are fine *porcelain* decorated with tiny flowers and trimmed in gold. *Porcelain* means _____.

15. I will go to see my aunt, *Tante* Lena, to celebrate her birthday. *Tante* means _____.

16. I love the large yellow *chrysanthemums* that bloom in a fall garden. *Chrysanthemum* means _____.

PRE-READING VOCABULARY
STRUCTURAL ATTACK

Define these words by solving the parts. Use the Glossary or a dictionary as needed.

The **Pre-reading Vocabulary—Structural Attack** exercises present words that you know but that may look strange or have altered meanings because of added parts. Here you will want to look for and define the **root** or core, word. Then look for and define the **prefix,** or part added to the front of the word. Finally, look for and define the **suffix,** or part added to the end of the word.

Prefixes (added to the front) and suffixes (added to the end) are called **affixes.** By defining the root and the affixes, you should be able to define each of these words with little trouble. For instance, look at the first vocabulary word. The very simple word "ripe" has two suffixes (-en, -ing) that can be added to it, which change the word's meaning from "ready" or "mature" to "getting ready" or "maturing." Or look at the fourth word. Here two words form a new word. This is called a **compound word**. "Summer" and "time" combine to mean "the warm part of the year." Using this same strategy, take each word apart, and define it by using the roots and affixes. The next two words are defined for you also. Try the last three on your own. See the Glossary (page 355) for affix definitions.

1. ripening becoming ripe or mature
2. la Madone mother or Holy Mother
3. restless active; cannot rest
4. summertime
5. godmother
6. plumpest

PRE-READING QUESTIONS

Try answering these questions as you read.

Now that you have defined words that might otherwise prevent you from understanding the reading, you are ready to turn to the narrative. Before reading, it is always helpful to start with a purpose. Use the reading's title and any other relevant information to set up questions to answer while you are reading. Answering these questions will make your reading easier and more efficient, so that you do not have to reread and reread to understand the narrative.

Each reading starts with **Pre-reading Questions** to set your purpose. Keep these questions in mind as you read.

Who are the main characters? Supporting characters?
What does Babette want?
What does Maman want?
What does the title mean?

RIPE FIGS

KATE CHOPIN

To begin, a brief **biography** provides some information about the author. In addition to learning about the author's life, you may also pick up information that will help you in reading the narrative. The biography may also list other works by the author, in case you would like to read more by that author.

Here, read Kate Chopin's biography. It tells you, among other things, that she writes about the people she met in Louisiana and that she likes to use "symbols and images from nature." Both of these pieces of information will come in handy as you read "Ripe Figs."

Kate O'Flaherty Chopin was born in St. Louis in 1851 to an affluent family. Although her father died when she was young, her widowed mother gave young Kate a taste of independence. In 1870 Kate married Oscar Chopin and moved to New Orleans and then Natchitoches Parish. Here she met the Creoles, Acadians, and African Americans she would later write about. However, Oscar died in 1882, and by 1884 she sold the plantation, gathered her five children, and returned home to St. Louis, where she began to write for popular women's magazines. Influenced noticeably by Guy de Maupassant's sense of irony and Henrik Ibsen's social comment, Chopin wrote stories, often touched with rich symbols and images from nature, that question societal assumptions and dictates. The Awakening remains her master work, although short stories such as "Desiree's Baby" and "The Kiss" offer Chopin at her most terse. Chopin died in 1904.

Now it is time to turn to the reading. As you read, keep the following suggestions in mind. Don't just let your eyes go over words. Instead, *get involved—get out a pen or pencil and highlighters, and use them!*

1. First, *circle the name of each character*, or highlight each in a different color. The first step in understanding a narrative is knowing *whom* it is about.
2. Second, underline or highlight in yet another color all the hints that let you know *where and when the narrative takes place*. The second step in understanding a narrative is knowing *where* and *when* it takes place.
3. Third, *number each event* in the narrative as it occurs. Number these events in the margin or right in the text. The third step in understanding a narrative is knowing *what* is happening.
4. Fourth, *make notes*—ideas, questions to be answered later, and so on—in the margin. These are ideas you can return to later, and they may help you understand the *how* and/or *why* of the narrative.
5. Fifth, but certainly not least, always *reread the title*. The title often gives you information that is helpful in understanding the narrative.

Maman-Nainaine said that when the figs were ripe Babette might go to visit her cousins down on the Bayou-Lafourche where the sugar cane grows. Not that the ripening of figs had the least thing to do with it, but that is the way Maman-Nainaine was.

2 It seemed to Babette a very long time to wait; for the leaves upon the trees were tender yet, and the figs were like little hard, green marbles.

3 But warm rains came along and plenty of strong sunshine, and though Maman-Nainaine was as patient as the statue of la Madone, and Babette as

restless as a humming-bird, the first thing they both knew it was hot summer-time. Every day Babette danced out to where the fig-trees were in a long line against the fence. She walked slowly beneath them, carefully peering between the gnarled, spreading branches. But each time she came away disconsolate again. What she saw there finally was something that made her sing and dance the whole day long.

4   When Maman-Nainaine sat down in her stately way to breakfast, the following morning, her muslin cap standing like an aureole around her white, placid face, Babette approached. She bore a dainty porcelain platter, which she set down before her godmother. It contained a dozen purple figs, fringed around with their rich, green leaves.

5   "Ah," said Maman-Nainaine arching her eyebrows, "how early the figs have ripened this year!"

6   "Oh," said Babette. "I think they have ripened very late."

7   "Babette," continued Maman-Nainaine, as she peeled the very plumpest figs with her pointed silver fruit-knife, "you will carry my love to them all down on Bayou-Lafourche. And tell your Tante Frosine I shall look for her at Toussaint— when the chrysanthemums are in bloom."

Now turn to the marked copy of "Ripe Figs" in Figure 1. The first half has already been noted for you. Take out your pen, pencil, and/or highlighters, and using the strategies listed above, complete the notes on "Ripe Figs." Note how effective the notations in Figure 1 are. It's important to know that Chopin uses nature to reflect life, so this is underlined in the biography. The title is "Ripe Figs," so figs (which are a delicate fruit) must somehow relate to the story. Babette and Maman-Nainaine are in the center of the story, and the cousins and Tante Frosine are also involved. Hints like "figs" and "Bayou," as well as information in the biography, all indicate that this story is probably taking place in the South, in Louisiana. The events are numbered in sequence: (1) Babette wants to go visiting, but Maman says not yet; (2) Babette must wait for the figs to ripen; (3) the figs ripen, and Babette now can go; and (4) Maman will go in the fall. Now it is easier to see that two things are ripening or maturing here: Babette and the figs. Thus, the ripening figs reflect Babette's maturing. When the figs are ripe, she is also ripe, or mature enough to go visiting. By using the information from the biography and title and combining this information with the story's characters, setting, and events, you can see that as the figs ripen, Babette grows older and becomes ready to travel. Add your own notes in paragraphs 4 through 7.

FIGURE 1
Marked Copy of "Ripe Figs"

Ripe Figs

KATE CHOPIN

Kate O'Flaherty Chopin was born in St. Louis in 1851 to an affluent family. Although her father died when she was young, her widowed mother gave young Kate a taste of independence. In 1870 Kate married Oscar Chopin and moved to New Orleans and then Natchitoches Parish. Here she met the Creoles, Acadians, and African Americans she would later write about. However, Oscar died in 1882, and by 1884 she sold the plantation, gathered her five children, and returned home to St. Louis, where she began to write for popular women's magazines. Influenced noticeably by Guy de Maupassant's sense of irony and Henrik Ibsen's social comment, Chopin wrote stories, often touched with rich symbols and <u>images from nature,</u> that question societal assumptions and dictates. Her brief novel <u>The Awakening</u> remains her master work, although stories such as "Desiree's Baby" and "The Kiss" offer Chopin at her most terse. Chopin died in 1904.

Maman-Nainaine said that when the figs were ripe Babette might go to visit her cousins down on the <u>Bayou-Lafourche</u> where the <u>sugar cane grows</u>. Not that the ripening of figs had the least thing to do with it, but that is the way Maman-Nainaine was.   *1. CAN VISIT WHEN FIGS RIPEN*

2   It seemed to Babette a very long time to wait, for the leaves upon the trees were tender yet, and the figs were like little hard, green marbles.

3   But <u>warm rains</u> came along and plenty of <u>strong sunshine</u>, and though Maman-Nainaine was as patient as the statue of la Madone, and Babette as restless as a humming-bird, the first thing they both knew it was <u>hot summertime</u>. Every day Babette danced out to where the fig-trees were in a long line against the fence. She walked slowly beneath them, carefully peering between the gnarled, spreading branches. But each time she came away disconsolate again. What she saw there finally was something that made her sing and dance the whole day long.   *2. WAIT FOR FIGS TO GROW*

4   When Maman-Nainaine sat down in her stately way to breakfast, the following morning, her muslin cap standing like an aureole around her white, placid face, Babette approached. She bore a dainty porcelain platter, which she set down before her godmother. It contained a dozen purple figs, fringed around with their rich, green leaves.

5   "Ah," said Maman-Nainaine arching her eyebrows, "how early the figs have ripened this year!"

6   "Oh," said Babette. "I think they have ripened very late."

7   "Babette," continued Maman-Nainaine, as she peeled the very plumpest figs with her pointed silver fruit-knife, "you will carry my love to them all down on Bayou-Lafourche. And tell your Tante Frosine I shall look for her at Toussaint—when the chrysanthemums are in bloom."

RIPE FIGS

JOURNAL

Once you have finished reading and making your notes on the reading, the **Journal** allows you to record and organize all the relevant information. Here you will be able to record, to organize, to reflect upon, and to make sense of all the details that can make a reading challenging.

1. MLA Works Cited *Using this model, record this book.*
   Author's Last Name, First Name. "Title of the Story." <u>Title of This Book</u>.
   Ed. First Name Last Name. City: Publisher, year. Pages of the story.

Whenever you refer to or use anyone else's words or ideas, you must give that person credit. Failing to give credit is called **plagiarism**. Plagiarism can result in failing an assignment, failing a course, and even being removed from school.

   To give credit appropriately, it is helpful to learn the format used to credit works of literature. This format has been created by the Modern Language Association, or MLA. The **MLA Works Cited entry** you use here is the same basic form you will be using in your other English classes.

   The MLA entry is really a very simple form. All you have to do is follow the model given. Note that, unlike paragraphs, the first line starts at the left margin and each line *after* that is indented. Try doing this on your own. When you finish, your MLA Works Cited entry for "Ripe Figs" should look like the following:

   Chopin, Kate. "Ripe Figs." <u>The Scarlet Letter: Annotated Edition</u>. Ed. Gertrude Coleman.
      New York: Pearson Longman, 2008. 7.

However, in this book you are not only reading a short story but you will be reading a novel. The correct form for the novel that you will be reading throughout this book is this model:

   Author's Last Name, First Name. <u>Title of the Novel</u>. Year of the novel's first publi-
      cation. <u>Title of This Book</u>. Ed. First Name Last Name. City: Publisher, year.

Try following this model on your own. When you finish, your MLA Works Cited entry for the novel should look like this:

   Hawthorne, Nathaniel. <u>The Scarlet Letter</u>. 1850. <u>The Scarlet Letter: Annotated Edition</u>.
      Ed. Gertrude Coleman. New York: Pearson Longman, 2008.

2. Main Character(s)

Characters are the creatures that create, move, or experience the actions of a narrative. We normally think of characters as alive, animated beings, such as humans or animals, who can participate in the action, although some characters will surprise you. A character may also be called an **actor, player, person, personage,** or **persona.**

Characters fall into two categories: **main characters** and **supporting characters.** Generally, a main character is central to the action. A supporting character may encourage the action and is usually not present as much, or as central to the action, as the main character. Sometimes it is difficult to decide if a character is main or supporting. For instance, in a murder mystery, the victim may appear at the beginning or not at all, but the entire narrative is about solving her or his murder. Is the victim a main character because the entire narrative is all about her or him, or is s/he a supporting character because s/he is simply not around much? Both answers may be correct. In literature there are not always so much right or wrong answers as there are explanations, analyses, and debates. The correctness of your answers may depend on how well you explain your choices.

Characters may also be considered protagonists or antagonists. "Pro" means "for," and the **protagonist** is the hero or heroine, the character we **empathize** with or share feelings with, the character we root for. "Anti" means "against," and the **antagonist** is the villain, the enemy of the protagonist, the character we do not like, the character we root against. In "Ripe Figs," our sympathies are with Babette and her longing for adventure; she is the protagonist. Maman, who sets limits on Babette, is the antagonist. Here, these two characters are members of a seemingly close family and love each other, but in other narratives the protagonist and antagonist may not be such close relatives or friends.

The author speaks to us through her or his characters. When an author writes using "I" or "we," this is called a **first-person narrative.** The first-person makes a story very immediate. The character who tells the story is called the **narrator.** If the author addresses the reader directly using "you," this narrative technique is called a **second-person narrative.** Second-person is not used often today. Finally, if the author uses "he," "she," "it," or "they" to tell the narrative, this narrative technique is called a **third-person narrative.** This is the most common narrative form, with the author seeming to be more of an observer and less of a participant in the story. In "Ripe Figs," both Babette and Maman are observed as "she." The story is thus told in the third-person; the author is the narrator who observes but does not enter the narrative.

With these understandings, turn to the **Main Character(s)** and **Supporting Characters** entries in the Journal. Note that we have already filled in Babette, briefly describing her and noting her important place in the story. Who else should be here? Add an entry in which you describe and defend Maman as a main character.

Note: When discussing literature, always use the present tense. Although a narrative may have been written a thousand years ago, each time a narrative is read the characters and actions come to life and are alive right now, so keep your discussion of the characters and events in the present tense.

Describe each main character, and explain why you think each is a main character.

Babette is a young girl who lives with her godmother and wants to go visit her cousins. She is a main character because the story is about her wants and her godmother's rules.

3. Supporting Characters

Now fill in the **Supporting Characters** entry. This has been started for you. Certainly, the cousins support the action because they are the reason Babette wants to travel. Who else should be here? Add an entry in which you describe and defend Tante Frosine as a supporting character. Remember from your context studies that "tante" means "aunt," so Tante Frosine is probably the cousins' mother.

Describe each supporting character, and explain why you think each is a supporting character.

Babette's cousins are supporting characters. Although we never see them, they are the reason for the story's conflict.

4. Setting

Setting is a catch-all term that describes the **time, place,** and surroundings of a narrative. In a short story, the setting is usually, although not always, limited. The story usually takes place in a shorter amount of time than in a longer work, and fewer places are involved. In a novel, there may be more time and more places.

Props go along with the setting. Props (short for "properties") are the inanimate objects in a narrative. Props sometimes take on the qualities of characters.

Now turn to the **Setting** entry. You already have a head start because the place, Louisiana, is described. But you still have several things to do. First, you need to add when the story takes place. Check the biography for when Chopin lived, and remember that traveling seems to be a very big accomplishment in this story, unlike it is in today's world of easy car transportation. Second, think about props and mention the figs, which are certainly part of this story.

Describe the setting(s) and any relevant prop(s).

This must be set in the South because figs are a delicate fruit, because the French words sound like words spoken in Louisiana, and because the biography says that Chopin wrote about the South.

5. Sequence

A narrative is based around a simple skeleton of events called a **plot**. Around this basic plot, a logical order of events or **sequence** occurs that builds tension or in mysteries, suspense. In narratives we call all the events in the sequence a **story line**. The plot is the bare framework, while the sequence supplies the details that make each narrative unique.

Have you ever gone to the movies and watched the end credits roll while you were still waiting for the movie to get going? You looked at the person sitting next to you, felt cheated, and asked, "What happened?" What happened is that, somewhere along the line, the storyteller failed.

In a well-written narrative, one event logically leads to another, and then to another, and so on, so that each word and action counts and builds tension that carries your interest. The tension peaks at the **climax** and then resolves in the **dénouement**. When any of these pieces are missing, poorly developed, or unbelievable, we are disappointed. (Movie sequels, in fact, purposely stop at the climax and before the dénouement so that we will return for the next episode.) A very simple story line appears in Figure 2.

FIGURE 2
Simple Story Line

Use information about sequence and plot in the Journal. In the **Sequence** entry, you are asked to outline all the events in order. The outline is started for you, with Babette's desire to go visiting and Maman's restriction. Now look at your numbered notes on the story, and complete the outline. Add as many events as you feel are necessary.

Outline the events of the story in order.

   I. Babette wants to go visiting, but Maman-Nainaine says she must wait for the figs to ripen.

   II.

   III.

   IV.

6. Plot

Next, in the **Plot** entry, summarize all these events into one sentence. Summarizing makes you look back over the reading and reflect on what you have read. Remember, this is the bare framework of the narrative, so keep it short.

Tell the story in no more than one sentence.

7. Conflicts

Conflicts are the disagreements between the characters. Conflicts build the tension in a narrative. Many types of conflicts are possible. The conflict may be **human versus human,** as when a character(s) is pitted against another character(s). The conflict may be **human versus society,** as when a character(s) struggles against a group, community, or social structure. The conflict may be **human versus technology,** as when a character(s) vies with the tools of science or machines of her/his society. The conflict may be **human versus nature,** as when a character(s) battles with the forces of nature. The conflict may be **human versus the supernatural,** as when a character(s) vies with God or gods or demons. Finally, the conflict may be **human versus her/himself,** as when a character wrestles with her or his own internal and self-defeating **flaw.** More often than not, a story will contain a combination of these conflicts.

    Let's now turn to the **Conflicts** entry. Human versus human, in Babette's struggle with Maman's restriction, is already noted. What other types of conflicts are present in the story? How about human versus nature in Babette's wanting the figs to mature rapidly, and human versus herself in Babette's impatience? Add these and explain them in your Journal entry.

Identify and explain the conflicts involved here.

Human versus human applies to Babette wanting to go and Maman-Nainaine stopping her.

8. Significant Quotations

By now, you already understand the narrative well. You have identified the pieces and pulled them together. Now you need to reflect on the narrative. In this section, you will find quotations from key parts of the narrative. By explaining why each quotation is important to the reading, you can deepen your understanding.

First, look up the quotation in the reading text. Underline it and note what is important about this moment in the reading. Then, record the importance of this moment. Tell who is speaking and why this quotation is important to the action in the reading. The first one has been done for you. Now, complete the rest. Record the page number for practice with **MLA parenthetical citation**.

Explain the importance of each of these quotations. Record the page number in the parentheses.

a. "Maman-Nainaine said that when the figs were ripe Babette might go to visit her cousins down on the Bayou-Lafourche where the sugar cane grows" (7).

   This quotation sets the tension in the story between Babette and Maman-Nainaine and between Babette and nature. Babette wants to visit her cousins, but she must wait until the figs—and she—are ripe or mature enough to go.

b. "Every day Babette danced out to where the fig-trees were in a long line against the fence" (   ).

c. "What she saw there finally was something that made her sing and dance the whole day long" (   ).

d. " 'Ah,' said Maman-Nainaine arching her eyebrows, 'how early the figs have ripened this year!' " (   ).

e. " 'And tell your Tante Frosine I shall look for her at Toussaint—when the chrysanthemums are in bloom' " (   ).

9. Foreshadowing, Irony, or Symbolism

Other elements that may enhance a narrative are foreshadowing, irony, and symbolism.

Foreshadowing is a technique some authors use to help explain or predict events to come. The author may sprinkle information or hints throughout the narrative to help predict actions that are yet to happen.

Irony is found in the difference between what *is* and what *should be*. Irony may be bitter—you work and work, and someone new, who has done nothing, arrives at your job and gets the promotion you deserve. Irony may be humorous—you wake up late and race around knowing you will be late for class, only to get to school and find out that your class has been canceled. Irony may even be providential—you sleep in and miss your bus only to find out that the bus was in an accident and you are still safe at home. Think of ironies as unexpected twists in time, places, or events.

Symbols are objects or characters that represent something beyond their face value. For instance, an American flag is really nothing more than pieces of cloth sewn together, but the American flag represents the pride and glory and industry of America. By looking beyond the surface, you may find many symbols in literature.

In **Foreshadowing, Irony, or Symbolism,** you will often be asked to discuss one of these elements. Here, you are asked to discuss the symbols in this story, and there are several. First and foremost, the figs represent maturity and reflect Babette's growth. Second, the **seasons** are relevant here. Summer is youthful Babette's time, while fall is the older Maman's and Tante Frosine's time. In literature, spring may represent birth or rebirth or youth; summer may represent youth or the full blossom of life; fall may represent middle age; and winter may represent the later years. Here Chopin gives us clues to the characters' ages by using the seasons. The chrysanthemums (flowers that bloom in the fall) represent the time for Babette's elders.

Although foreshadowing and irony are not particularly relevant to this story, be aware that Kate Chopin is known for her ironic twists. And, of course, here the ripening figs foreshadow Babette's growth.

Identify and explain the symbols Kate Chopin uses.

FOLLOW-UP QUESTIONS

10 SHORT QUESTIONS

Follow-up questions are designed to measure your comprehension of each reading. In the first set of questions you will see multiple-choice entries aimed at measuring your comprehension.

Notice that you are instructed to "select the *best* answer." In some readings, more than one answer will be correct; it is your job to choose the *best* answer. The first five have been done for you here.

The answer to question 1 is "a" because Babette is the younger of the two. We know this because Babette's actions and the information from the story—Maman means "mother" and Maman is Babette's godmother—imply that Babette is younger and Maman is older. The answer to question 2 is "b" for the same reasons listed in the answer to question 1. The answer to question 3 is "c" because we are clearly told that Maman is the godmother. The cousins are in Babette's age group and are whom she wants to visit; there is no mention of a sister in the story. The answer to question 4 is "a" because, as the story implies, figs need a warm summer and rain to grow; neither "cold" nor "desert" fit the story's setting. The answer to question 5 is "c," because we are clearly told about Babette's "restlessness" as opposed to Maman's "patience."

Now complete questions 6 through 10 on your own. The correct answers appear on page 20.

Select the <u>best</u> answer for each.

<u>a</u> 1. Babette is
   a. younger than Maman.
   b. older than Maman.
   c. the same age as Maman.

<u>b</u> 2. Maman-Nainaine is
   a. younger than Babette.
   b. older than Babette.
   c. the same age as Babette.

<u>c</u> 3. Maman-Nainaine is Babette's
   a. sister.
   b. cousin.
   c. godmother.

<u>a</u> 4. "Ripe Figs" is probably set in
   a. a warm climate.
   b. a cold climate.
   c. a desert climate.

<u>c</u> 5. Babette
   a. does not wait for the figs.
   b. waits calmly for the figs.
   c. waits impatiently for the figs.

___ 6. Maman
   a. does not wait for the figs.
   b. waits calmly for the figs.
   c. waits impatiently for the figs.

___ 7. The figs symbolize
   a. Maman's maturing.
   b. Babette's maturing.
   c. Babette's cousins' maturing.

___ 8. We can infer that Maman is relatively
   a. poor.
   b. middle class.
   c. well off.

___ 9. We can infer that the cousins live
   a. nearby.
   b. a distance away.
   c. very, very far away.

___ 10. The chrysanthemums tell us that Maman is
   a. very young.
   b. very old.
   c. in her middle years.

5 SIGNIFICANT QUOTATIONS

Approach these **5 Significant Quotations** by reflecting on the reading. The quotations are important and central to the reading. Remember you are demonstrating how well you have understood the reading, so explain why each quotation is important as completely as you can.

The first quotation here has already been done for you. Now, explain the significance of the remaining four. (The answers are on page 20.)

Explain the importance of each of these quotations.

1. "Maman-Nainaine said that when the figs were ripe Babette might go to visit her cousins down on the Bayou-Lafourche where the sugar cane grows."
   This sentence sets the tension in the story between Babette and Maman-Nainaine and between Babette and nature. Babette wants to visit her cousins, but she must wait until the figs—and she—are ripe or mature enough.

2. "It seemed to Babette a very long time to wait [. . .]."

3. "But warm rains came along and plenty of strong sunshine, and though Maman-Nainaine was as patient as the statue of la Madone, and Babette as restless as a humming-bird, the first thing they knew it was hot summertime."

4. "It [the platter] contained a dozen purple figs, fringed around with their rich, green leaves."

5. " 'Babette,' continued Maman-Nainaine, as she peeled the very plumpest figs with her pointed silver fruit-knife, 'you will carry my love to them all down on Bayou-LaFourche.' "

2 COMPREHENSION ESSAY QUESTIONS

The **2 Comprehension Essay Questions** offer opportunities for extended essays. Your teacher may assign one or both for individual assignment or for group discussion. Gather your thoughts and respond, demonstrating what you have learned from the reading. Note that none of these questions asks how well you liked the reading or even if you liked it at all. The intention here is very simply to find out what you have understood in the reading.

Note that the directions ask you to "use specific details and information from the story." This does not mean that you have to memorize the reading, but it does mean that you should know the characters and events in the reading. Look at question 1. It asks you to explain the title, so for this essay question, you will want to review the story's events and the relevance of the figs. Now look at question 2. It asks you to focus on the ages involved in the story, and for this you will want to discuss the ages of Babette and her cousins as opposed to those of Maman and Tante Frosine, remembering the references to summer and fall in the story.

Use specific details and information from the story to answer these questions as completely as possible.

1. How does the title relate to the story? Explain the significance of the title using specific details and information from the story.
2. What is the relevance of age in this story? Use specific details and information from the story to support your explanation.

DISCUSSION QUESTIONS

Now that you have read and studied the narrative, **Discussion Questions** are two questions that are always focused on the narrative and that are designed to help you think about the narrative. Here, you may be asked to share your opinions or reactions to elements in the narrative. Notice that you are instructed to "be prepared to discuss these in class." Although your teacher may ask you to discuss these questions as a class or to write the answers independently, your thoughtful answers should reflect what you have learned about the reading. The first one has been started for you.

Here, you need to reflect on the story and on your own youth. You need to identify and explain what characteristics you think Babette possesses that are youthful. Of course, when one thinks of youth, one thinks of energy, and you might want to discuss Babette's activities that require lots of energy, such as being physically busy and active, surrounding oneself with busy friends, and so forth. Related to energy, one thinks of impatience when one thinks of youth, and you may want to discuss Babette's impatience with the figs and Maman and travelling. Finally, the curiosity to explore, or in this case to travel, may also be a sign of youth, and you may want to discuss Babette's desire to travel. Think if there is anything else you might want to add to question 1.

Then, reflect on the story and on your own observations of mature people. Complete question 2 on your own.

Be prepared to discuss these questions in class.

1. What characteristics mark Babette's youth?
   One characteristic of youth is having lots of energy. Babette is continually in motion, expending a great deal of physical energy. She is also looking forward to visiting with her cousins, and visiting also requires a great deal of energy. With all this energy, another characteristic of youth is impatience. Babette is impatient with Maman, wanting to speed the ripening of the figs to suit Maman's rules. Babette is also impatient with the figs themselves, as she spends much time and energy checking and wishing them into ripening. And Babette is impatient to travel. Curiosity and inquisitiveness are often associated with the young, and Babette has both the energy and the curiosity to look forward to this trip.
2. What characteristics mark Maman's maturity?

WRITING

Chapter groups end with a final section of **Writing** prompts. The first two prompts offer suggestions for personal writing. The prompts under Further Writing are designed with research in mind. These may suggest comparing and contrasting the reading with other readings in this book or with other narratives the author or another author has written, or they may suggest other research topics. Your teacher will guide you through the writing process.

At this point, a few words about the writing process are in order. Writing does not start with a pen or pencil; it starts with ideas. Before you start writing, jot down ideas, and then organize them. Here are two **pre-writing strategies** to get the ideas flowing:

1. On a clean sheet of paper, write one key word based on the topic you plan to write about. Now look at the key word, and start listing every word that this key word brings to mind. Avoid sentences or even phrases, as they take longer to write and can break your train of thought. Just write words—lots of words, the more the merrier. When you run out of words, look back at the key word, and write more words. When you finish, you will have a whole list of ideas to start thinking about for your essay. This process is called **free associating** or **brainstorming**.
2. On a clean sheet of paper, draw a circle. Inside that circle, write one key word from the topic you plan to write about. Now look at the key word, and start tagging other, related words onto the circle. Then tag words onto the tag words, and so on. When you get stuck, look back at the key word, and add more words. When you finish, you will have groups of words—ideas—to start thinking about for your essay. This process is called **grouping, networking, or clustering.**

Once you have the ideas—and you should have plenty from either of these prewriting strategies—the next step is to organize them into an **outline.** Do not worry about Roman numerals at this stage. Rather, develop logical groupings of these ideas into a working outline. You may find that there are words/ideas in your pre-write that you do not want to use. Cross these out. You may also find ideas in your outline that are out of place. Number and renumber the groups to make them work for you. (Your instructor may want you to formalize your outline later, but at this point the important thing is to find an organization that works for you.)

Look at the first writing prompt below. It asks you, first, to discuss one specific maturing process you have experienced and, second, to relate this process to a reflective image, much like the figs in our story. In Figure 3 both a cluster and an outline on the topic, "Getting a License," are demonstrated, but you may want to try "Learning to Ride a Bike" or "Graduating from High School" or any other maturing process you prefer.

FIGURE 3
Sample Cluster and Outline

To prepare the pre-writing cluster and outline shown in Figure 3, we first tagged ideas onto "License" and then tagged ideas onto ideas. Second, we looked for a logical order and numbered and renumbered the cluster. Third, we transferred these numbers into the informal, working outline. Finally, we looked back over what we had and decided that getting a license was like attending high school, because of all the preparation and responsibility involved in getting a license. With these ideas initiated and organized, we are now ready to write an intelligent and orderly essay.

Now try your hand at the other writing prompts.

Use each of these ideas for writing an essay.

1. We all go through maturing processes. Think of a specific process you have experienced. Then think of something that reflects your process, much like the figs reflect Babette's growth. Write an essay on your growing up process, relating it to a continuing symbol.
2. Age has an effect on all of us. Write about a specific incident when age affected you or someone you know.

FURTHER WRITING

1. Read Kate Chopin's "The Storm" (available in a library), and compare and contrast the images of nature in "The Storm" with those in "Ripe Figs."
2. Read Kate Chopin's "The Kiss" (available in a library), and compare the women in "The Kiss" and those in "The Storm."

ANSWERS TO
10 SHORT QUESTIONS

6. b. We are clearly told Maman is "patient" and not "impatient."
7. b. We know Babette is the one growing and "maturing."
8. c. Their genteel life, her leisurely breakfast, and the "silver fruit-knife" all imply wealth.
9. b. Bayou-Lafourche, in Louisiana, and Maman's reluctance to let Babette go at all both imply that this is, on the one hand, not "near by" and, on the other hand, not "very, very far away." The middle choice is the *best* choice here.
10. c. Again, we have discussed literary seasons and the middle choice is the *best* choice here. Spring or summer would refer to youth, and winter would refer to old age. Chrysanthemums are fall, and fall is middle age.

ANSWERS TO
5 SIGNIFICANT QUOTATIONS

2. You should note that this sets up the central tension of Babette having to wait for the figs to ripen so that she can go visiting.
3. You should comment on Babette's "restlessness" and Maman's patience. This is not an easy wait for Babette.
4. You should explain that this is the moment of climax. The figs are ripe. You should explain that the ripe figs represent Babette's maturing and she now is old enough/mature enough/ripe enough to travel to her cousins'.
5. You should note that this is the story's resolution, the dénouement. Babette may now travel.

Yvonne Collioud Sisko

THE SCARLET LETTER

NATHANIEL HAWTHORNE

Nathaniel Hawthorne (1804–1864) was born of New England Puritan ancestry in Salem, Massachusetts. The Puritan influence and his response to it are evident in many of his works, particularly The Scarlet Letter and The House of Seven Gables. Nathaniel Hawthorne added a "w" to his name to distance himself from his stern Puritan ancestors, particularly Judge John Hathorne, who sentenced many people to death during the 1692 Salem witchcraft trials.

Hawthorne attended Bowdoin College in Maine, becoming friends with Franklin Pierce, later the fourteenth president of the United States, and American poet Henry Wadsworth Longfellow. Barely able to make a living as a writer, Hawthorne accepted political appointments from his friends, working at both the Boston and Salem custom houses, and later traveling as an American consul to England. In 1846 when Hawthorne was appointed surveyor at the Salem Custom House where he determined the quantity and value of imported goods, he conceived the idea for The Scarlet Letter. Hawthorne's essay included in this book, "The Custom-House," satirizes the spoils system and depicts the transitory nature of such positions.

After a brief sojourn in 1841 at the Brook Farm Utopian Commune, he married Sophia Peabody in 1842. They had three children and lived mainly in New England, where they were neighbors to Transcendentalists Ralph Waldo Emerson and Henry David Thoreau in Concord, Massachusetts. Hawthorne's work embodies many of the Transcendentalist ideals, including an emphasis on nature and a philosophical preference for intuition over scientific and empirical explanation. Hawthorne's major works include Twice-Told Tales (1837), Mosses from an Old Manse (1846), The Scarlet Letter (1850), The House of Seven Gables (1851), The Blithedale Romance (1852), and The Marble Faun (1860).

The Scarlet Letter is a tale of obsession and revenge, conscience and consequences, and strength and weakness set in Puritan New England. This tale of redemption and love is set in the 1640s but told two hundred years later. Hester Prynne has been seen as a major heroine in American literature. Like Edgar Allan Poe, Hawthorne reveals a dark view of human nature in the depiction of his characters' hidden motivations, particularly Roger Chillingworth and Arthur Dimmesdale. His dark, introspective stories are set in colonial New England and address the moral and spiritual issues within society and the individual. Hawthorne psychologically explores universal themes such as hypocrisy (particularly of the Puritans), guilt, shame, and anxiety.

Editor's Note: Hawthorne's essay "The Custom-House" is always included with the text for <u>The Scarlet Letter</u>. However, "The Custom-House" is not necessary for understanding <u>The Scarlet Letter</u>. Therefore, "The Custom-House" is treated as a separate entity.

THE CUSTOM-HOUSE

PRE-READING VOCABULARY
CONTEXT

Use context clues to define these words before reading. Use a dictionary as needed.

1. Hawthorne's *autobiographical* essay is a personal account of his life and times. *Autobiographical* means _story written of someone person's life by that person_

2. The *revelation* scene occurs at the end of a murder mystery when the detective finally reveals the name of the murderer. *Revelation* means _concluding something revealed or disclosed_

3. Colleen is a wonderful doctor and always takes time to offer understanding and *sympathy* to her patients. *Sympathy* means _compassion sharing the feelings of another_.

4. Jimmy was so amazed by the number of buildings on the city street that he was not sure what *edifice* he was looking for. *Edifice* means _a building_ ____

5. The cold wind made Valerie *shudder* and shiver uncontrollably, so she went back into the house for warmer clothes. *Shudder* means _to tremble w/ a sudden convulsive movement_

6. The learned wisdom and great dignity of the judge made him a *venerable* person. *Venerable* means _respectable_ ____

7. The elderly man was old and *decrepit* and could hardly walk without assistance. *Decrepit* means _weakened_ ____

8. Christine's *ancestors* came to America one hundred years ago and settled in Texas. *Ancestors* means _a person from whom one is descended_.

9. When Haynes retired as director of the bank, he reviewed the duties and responsibilities with his *successor*, who took over the job from him. *Successor* means _a person who succeeds or follows next in the possition_.

10. The *Puritans* were a group of English Protestants in the sixteenth and seventeenth centuries who believed in strict laws and simplification of religious worship. *Puritans* means _one who lives in accordance w/ protestant precepts, especially one who regards pleasure or luxuryas sinful_.

11. The elderly dog was *accustomed* to sleeping on the couch and did not want to change his ways when we bought a new couch. *Accustomed* means _habituated_.

12. During her *incumbency*, the president made many speeches and passed many laws; after her *incumbency*, she returned to being a private citizen. *Incumbency* means _a duty or obligation job_.

13. When Barbara was a new teacher, she regularly asked the *veteran* teachers for advice and teaching tips. *Veteran* means _a person who has more experience in an occupation_.

14. Childhood is only a *transitory* state because it gives way to adulthood in a relatively short time. *Transitory* means _brief, short lived_.

15. Before the party, Isabelle *toiled* all day cleaning the house and weeding the garden. *Toil* means _exausting labor effort_.

16. The writer Nathaniel Hawthorne was a *descendant* of the Puritans who had settled in New England two hundred years earlier. *Descendant* means _____.

17. *Foolscap* is a size of paper in Britain that is slightly larger than standard American typing paper. *Foolscap* means _an offspring_.

18. Phyllis has the most *singular* laugh and no one else in the world can laugh the way she does. *Singular* means _unique/extraordinary_.

19. In an attempt to verify that her house was two hundred years old, Gert looked at the old maps and deeds in the town's historical *archives*. *Archives* means _a place were public records or other historical documents are kept_.

20. The Custom-House is a part of the *civil* government, dealing with social and economic issues like shipping and sea travel. *Civil* means _of the commonwealth or state._

PRE-READING VOCABULARY
STRUCTURAL ATTACK

Define these words by solving the parts. Use the Glossary or a dictionary as needed.

1. disinclined	21. flourished	41. valorous
2. indulge	22. corpsmen	42. dreary
3. intrusive	23. functionary	43. dignitaries
4. exclusive	24. dotage	44. festooned
5. emigrant	25. vicissitudes	45. gourmandism
6. spacious	26. abbreviate	46. decipherable
7. schooner	27. sagacious	47. antiquarian
8. barbed	28. vigilance	48. frayed
9. fiddler	29. alacrity	49. sacrilegious
10. tarnished	30. countenance	50. evaded
11. feebly	31. florid	51. cogitate
12. subsist	32. quaver	52. commodities
13. alms-houses	33. nonentity	53. unobtrusive
14. dingy	34. bygone	54. henceforth
15. slovenliness	35. detriment	55. methinks
16. sanctuary	36. customary	56. perchance
17. infirm	37. repose	57. tinged
18. quaintly	38. reprimand	58. folly
19. patriarchal	39. bipeds	59. irksome
20. severity	40. stalwart	60. attribute

PRE-READING QUESTIONS

Try answering these questions as you read.

Who are Nathaniel Hawthorne's ancestors?
How does he get his job at the Custom-House and what does he do there?
Who else works at the Custom-House?
What does he find?
Why does he leave the Custom-House?
How does this job affect his life as a writer?

PREFACE
To The Second Edition

Much to the author's surprise, and (if he may say so without additional offence) considerably to his amusement, he finds that his sketch of official life, introductory to THE SCARLET LETTER, has created an unprecedented excitement in the respectable community immediately around him. It could hardly have been more violent, indeed, had he burned down the Custom-House, and quenched its last smoking ember in the blood of a certain venerable personage, against whom he is supposed to cherish a peculiar malevolence. As the public disapprobation would weigh very heavily on him, were he conscious of deserving it, the author begs leave to say, that he has carefully read over the introductory pages, with a purpose to alter or expunge whatever might be found amiss, and to make the best reparation in his power for the atrocities of which he has been adjudged guilty. But it appears to him, that the only remarkable features of the sketch are its frank and genuine good-humor, and the general accuracy with which he has conveyed his sincere impressions of the characters therein described. As to enmity, or ill-feeling of any kind, personal or political, he utterly disclaims such motives. The sketch might, perhaps, have been wholly omitted, without loss to the public, or detriment to the book; but, having undertaken to write it, he conceives that it could not have been done in a better or a kindlier spirit, nor, so far as his abilities availed, with a livelier effect of truth.

The author is constrained, therefore, to republish his introductory sketch without the change of a word.

SALEM, *March 30, 1850*

THE CUSTOM-HOUSE

Introductory to "The Scarlet Letter"

It is a little remarkable, that—though disinclined to talk overmuch of myself and my affairs at the fireside, and to my personal friends—an autobiographical impulse should twice in my life have taken possession of me, in addressing the public. The first time was three or four years since, when I favored the reader— inexcusably, and for no earthly reason, that either the indulgent reader or the intrusive author could imagine—with a description of my way of life in the deep quietude of an Old Manse. And now—because, beyond my deserts, I was happy enough to find a listener or two on the former occasion—I again seize the public by the button, and talk of my three years' experience in a Custom-House. The example of the famous "P.P., Clerk of this Parish," was never more faithfully fol-lowed. The truth seems to be, however, that, when he casts his leaves forth upon the wind, the author addresses, not the many who will fling aside his volume, or never take it up, but the few who will understand him, better than most of his schoolmates and lifemates. Some authors, indeed, do far more than this, and indulge themselves in such confidential depths of revelation as could fittingly be addressed, only and exclusively, to the one heart and mind of perfect sympathy; as if the printed book, thrown at large on the wide world, were certain to find out the divided segment of the writer's own nature, and complete his circle of exis-tence by bringing him into communion with it. It is scarcely decorous, however, to speak all, even where we speak impersonally. But—as thoughts are frozen and utterance benumbed, unless the speaker stand in some true relation with his audience—it may be pardonable to imagine that a friend, a kind and apprehen-sive, though not the closest friend, is listening to our talk; and then, a native reserve being thawed by this genial consciousness, we may prate of the circum-stances that lie around us, and even of ourself, but still keep the inmost Me behind its veil. To this extent and within these limits, an author, methinks, may be autobiographical, without violating either the reader's rights or his own.

It will be seen, likewise, that this Custom-House sketch has a certain propri-ety, of a kind always recognized in literature, as explaining how a large portion of the following pages came into my possession, and as offering proofs of the authenticity of a narrative therein contained. This, in fact,—a desire to put myself in my true position as editor, or very little more, of the most prolix among the tales that make up my volume,—this, and no other, is my true reason for assuming a personal relation with the public. In accomplishing the main pur-pose, it has appeared allowable, by a few extra touches, to give a faint representa-tion of a mode of life not heretofore described, together with some of the characters that move in it, among whom the author happened to make one.

In my native town of Salem, at the head of what, half a century ago, in the days of old King Derby, was a bustling wharf,—but which is now burdened with decayed wooden warehouses, and exhibits few or no symptoms of commercial life; except, perhaps, a bark or brig, half-way down its melancholy length, discharging hides; or, nearer at hand, a Nova Scotia schooner, pitching out her cargo of firewood,—at the head, I say, of this dilapidated wharf, which the tide often over-flows, and along which, at the base and in the rear of the row of buildings, the track of many languid years is seen in a border of unthrifty grass,—here, with a view from its front windows adown this not very enlivening prospect, and thence across the harbour, stands a spacious edifice of brick. From the loftiest point of its roof, during precisely three and a half hours of each forenoon, floats or droops, in breeze or calm, the banner of the republic; but with the thirteen stripes turned vertically, instead of horizontally, and thus indicating that a civil, and not a mili-tary post of Uncle Sam's government, is here established. Its front is ornamented with a portico of half a dozen wooden pillars, supporting a balcony, beneath which a flight of wide granite steps descends towards the street. Over the entrance hovers an enormous specimen of the American eagle, with outspread wings, a shield before her breast, and, if I recollect aright, a bunch of intermingled thunderbolts and barbed arrows in each claw. With the customary infirmity of temper that characterizes this unhappy fowl, she appears, by the fierceness of her beak and eye and the general truculency of her attitude, to threaten mischief to the inoffensive community; and especially to warn all citizens, careful of their safety, against intruding on the premises which she overshadows with her wings. Nevertheless, vixenly as she looks, many people are seeking, at this very moment, to shelter themselves under the wing of the federal eagle; imagining, I presume, that her bosom has all the softness and snugness of an eider-down pillow. But she has no great tenderness, even in her best of moods, and, sooner or later,—oftener soon than late,—is apt to fling off her nestlings with a scratch of her claw, a dab of her beak, or a rankling wound from her barbed arrows.

The pavement round about the above-described edifice—which we may as well name at once as the Custom-House of the port—has grass enough growing in its chinks to show that it has not, of late days, been worn by any multitudi-nous resort of business. In some months of the year, however, there often chances a forenoon when affairs move onward with a livelier tread. Such occasions might remind the elderly citizen of that period, before the last war with England, when Salem was a port by itself; not scorned, as she is now, by her own merchants and ship-owners, who permit her wharves to crumble to ruin, while their ventures go to swell, needlessly and imperceptibly, the mighty flood of commerce at New York or Boston. On some such morning, when three or four vessels happen to have arrived at once,—usually from Africa or South America,—or to be on the verge of their departure thitherward, there is a sound of frequent feet, passing briskly up and down the granite steps. Here, before his own wife has greeted him, you may greet the sea-flushed ship-master, just in port, with his vessel's papers under his arm in a tarnished tin box. Here, too, comes his owner, cheerful or somber, gracious or in the sulks, accordingly as his scheme of the now accom-plished voyage has been realized in merchandise that will readily be turned to gold, or has buried him under a bulk of incommodities, such as nobody will care to rid him of. Here, likewise,—the germ of the wrinkle-browed, grizzly-bearded, careworn merchant,—we have the smart young clerk, who gets the taste of traffic as a wolf-cub does of blood, and already sends adventures in his master's ships, when he had better be sailing mimic boats upon a mill-pond. Another figure in the scene is the outward-bound sailor, in quest of a protection; or the recently arrived one, pale and feeble, seeking a passport to the hospital. Nor must we forget the captains of the rusty little schooners that bring firewood from the British provinces; a rough-looking set of tarpaulins, without the alertness of the Yankee aspect, but contributing an item of no slight importance to our decaying trade.

Cluster all these individuals together, as they sometimes were, with other miscellaneous ones to diversify the group, and, for the time being, it made the Custom-House a stirring scene. More frequently, however, on ascending the steps, you would discern—in the entry, if it were summer time, or in their appropriate rooms, if wintry or inclement weather—a row of venerable figures, sitting in old-fashioned chairs, which were tipped on their hind legs back against the wall. Oftentimes they were asleep, but occasionally might be heard talking together, in voices between speech and a snore, and with that lack of energy that distinguishes the occupants of alms-houses, and all other human beings who depend for subsistence on charity, on monopolized labor; or any thing else but their own independent exertions. These old gentlemen—seated, like Matthew, at the receipt of custom, but not very liable to be summoned thence, like him, for apostolic errands—were Custom-House officers.

Furthermore, on the left hand as you enter the front door, is a certain room or office, about fifteen feet square, and of a lofty height; with two of its arched windows commanding a view of the aforesaid dilapidated wharf, and the third looking across a narrow lane, and along a portion of Derby Street. All three give glimpses of the shops of grocers, block-makers, slop-sellers, and ship-chandlers; around the doors of which are generally to be seen, laughing and gossiping, clusters of old salts, and such other wharf-rats as haunt the Wapping of a seaport. The room itself is cobwebbed, and dingy with old paint; its floor is strewn with gray sand, in a fashion that has elsewhere fallen into long disuse; and it is easy to conclude, from the general slovenliness of the place, that this is a sanctuary into which womankind, with her tools of magic, the broom and mop, has very infrequent access. In the way of furniture, there is a stove with a voluminous funnel; an old pine desk, with a three-legged stool beside it; two or three wooden-bottom chairs, exceedingly decrepit and infirm; and,—not to forget the library,—on some shelves, a score or two of volumes of the Acts of Congress, and a bulky Digest of the Revenue Laws. A tin pipe ascends through the ceiling, and forms a medium of vocal communication with other parts of the edifice. And here, some six months ago,—pacing from corner to corner, or lounging on the long-legged stool, with his elbow on the desk, and his eyes wandering up and down the columns of the morning newspaper,—you might have recognized, honored reader, the same individual who welcomed you into his cheery little study, where the sunshine glimmered so pleasantly through the willow branches, on the western side of the Old Manse. But now, should you go thither to seek him, you would inquire in vain for the Loco-foco Surveyor. The besom of reform has swept him out of office; and a worthier successor wears his dignity and pockets his emoluments.

This old town of Salem—my native place, though I have dwelt much away from it, both in boyhood and maturer years—possesses, or did possess, a hold on my affections, the force of which I have never realized during my seasons of actual residence here. Indeed, so far as its physical aspect is concerned, with its flat, unvaried surface, covered chiefly with wooden houses, few or none of which pretend to architectural beauty,—its irregularity, which is neither picturesque nor quaint, but only tame,—its long and lazy street, lounging wearisomely through the whole extent of the peninsula, with Gallows Hill and New Guinea at one end, and a view of the alms-house at the other,—such being the features of my native town, it would be quite as reasonable to form a sentimental attachment to a disarranged checkerboard. And yet, though invariably happiest elsewhere, there is within me a feeling for old Salem, which, in lack of a better phrase, I must be content to call affection. The sentiment is probably assignable to the deep and aged roots which my family has struck into the soil. It is now nearly two centuries and a quarter since the original Briton, the earliest emigrant of my name, made his appearance in the wild and forest-bordered settlement, which has since become a city. And here his descendants have been born and died, and have mingled their earthy substance with the soil; until no small portion of it must necessarily be akin to the mortal frame wherewith, for a little while, I walk the streets. In part, therefore, the attachment which I speak of is the mere sensuous sympathy of dust for dust. Few of my countrymen can know what it is; nor, as frequent transplantation is perhaps better for the stock, need they consider it desirable to know.

But the sentiment has likewise its moral quality. The figure of that first ancestor, invested by family tradition with a dim and dusky grandeur, was present to my boyish imagination, as far back as I can remember. It still haunts me, and induces a sort of home-feeling with the past, which I scarcely claim in reference to the present phase of the town. I seem to have a stronger claim to a residence here on account of this grave, bearded, sable-cloaked, and steeple-crowned progenitor,—who came so early, with his Bible and his sword, and trode the unworn street with such a stately port, and made so large a figure, as a man of war and peace,—a stronger claim than for myself, whose name is seldom heard and my face hardly known. He was a soldier, legislator, judge; he was a ruler in the Church; he had all the Puritanic traits, both good and evil. He was likewise a bitter persecutor; as witness the Quakers, who have remembered him in their histories, and relate an incident of his hard severity towards a woman of their sect, which will last longer, it is to be feared, than any record of his better deeds, although these were many. His son, too, inherited the persecuting spirit, and made himself so conspicuous in the martyrdom of the witches, that their blood may fairly be said to have left a stain upon him. So deep a stain, indeed, that his old dry bones, in the Charter Street burial-ground, must still retain it, if they have not crumbled utterly to dust! I know not whether these ancestors of mine bethought themselves to repent, and ask pardon of Heaven for their cruelties; or whether they are now groaning under the heavy consequences of them, in another state of being. At all events, I, the present writer, as their representative, hereby take shame upon myself for their sakes, and pray that any curse incurred by them—as I have heard, and as the dreary and unprosperous condition of the race, for many a long year back, would argue to exist—may be now and henceforth removed.

Doubtless, however, either of these stern and black-browed Puritans would have thought it quite a sufficient retribution for his sins, that, after so long a lapse of years, the old trunk of the family tree, with so much venerable moss upon it, should have borne, as its topmost bough, an idler like myself. No aim, that I have ever cherished, would they recognize as laudable; no success of mine—if my life, beyond its domestic scope, had ever been brightened by success—would they deem otherwise than worthless, if not positively disgraceful. "What is he?" murmurs one gray shadow of my forefathers to the other. "A writer of storybooks! What kind of a business in life,—what mode of glorifying God, or being serviceable to mankind in his day and generation,—may that be? Why, the degenerate fellow might as well have been a fiddler!" Such are the compliments bandied between my great-grandsires and myself, across the gulf of time! And yet, let them scorn me as they will, strong traits of their nature have intertwined themselves with mine.

Planted deep, in the town's earliest infancy and childhood, by these two earnest and energetic men, the race has ever since subsisted here; always, too, in respectability; never, so far as I have known, disgraced by a single unworthy member; but seldom or never, on the other hand, after the first two generations, performing any memorable deed, or so much as putting forward a claim to public notice. Gradually, they have sunk almost out of sight; as old houses, here and there about the streets, get covered half-way to the eaves by the accumulation of new soil. From father to son, for above a hundred years, they followed the sea; a gray-headed shipmaster, in each generation, retiring from the quarter-deck to the homestead, while a boy of fourteen took the hereditary place before the mast, confronting the salt spray and the gale, which had blustered against his sire and grandsire. The boy, also, in due time, passed from the forecastle to the cabin, spent a tempestuous manhood, and returned from his world-wanderings, to grow old, and die, and mingle his dust with the natal earth. This long connection of a family with one spot, as its place of birth and burial, creates a kindred between the human being and the locality, quite independent of any charm in the scenery or moral circumstances that surround him. It is not love, but instinct. The new inhabitant—who came himself from a foreign land, or whose father or grandfather came—has little claim to be called a Salemite; he has no conception of the oyster-like tenacity with which an old settler, over whom his third century is creeping, clings to the spot where his successive generations have been imbedded. It is no matter that the place is joyless for him; that he is weary of the old wooden houses, the mud and dust, the dead level of site and sentiment, the chill east wind, and the chillest of social atmospheres;—all these, and whatever faults besides he may see or imagine, are nothing to the purpose. The spell survives, and just as powerfully as if the natal spot were an earthly paradise. So has it been in my case. I felt it almost as a destiny to make Salem my home; so that the mould of features and cast of character which had all along been familiar here—ever, as one representative of the race lay down in his grave, another assuming, as it were, his sentry-march along the Main Street—might still in my little day be seen and recognized in the old town. Nevertheless, this very sentiment is an evidence that the connection, which has become an unhealthy one, should at last be severed. Human nature will not flourish, any more than a potato, if it be planted and replanted, for too long a series of generations, in the same worn-out soil. My children have had other birthplaces, and, so far as their fortunes may be within my control, shall strike their roots into unaccustomed earth.

On emerging from the Old Manse, it was chiefly this strange, indolent, unjoyous attachment for my native town, that brought me to fill a place in Uncle Sam's brick edifice, when I might as well, or better, have gone somewhere else. My doom was on me. It was not the first time, nor the second, that I had gone away,—as it seemed, permanently,—but yet returned, like the bad half-penny; or as if Salem were for me the inevitable centre of the universe. So, one fine morning, I ascended the flight of granite steps, with the President's commission in my pocket, and was introduced to the corps of gentlemen who were to aid me in my weighty responsibility, as chief executive officer of the Custom-House.

I doubt greatly—or rather, I do not doubt at all—whether any public functionary of the United States, either in the civil or military line, has ever had such a patriarchal body of veterans under his orders as myself. The whereabouts of the Oldest Inhabitant was at once settled, when I looked at them. For upwards of twenty years before this epoch, the independent position of the Collector had kept the Salem Custom-House out of the whirlpool of political vicissitude, which makes the tenure of office generally so fragile: A soldier,—New England's most distinguished soldier,—he stood firmly on the pedestal of his gallant services; and, himself secure in the wise liberality of the successive administrations through which he had held office, he had been the safety of his subordinates in many an hour of danger and heart-quake. General Miller was radically conservative; a man over whose kindly nature habit had no slight influence; attaching himself strongly to familiar faces, and with difficulty moved to change, even when change might have brought unquestionable improvement. Thus, on taking charge of my department, I found few but aged men. They were ancient sea-captains, for the most part, who, after being tost on every sea, and standing up sturdily against life's tempestuous blast, had finally drifted into this quiet nook; where, with little to disturb them, except the periodical terrors of a Presidential election, they one and all acquired a new lease of existence. Though by no means less liable than their fellow-men to age and infirmity, they had evidently some talisman or other that kept death at bay. Two or three of their number, as I was assured, being gouty and rheumatic, or perhaps bed-ridden, never dreamed of making their appearance at the Custom-House, during a large part of the year; but, after a torpid winter, would creep out into the warm sunshine of May or June, go lazily about what they termed duty, and, at their own leisure and convenience, betake themselves to bed again. I must plead guilty to the charge of abbreviating the official breath of more than one of these venerable servants of the republic. They were allowed, on my representation, to rest from their arduous labors, and soon afterwards—as if their sole principle of life had been zeal for their country's service; as I verily believe it was—withdrew to a better world. It is a pious consolation to me, that, through my interference, a sufficient space was allowed them for repentance of the evil and corrupt practices, into which, as a matter of course, every Custom-House officer must be supposed to fall. Neither the front nor the back entrance of the Custom-House opens on the road to Paradise.

The greater part of my officers were Whigs. It was well for their venerable brotherhood, that the new Surveyor was not a politician, and, though a faithful Democrat in principle, neither received nor held his office with any reference to political services. Had it been otherwise,—had an active politician been put into this influential post, to assume the easy task of making head against a Whig Collector, whose infirmities withheld him from the personal administration of his office,—hardly a man of the old corps would have drawn the breath of official life, within a month after the exterminating angel had come up the Custom-House steps. According to the received code in such matters, it would have been nothing short of duty, in a politician, to bring every one of those white heads under the axe of the guillotine. It was plain enough to discern, that the old fellows dreaded some such discourtesy at my hands. It pained, and at the same time amused me, to behold the terrors that attended my advent; to see a furrowed cheek, weather-beaten by half a century of storm, turn ashy pale at the glance of so harmless an individual as myself; to detect, as one or another addressed me, the tremor of a voice, which, in long-past days, had been wont to bellow through a speaking-trumpet, hoarsely enough to frighten Boreas himself to silence. They knew, these excellent old persons, that, by all established rule,—and, as regarded some of them, weighted by their own lack of efficiency for business,—they ought to have given place to younger men, more orthodox in politics, and altogether fitter than themselves to serve our common Uncle. I knew it too, but could never quite find in my heart to act upon the knowledge. Much and deservedly to my own discredit, therefore, and considerably to the detriment of my official conscience, they continued, during my incumbency, to creep about the wharves, and loiter up and down the Custom-House steps. They spent a good deal of time, also, asleep in their accustomed corners, with their chairs tilted back against the wall; awaking, however, once or twice in a forenoon, to bore one another with the several thousandth repetition of old sea-stories, and mouldy jokes, that had grown to be pass-words and countersigns among them.

The discovery was soon made, I imagine, that the new Surveyor had no great harm in him. So, with lightsome hearts, and the happy consciousness of being usefully employed,—in their own behalf, at least, if not for our beloved country,—these good old gentlemen went through the various formalities of office. Sagaciously, under their spectacles, did they peep into the holds of vessels! Mighty was their fuss about little matters, and marvellous, sometimes, the obtuseness that allowed greater ones to slip between their fingers! Whenever such a mischance occurred,—when a wagon-load of valuable merchandise had been smuggled ashore, at noonday, perhaps, and directly beneath their unsuspicious noses,—nothing could exceed the vigilance and alacrity with which they proceeded to lock, and double-lock, and secure with tape and sealing-wax, all the avenues of the delinquent vessel. Instead of a reprimand for their previous negligence, the case seemed rather to require an eulogium on their praiseworthy caution, after the mischief had happened; a grateful recognition of the promptitude of their zeal, the moment that there was no longer any remedy!

Unless people are more than commonly disagreeable, it is my foolish habit to contract a kindness for them. The better part of my companion's character, if it have a better part, is that which usually comes uppermost in my regard, and forms the type whereby I recognize the man. As most of these old Custom-House officers had good traits, and as my position in reference to them, being paternal and protective, was favorable to the growth of friendly sentiments, I soon grew to like them all. It was pleasant, in the summer forenoons,—when the fervent heat, that almost liquefied the rest of the human family, merely communicated a genial warmth to their half-torpid systems,—it was pleasant to hear them chatting in the back entry, a row of them all tipped against the wall, as usual; while the frozen witticisms of past generations were thawed out, and came bubbling with laughter from their lips. Externally, the jollity of aged men has much in common with the mirth of children; the intellect, any more than a deep sense of humor, has little to do with the matter; it is, with both, a gleam that plays upon the surface, and imparts a sunny and cheery aspect alike to the green branch, and gray, mouldering trunk. In one case, however, it is real sunshine; in the other, it more resembles the phosphorescent glow of decaying wood.

It would be sad injustice, the reader must understand, to represent all my excellent old friends as in their dotage. In the first place, my coadjutors were not invariably old; there were men among them in their strength and prime, of marked ability and energy, and altogether superior to the sluggish and dependent mode of life on which their evil stars had cast them. Then, moreover, the white locks of age were sometimes found to be the thatch of an intellectual tenement in good repair. But, as respects the majority of my corps of veterans, there will be no wrong done, if I characterize them generally as a set of wearisome old souls, who had gathered nothing worth preservation from their varied experience of life. They seemed to have flung away all the golden grain of practical wisdom, which they had enjoyed so many opportunities of harvesting, and most carefully to have stored their memories with the husks. They spoke with far more interest and unction of their morning's breakfast, or yesterday's, to-day's, or to-morrow's dinner, than of the shipwreck of forty or fifty years ago, and all the world's wonders which they had witnessed with their youthful eyes.

The father of the Custom-House—the patriarch, not only of this little squad of officials, but, I am bold to say, of the respectable body of tide-waiters all over the United States—was a certain permanent Inspector. He might truly be termed a legitimate son of the revenue system, dyed in the wool, or rather, born in the purple; since his sire, a Revolutionary colonel, and formerly collector of the port, had created an office for him, and appointed him to fill it, at a period of the early ages which few living men can now remember. This Inspector, when I first knew him, was a man of fourscore years, or thereabouts, and certainly one of the most wonderful specimens of winter-green that you would be likely to discover in a lifetime's search. With his florid cheek, his compact figure, smartly arrayed in a bright-buttoned blue coat, his brisk and vigorous step, and his hale and hearty aspect, altogether, he seemed—not young, indeed—but a kind of new contrivance of Mother Nature in the shape of man, whom age and infirmity had no business to touch. His voice and laugh, which perpetually reëchoed through the Custom-House, had nothing of the tremulous quaver and cackle of an old man's utterance; they came strutting out of his lungs, like the crow of a cock, or the blast of a clarion. Looking at him merely as an animal,—and there was very little else to look at,—he was a most satisfactory object, from the thorough healthfulness and wholesomeness of his system, and his capacity, at that extreme age, to enjoy all, or nearly all, the delights which he had ever aimed at, or conceived of. The careless security of his life in the Custom-House, on a regular income, and with but slight and infrequent apprehensions of removal, had no doubt contributed to make time pass lightly over him. The original and more potent causes, however, lay in the rare perfection of his animal nature, the moderate proportion of intellect, and the very trifling admixture of moral and spiritual ingredients; these latter qualities, indeed, being in barely enough measure to keep the old gentleman from walking on all-fours. He possessed no power of thought, no depth of feeling, no troublesome sensibilities; nothing, in short, but a few commonplace instincts, which, aided by the cheerful temper that grew inevitably out of his physical well-being, did duty very respectably, and to general acceptance, in lieu of a heart. He had been the husband of three wives, all long since dead; the father of twenty children, most of whom, at every age of childhood or maturity, had likewise returned to dust. Here, one would suppose, might have been sorrow enough to imbue the sunniest disposition, through and through, with a sable tinge. Not so with our old Inspector! One brief sigh sufficed to carry off the entire burden of these dismal reminiscences. The next moment, he was as ready for sport as any unbreeched infant; far readier than the Collector's junior clerk, who, at nineteen years, was much the elder and graver man of the two.

I used to watch and study this patriarchal personage with, I think, livelier curiosity than any other form of humanity there presented to my notice. He was, in truth, a rare phenomenon; so perfect in one point of view; so shallow, so delusive, so impalpable, such an absolute nonentity, in every other. My conclusion was that he had no soul, no heart, no mind; nothing, as I have already said, but instincts; and yet, withal, so cunningly had the few materials of his character been put together, that there was no painful perception of deficiency, but, on my part, an entire contentment with what I found in him. It might be difficult—and it was so—to conceive how he should exist hereafter, so earthy and sensuous did he seem; but surely his existence here, admitting that it was to terminate with his last breath, had been not unkindly given; with no higher moral responsibilities than the beasts of the field, but with a larger scope of enjoyment than theirs, and with all their blessed immunity from the dreariness and duskiness of age.

One point, in which he had vastly the advantage over his four-footed brethren, was his ability to recollect the good dinners which it had made no small portion of the happiness of his life to eat. His gourmandism was a highly agreeable trait; and to hear him talk of roast-meat was as appetizing as a pickle or an oyster. As he possessed no higher attribute, and neither sacrificed nor vitiated any spiritual endowment by devoting all his energies and ingenuities to subserve the delight and profit of his maw, it always pleased and satisfied me to hear him expatiate on fish, poultry, and butcher's meat, and the most eligible methods of preparing them for the table. His reminiscences of good cheer, however ancient the date of the actual banquet, seemed to bring the savor of pig or turkey under one's very nostrils. There were flavors on his palate, that had lingered there not less than sixty or seventy years, and were still apparently as fresh as that of the mutton-chop which he had just devoured for his breakfast. I have heard him smack his lips over dinners, every guest at which, except himself, had long been food for worms. It was marvellous to observe how the ghosts of bygone meals were continually rising up before him; not in anger or retribution, but as if grateful for his former appreciation, and seeking to reduplicate an endless series of enjoyment, at once shadowy and sensual. A tenderloin of beef, a hind-quarter of veal, a spare-rib of pork, a particular chicken, or a remarkably praiseworthy turkey, which had perhaps adorned his board in the days of the elder Adams, would be remembered; while all the subsequent experience of our race, and all the events that brightened or darkened his individual career, had gone over him with as little permanent effect as the passing breeze. The chief tragic event of the old man's life, so far as I could judge, was his mishap with a certain goose, which lived and died some twenty or forty years ago; a goose of most promising figure, but which, at table, proved so inveterately tough that the carving-knife would make no impression on its carcass; and it could only be divided with an axe and handsaw.

But it is time to quit this sketch; on which, however, I should be glad to dwell at considerably more length, because, of all men whom I have ever known, this individual was fittest to be a Custom-House officer. Most persons, owing to causes which I may not have space to hint at, suffer moral detriment from this peculiar mode of life. The old Inspector was incapable of it, and, were he to continue in office to the end of time, would be just as good as he was then, and sit down to dinner with just as good an appetite.

There is one likeness, without which my gallery of Custom-House portraits would be strangely incomplete; but which my comparatively few opportunities for observation enable me to sketch only in the merest outline. It is that of the Collector, our gallant old General, who, after his brilliant military service, subsequently to which he had ruled over a wild Western territory, had come hither, twenty years before, to spend the decline of his varied and honorable life. The brave soldier had already numbered, nearly or quite, his threescore years and ten, and was pursuing the remainder of his earthly march, burdened with infirmities which even the martial music of his own spirit-stirring recollections could do little towards lightening. The step was palsied now, that had been foremost in the charge. It was only with the assistance of a servant, and by leaning his hand heavily on the iron balustrade, that he could slowly and painfully ascend the Custom-House steps, and, with a toilsome progress across the floor, attain his customary chair beside the fireplace. There he used to sit, gazing with a somewhat dim serenity of aspect at the figures that came and went; amid the rustle of papers, the administering of oaths, the discussion of business, and the casual talk of the office; all which sounds and circumstances seemed but indistinctly to impress his senses, and hardly to make their way into his inner sphere of contemplation. His countenance, in this repose, was mild and kindly. If his notice was sought, an expression of courtesy and interest gleamed out upon his features; proving that there was light within him, and that it was only the outward medium of the intellectual lamp that obstructed the rays in their passage. The closer you penetrated to the substance of his mind, the sounder it appeared. When no longer called upon to speak, or listen, either of which operations cost him an evident effort, his face would briefly subside into its former not uncheerful quietude. It was not painful to behold this look; for, though dim, it had not the imbecility of decaying age. The framework of his nature, originally strong and massive, was not yet crumbled into ruin.

To observe and define his character, however, under such disadvantages, was as difficult a task as to trace out and build up anew, in imagination, an old fortress, like Ticonderoga, from a view of its gray and broken ruins. Here and there, perchance, the walls may remain almost complete; but elsewhere may be only a shapeless mound, cumbrous with its very strength, and overgrown, through long years of peace and neglect, with grass and alien weeds.

Nevertheless, looking at the old warrior with affection,—for, slight as was the communication between us, my feeling towards him, like that of all bipeds and quadrupeds who knew him, might not improperly be termed so,—I could discern the main points of his portrait. It was marked with the noble and heroic qualities which showed it to be not by a mere accident, but of good right, that he had won a distinguished name. His spirit could never, I conceive, have been characterized by an uneasy activity; it must, at any period of his life, have required an impulse to set him in motion; but, once stirred up, with obstacles to overcome, and an adequate object to be attained, it was not in the man to give out or fail. The heat that had formerly pervaded his nature, and which was not yet extinct, was never of the kind that flashes and flickers in a blaze, but, rather, a deep, red glow, as of iron in a furnace. Weight, solidity, firmness; this was the expression of his repose, even in such decay as had crept untimely over him, at the period of which I speak. But I could imagine, even then, that, under some excitement which should go deeply into his consciousness,—roused by a trumpet-peal, loud enough to awaken all of his energies that were not dead, but only slumbering,—he was yet capable of flinging off his infirmities like a sick man's gown, dropping the staff of age to seize a battle-sword, and starting up once more a warrior. And, in so intense a moment, his demeanour would have still been calm. Such an exhibition, however, was but to be pictured in fancy; not to be anticipated, nor desired. What I saw in him—as evidently as the indestructible ramparts of Old Ticonderoga, already cited as the most appropriate simile—were the features of stubborn and ponderous endurance, which might well have amounted to obstinacy in his earlier days; of integrity, that, like most of his other endowments, lay in a somewhat heavy mass, and was just as unmalleable and unmanageable as a ton of iron ore; and of benevolence, which, fiercely as he led the bayonets on at Chippewa or Fort Erie, I take to be of quite as genuine a stamp as what actuates any or all the polemical philanthropists of the age. He had slain men with his own hand, for aught I know;—certainly, they had fallen, like blades of grass at the sweep of the scythe, before the charge to which his spirit imparted its triumphant energy;—but, be that as it might, there was never in his heart so much cruelty as would have brushed the down off a butterfly's wing. I have not known the man, to whose innate kindliness I would more confidently make an appeal.

Many characteristics—and those, too, which contribute not the least forcibly to impart resemblance in a sketch—must have vanished, or been obscured, before I met the General. All merely graceful attributes are usually the most evanescent; nor does Nature adorn the human ruin with blossoms of new beauty, that have their roots and proper nutriment only in the chinks and crevices of decay, as she sows wall-flowers over the ruined fortress of Ticonderoga. Still, even in respect of grace and beauty, there were points well worth noting. A ray of humor, now and then, would make its way through the veil of dim obstruction, and glimmer pleasantly upon our faces. A trait of native elegance, seldom seen in the masculine character after childhood or early youth, was shown in the General's fondness for the sight and fragrance of flowers. An old soldier might be supposed to prize only the bloody laurel on his brow; but here was one, who seemed to have a young girl's appreciation of the floral tribe.

There, beside the fireplace, the brave old General used to sit; while the Surveyor—though seldom, when it could be avoided, taking upon himself the difficult task of engaging him in conversation—was fond of standing at a distance, and watching his quiet and almost slumberous countenance. He seemed away from us, although we saw him but a few yards off; remote, though we passed close beside his chair; unattainable, though we might have stretched forth our hands and touched his own. It might be, that he lived a more real life within his thoughts, than amid the unappropriate environment of the Collector's office. The evolutions of the parade; the tumult of the battle; the flourish of old, heroic music, heard thirty years before;—such scenes and sounds, perhaps, were all alive before his intellectual sense. Meanwhile, the merchants and ship-masters, the spruce clerks, and uncouth sailors, entered and departed; the bustle of this commercial and Custom-House life kept up its little murmur roundabout him; and neither with the men nor their affairs did the General appear to sustain the most distant relation. He was as much out of place as an old sword—now rusty, but which had flashed once in the battle's front, and showed still a bright gleam along its blade—would have been, among the inkstands, paper-folders, and mahogany rulers, on the Deputy Collector's desk.

There was one thing that much aided me in renewing and recreating the stalwart soldier of the Niagara frontier,—the man of true and simple energy. It was the recollection of those memorable words of his,—"I'll try, Sir!"—spoken on the very verge of a desperate and heroic enterprise, and breathing the soul and spirit of New England hardihood, comprehending all perils, and encountering all. If, in our country, valor were rewarded by heraldic honor, this phrase—which it seems so easy to speak, but which only he, with such a task of danger and glory before him, has ever spoken—would be the best and fittest of all mottoes for the General's shield of arms.

It contributes greatly towards a man's moral and intellectual health, to be brought into habits of companionship with individuals unlike himself, who care little for his pursuits, and whose sphere and abilities he must go out of himself to appreciate. The accidents of my life have often afforded me this advantage, but never with more fulness and variety than during my continuance in office. There was one man, especially, the observation of whose character gave me a new idea of talent. His gifts were emphatically those of a man of business; prompt, acute, clear-minded; with an eye that saw through all perplexities, and a faculty of arrangement that made them vanish, as by the waving of an enchanter's wand. Bred up from boyhood in the Custom-House, it was his proper field of activity; and the many intricacies of business, so harassing to the interloper, presented themselves before him with the regularity of a perfectly comprehended system. In my contemplation, he stood as the ideal of his class. He was, indeed, the Custom-House in himself; or, at all events, the main-spring that kept its variously revolving wheels in motion; for, in an institution like this, where its officers are appointed to subserve their own profit and convenience, and seldom with a leading reference to their fitness for the duty to be performed, they must perforce seek elsewhere the dexterity which is not in them. Thus, by an inevitable necessity, as a magnet attracts steel-filings, so did our man of business draw to himself the difficulties which everybody met with. With an easy condescension, and kind forbearance towards our stupidity,— which, to his order of mind, must have seemed little short of crime,—would he forthwith, by the merest touch of his finger, make the incomprehensible as clear as daylight. The merchants valued him not less than we, his esoteric friends. His integrity was perfect; it was a law of nature with him, rather than a choice or a principle; nor can it be otherwise than the main condition of an intellect so remarkably clear and accurate as his, to be honest and regular in the administration of affairs. A stain on his conscience, as to any thing that came within the range of his vocation, would trouble such a man very much in the same way, though to a far greater degree, than an error in the balance of an account, or an ink-blot on the fair page of a book of record. Here, in a word,—and it is a rare instance in my life,—I had met with a person thoroughly adapted to the situation which he held.

Such were some of the people with whom I now found myself connected. I took it in good part at the hands of Providence, that I was thrown into a position so little akin to my past habits; and set myself seriously to gather from it whatever profit was to be had. After my fellowship of toil and impracticable schemes, with the dreamy brethren of Brook Farm, after living for three years within the subtile influence of an intellect like Emerson's; after those wild, free days on the Assabeth, indulging fantastic speculations beside our fire of fallen boughs, with Ellery Channing; after talking with Thoreau about pine-trees and Indian relics, in his hermitage at Walden; after growing fastidious by sympathy with the classic refinement of Hillard's culture; after becoming imbued with poetic sentiment at Longfellow's hearth-stone;—it was time, at length, that I should exercise other faculties of my nature, and nourish myself with food for which I had hitherto had little appetite. Even the old Inspector was desirable, as a change of diet, to a man who had known Alcott. I looked upon it as an evidence, in some measure, of a system naturally well balanced, and lacking no essential part of a thorough organization, that, with such associates to remember, I could mingle at once with men of altogether different qualities, and never murmur at the change.

Literature, its exertions and objects, were now of little moment in my regard. I cared not, at this period, for books; they were apart from me. Nature,—except it were human nature,—the nature that is developed in earth and sky, was, in one sense, hidden from me; and all the imaginative delight, wherewith it had been spiritualized, passed away out of my mind. A gift, a faculty, if it had not departed, was suspended and inanimate within me. There would have been something sad, unutterably dreary, in all this, had I not been conscious that it lay at my own option to recall whatever was valuable in the past. It might be true, indeed, that this was a life which could not, with impunity, be lived too long; else, it might make me permanently other than I had been, without transforming me into any shape which it would be worth my while to take. But I never considered it as other than a transitory life. There was always a prophetic instinct, a low whisper in my ear, that, within no long period, and whenever a new change of custom should be essential to my good, a change would come.

Meanwhile, there I was, a Surveyor of the Revenue, and, so far as I have been able to understand, as good a Surveyor as need be. A man of thought, fancy, and sensibility, (had he ten times the Surveyor's proportion of those qualities,) may, at any time, be a man of affairs, if he will only choose to give himself the trouble. My fellow-officers, and the merchants and sea-captains with whom my official duties brought me into any manner of connection, viewed me in no other light, and probably knew me in no other character. None of them, I presume, had ever read a page of my inditing, or would have cared a fig the more for me, if they had read them all; nor would it have mended the matter, in the least, had those same unprofitable pages been written with a pen like that of Burns or of Chaucer, each of whom was a Custom-House officer in his day, as well as I. It is a good lesson—though it may often be a hard one—for a man who has dreamed of literary fame, and of making for himself a rank among the world's dignitaries by such means, to step aside out of the narrow circle in which his claims are recognized, and to find how utterly devoid of significance, beyond that circle, is all that he achieves, and all he aims at. I know not that I especially needed the lesson, either in the way of warning or rebuke; but, at any rate, I learned it thoroughly; nor, it gives me pleasure to reflect, did the truth, as it came home to my perception, ever cost me a pang, or require to be thrown off in a sigh. In the way of literary talk, it is true, the Naval Officer—an excellent fellow, who came into office with me, and went out only a little later —would often engage me in a discussion about one or the other of his favorite topics, Napoleon or Shakspeare. The Collector's junior clerk, too,—a young gentleman who, it was whispered, occasionally covered a sheet of Uncle Sam's letter-paper with what, (at the distance of a few yards,) looked very much like poetry,—used now and then to speak to me of books, as matters with which I might possibly be conversant. This was my all of lettered intercourse; and it was quite sufficient for my necessities.

No longer seeking nor caring that my name should be blazoned abroad on title-pages, I smiled to think that it had now another kind of vogue. The Custom-House marker imprinted it, with a stencil and black paint, on pepper-bags, and baskets of anatto, and cigar-boxes, and bales of all kinds of dutiable merchandise, in testimony that these commodities had paid the impost, and gone regularly through the office. Borne on such queer vehicle of fame, a knowledge of my existence, so far as a name conveys it, was carried where it had never been before, and, I hope, will never go again.

But the past was not dead. Once in a great while, the thoughts, that had seemed so vital and so active, yet had been put to rest so quietly, revived again. One of the most remarkable occasions, when the habit of bygone days awoke in me, was that which brings it within the law of literary propriety to offer the public the sketch which I am now writing.

In the second story of the Custom-House, there is a large room, in which the brick-work and naked rafters have never been covered with panelling and plaster. The edifice—originally projected on a scale adapted to the old commercial enterprise of the port, and with an idea of subsequent prosperity destined never to be realized—contains far more space than its occupants know what to do with. This airy hall, therefore, over the Collector's apartments, remains unfinished to this day, and, in spite of the aged cobwebs that festoon its dusky beams, appears still to await the labor of the carpenter and mason. At one end of the room, in a recess, were a number of barrels, piled one upon another, containing bundles of official documents. Large quantities of similar rubbish lay lumbering the floor. It was sorrowful to think how many days, and weeks, and months, and years of toil, had been wasted on these musty papers, which were now only an encumbrance on earth, and were hidden away in this forgotten corner, never more to be glanced at by human eyes. But, then, what reams of other manuscripts—filled, not with the dullness of official formalities, but with the thought of inventive brains and the rich effusion of deep hearts—had gone equally to oblivion; and that, moreover, without serving a purpose in their day, as these heaped-up papers had, and—saddest of all—without purchasing for their writers the comfortable livelihood which the clerks of the Custom-House had gained by these worthless scratchings of the pen! Yet not altogether worthless, perhaps, as materials of local history. Here, no doubt, statistics of the former commerce of Salem might be discovered, and memorials of her princely merchants,—old King Derby,—old Billy Gray,—old Simon Forrester,—and many another magnate in his day; whose powdered head, however, was scarcely in the tomb, before his mountain-pile of wealth began to dwindle. The founders of the greater part of the families which now compose the aristocracy of Salem might here be traced, from the petty and obscure beginning of their traffic, at periods generally much posterior to the Revolution, upward to what their children look upon as long-established rank.

Prior to the Revolution, there is a dearth of records; the earlier documents and archives of the Custom-House having, probably, been carried off to Halifax, when all the King's officials accompanied the British army in its flight from Boston. It has often been a matter of regret with me; for, going back, perhaps, to the days of the Protectorate, those papers must have contained many references to forgotten or remembered men, and to antique customs, which would have affected me with the same pleasure as when I used to pick up Indian arrow-heads in the field near the Old Manse.

But, one idle and rainy day, it was my fortune to make a discovery of some little interest. Poking and burrowing into the heaped-up rubbish in the corner; unfolding one and another document, and reading the names of vessels that had long ago foundered at sea or rotted at the wharves, and those of merchants, never heard of now on 'Change, nor very readily decipherable on their mossy tombstones; glancing at such matters with the saddened, weary, half-reluctant interest which we bestow on the corpse of dead activity,—and exerting my fancy, sluggish with little use, to raise up from these dry bones an image of the old town's brighter aspect, when India was a new region, and only Salem knew the way thither,—I chanced to lay my hand on a small package, carefully done up in a piece of ancient yellow parchment. This envelope had the air of an official record of some period long past, when clerks engrossed their stiff and formal chirography on more substantial materials than at present. There was something about it that quickened an instinctive curiosity, and made me undo the faded red tape, that tied up the package, with the sense that a treasure would here be brought to light.

Unbending the rigid folds of the parchment cover, I found it to be a commission, under the hand and seal of Governor Shirley, in favor of one Jonathan Pue, as Surveyor of his Majesty's Customs for the port of Salem, in the Province of Massachusetts Bay. I remembered to have read (probably in Felt's Annals) a notice of the decease of Mr. Surveyor Pue, about fourscore years ago; and likewise, in a newspaper of recent times, an account of the digging up of his remains in the little grave-yard of St. Peter's Church, during the renewal of that edifice. Nothing, if I rightly call to mind, was left of my respected predecessor, save an imperfect skeleton, and some fragments of apparel, and a wig of majestic frizzle; which, unlike the head that it once adorned, was in very satisfactory preservation. But, on examining the papers which the parchment commission served to envelop, I found more traces of Mr. Pue's mental part, and the internal operations of his head, than the frizzled wig had contained of the venerable skull itself.

They were documents, in short, not official, but of a private nature, or, at least, written in his private capacity, and apparently with his own hand. I could account for their being included in the heap of Custom-House lumber only by the fact, that Mr. Pue's death had happened suddenly; and that these papers, which he probably kept in his official desk, had never come to the knowledge of his heirs, or were supposed to relate to the business of the revenue. On the transfer of the archives to Halifax, this package, proving to be of no public concern, was left behind, and had remained ever since unopened.

The ancient Surveyor—being little molested, I suppose, at that early day, with business pertaining to his office—seems to have devoted some of his many leisure hours to researches as a local antiquarian, and other inquisitions of a similar nature. These supplied material for petty activity to a mind that would otherwise have been eaten up with rust. A portion of his facts, by the by, did me good service in the preparation of the article entitled "MAIN STREET," included in the present volume. The remainder may perhaps be applied to purposes equally valuable, hereafter; or not impossibly may be worked up, so far as they go, into a regular history of Salem, should my veneration for the natal soil ever impel me to so pious a task. Meanwhile, they shall be at the command of any gentleman, inclined, and competent, to take the unprofitable labor off my hands. As a final disposition, I contemplate depositing them with the Essex Historical Society.

But the object that most drew my attention, in the mysterious package, was a certain affair of fine red cloth, much worn and faded. There were traces about it of gold embroidery, which, however, was greatly frayed and defaced; so that none, or very little, of the glitter was left. It had been wrought, as was easy to perceive, with wonderful skill of needlework; and the stitch (as I am assured by ladies conversant with such mysteries) gives evidence of a now forgotten art, not to be recovered even by the process of picking out the threads. This rag of scarlet cloth,—for time, and wear, and a sacrilegious moth, had reduced it to little other than a rag,—on careful examination, assumed the shape of a letter. It was the capital letter A. By an accurate measurement, each limb proved to be precisely three inches and a quarter in length. It had been intended, there could be no doubt, as an ornamental article of dress; but how it was to be worn, or what rank, honor, and dignity, in by-past times, were signified by it, was a riddle which (so evanescent are the fashions of the world in these particulars) I saw little hope of solving. And yet it strangely interested me. My eyes fastened themselves upon the old scarlet letter, and would not be turned aside. Certainly, there was some deep meaning in it, most worthy of interpretation, and which, as it were, streamed forth from the mystic symbol, subtly communicating itself to my sensibilities, but evading the analysis of my mind.

While thus perplexed,—and cogitating, among other hypotheses, whether the letter might not have been one of those decorations which the white men used to contrive, in order to take the eyes of Indians,—I happened to place it on my breast. It seemed to me,—the reader may smile, but must not doubt my word,—it seemed to me, then, that I experienced a sensation not altogether physical, yet almost so, as of burning heat; and as if the letter were not of red cloth, but red-hot iron. I shuddered, and involuntarily let it fall upon the floor.

In the absorbing contemplation of the scarlet letter, I had hitherto neglected to examine a small roll of dingy paper, around which it had been twisted. This I now opened, and had the satisfaction to find, recorded by the old Surveyor's pen, a reasonably complete explanation of the whole affair. There were several foolscap sheets, containing many particulars respecting the life and conversation of one Hester Prynne, who appeared to have been rather a noteworthy personage in the view of our ancestors. She had flourished during a period between the early days of Massachusetts and the close of the seventeenth century. Aged persons, alive in the time of Mr. Surveyor Pue, and from whose oral testimony he had made up his narrative, remembered her, in their youth, as a very old, but not decrepit woman, of a stately and solemn aspect. It had been her habit, from an almost immemorial date, to go about the country as a kind of voluntary nurse, and doing whatever miscellaneous good she might; taking upon herself, likewise, to give advice in all matters, especially those of the heart; by which means, as a person of such propensities inevitably must, she gained from many people the reverence due to an angel, but, I should imagine, was looked upon by others as an intruder and a nuisance. Prying farther into the manuscript, I found the record of other doings and sufferings of this singular woman, for the most of which the reader is referred to the story entitled "THE SCARLET LETTER"; and it should be borne carefully in mind, that the main facts of that story are authorized and authenticated by the document of Mr. Surveyor Pue. The original papers, together with the scarlet letter itself,—a most curious relic,—are still in my possession, and shall be freely exhibited to whomsoever, induced by the great interest of the narrative, may desire a sight of them. I must not be understood as affirming, that, in the dressing up of the tale, and imagining the motives and modes of passion that influenced the characters who figure in it, I have invariably confined myself within the limits of the old Surveyor's half a dozen sheets of foolscap. On the contrary, I have allowed myself, as to such points, nearly or altogether as much license as if the facts had been entirely of my own invention. What I contend for is the authenticity of the outline.

This incident recalled my mind, in some degree, to its old track. There seemed to be here the groundwork of a tale. It impressed me as if the ancient Surveyor, in his garb of a hundred years gone by, and wearing his immortal wig,—which was buried with him, but did not perish in the grave,—had met me in the deserted chamber of the Custom-House. In his port was the dignity of one who had borne his Majesty's commission, and who was therefore illuminated by a ray of the splendor that shone so dazzlingly about the throne. How unlike, alas! the hang-dog look of a republican official, who, as the servant of the people, feels himself less than the least, and below the lowest, of his masters. With his own ghostly hand, the obscurely seen, but majestic, figure had imparted to me the scarlet symbol, and the little roll of explanatory manuscript. With his own ghostly voice, he had exhorted me, on the sacred consideration of my filial duty and reverence towards him,—who might reasonably regard himself as my official ancestor,—to bring his mouldy and moth-eaten lucubrations before the public. "Do this," said the ghost of Mr. Surveyor Pue, emphatically nodding the head that looked so imposing within its memorable wig, "do this, and the profit shall be all your own! You will shortly need it; for it is not in your days as it was in mine, when a man's office was a life-lease, and often-times an heirloom. But, I charge you, in this matter of old Mistress Prynne, give to your predecessor's memory the credit which will be rightfully its due!" And I said to the ghost of Mr. Surveyor Pue,—"I will!"

On Hester Prynne's story, therefore, I bestowed much thought. It was the subject of my meditations for many an hour, while pacing to and fro across my room, or traversing, with a hundredfold repetition, the long extent from the front-door of the Custom-House to the side-entrance, and back again. Great were the weariness and annoyance of the old Inspector and the Weighers and Gaugers, whose slumbers were disturbed by the unmercifully lengthened tramp of my passing and returning footsteps. Remembering their own former habits, they used to say that the Surveyor was walking the quarter-deck. They probably fancied that my sole object—and, indeed, the sole object for which a sane man could ever put himself into voluntary motion—was, to get an appetite for dinner. And to say the truth, an appetite, sharpened by the east-wind that generally blew along the passage, was the only valuable result of so much indefatigable exercise. So little adapted is the atmosphere of a Custom-House to the delicate harvest of fancy and sensibility, that, had I remained there through ten Presidencies yet to come, I doubt whether the tale of "The Scarlet Letter" would ever have been brought before the public eye. My imagination was a tarnished mirror. It would not reflect, or only with miserable dimness, the figures with which I did my best to people it. The characters of the narrative would not be warmed and rendered malleable, by any heat that I could kindle at my intellectual forge. They would take neither the glow of passion nor the tenderness of sentiment, but retained all the rigidity of dead corpses, and stared me in the face with a fixed and ghastly grin of contemptuous defiance. "What have you to do with us?" that expression seemed to say. "The little power you might once have possessed over the tribe of unrealities is gone! You have bartered it for a pittance of the public gold. Go, then, and earn your wages!" In short, the almost torpid creatures of my own fancy twitted me with imbecility, and not without fair occasion.

It was not merely during the three hours and a half which Uncle Sam claimed as his share of my daily life, that this wretched numbness held possession of me. It went with me on my sea-shore walks and rambles into the country, whenever—which was seldom and reluctantly—I bestirred myself to seek that invigorating charm of Nature, which used to give me such freshness and activity of thought, the moment that I stepped across the threshold of the Old Manse. The same torpor, as regarded the capacity for intellectual effort, accompanied me home, and weighed upon me in the chamber which I most absurdly termed my study. Nor did it quit me, when, late at night, I sat in the deserted parlour, lighted only by the glimmering coal-fire and the moon, striving to picture forth imaginary scenes, which, the next day, might flow out on the brightening page in many-hued description.

If the imaginative faculty refused to act at such an hour, it might well be deemed a hopeless case. Moonlight, in a familiar room, falling so white upon the carpet, and showing all its figures so distinctly,—making every object so minutely visible, yet so unlike a morning or noontide visibility,—is a medium the most suitable for a romance-writer to get acquainted with his illusive guests. There is the little domestic scenery of the well-known apartment; the chairs, with each its separate individuality; the centre-table, sustaining a work-basket, a volume or two, and an extinguished lamp; the sofa; the book-case; the picture on the wall; all these details, so completely seen, are so spiritualized by the unusual light, that they seem to lose their actual substance, and become things of intellect. Nothing is too small or too trifling to undergo this change, and acquire dignity thereby. A child's shoe; the doll, seated in her little wicker carriage; the hobby-horse;—whatever, in a word, has been used or played with, during the day, is now invested with a quality of strangeness and remoteness, though still almost as vividly present as by daylight. Thus, therefore, the floor of our familiar room has become a neutral territory, somewhere between the real world and fairy-land, where the Actual and the Imaginary may meet, and each imbue itself with the nature of the other. Ghosts might enter here, without affrighting us. It would be too much in keeping with the scene to excite surprise, were we to look about us and discover a form, beloved, but gone hence, now sitting quietly in a streak of this magic moonshine, with an aspect that would make us doubt whether it had returned from afar, or had never once stirred from our fireside.

The somewhat dim coal-fire has an essential influence in producing the effect which I would describe. It throws its unobtrusive tinge throughout the room, with a faint ruddiness upon the walls and ceiling, and a reflected gleam from the polish of the furniture. This warmer light mingles itself with the cold spirituality of the moonbeams, and communicates, as it were, a heart and sensibilities of human tenderness to the forms which fancy summons up. It converts them from snow-images into men and women. Glancing at the looking-glass, we behold—deep within its haunted verge—the smouldering glow of the half-extinguished anthracite, the white moonbeams on the floor, and a repetition of all the gleam and shadow of the picture, with one remove farther from the actual, and nearer to the imaginative. Then, at such an hour, and with this scene before him, if a man, sitting all alone, cannot dream strange things, and make them look like truth, he need never try to write romances.

But, for myself, during the whole of my Custom-House experience, moonlight and sunshine, and the glow of firelight, were just alike in my regard; and neither of them was of one whit more avail than the twinkle of a tallow-candle. An entire class of susceptibilities, and a gift connected with them,—of no great richness or value, but the best I had,—was gone from me.

It is my belief, however, that, had I attempted a different order of composition, my faculties would not have been found so pointless and inefficacious. I might, for instance, have contented myself with writing out the narratives of a veteran shipmaster, one of the Inspectors, whom I should be most ungrateful not to mention; since scarcely a day passed that he did not stir me to laughter and admiration by his marvellous gifts as a story-teller. Could I have preserved the picturesque force of his style, and the humorous coloring which nature taught him how to throw over his descriptions, the result, I honestly believe, would have been something new in literature. Or I might readily have found a more serious task. It was a folly, with the materiality of this daily life pressing so intrusively upon me, to attempt to fling myself back into another age; or to insist on creating the semblance of a world out of airy matter, when, at every moment, the impalpable beauty of my soap-bubble was broken by the rude contact of some actual circumstance. The wiser effort would have been, to diffuse thought and imagination through the opaque substance of to-day, and thus to make it a bright transparency; to spiritualize the burden that began to weigh so heavily; to seek, resolutely, the true and indestructible value that lay hidden in the petty and wearisome incidents, and ordinary characters, with which I was now conversant. The fault was mine. The page of life that was spread out before me seemed dull and commonplace, only because I had not fathomed its deeper import. A better book than I shall ever write was there; leaf after leaf presenting itself to me, just as it was written out by the reality of the flitting hour, and vanishing as fast as written, only because my brain wanted the insight and my hand the cunning to transcribe it. At some future day, it may be, I shall remember a few scattered fragments and broken paragraphs, and write them down, and find the letters turn to gold upon the page.

These perceptions have come too late. At the instant, I was only conscious that what would have been a pleasure once was now a hopeless toil. There was no occasion to make much moan about this state of affairs. I had ceased to be a writer of tolerably poor tales and essays, and had become a tolerably good Surveyor of the Customs. That was all. But, nevertheless, it is any thing but agreeable to be haunted by a suspicion that one's intellect is dwindling away; or exhaling, without your consciousness, like ether out of a phial; so that, at every glance, you find a smaller and less volatile residuum. Of the fact, there could be no doubt; and, examining myself and others, I was led to conclusions in reference to the effect of public office on the character, not very favorable to the mode of life in question. In some other form, perhaps, I may hereafter develop these effects. Suffice it here to say, that a Custom-House officer, of long continuance, can hardly be a very praiseworthy or respectable personage, for many reasons; one of them, the tenure by which he holds his situation, and another, the very nature of his business, which—though, I trust, an honest one—is of such a sort that he does not share in the united effort of mankind.

An effect—which I believe to be observable, more or less, in every individual who has occupied the position—is, that, while he leans on the mighty arm of the Republic, his own proper strength departs from him. He loses, in an extent proportioned to the weakness or force of his original nature, the capability of self-support. If he possess an unusual share of native energy, or the enervating magic of place do not operate too long upon him, his forfeited powers may be redeemable. The ejected officer—fortunate in the unkindly shove that sends him forth betimes, to struggle amid a struggling world—may return to himself, and become all that he has ever been. But this seldom happens. He usually keeps his ground just long enough for his own ruin, and is then thrust out, with sinews all unstrung, to totter along the difficult footpath of life as he best may. Conscious of his own infirmity,—that his tempered steel and elasticity are lost,—he for ever afterwards looks wistfully about him in quest of support external to himself. His pervading and continual hope—a hallucination, which, in the face of all discouragement, and making light of impossibilities, haunts him while he lives, and, I fancy, like the convulsive throes of the cholera, torments him for a brief space after death—is, that, finally, and in no long time, by some happy coincidence of circumstances, he shall be restored to office. This faith, more than any thing else, steals the pith and availability out of whatever enterprise he may dream of undertaking. Why should he toil and moil, and be at so much trouble to pick himself up out of the mud, when, in a little while hence, the strong arm of his Uncle will raise and support him? Why should he work for his living here, or go to dig gold in California, when he is so soon to be made happy, at monthly intervals, with a little pile of glittering coin out of his Uncle's pocket? It is sadly curious to observe how slight a taste of office suffices to infect a poor fellow with this singular disease. Uncle Sam's gold—meaning no disrespect to the worthy old gentleman—has, in this respect, a quality of enchantment like that of the Devil's wages. Whoever touches it should look well to himself, or he may find the bargain to go hard against him, involving, if not his soul, yet many of its better attributes; its sturdy force, its courage and constancy, its truth, its self-reliance, and all, that gives the emphasis to manly character.

Here was a fine prospect in the distance! Not that the Surveyor brought the lesson home to himself, or admitted that he could be so utterly undone, either by continuance in office, or ejectment. Yet my reflections were not the most comfortable. I began to grow melancholy and restless; continually prying into my mind, to discover which of its poor properties were gone, and what degree of detriment had already accrued to the remainder. I endeavoured to calculate how much longer I could stay in the Custom-House, and yet go forth a man. To confess the truth, it was my greatest apprehension,—as it would never be a measure of policy to turn out so quiet an individual as myself, and it being hardly in the nature of a public officer to resign,—it was my chief trouble, therefore, that I was likely to grow gray and decrepit in the Surveyorship, and become much such another animal as the old Inspector. Might it not, in the tedious lapse of official life that lay before me, finally be with me as it was with this venerable friend,— to make the dinner-hour the nucleus of the day, and to spend the rest of it, as an old dog spends it, asleep in the sunshine or the shade? A dreary look-forward this, for a man who felt it to be the best definition of happiness to live throughout the whole range of his faculties and sensibilities! But, all this while, I was giving myself very unnecessary alarm. Providence had meditated better things for me than I could possibly imagine for myself.

A remarkable event of the third year of my Surveyorship—to adopt the tone of "P.P."—was the election of General Taylor to the Presidency. It is essential, in order to form a complete estimate of the advantages of official life, to view the incumbent at the in-coming of a hostile administration. His position is then one of the most singularly irksome, and, in every contingency, disagreeable, that a wretched mortal can possibly occupy, with seldom an alternative of good, on either hand, although what presents itself to him as the worst event may very probably be the best. But it is a strange experience, to a man of pride and sensibility, to know that his interests are within the control of individuals who neither love nor understand him, and by whom, since, one or the other must needs happen, he would rather be injured than obliged. Strange, too, for one who has kept his calmness throughout the contest, to observe the bloodthirstiness that is developed in the hour of triumph, and to be conscious that he is himself among its objects! There are few uglier traits of human nature than this tendency—which I now witnessed in men no worse than their neighbours—to grow cruel, merely because they possessed the power of inflicting harm. If the guillotine, as applied to office-holders, were a literal fact, instead of one of the most apt of metaphors, it is my sincere belief, that the active members of the victorious party were sufficiently excited to have chopped off all our heads, and have thanked Heaven for the opportunity! It appears to me—who have been a calm and curious observer, as well in victory as defeat—that this fierce and bitter spirit of malice and revenge has never distinguished the many triumphs of my own party as it now did that of the Whigs. The Democrats take the offices, as a general rule, because they need them, and because the practice of many years has made it the law of political warfare, which, unless a different system be proclaimed, it were weakness and cowardice to murmur at. But the long habit of victory has made them generous. They know how to spare, when they see occasion; and when they strike, the axe may be sharp, indeed, but its edge is seldom poisoned with ill-will; nor is it their custom ignominiously to kick the head which they have just struck off.

In short, unpleasant as was my predicament, at best, I saw much reason to congratulate myself that I was on the losing side, rather than the triumphant one. If, heretofore, I had been none of the warmest of partisans, I began now, at this season of peril and adversity, to be pretty acutely sensible with which party my predilections lay; nor was it without something like regret and shame, that, according to a reasonable calculation of chances, I saw my own prospect of retaining office to be better than those of my Democratic brethren. But who can see an inch into futurity, beyond his nose? My own head was the first that fell!

The moment when a man's head drops off is seldom or never, I am inclined to think, precisely the most agreeable of his life. Nevertheless, like the greater part of our misfortunes, even so serious a contingency brings its remedy and consolation with it, if the sufferer will but make the best, rather than the worst, of the accident which has befallen him. In my particular case, the consolatory topics were close at hand, and, indeed, had suggested themselves to my meditations a considerable time before it was requisite to use them. In view of my previous weariness of office, and vague thoughts of resignation, my fortune somewhat resembled that of a person who should entertain an idea of committing suicide, and, altogether beyond his hopes, meet with the good hap to be murdered. In the Custom-House, as before in the Old Manse, I had spent three years; a term long enough to rest a weary brain; long enough to break off old intellectual habits, and make room for new ones; long enough, and too long, to have lived in an unnatural state, doing what was really of no advantage nor delight to any human being, and withholding myself from toil that would, at least, have stilled an unquiet impulse in me. Then, moreover, as regarded his unceremonious ejectment, the late Surveyor was not altogether ill-pleased to be recognized by the Whigs as an enemy; since his inactivity in political affairs,—his tendency to roam, at will, in that broad and quiet field where all mankind may meet, rather than confine himself to those narrow paths where brethren of the same household must diverge from one another,—had sometimes made it questionable with his brother Democrats whether he was a friend. Now, after he had won the crown of martyrdom, (though with no longer a head to wear it on,) the point might, be looked upon as settled. Finally, little heroic as he was, it seemed more decorous to be overthrown in the downfall of the party with which he had been content to stand, than to remain a forlorn survivor, when so many worthier men were falling; and, at last, after subsisting for four years on the mercy of a hostile administration, to be compelled then to define his position anew, and claim the yet more humiliating mercy of a friendly one.

Meanwhile, the press had taken up my affair, and kept me, for a week or two, careering through the public prints, in my decapitated state, like Irving's Headless Horseman ghastly and grim, and longing to be buried, as a politically dead man ought. So much for my figurative self. The real human being, all this time, with his head safely on his shoulders, had brought himself to the comfortable conclusion, that every thing was for the best; and, making an investment in ink, paper, and steel-pens, had opened his long-disused writing-desk, and was again a literary man.

Now it was, that the lucubrations of my ancient predecessor, Mr. Surveyor Pue, came into play. Rusty through long idleness, some little space was requisite before my intellectual machinery could be brought to work upon the tale, with an effect in any degree satisfactory. Even yet, though my thoughts were ultimately much absorbed in the task, it wears, to my eye, a stern and sombre aspect; too much ungladdened by genial sunshine; too little relieved by the tender and familiar influences which soften almost every scene of nature and real life, and, undoubtedly, should soften every picture of them. This uncaptivating effect is perhaps due to the period of hardly accomplished revolution, and still seething turmoil, in which the story shaped itself. It is no indication, however, of a lack of cheerfulness in the writer's mind; for he was happier, while straying through the gloom of these sunless fantasies, than at any time since he had quitted the Old Manse. Some of the briefer articles, which contribute to make up the volume, have likewise been written since my involuntary withdrawal from the toils and honors of public life, and the remainder are gleaned from annuals and magazines, of such antique date that they have gone round the circle, and come back to novelty again.* Keeping up the metaphor of the political guillotine, the whole may be considered as the POST HUMOUS PAPERS OF A DECAPITATED SURVEYOR; and the sketch which I am now bringing to a close, if too autobiographical for a modest person to publish in his lifetime, will readily be excused in a gentleman who writes from beyond the grave. Peace be with all the world! My blessing on my friends! My forgiveness to my enemies! For I am in the realm of quiet!

The life of the Custom-House lies like a dream behind me. The old Inspector,—who, by the by, I regret to say, was overthrown and killed by a horse, some time ago; else he would certainly have lived for ever,—he, and all those other venerable personages who sat with him at the receipt of custom, are but shadows in my view; white-headed and wrinkled images, which my fancy used to sport with, and has now flung aside for ever. The merchants,—Pingree, Phillips, Shepard, Upton, Kimball, Bertram, Hunt,—these, and many other names, which had such a classic familiarity for my ear six months ago,—these men of traffic, who seemed to occupy so important a position in the world,—how little time has it required to disconnect me from them all, not merely in act, but recollection! It is with an effort that I recall the figures and appellations of these few. Soon, likewise, my old native town will loom upon me through the haze of memory, a mist brooding over and around it; as if it were no portion of the real earth, but an overgrown village in cloud-land, with only imaginary inhabitants to people its wooden houses, and walk its homely lanes, and the unpicturesque prolixity of its main street. Henceforth, it ceases to be a reality of my life. I am a citizen of somewhere else. My good townspeople will not much regret me; for—though it has been as dear an object as any, in my literary efforts, to be of some importance in their eyes, and to win myself a pleasant memory in this abode and burial-place of so many of my forefathers—there has never been, for me, the genial atmosphere which a literary man requires, in order to ripen the best harvest of his mind.

---

* At the time of writing this article, the author intended to publish, along with "The Scarlet Letter," several shorter tales and sketches. These it has been thought advisable to defer.

I shall do better amongst other faces; and these familiar ones, it need hardly be said, will do just as well without me.

It may be, however,—O, transporting and triumphant thought!—that the great-grandchildren of the present race may sometimes think kindly of the scribbler of bygone days, when the antiquary of days to come, among the sites memorable in the town's history, shall point out the locality of THE TOWN-PUMP!

THE CUSTOM-HOUSE

JOURNAL

1. **MLA Works Cited** *Using this model, record this book.*
   Author's Last Name, First Name. The Scarlet Letter. 1850. Title of This Book.
   Ed. First Name Last Name. City: Publisher, year.
2. **Main Character(s)** *Describe each main character and explain why you think each is a main character.*
3. **Supporting Characters** *Describe each supporting character and explain why you think each is a supporting character.*
4. **Setting** *Describe the setting(s) and any relevant prop(s).*
5. **Sequence** *Outline the events in this chapter in order.*
6. **Plot** *Summarize this chapter's events in no more than five sentences.*
7. **Conflicts** *Identify and explain all conflicts involved in this chapter.*
8. **Significant Quotations** *Explain the importance of each of these quotations. Record the page number in the parentheses.*
   a. " 'A writer of storybooks! What kind of a business in life,—what mode of glorifying God, or being serviceable to mankind in his day and generation,—may that be? Why, the degenerate fellow might as well have been a fiddler!' " ( ).
   b. "They spent a good deal of time, also, asleep in their accustomed corners, with their chairs tilted back against the wall; awaking, however, once or twice in a forenoon, to bore one another with the several thousandth repetition of old sea-stories, and mouldy jokes, that had grown to be pass-words and countersigns among them" ( ).
   c. "The original papers, together with the scarlet letter itself,—a most curious relic,—are still in my possession, and shall be freely exhibited to whomsoever, induced by the great interest of the narrative, may desire a sight of them. . . ." ( ).
   d. "[A]ccording to a reasonable calculation of chances, I saw my own prospect of retaining office to be better than those of my Democratic brethren. But who can see an inch into futurity, beyond his nose? My own head was the first that fell!" ( ).
   e. "The life of the Custom-House lies like a dream behind me" ( ).
9. **Recap** *Summarize what has happened so far, from the beginning of the book through this chapter.*

FOLLOW-UP QUESTIONS

6 SHORT QUESTIONS

Select the <u>best</u> answer for each.

____ 1. Hawthorne worked in the
Custom-House for
   a. seven years.
   b. three years.
   c. one and a half years.

____ 2. The Custom-House is
located in
   a. Boston.
   b. New York.
   c. Salem.

____ 3. The narrator's hometown is
   a. Boston.
   b. New York.
   c. Salem.

____ 4. In an old box, the narrator
says he found
   a. the scarlet letter.
   b. military uniforms.
   c. alcoholic beverages.

____ 5. Hester Prynne lived in the
   a. sixteenth century.
   b. seventeenth century.
   c. eighteenth century.

____ 6. Hawthorne left the Custom-
House because
   a. he wanted to pursue his
      writing.
   b. he was fired.
   c. he found it boring.

5 SIGNIFICANT QUOTATIONS

Explain the importance of each of these quotations.

1. "It is now nearly two centuries and a quarter since the original Briton, the earliest emigrant of my name, made his appearance in the wild and forest-bordered settlement, which has since become a city. And here his descendants have been born and died, and have mingled their earthy substance with the soil [. . .]."

2. "At all events, I, the present writer, as [my Puritan ancestors'] representative, hereby take shame upon myself for their sakes, and pray that any curse incurred by them [. . .] may be now and henceforth removed."

3. "As most of these old Custom-House officers had good traits, and as my position in reference to them, being paternal and protective, was favorable to the growth of friendly sentiments, I soon grew to like them all [. . .]."

4. "But the object that most drew my attention, in the mysterious package, was a certain affair of fine red cloth, much worn and faded. [. . .]. This rag of scarlet cloth, [. . .] on careful examination, assumed the shape of a letter. It was the capital letter A [. . .]."

5. "I happened to place it on my breast. [. . .] [I]t seemed to me, then, that I experienced a sensation not altogether physical, yet almost so, as of burning heat; and as if the letter were not of red cloth, but red-hot iron. I shuddered, and involuntarily let it fall upon the floor."

2 COMPREHENSION ESSAY QUESTIONS

Use specific details and information from the essay to answer these questions as completely as possible.

1. How does Hawthorne feel about his Puritan ancestors? Use specific details and information from the essay in your explanation.
2. How does Hawthorne both get and leave his job at the Custom-House? Use specific details and information from the essay in your explanation.

DISCUSSION QUESTIONS

Be prepared to discuss these questions in class.

1. What does the narrator find in a box and how does it make him feel about his ancestors? What do you know about the Puritans?
2. What are the advantages and disadvantages of the narrator's job at the Custom-House? Do people receive jobs in this manner today?

WRITING

Use each of these ideas for writing an essay.

1. Hawthorne wanted to be a writer but found that his job at the Custom-House affected his goal. Have you ever wanted to do or be something but were influenced by circumstances from doing it? What did you want to do, what got in your way, and what did you do about it?
2. Hawthorne discusses politics and how it affects his life and his job. How much do politics and the workings of government affect your life and the lives of your friends and family?

FURTHER WRITING

1. If you look carefully at the word *"Puritans,"* you will see that the word "pure" is embedded within it. What did the Puritans want to make pure? Research the laws, customs, religion, and clothing of the Puritans as well as their historical background. What influences have they had on American culture?
2. Hawthorne can trace his lineage back to the Puritans in Massachusetts and earlier to England. How far back can you trace your ancestors? Create a family tree and summarize the lives of your parents, grandparents, and great-grandparents, or as far back as possible. Are there similarities in names and professions?

CHAPTER 1

THE PRISON-DOOR

Use context clues to define these words before reading. Use a dictionary as needed.

1. Looking at the *throng* of travelers waiting on the platform, I knew the train would be too crowded to get a seat. *Throng* means _____ _____.

2. John was so amazed by the number of buildings on the city street that he was not sure what *edifice* he was looking for. *Edifice* means _____ _____.

3. The community honored the *virtuous* clergyman for his good works. *Virtuous* means _____ _____.

4. The team of movers rested after they had *borne* numerous boxes of heavy furniture up seven flights of stairs. *Borne* means _____ _____.

5. The residents were required to sort their recyclables *in accordance* with town rules—glass in blue bins, paper in orange bins, and plastic in yellow bins. *In accordance* means _____ _____.

6. At the cemetery, Carol visited the large stone *sepulchre* that housed her deceased grandparents and great-grandparents. *Sepulchre* means _____ _____.

7. The day was so dark and *gloomy* that we turned on the lights to cheer ourselves up. *Gloomy* means _____ _____.

8. The *ponderous* furniture was so heavy that it took four strong men to move it across the room. *Ponderous* means _____ _____.

9. Kevin's beautiful gold watch, passed down through his family for over one hundred years, was old enough to be called an *antique*. *Antique* means _____
_____.

10. The lush *vegetation* of grasses, bushes, and flowers provided a colorful contrast to the six-lane concrete highway. *Vegetation* means _____
_____.

11. Ian has learned to *allot* parts of his paycheck, setting aside some money to pay car insurance and some money to pay his rent. *Allot* means _____
_____.

12. Cecelia's *forefathers* came to America over two hundred years ago and settled in New York. *Forefathers* means _____
_____.

13. When the large new mall with lots of parking opened outside of town, it meant *doom* for the businesses in the old part of town. *Doom* means
_____.

14. The Puritans believed that a set of rules, with strict enforcement and harsh punishment for breaking them, would *civilize* their colony in the New World. *Civilize* means _____
_____.

15. Susan stood on the *threshold* of the doorway, trying to decide if she should enter the room. *Threshold* means _____
_____.

16. The *stern* professor ignored the student's joke and unsmilingly continued explaining the rules of his classroom. *Stern* means _____
_____.

17. Gert is very interested in learning about herbs and everything that *pertains* to them. *Pertains* means _____
_____.

18. To enter the Empire State Building, one must pass through the *portal* on Fifth Avenue. *Portal* means _____
_____.

19. The patient, weakened by his illness to the point of *frailty*, could barely stand up. *Frailty* means _____
_____.

20. The Puritans hoped that their colony in New England would be a *utopia*, perfect in all social and moral aspects. *Utopia* means _____

_____.

PRE-READING VOCABULARY
STRUCTURAL ATTACK

Define these words by solving the parts. Use the Glossary or a dictionary as needed.

1. unsightly	10. condemned	19. nucleus
2. invariably	11. overshadowed	20. assembled
3. congenial	12. inhabitants	21. delicately
4. inauspicious	13. intermixed	22. gemstone
5. cemetery	14. timbered	23. survived
6. wilderness	15. studded	24. gigantic
7. scarlet	16. weather-stained	25. authority
8. youthful	17. overgrown	26. assembled
9. wheel-track	18. fragrance	27. gazed

PRE-READING QUESTIONS

Try answering these questions as you read.

What kind of people make up this town?
What kinds of buildings and places exist here?
Which building is focused on the most, and why?

CHAPTER 1

THE SCARLET LETTER
The Prison-Door

1 A throng of bearded men, in sad-colored garments and gray, steeple-crowned hats, intermixed with women, some wearing hoods, and others bareheaded, was assembled in front of a wooden edifice, the door of which was heavily timbered with oak, and studded with iron spikes.

2 The founders of a new colony, whatever Utopia of human virtue and happiness they might originally project, have invariably recognized it among their earliest practical necessities to allot a portion of the virgin soil as a cemetery, and another portion as the site of a prison. In accordance with this rule, it may safely be assumed that the forefathers of Boston had built the first prison-house, somewhere

in the vicinity of Cornhill, almost as seasonably as they marked out the first burial-ground, on Issac Johnson's lot, and round about his grave, which subsequently became the nucleus of all the congregated sepulchres in the old churchyard of King's Chapel. Certain it is, that, some fifteen or twenty years after the settlement of the town, the wooden jail was already marked with weather-stains and other indications of age, which gave a yet darker aspect to its beetle-browed and gloomy front. The rust on the ponderous ironwork of its oaken door looked more antique than any thing else in the new world. Like all that pertains to crime, it seemed never to have known a youthful era. Before this ugly edifice, and between it and the wheel-track of the street, was a grass-plot, much overgrown with burdock, pig-weed, apple-peru, and such unsightly vegetation, which evidently found some-thing congenial in the soil that had so early borne the black flower of civilized society, a prison. But on one side of the portal, and rooted almost at the threshold, was a wild rose-bush, covered, in this month of June, with its delicate gems, which might be imagined to offer their fragrance and fragile beauty to the prisoner as he went in, and to the condemned criminal as he came forth to his doom, in token that the deep heart of Nature could pity and be kind to him.

3   This rose-bush, by a strange chance, has been kept alive in history; but whether it had merely survived out of the stern old wilderness, so long after the

fall of the gigantic pines and oaks that originally overshadowed it,—or whether, as there is fair authority for believing, it had spring up under the footsteps of the sainted Ann Hutchinson, as she entered the prison door,—we shall not take upon us to determine. Finding it so directly on the threshold of our narrative, which is now about to issue from that inauspicious portal, we could hardly do otherwise than pluck one of its flowers and present it to the reader. It may serve, let us hope, to symbolize some sweet moral blossom, that may be found along the track, or relieve the darkening close of a tale of human frailty and sorrow.

CHAPTER 1

JOURNAL

1. **MLA Works Cited** *Using this model, record this book.*
   Author's Last Name, First Name. The Scarlet Letter. 1850. Title of This Book.
   Ed. First Name Last Name. City: Publisher, year.
2. **Main Character(s)** *Describe each main character and explain why you think each is a main character.*
3. **Supporting Characters** *Describe each supporting character and explain why you think each is a supporting character.*
4. **Setting** *Describe the setting(s) and any revelant prop(s).*
5. **Sequence** *Outline the events in this chapter in order.*
6. **Plot** *Summarize this chapter's events in no more than two sentences.*
7. **Conflicts** *Identify and explain all conflicts involved in this chapter.*
8. **Significant Quotations** *Explain the importance of each of these quotations. Record the page number in the parentheses.*
   a. "A throng of bearded men, in sad-colored garments and gray, steeple-crowned hats, intermixed with women, some wearing hoods, and others bareheaded, was assembled in front of a wooden edifice [. . .]" (   ).
   b. "[T]he door [. . .] was heavily-timbered with oak, and studded with iron spikes" (   ).
   c. "The founders of a new colony [. . .] have invariably recognized it among their earliest practical necessities to allot a portion of the virgin soil as a cemetery, and another as the site of a prison" (   ).
   d. "Like all that pertains to crime, [the jail] seemed never to have known a youthful era" (   ).
   e. "[O]n one side of the portal, and rooted almost at the threshold was a wild rose-bush, covered, in this month of June, with its delicate gems [. . .]" (   ).
9. **Recap** *Summarize what has happened so far, from the beginning of the book through this chapter.*

FOLLOW-UP QUESTIONS

6 SHORT QUESTIONS

*Select the **best** answer for each.*

____ 1. The building this chapter
focuses on is a
a. church.
b. prison.
c. hospital.

____ 2. The name of the new Puritan
colony is
a. Boston.
b. Salem.
c. Utopia.

____ 3. The prison door looks
a. open.
b. new.
c. old.

____ 4. Next to the prison door is a
a. tall oak tree.
b. rosebush.
c. pine tree.

____ 5. The story begins in the
month of
a. November.
b. August.
c. June.

____ 6. The rosebush seems to suggest
a. sorrow and pain.
b. human frailty and
suffering.
c. hope and kindness.

5 SIGNIFICANT QUOTATIONS

Explain the importance of each of these quotations.

1. "[S]ome fifteen or twenty years after the settlement of the town, the wooden jail was already marked with weather-stains and other indications of age, which gave a yet darker aspect to its beetle-browed and gloomy front."
2. "The rust on the ponderous ironwork of [the prison's] oaken door looked more antique than anything else in the new world [. . .]."
3. "Before this ugly edifice, and between it and the wheel-track of the street, was a grass-plot, much overgrown with burdock, pig-weed, apple-peru, and such unsightly vegetation, which evidently found something congenial in the soil that had so early borne the black flower of civilized society, a prison [. . .]."
4. "[The flowers on the rose-bush] might be imagined to offer their fragrance and fragile beauty to the prisoner as he went in, and to the condemned criminal as he came forth to his doom, in token that the deep heart of Nature could pity and be kind to him."
5. "This rose-bush [. . .] may [. . .] symbolize some sweet moral blossom, that may be found along the track, or relieve the darkening close of a tale of human frailty and sorrow."

2 COMPREHENSION ESSAY QUESTIONS

Use specific details and information from the chapter to answer these questions as completely as possible.

1. The setting of a story often includes both physical and psychological aspects. Using specific details and information from the story, how would you describe the setting?
2. How is the title of the chapter relevant to the story so far? Use specific details and information from the story in your explanation.

DISCUSSION QUESTIONS

Be prepared to discuss these questions in class.

1. What values or ideas seem important to this town? What do you think the people are like?
2. What is important about the prison?

CHAPTER 2

THE MARKET-PLACE

PRE-READING VOCABULARY
CONTEXT

Use context clues to define these words before reading. Use a dictionary as needed.

1. The *grim* news about the hurricane included descriptions of property destruction and loss of human life. *Grim* means _____
   _____.

2. The *rigid* steel structure created a strong, enduring bridge for trucks and cars. *Rigid* means _____
   _____.

3. The smile on the clown's *physiognomy*, painted brightly on his face, made the children laugh. *Physiognomy* means _____
   _____.

4. Getting a snowstorm very early in the season *augurs*, or predicts, a cold and snowy winter. *Augur* means _____
   _____.

5. When Mother saw the ripped papers all over the floor, she knew the puppy was the *culprit*. *Culprit* means _____
   _____.

6. Health care professionals who work in the emergency room at the hospital try to maintain a calm *demeanor* to reassure patients. *Demeanor* means _____
   _____.

7. Bathing suits are the proper *attire* to wear at the beach or the pool. *Attire* means _____
   _____.

8. As part of her punishment, Hester Prynne stood on the *scaffold*, a wooden structure in the town square, for everyone to see. *Scaffold* means _____
   _____.

9. It is up to the jury to decide if the accused has *transgressed* the law; the judge then sentences the *transgressor* accordingly. *Transgressed* and *transgressor* mean

_____.

10. The elderly woman walked with *dignity*, her back straight and her head held high, nodding in a *dignified* way to her neighbors. *Dignity* and *dignified* mean

_____.

11. The *penal* system is a code of rules and laws. The person who breaks a law must pay a *penalty*. *Penal* and *penalty* mean _____

_____.

12. From the look on Becky's *countenance*, we could see that she was very happy to see us. *Countenance* means _____

_____.

13. Fashion models learn good *deportment*, or how to carry themselves in public. *Deportment* means _____

_____.

14. Jody is a good friend and never *ridicules* or makes fun of any of her friends. *Ridicule* means _____

_____.

15. Many people wear hats and sunscreen at the beach because the strong sun can *inflict* much damage to the skin. *Inflict* means _____

_____.

16. One punishment the Puritans used was public humiliation, when they would lock the offender into a *pillory*, a wooden framework with holes for the head and hands, for several hours on public display. *Pillory* means _____

_____.

17. Jamie's married sister, Tonie, will be the *matron* of honor at her wedding. *Matron* means _____

_____.

18. The mayor and the town council members are usually considered to be the *magistrates* of the town. *Magistrate* means _____

_____.

19. In the American Old West, to demonstrate ownership, cowboys used to *brand* the symbol of their ranch into the hides of their cattle, using a hot *branding* iron. *Brand* and *branding* mean _____

_____.

20. When Joyce tripped over the wire, she splashed coffee down the *bodice* of her dress, staining it from the neck to the waist. *Bodice* means _____
_____.

PRE-READING VOCABULARY
STRUCTURAL ATTACK

Define these worth by solving the parts. Use the Glossary or a dictionary as needed.

1. infamy	14. prefigured	27. flourishes
2. betokened	15. repelled	28. sluggish
3. spectator/spectacle	16. market-place	29. heretofore
4. severity	17. intently	30. meager
5. solemnity	18. grisly	31. vividly
6. repressed	19. statute	32. wont
7. astray	20. brooch	33. twilight
8. indubitably	21. sphere	34. dungeon
9. restrained	22. embroidered	35. blushed
10. minister	23. perchance	36. haughty
11. impropriety	24. petrified	37. winced
12. transmit	25. fastened	
13. malefactor	26. elaborate	

PRE-READING QUESTIONS

Try answering these questions as you read.

Who is released from the prison?
What crime has the prisoner committed?
How do members of the crowd react to the prisoner and the crime?
What does the prisoner think about while standing before the crowd?

CHAPTER 2

THE MARKET-PLACE

1   The grass-plot before the jail, in Prison Lane, on a certain summer morning, not less than two centuries ago, was occupied by a pretty large number of the inhabitants of Boston; all with their eyes intently fastened on the iron-clamped oaken door. Amongst any other population, or at a later period in the history of New England, the grim rigidity that petrified the bearded physiognomies of these good people would have augured some awful business in hand. It could have

betokened nothing short of the anticipated execution of some noted culprit, on whom the sentence of a legal tribunal had but confirmed the verdict of public sentiment. But, in that early severity of the Puritan character, an inference of this kind could not so indubitably be drawn. It might be that a sluggish bond-servant, or an undutiful child, whom his parents had given over to the civil authority, was to be corrected at the whipping-post. It might be, that an Antinomian, a Quaker, or other heterodox religionist, was to be scourged out of the town, or an idle and vagrant Indian, whom the white man's fire-water had made riotous about the streets, was to be driven with stripes into the shadow of the forest. It might be, too, that a witch, like old Mistress Hibbins, the bitter-tempered widow of the magistrate, was to die upon the gallows. In either case, there was very much the same solemnity of demeanour on the part of the spectators; as befitted a people amongst whom religion and law were almost identical, and in whose character both were so thoroughly interfused, that the mildest and the severest acts of public discipline were alike made venerable and awful. Meagre, indeed, and cold, was the sympathy that a transgressor might look for, from such bystanders at the scaffold. On the other hand, a penalty which, in our days, would infer a degree of mocking infamy and ridicule, might then be invested with almost as stern a dignity as the punishment of death itself.

2   It was a circumstance to be noted, on the summer morning when our story begins its course, that the women, of whom there were several in the crowd, appeared to take a peculiar interest in whatever penal infliction might be expected to ensue. The age had not so much refinement, that any sense of impropriety restrained the wearers of petticoat and farthingale from stepping forth into the public ways, and wedging their not unsubstantial persons, if occasion were, into the throng nearest to the scaffold at an execution. Morally, as well as materially, there was a coarser fibre in those wives and maidens of old English birth and breeding, than in their fair descendants, separated from them by a series of six or seven generations; for, throughout that chain of ancestry, every successive mother has transmitted to her child a fainter bloom, a more delicate and briefer beauty, and a slighter physical frame, if not a character of less force and solidity, than her own. The women, who were now standing about the prison-door, stood within less than half a century of the period when the man-like Elizabeth had been the not altogether unsuitable representative of the sex. They were her countrywomen; and the beef and ale of their native land, with a moral diet not a whit more refined, entered largely into their composition. The bright morning sun, therefore, shone on broad shoulders and well-developed busts, and on round and ruddy cheeks, that had ripened in the far-off island, and had hardly yet grown paler or thinner in the atmosphere of New England. There was, moreover, a boldness and rotundity of speech among these matrons, as most of them seemed to be, that would startle us at the present day, whether in respect to its purport or its volume of tone.

3   "Goodwives," said a hard-featured dame of fifty, "I'll tell ye a piece of my mind. It would be greatly for the public behoof, if we women, being of mature

age and church-members in good repute, should have the handling of such male-factresses as this Hester Prynne. What think ye, gossips? If the hussy stood up for judgment before us five, that are now here in a knot together, would she come off with such a sentence as the worshipful magistrates have awarded? Marry, I trow not!"

4   "People say," said another, "that the Reverend Master Dimmesdale, her godly pastor, takes it very grievously to heart that such a scandal should have come upon his congregation."

5   "The magistrates are God-fearing gentlemen, but merciful overmuch,—that is a truth," added a third autumnal matron. "At the very least, they should have put the brand of a hot iron on Hester Prynne's forehead. Madam Hester would have winced at that, I warrant me. But she,—the naughty baggage,—little will she care what they put upon the bodice of her gown! Why, look you, she may cover it with a brooch, or such like heathenish adornment, and so walk the streets as brave as ever!"

6   "Ah, but," interposed, more softly, a young wife, holding a child by the hand, "let her cover the mark as she will, the pang of it will be always in her heart."

7   "What do we talk of marks and brands, whether on the bodice of her gown, or the flesh of her forehead?" cried another female, the ugliest as well as the most pitiless of these self-constituted judges. "This woman has brought shame upon us all, and ought to die. Is there not law for it? Truly there is, both in the Scripture and the stature-book. Then let the magistrates, who have made it of no effect, thank themselves if their own wives and daughters go astray!"

8   "Mercy on us, goodwife," exclaimed a man in the crowd, "is there no virtue in woman, save what springs from a wholesome fear of the gallows? That is the hardest word yet! Hush, now, gossips; for the lock is turning in the prison-door, and here comes Mistress Prynne herself."

9   The door of the jail being flung open from within, there appeared, in the first place, like a black shadow emerging into the sunshine, the grim and grisly presence of the town-beadle, with a sword by his side and his staff of office in his hand. This personage prefigured and represented in his aspect the whole dismal severity of the Puritanic code of law, which it was his business to administer in its final and closest application to the offender. Stretching forth the official staff in his left hand, he laid his right upon the shoulder of a young woman, whom he thus drew forward; until, on the threshold of the prison-door, she repelled him, by an action marked with natural dignity and force of character, and stepped into the open air, as if by her own free-will. She bore in her arms a child, a baby of some three months old, who winked and turned aside its little face from the too vivid light of day; because its existence, heretofore, had brought it acquainted only with the gray twilight of a dungeon, or other darksome apartment of the prison.

10   When the young woman—the mother of this child—stood fully revealed before the crowd, it seemed to be her first impulse to clasp the infant closely to her bosom; not so much by an impulse of motherly affection, as that she might thereby conceal a certain token, which was wrought or fastened into her dress.

In a moment, however, wisely judging that one token of her shame would but poorly serve to hide another, she took the baby on her arm, and, with a burning blush, and yet a haughty smile, and a glance that would not be abashed, looked around at her townspeople and neighbours. On the breast of her gown, in fine red cloth, surrounded with an elaborate embroidery and fantastic flourishes of gold thread, appeared the letter A. It was so artistically done, and with so much fertility and gorgeous luxuriance of fancy, that it had all the effect of a last and fitting decoration to the apparel which she wore; and which was of a splendor in accordance with the taste of the age, but greatly beyond what was allowed by the sumptuary regulations of the colony.

11   The young woman was tall, with a figure of perfect elegance, on a large scale. She had dark and abundant hair, so glossy that it threw off the sunshine with a gleam, and a face which, besides being beautiful from regularity of feature and richness of complexion, had the impressiveness belonging to a marked brow and deep black eyes. She was lady-like, too, after the manner of the feminine gentility of those days; characterized by a certain state and dignity, rather than by the delicate, evanescent, and indescribable grace, which is now recognized as its indication. And never had Hester Prynne appeared more lady-like, in the antique interpretation of the term, than as she issued from the prison. Those who had before known her, and had expected to behold her dimmed and obscured by a disastrous cloud, were astonished, and even startled, to perceive how her beauty shone out, and made a halo of the misfortune and ignominy in which she was enveloped. It may be true, that, to a sensitive observer, there was something exquisitely painful in it. Her attire, which, indeed, she had wrought for the occasion, in prison, and had modelled much after her own fancy, seemed to express the attitude of her spirit, the desperate recklessness of her mood, by its wild and picturesque peculiarity. But the point which drew all eyes, and, as it were, transfigured the wearer,—so that both men and women, who had been familiarly acquainted with Hester Prynne, were now impressed as if they beheld her for the first time,—was that SCARLET LETTER, so fantastically embroidered and illuminated upon her bosom. It had the effect of a spell, taking her out of the ordinary relations with humanity, and inclosing her in a sphere by herself.

12   "She hath good skill at her needle, that's certain," remarked one of the female spectators; "but did ever a woman, before this brazen hussy, contrive such a way of showing it! Why, gossips, what is it but to laugh in the faces of our godly magistrates, and make a pride out of what they, worthy gentlemen, meant for a punishment?"

13   "It were well," muttered the most iron-visaged of the old dames, "if we stripped Madam Hester's rich gown off her dainty shoulders; and as for the red letter, which she hath stitched so curiously, I'll bestow a rag of mine own rheumatic flannel, to make a fitter one!"

14   "O, peace, neighbours, peace!" whispered their youngest companion. "Do not let her hear you! Not a stitch in that embroidered letter, but she has felt it in her heart."

15   The grim beadle now made a gesture with his staff.

16   "Make way, good people, make way, in the King's name," cried he. "Open a passage; and, I promise ye, Mistress Prynne shall be set where man, woman, and child may have a fair sight of her brave apparel, from this time till an hour past meridian. A blessing on the righteous Colony of the Massachusetts, where iniquity is dragged out into the sunshine! Come along, Madam Hester, and show your scarlet letter in the market-place!"

17   A lane was forth with opened through the crowd of spectators. Preceded by the beadle, and attended by an irregular procession of stern-browed men and unkindly-visaged women, Hester Prynne set forth towards the place appointed for her punishment. A crowd of eager and curious schoolboys, understanding little of the matter in hand, except that it gave them a half-holiday, ran before her progress, turning their heads continually to stare into her face, and at the winking baby in her arms, and at the ignominious letter on her breast. It was no great distance, in those days, from the prison-door to the market-place. Measured by the prisoner's experience, however, it might be reckoned a journey of some length; for, haughty as her demeanour was, she perchance underwent an agony from every footstep of those that thronged to see her, as if her heart had been flung into the street for them all to spurn and trample upon. In our nature, however, there is a provision, alike marvellous and merciful, that the sufferer should never know the intensity of what he endures by its present torture, but chiefly by the pang that rankles after it. With almost a serene deportment, therefore, Hester Prynne passed through this portion of her ordeal, and came to a sort of scaffold, at the western extremity of the market-place. It stood nearly beneath the eaves of Boston's earliest church, and appeared to be a fixture there.

18   In fact, this scaffold constituted a portion of a penal machine, which now, for two or three generations past, has been merely historical and traditionary among us, but was held, in the old time, to be as effectual an agent in the promotion of good citizenship, as ever was the guillotine among the terrorists of France. It was, in short, the platform of the pillory; and above it rose the framework of that instrument of discipline, so fashioned as to confine the human head in its tight grasp, and thus hold it up to the public gaze. The very ideal of ignominy was embodied and made manifest in this contrivance of wood and iron. There can be no outrage, methinks, against our common nature,—whatever be the delinquencies of the individual,—no outrage more flagrant than to forbid the culprit to hide his face for shame; as it was the essence of this punishment to do. In Hester Prynne's instance, however, as not unfrequently in other cases, her sentence bore, that she should stand a certain time upon the platform, but without undergoing that gripe about the neck and confinement of the head, the proneness to which was the most devilish characteristic of this ugly engine. Knowing well her part, she ascended a flight of wooden steps, and was thus displayed to the surrounding multitude, at about the height of a man's shoulders above the street.

19   Had there been a Papist among the crowd of Puritans, he might have seen in this beautiful woman, so picturesque in her attire and mien, and with the infant at her bosom, an object to remind him of the image of Divine Maternity, which

so many illustrious painters have vied with one another to represent; something which should remind him, indeed, but only by contrast, of that sacred image of sinless motherhood, whose infant was to redeem the world. Here, there was the taint of deepest sin in the most sacred quality of human life, working such effect, that the world was only the darker for this woman's beauty, and the more lost for the infant that she had borne.

20   The scene was not without a mixture of awe, such as must always invest the spectacle of guilt and shame in a fellow creature, before society shall have grown corrupt enough to smile, instead of shuddering, at it. The witnesses of Hester Prynne's disgrace had not yet passed beyond their simplicity. They were stern enough to look upon her death, had that been the sentence, without a murmur at its severity, but had none of the heartlessness of another social state, which would find only a theme for jest in an exhibition like the present. Even had there been a disposition to turn the matter into ridicule, it must have been repressed and overpowered by the solemn presence of men no less dignified than the Governor, and several of his counsellors, a judge, a general, and the ministers of the town; all of whom sat or stood in a balcony of the meeting-house, looking down upon the platform. When such personages could constitute a part of the spectacle, without risking the majesty or reverence of rank and office, it was safely to be inferred that the infliction of a legal sentence would have an earnest and effectual meaning. Accordingly, the crowd was sombre and grave. The unhappy culprit sustained herself as best a woman might, under the heavy weight of a thousand unrelenting eyes, all fastened upon her, and concentred at her bosom. It was almost intolerable to be borne. Of an impulsive and passionate nature, she had fortified herself to encounter the stings and venomous stabs of public contumely, wreaking itself in every variety of insult; but there was a quality so much more terrible in the solemn mood of the popular mind, that she longed rather to behold all those rigid countenances contorted with scornful merriment, and herself the object. Had a roar of laughter burst from the multitude,—each man, each woman, each little shrill-voiced child, contributing their individual parts,—Hester Prynne might have repaid them all with a bitter and disdainful smile. But, under the leaden infliction which it was her doom to endure, she felt, at moments, as if she must needs shriek out with the full power of her lungs, and cast herself from the scaffold down upon the ground, or else go mad at once.

21   Yet there were intervals when the whole scene, in which she was the most conspicuous object, seemed to vanish from her eyes, or, at least, glimmered indistinctly before them, like a mass of imperfectly shaped and spectral images. Her mind, and especially her memory, was preternaturally active, and kept bringing up other scenes than this roughly hewn street of a little town, on the edge of the Western wilderness; other faces than were lowering upon her from beneath the brims of those steeple-crowned hats. Reminiscences, the most trifling and immaterial, passages of infancy and school-days, sports, childish quarrels, and the little domestic traits of her maiden years, came swarming back upon her, intermingled with recollections of whatever was gravest in her subsequent life; one picture precisely as vivid as another; as if all were of similar importance, or all alike a play. Possibly,

it was an instinctive device of her spirit, to relieve itself, by the exhibition of
these phantasmagoric forms, from the cruel weight and hardness of the reality.

22   Be that as it might, the scaffold of the pillory was a point of view that
revealed to Hester Prynne the entire track along which she had been treading,
since her happy infancy. Standing on that miserable eminence, she saw again her
native village, in Old England, and her paternal home; a decayed house of gray
stone, with a poverty-stricken aspect, but retaining a half-obliterated shield of
arms over the portal, in token of antique gentility. She saw her father's face, with
its bald brow, and reverend white beard, that flowed over the old-fashioned Elizabethan ruff; her mother's, too, with the look of heedful and anxious love which
it always wore in her remembrance, and which, even since her death, had so often
laid the impediment of a gentle remonstrance in her daughter's pathway. She saw
her own face, glowing with girlish beauty, and illuminating all the interior of
the dusky mirror in which she had been wont to gaze at it. There she beheld
another countenance, of a man well stricken in years, a pale, thin, scholar-like
visage, with eyes dim and bleared by the lamp-light that had served them to pore
over many ponderous books. Yet those same bleared optics had a strange, pene-
trating power, when it was their owner's purpose to read the human soul. This
figure of the study and the cloister, as Hester Prynne's womanly fancy failed not
to recall, was slightly deformed, with the left shoulder a trifle higher than the
right. Next rose before her, in memory's picture-gallery, the intricate and narrow
thoroughfares, the tall, gray houses, the huge cathedrals, and the public edifices,
ancient in date and quaint in architecture, of a Continental city; where a new life
had awaited her, still in connection with the misshapen scholar; a new life, but
feeding itself on time-worn materials, like a tuft of green moss on a crumbling
wall. Lastly, in lieu of these shifting scenes, came back the rude market-place of
the Puritan settlement, with all the townspeople assembled and levelling their
stern regards at Hester Prynne,—yes, at herself,—who stood on the scaffold of
the pillory, an infant on her arm, and the letter A, in scarlet, fantastically embroidered with gold thread, upon her bosom!

23   Could it be true? She clutched the child so fiercely to her breast, that it sent
forth a cry; she turned her eyes downward at the scarlet letter, and even touched
it with her finger, to assure herself that the infant and the shame were real.
Yes!—these were her realities,—all else had vanished!

CHAPTER 2

JOURNAL

1. **MLA Works Cited** *Using this model, record this book.*
   Author's Last Name, First Name. The Scarlet Letter. *1850.* Title of This Book.
   Ed. First Name Last Name. City: Publisher, year.
2. **Main Character(s)** *Describe each main character and explain why you think each
   is a main character.*

3. **Supporting Characters** *Describe each supporting character and explain why you think each is a supporting character.*
4. **Setting** *Describe the setting(s) and any relevant prop(s).*
5. **Sequence** *Outline the events in this chapter in order.*
6. **Plot** *Summarize this chapter's events in no more than two sentences.*
7. **Conflicts** *Identify and explain all conflicts involved in this chapter.*
8. **Significant Quotations** *Explain the importance of each of these quotations. Record the page number in the parentheses.*
   a. "Amongst any other population, or at a later period in the history of New England, the grim rigidity that petrified the bearded physiognomies of these good people would have augured some awful business in hand [. . .]" (   ).
   b. "Meagre, indeed, and cold, was the sympathy that a transgressor might look for, from such by-standers at the scaffold [. . .]" (   ).
   c. "On the other hand, a penalty which, in our days, would infer a degree of mocking infamy and ridicule, might then be invested with almost as stern a dignity as the punishment of death itself" (   ).
   d. "[T]he women, of whom there were several in the crowd, appeared to take a peculiar interest in whatever penal infliction might be expected to ensue [. . .]" (   ).
   e. "On the breast of her gown, in fine red cloth, surrounded with elaborate embroidery and fantastic flourishes of gold thread, appeared the letter A [. . .]" (   ).
9. **Recap** *Summarize what has happened so far, from the beginning of the book through this chapter.*

FOLLOW-UP QUESTIONS

6 SHORT QUESTIONS

Select the __best__ answer for each.

____ 1. Hester Prynne is
    a. the prisoner.
    b. the minister.
    c. a member of the crowd.

____ 2. Hester Prynne is holding
    a. a book.
    b. a sword.
    c. a baby.

____ 3. The harshest comments in the crowd are made by
    a. magistrates.
    b. ministers.
    c. women.

____ 4. The punishment includes
    a. a public whipping.
    b. wearing a red letter A.
    c. asking for forgiveness.

____ 5. On the scaffold, Hester Prynne
    a. cries.
    b. begs to get down.
    c. thinks about her past life.

____ 6. Despite the ordeal of punishment, the prisoner appears
    a. beautiful.
    b. tearful.
    c. asleep.

5 SIGNIFICANT QUOTATIONS

Explain the importance of each of these quotations.

1. "In either case, there was very much the same solemnity of demeanor on the part of the spectators; as befitted a people amongst whom religion and law were almost identical, and in whose character both were so thoroughly inter-fused, that the mildest and the severest acts of public discipline were alike made venerable and awful [. . .]."
2. " 'This woman has brought shame upon us all, and ought to die. Is there not law for it? Truly there is, both in the Scripture and the statute-book. Then let the magistrates, who have made it of no effect, thank themselves if their own wives and daughters go astray' "
3. "[L]ike a black shadow emerging into the sunshine, the grim and grisly presence of the town-beadle, with a sword by his side and his staff of office in his hand [. . .] represented in his aspect the whole dismal severity of the Puritanic code of law [. . .]."
4. "But the point which drew all eyes, and, as it were, transfigured the wearer,— so that both men and women, who had been familiarly acquainted with Hester Prynne, were now impressed as if they beheld her for the first time,—was that SCARLET LETTER, so fantastically embroidered and illuminated upon her bosom [. . .]."
5. " 'Do not let her hear you! Not a stitch in that embroidered letter, but she has felt it in her heart.' "

2 COMPREHENSION ESSAY QUESTIONS

Use specific details and information from the chapter to answer these questions as completely as possible.

1. How do members of the crowd react to Hester Prynne and her punishment? Use specific details and information from the chapter to support your explanation.
2. How does Hester Prynne endure her public punishment? Use specific details and information from the chapter to support your explanation.

DISCUSSION QUESTIONS

Be prepared to discuss these questions in class.

How do the people of this town feel about punishment?
Why are the women in the crowd such harsh critics?

CHAPTER 3

THE RECOGNITION

Use context clues to define these words before reading. Use a dictionary as needed.

1. With the shock of *recognition*, I realized that the woman in the grocery store was my first grade teacher, whom I had not seen in years. *Recognition* means

   _____.

2. French cosmetic companies sell *visage* creams that are supposed to erase facial wrinkles and soften facial skin. *Visage* means _____

   _____.

3. The flu sometimes *manifests* itself as fever, chills, and dizziness. *Manifest* means _____.

4. Even with her glasses on, Aunt Clara has trouble *discerning* the small print in the newspaper. *Discern* means _____

   _____.

5. Advancing technology, from cars and televisions to computers and cell phones, has *wrought* many changes in our lives. *Wrought* means _____

   _____.

6. Marshall *writhed* in pain when someone accidentally touched his sunburn. *Writhe* means _____

   _____.

7. After getting two D's the first semester, Jeffrey realized that it *behooved* him to study several hours a week. *Behoove* means _____

   _____.

8. Carmella is very *conscious* of everything around her and always seems to know what everyone is saying. *Conscious* means _____

   _____.

9. After his accident, the patient *convulsed* in pain, twisting and jerking his body violently. *Convulse* means _____
_____.

10. Professor Sisko's *passion* for her subject matter is so strong that all who listen to her are inspired to learn more. *Passion* means _____
_____.

11. Leslie was so nervous about speaking in front of a full auditorium that her hands shook *tremulously*. *Tremulously* means _____
_____.

12. Lourdes *concealed* her wallet in the zippered pocket of her purse so that no one could see it. *Conceal* means _____
_____.

13. Evan is guilty of *hypocrisy*, telling others to do one thing while he takes the easy way out and does another. *Hypocrisy* means _____
_____.

14. Using evidence and clear arguments, the defense lawyer *exhorted* the court to find his client innocent of all charges. *Exhort* means _____
_____.

15. After the funeral, a *somber* group of mourners gathered at the cemetery to pay their respects. *Somber* means _____
_____.

16. Lorraine was so *repentant* after losing her mother's watch that she went to the store to replace it. *Repentant* means _____
_____.

17. Donald committed *adultery* when he cheated on his wife by dating another woman. *Adultery* means _____
_____.

18. Circus entertainers are noted for their eye-catching *garb*: brightly colored shirts, tight-fitting pants with sequins, and hats with feathers. *Garb* means
_____.

19. The released prisoner was glad to be free after months of *captivity*. *Captivity* means _____
_____.

20. Mary Victoria is a wonderful doctor and always takes time to offer understanding and *sympathy* to her patients. *Sympathy* means _____

_____.

PRE-READING VOCABULARY
STRUCTURAL ATTACK

Define these words by solving the parts. Use the Glossary or a dictionary as needed.

1. irresistibly	13. multitude	25. riddled
2. infrequent	14. temperament	26. ignominy
3. excluded	15. insensibility	27. audible
4. heterogeneous	16. remorseless	28. strived
5. heathen	17. consciousness	29. endeavor
6. subside	18. pedestal	30. penetrative
7. redeem	19. universal	31. sojourn
8. iniquity	20. savagely	32. wilderness
9. intense	21. clergyman	33. disarray
10. amidst	22. furrowed	34. mishaps
11. ill-fitted	23. uttered	35. wanderer
12. self-congratulation	24. keenly	

PRE-READING QUESTIONS

Try answering these questions as you read.

Whom does Hester Prynne recognize in the crowd?
Who is Master Dimmesdale?
What crime has Hester Prynne committed?
Why does she not receive the death penalty for her crime?

CHAPTER 3

THE RECOGNITION

1 From this intense consciousness of being the object of severe and universal observation, the wearer of the scarlet letter was at length relieved by discerning, on the outskirts of the crowd, a figure which irresistibly took possession of her thoughts. An Indian, in his native garb, was standing there; but the red men were not so infrequent visitors of the English settlements, that one of them would have attracted any notice from Hester Prynne, at such a time; much less would he have excluded all other objects and ideas from her mind. By the Indian's side,

and evidently sustaining a companionship with him, stood a white man, clad in a strange disarray of civilized and savage costume.

2   He was small in stature, with a furrowed visage, which, as yet, could hardly be termed aged. There was a remarkable intelligence in his features, as of a person who had so cultivated his mental part that it could not fail to mould the physical to itself, and become manifest by unmistakable tokens. Although, by a seemingly careless arrangement of his heterogeneous garb, he had endeavoured to conceal or abate the peculiarity, it was sufficiently evident to Hester Prynne, that one of this man's shoulders rose higher than the other. Again, at the first instant of perceiving that thin visage, and the slight deformity of the figure, she pressed her infant to her bosom, with so convulsive a force that the poor babe uttered another cry of pain. But the mother did not seem to hear it.

3   At his arrival in the market-place, and some time before she saw him, the stranger had bent his eyes on Hester Prynne. It was carelessly, at first, like a man chiefly accustomed to look inward, and to whom external matters are of little value and import, unless they bear relation to something within his mind. Very soon, however, his look became keen and penetrative. A writhing horror twisted itself across his features, like a snake gliding swiftly over them, and making one little pause, with all its wreathed intervolutions in open sight. His face darkened with some powerful emotion, which, nevertheless, he so instantaneously controlled by an effort of his will, that, save at a single moment, its expression might have passed for calmness. After a brief space, the convulsion grew almost imperceptible, and finally subsided into the depths of his nature. When he found the eyes of Hester Prynne fastened on his own, and saw that she appeared to recognize him, he slowly and calmly raised his finger, made a gesture with it in the air, and laid it on his lips.

4   Then, touching the shoulder of a townsman who stood next to him, he addressed him in a formal and courteous manner.

5   "I pray you, good Sir," said he, "who is this woman?—and wherefore is she here set up to public shame?"

6   "You must needs be a stranger in this region, friend," answered the townsman, looking curiously at the questioner and his savage companion; "else you would surely have heard of Mistress Hester Prynne, and her evil doings. She hath raised a great scandal, I promise you, in godly Master Dimmesdale's church."

7   "You say truly," replied the other. "I am a stranger, and have been a wanderer, sorely against my will. I have met with grievous mishaps by sea and land, and have been long held in bonds among the heathen-folk, to the southward; and am now brought hither by this Indian, to be redeemed out of my captivity. Will it please you, therefore, to tell me of Hester Prynne's,—have I her name rightly?— of this woman's offences, and what has brought her to yonder scaffold?"

8   "Truly, friend, and methinks it must gladden your heart, after your troubles and sojourn in the wilderness," said the townsman, "to find yourself, at length, in a land where iniquity is searched out, and punished in the sight of rulers and people; as here in our godly New England. Yonder woman, Sir, you must know,

was the wife of a certain learned man, English by birth, but who had long dwelt in Amsterdam, whence, some good time agone, he was minded to cross over and cast in his lot with us of the Massachusetts. To this purpose, he sent his wife before him, remaining himself to look after some necessary affairs. Marry, good Sir, in some two years, or less, that the woman has been a dweller here in Boston, no tidings have come of this learned gentleman, Master Prynne; and his young wife, look you, being left to her own misguidance—"

9   "Ah!—aha!—I conceive you," said the stranger, with a bitter smile. "So learned a man as you speak of should have learned this too in his books. And who, by your favor, Sir, may be the father of yonder babe—it is some three or four months old, I should judge—which Mistress Prynne is holding in her arms?"

10   "Of a truth, friend, that matter remaineth a riddle; and the Daniel who shall expound it is yet a-wanting," answered the townsman. "Madam Hester absolutely refuseth to speak, and the magistrates have laid their heads together in vain. Peradventure the guilty one stands looking on at this sad spectacle, unknown of man, and forgetting that God sees him."

11   "The learned man," observed the stranger, with another smile, "should come himself to look into the mystery."

12   "It behooves him well, if he be still in life," responded the townsman. "Now, good Sir, our Massachusetts magistracy, bethinking themselves that this woman is youthful and fair, and doubtless was strongly tempted to her fall;—and that, moreover, as is most likely, her husband may be at the bottom of the sea;—they have not been bold to put in force the extremity of our righteous law against her. The penalty thereof is death. But, in their great mercy and tenderness of heart, they have doomed Mistress Prynne to stand only a space of three hours on the platform of the pillory, and then and thereafter, for the remainder of her natural life, to wear a mark of shame upon her bosom."

13   "A wise sentence!" remarked the stranger, gravely bowing his head. "Thus she will be a living sermon against sin, until the ignominious letter be engraved upon her tombstone. It irks me, nevertheless, that the partner of her iniquity should not, at least, stand on the scaffold by her side. But he will be known!—he will be known!—he will be known!"

14   He bowed courteously to the communicative townsman, and, whispering a few words to his Indian attendant, they both made their way through the crowd.

15   While this passed, Hester Prynne had been standing on her pedestal, still with a fixed gaze towards the stranger; so fixed a gaze, that, at moments of intense absorption, all other objects in the visible world seemed to vanish, leaving only him and her. Such an interview, perhaps, would have been more terrible than ever to meet him as she now did, with the hot, mid-day sun burning down upon her face, and lighting up its shame; with the scarlet token of infamy on her breast; with the sin-born infant in her arms; with a whole people, drawn forth as to a festival, staring at the features that should have been seen only in the quiet gleam of the fireside, in the happy shadow of a home, or beneath a matronly veil, at church. Dreadful as it was, she was conscious of a shelter in the presence of

ousand witnesses. It was better to stand thus, with so many betwixt him and her, than to greet him, face to face, they two alone. She fled for refuge, as it were, to the public exposure, and dreaded the moment when its protection should be withdrawn from her. Involved in these thoughts, she scarcely heard a voice behind her, until it had repeated her name more than once, in a loud and solemn tone, audible to the whole multitude.

16   "Hearken unto me, Hester Prynne!" said the voice.

17   It has already been noticed, that directly over the platform on which Hester Prynne stood was a kind of balcony, or open gallery, appended to the meeting-house. It was the place whence proclamations were wont to be made, amidst an assemblage of the magistracy, with all the ceremonial that attended such public observances in those days. Here, to witness the scene which we are describing, sat Governor Bellingham himself, with four sergeants about his chair, bearing halberds, as a guard of honor. He wore a dark feather in his hat, a border of embroidery on his cloak, and a black velvet tunic beneath; a gentleman advanced in years, and with a hard experience written in his wrinkles. He was not ill fitted to be the head and representative of a community, which owed its origin and progress, and its present state of development, not to the impulses of youth, but to the stern and tempered energies of manhood, and the sombre sagacity of age; accomplishing so much, precisely because it imagined and hoped so little. The other eminent characters, by whom the chief ruler was surrounded, were distinguished by a dignity of mien, belonging to a period when the forms of authority were felt to possess the sacredness of divine institutions. They were, doubtless, good men, just, and sage. But, out of the whole human family, it would not have been easy to select the same number of wise and virtuous persons, who should be less capable of sitting in judgment on an erring woman's heart, and disentangling its mesh of good and evil, than the sages of rigid aspect towards whom Hester Prynne now turned her face. She seemed conscious, indeed, that whatever sympathy she might expect lay in the larger and warmer heart of the multitude; for, as she lifted her eyes towards the balcony, the unhappy woman grew pale and trembled.

18   The voice which had called her attention was that of the reverend and famous John Wilson, the eldest clergyman of Boston, a great scholar, like most of his contemporaries in the profession, and withal a man of kind and genial spirit. This last attribute, however, had been less carefully developed than his intellectual gifts, and was, in truth, rather a matter of shame than self-congratulation with him. There he stood, with a border of grizzled locks beneath his skull-cap; while his gray eyes, accustomed to the shaded light of his study, were winking, like those of Hester's infant, in the unadulterated sunshine. He looked like the darkly engraved portraits which we see prefixed to old volumes of sermons; and had no more right than one of those portraits would have, to step forth, as he now did, and meddle with a question of human guilt, passion, and anguish.

19   "Hester Prynne," said the clergyman, "I have striven with my young brother here, under whose preaching of the word you have been privileged to sit,"—here Mr. Wilson laid his hand on the shoulder of a pale young man beside him,—"I

have sought, I say, to persuade this godly youth, that he should deal with you, here in the face of Heaven, and before these wise and upright rulers, and in hearing of all the people, as touching the vileness and blackness of your sin. Knowing your natural temper better than I, he could the better judge what arguments to use, whether of tenderness or terror, such as might prevail over your hardness and obstinacy; insomuch that you should no longer hide the name of him who tempted you to this grievous fall. But he opposes to me, (with a young man's oversoftness, albeit wise beyond his years,) that it were wronging the very nature of woman to force her to lay open her heart's secrets in such broad daylight, and in presence of so great a multitude. Truly, as I sought to convince him, the shame lay in the commission of the sin, and not in the showing of it forth. What say you to it, once again, brother Dimmesdale? Must it be thou or I that shall deal with this poor sinner's soul?"

20 There was a murmur among the dignified and reverend occupants of the balcony; and Governor Bellingham gave expression to its purport, speaking in an authoritative voice, although tempered with respect towards the youthful clergyman whom he addressed.

21 "Good Master Dimmesdale," said he, "the responsibility of this woman's soul lies greatly with you. It behooves you, therefore, to exhort her to repentance, and to confession, as a proof and consequence thereof."

22 The directness of his appeal drew the eyes of the whole crowd upon the Reverend Mr. Dimmesdale; a young clergyman, who had come from one of the great English universities, bringing all the learning of the age into our wild forest-land. His eloquence and religious fervor had already given the earnest of high eminence in his profession. He was a person of very striking aspect, with a white, lofty, and impending brow, large, brown, melancholy eyes, and a mouth which, unless when he forcibly compressed it, was apt to be tremulous, expressing both nervous sensibility and a vast power of self-restraint. Notwithstanding his high native gifts and scholar-like attainments, there was an air about this young minister,—an apprehensive, a startled, a half-frightened look,—as of a being who felt himself quite astray and at a loss in the pathway of human existence, and could only be at ease in some seclusion of his own. Therefore, so far as his duties would permit, he trode in the shadowy by-paths, and thus kept himself simple and childlike; coming forth, when occasion was, with a freshness, and fragrance, and dewy purity of thought, which, as many people said, affected them like the speech of an angel.

23 Such was the young man whom the Reverend Mr. Wilson and the Governor had introduced so openly to the public notice, bidding him speak, in the hearing of all men, to that mystery of a woman's soul, so sacred even in its pollution. The trying nature of his position drove the blood from his cheek, and made his lips tremulous.

24 "Speak to the woman, my brother," said Mr. Wilson. "It is of moment to her soul, and therefore, as the worshipful Governor says, momentous to thine own, in whose charge hers is. Exhort her to confess the truth!"

25   The Reverend Mr. Dimmesdale bent his head, in silent prayer, as it seemed, and then, came forward.

26   "Hester Prynne," said he, leaning over the balcony, and looking down stedfastly into her eyes, "thou hearest what this good man says, and seest the accountability under which I labor. If thou feelest it to be for thy soul's peace, and that thy earthly punishment will thereby be more effectual to salvation, I charge thee to speak out the name of thy fellow-sinner and fellow-sufferer! Be not silent from any mistaken pity and tenderness for him; for, believe me, Hester, though he were to step down from a high place, and stand there beside thee, on thy pedestal of shame, yet better were it so, than to hide a guilty heart through life. What can thy silence do for him, except it tempt him—yea, compel him, as it were—to add hypocrisy to sin? Heaven hath granted thee an open ignominy, that thereby thou mayest work out an open triumph over the evil within thee, and the sorrow without. Take heed how thou deniest to him—who, perchance, hath not the courage to grasp it for himself—the bitter, but wholesome, cup that is now presented to thy lips!"

27   The young pastor's voice was tremulously sweet, rich, deep, and broken. The feeling that it so evidently manifested, rather than the direct purport of the words, caused it to vibrate within all hearts, and brought the listeners into one accord of sympathy. Even the poor baby, at Hester's bosom, was affected by the same influence; for it directed its hitherto vacant gaze towards Mr. Dimmesdale, and held up its little arms, with a half pleased, half plaintive murmur. So powerful seemed the minister's appeal, that the people could not believe but that Hester Prynne would speak out the guilty name; or else that the guilty one himself, in whatever high or lowly place he stood, would be drawn forth by an inward and inevitable necessity, and compelled to ascend the scaffold.

28   Hester shook her head.

29   "Woman, transgress not beyond the limits of Heaven's mercy!" cried the Reverend Mr. Wilson, more harshly than before. "That little babe hath been gifted with a voice, to second and confirm the counsel which thou hast heard. Speak out the name! That, and thy repentance, may avail to take the scarlet letter off thy breast."

30   "Never!" replied Hester Prynne, looking, not at Mr. Wilson, but into the deep and troubled eyes of the younger clergyman. "It is too deeply branded. Ye cannot take it off. And would that I might endure his agony, as well as mine!"

31   "Speak, woman!" said another voice, coldly and sternly, proceeding from the crowd about the scaffold. "Speak; and give your child a father!"

32   "I will not speak!" answered Hester, turning pale as death, but responding to this voice, which she too surely recognized. "And my child must seek a heavenly Father; she shall never know an earthly one!"

33   "She will not speak!" murmured Mr. Dimmesdale, who, leaning over the balcony, with his hand upon his heart, had awaited the result of his appeal. He now drew back, with a long respiration. "Wondrous strength and generosity of a woman's heart! She will not speak!"

34   Discerning the impracticable state of the poor culprit's mind, the elder clergyman, who had carefully prepared himself for the occasion, addressed to the multitude a discourse on sin, in all its branches, but with continual reference to the
ignominious letter. So forcibly did he dwell upon this symbol, for the hour or more
during which his periods were rolling over the people's heads, that it assumed new
terrors in their imagination, and seemed to derive its scarlet hue from the flames of
the infernal pit. Hester Prynne, meanwhile, kept her place upon the pedestal of
shame, with glazed eyes, and an air of weary indifference. She had borne, that
morning, all that nature could endure; and as her temperament was not of the order
that escapes from too intense suffering by a swoon, her spirit could only shelter
itself beneath a stony crust of insensibility, while the faculties of animal life
remained entire. In this state, the voice of the preacher thundered remorselessly,
but unavailingly, upon her ears. The infant, during the latter portion of her ordeal,
pierced the air with its wailings and screams; she strove to hush it, mechanically,
but seemed scarcely to sympathize with its trouble. With the same hard
demeanour, she was led back to prison, and vanished from the public gaze within
its iron-clamped portal. It was whispered, by those who peered after her, that the
scarlet letter threw a lurid gleam along the dark passage-way of the interior.

CHAPTER 3

JOURNAL

1. **MLA Works Cited** *Using this model, record this book.*
   Author's Last Name, First Name. The Scarlet Letter. *1850.* Title of This Book.
   Ed. First Name Last Name. City: Publisher, year.
2. **Main Character(s)** *Describe each main character and explain why you think each
   is a main character.*
3. **Supporting Characters** *Describe each supporting character and explain why you
   think each is a supporting character.*
4. **Setting** *Describe the setting(s) and any relevant prop(s).*
5. **Sequence** *Outline the events in this chapter in order.*
6. **Plot** *Summarize this chapter's events in no more than two sentences.*
7. **Conflicts** *Identify and explain all conflicts involved in this chapter.*
8. **Significant Quotations** *Explain the importance of each of these quotations. Record
   the page number in the parentheses.*
   a. "'You must needs be a stranger in this region, friend,' answered the towns-
      man, looking curiously at the questioner and his savage companion; 'else
      you would surely have heard of Mistress Hester Prynne, and her evil
      doings. She hath raised a great scandal, I promise you, in godly Master
      Dimmesdale's church'" (   ).
   b. "'Truly, friend, and methinks it must gladden your heart, after your troubles
      and sojourn in the wilderness,' said the townsman, 'to find yourself, at

length, in a land where iniquity is searched out, and punished in the sight
of rulers and people; as here in godly New England [. . .]'" (   ).

c. "'[I]n some two years, or less, that the woman has been a dweller here in
Boston, no tidings have come of this learned gentleman, Master Prynne; and
his young wife, look you, being left to her own misguidance—'" (   ).

d. "'The learned man,' observed the stranger, with another smile, 'should
come himself to look into the mystery'" (   ).

e. "'Take heed how thou deniest to him—who, perchance, hath not the
courage to grasp it for himself—the bitter, but wholesome, cup that is now
presented to thy lips!'" (   ).

9. **Recap** *Summarize what has happened so far, from the beginning of the book through
this chapter.*

FOLLOW-UP QUESTIONS

6 SHORT QUESTIONS

Select the <u>best</u> answer for each.

_____ 1. The stranger at the edge of
the crowd
a. does not know Hester
Prynne.
b. is tall and well-built.
c. has been in Indian
captivity for a while.

_____ 2. Hester Prynne's crime is
a. adultery.
b. witchcraft.
c. robbery.

_____ 3. Hester Prynne does not receive
the death penalty because
a. the crime does not call for it.
b. her husband is missing
and presumed dead.
c. she reveals the name
of the baby's father.

_____ 4. Hester Prynne belongs to the
church led by
a. John Wilson.
b. Governor Bellingham.
c. Arthur Dimmesdale.

_____ 5. Hester Prynne is sentenced
to stand on the scaffold
a. for three days.
b. for three hours.
c. from dawn to sunset.

_____ 6. Arthur Dimmesdale seems
to be
a. old and deformed.
b. old and scholarly.
c. young and handsome.

5 SIGNIFICANT QUOTATIONS

Explain the importance of each of these quotations.

1. "By the Indian's side, and evidently sustaining a companionship with him,
stood a white man, clad in a strange disarray of civilized and savage costume."

2. "Again, at the first instant of perceiving that thin visage, and the slight deformity of the figure, she pressed her infant to her bosom, with so convulsive a force that the poor babe uttered another cry of pain. But the mother did not seem to hear it."
3. "Very soon, however, his look became keen and penetrative. A writhing horror twisted itself across his features, like a snake gliding swiftly over them [. . .]. Then his face darkened with some powerful emotion, which, nevertheless, he so instantaneously controlled by an effort of his will, that, save at a single moment, its expression might have passed for calmness [. . .]."
4. "When he found the eyes of Hester Prynne fastened on his own, and saw that she appeared to recognize him, he slowly and calmly raised his finger, made a gesture with it in the air, and laid it on his lips."
5. "'[. . .] I am a stranger and have been a wanderer, sorely against my will [. . .] and am now brought hither by this Indian, to be redeemed out of my captivity. Will it please you, therefore, to tell me of Hester Prynne's,—have I got her name rightly?—of this woman's offences, and what has brought her to yonder scaffold?'"

2 COMPREHENSION ESSAY QUESTIONS

Use specific details and information from the chapter to answer these questions as completely as possible.

1. Part of understanding a novel is keeping track of the characters. Which characters do you feel are important at this point?
2. How does the chapter title "The Recognition" relate to the story so far? Explain the significance of the title using specific details and information from the story thus far.

DISCUSSION QUESTIONS

Be prepared to discuss these questions in class.

1. What is the nature of Hester's crime and punishment? Do you think it is fair?
2. Who is the stranger at the edge of the crowd? What does he look like?

CHAPTER 4

THE INTERVIEW

PRE-READING VOCABULARY
CONTEXT

Use context clues to define these words before reading. Use a dictionary as needed.

1. Maria tried to *quell* her nervous laughter during the job interview by thinking of sad things. *Quell* means _____
_____.

2. In the military, soldiers who do not follow orders are guilty of *insubordination*. *Insubordination* means _____
_____.

3. In the hospital *maternity* ward, we visited new mother Laura and her new baby, Alex. *Maternity* means _____
_____.

4. The dog's ears and tail went down when his owner *rebuked* him for sleeping on the couch. *Rebuked* means _____
_____.

5. *Alchemy* is an old form of chemistry and natural science, used centuries ago to try to turn ordinary stones into gold. *Alchemy* means _____
_____.

6. We *sojourned* in the Bahamas for two weeks last winter. *Sojourned* means_____
_____.

7. We drank *draughts* of beer from the keg to celebrate our victory. *Draughts* means
_____.

8. Elizabeth was *apprehensive* about taking another biology test because she had failed the first two tests. *Apprehensive* means _____
_____.

9. The witness *pledged* an *oath* to tell the whole truth in court. *Pledge* and *oath* mean
_____.

10. The cold wind made me *shudder* and shiver uncontrollably, so I went back into the house for warmer clothes. *Shudder* means _____
_____ .

11. A marathon runner must *quaff* many glasses of water to avoid becoming dehydrated during a run. *Quaff* means _____
_____ .

12. Having lost the series to the Tigers last years, the Mets played with a *vengeance* in order to avoid a similar outcome. *Vengeance* means _____
_____ .

13. Some people think it is *folly* to buy lottery tickets because the chances of winning are so slim. *Folly* means _____
_____ .

14. A *multitude* of shoppers crowded the mall during the holiday sales. *Multitude* means _____ .

15. Despite being caught with lipstick on his collar, the adulterous husband would not name his *paramour. Paramour* means _____
_____ .

16. The farmer demanded money and materials as *retribution* when the motorist crashed into his fence. *Retribution* means _____
_____ .

17. Before the party, we sprayed the deck with insecticide to *repel* insects. *Repel* means _____ .

18. Michael *deluded* himself into thinking he had lost the race when, in fact, he had won. *Deluded* means _____
_____ .

19. The seas were in *turmoil* during the storm as waves knocked boats against each other and winds toppled sails. *Turmoil* means _____
_____ .

20. Because she did not want to talk to her roommate, Ashley *feigned* sleep by closing her eyes and pretending to snore. *Feign* means_____
_____ .

PRE-READING VOCABULARY
STRUCTURAL ATTACK

Define these words by solving the parts. Use the Glossary or a dictionary as needed.

1. involuntary	11. postpone	21. repute
2. misshapen	12. avenge	22. physician
3. foresee	13. potent	23. dishonor
4. sphere	14. sagely	24. despair
5. quietude	15. decayed	25. efficacy
6. impossible	16. veiled	26. dewy
7. bewildered	17. depressed	27. slumbering
8. singular	18. frankly	28. soothed
9. convenient	19. kindled	29. earnestly
10. ransom	20. blissful	30. outskirts

PRE-READING QUESTIONS

Try answering these questions as you read.

Who is Roger Chillingworth and what does he look like?
Why is Roger Chillingworth staying in the prison?
On whom does Roger Chillingworth want revenge?
What promise does Hester make to Roger Chillingworth?

CHAPTER 4
THE INTERVIEW

1 After her return to the prison, Hester Prynne was found to be in a state of nervous excitement that demanded constant watchfulness, lest she should perpetrate violence on herself, or do some half-frenzied mischief to the poor babe. As night approached, it proving impossible to quell her insubordination by rebuke or threats of punishment, Master Brackett, the jailer, thought fit to introduce a physician. He described him as a man of skill in all Christian modes of physical science, and likewise familiar with whatever the savage people could teach, in respect to medicinal herbs and roots that grew in the forest. To say the truth, there was much need of professional assistance, not merely for Hester herself, but still more urgently for the child; who, drawing its sustenance from the maternal bosom, seemed to have drank in with it all the turmoil, the anguish, and despair, which pervaded the mother's system. It now writhed in convulsions of pain, and was a forcible type, in its little frame, of the moral agony which Hester Prynne had borne throughout the day.

2   Closely following the jailer into the dismal apartment, appeared that individual, of singular aspect, whose presence in the crowd had been of such deep interest to the wearer of the scarlet letter. He was lodged in the prison, not as suspected of any offence, but as the most convenient and suitable mode of disposing of him, until the magistrates should have conferred with the Indian sagamores respecting his ransom. His name was announced as Roger Chillingworth. The jailer, after ushering him into the room, remained a moment, marvelling at the comparative quiet that followed his entrance; for Hester Prynne had immediately become as still as death, although the child continued to moan.

3   "Prithee, friend, leave me alone with my patient," said the practitioner. "Trust me, good jailer, you shall briefly have peace in your house; and, I promise you, Mistress Prynne shall hereafter be more amenable to just authority than you may have found her heretofore."

4   "Nay, if your worship can accomplish that," answered Master Brackett, "I shall own you for a man of skill indeed! Verily, the woman hath been like a possessed one; and there lacks little, that I should take in hand to drive Satan out of her with stripes."

5   The stranger had entered the room with the characteristic quietude of the profession to which he announced himself as belonging. Nor did his demeanour change, when the withdrawal of the prison-keeper left him face to face with the woman, whose absorbed notice of him, in the crowd, had intimated so close a relation between himself and her. His first care was given to the child; whose cries, indeed, as she lay writhing on the trundle-bed, made it of peremptory necessity to postpone all other business to the task of soothing her. He examined the infant carefully, and then proceeded to unclasp a leathern case, which he took from beneath his dress. It appeared to contain certain medical preparations, one of which he mingled with a cup of water.

6   "My old studies in alchemy," observed he, "and my sojourn, for above a year past, among a people well versed in the kindly properties of simples, have made a better physician of me than many that claim the medical degree. Here, woman! The child is yours,—she is none of mine,—neither will she recognize my voice or aspect as a father's. Administer this draught, therefore, with thine own hand."

7   Hester repelled the offered medicine, at the same time gazing with strongly marked apprehension into his face.

8   "Wouldst thou avenge thyself on the innocent babe?" whispered she.

9   "Foolish woman!" responded the physician, half coldly, half soothingly. "What should ail me to harm this misbegotten and miserable babe? The medicine is potent for good; and were it my child,—yea, mine own, as well as thine!—I could do no better for it."

10   As she still hesitated, being, in fact, in no reasonable state of mind, he took the infant in his arms, and himself administered the draught. It soon proved its efficacy, and redeemed the leech's pledge. The moans of the little patient subsided; its convulsive tossings gradually ceased; and in a few moments, as is the custom of young children after relief from pain, it sank into a profound and dewy

slumber. The physician, as he had a fair right to be termed, next bestowed his attention on the mother. With calm and intent scrutiny, he felt her pulse, looked into her eyes,—a gaze that made her heart shrink and shudder, because so familiar, and yet so strange and cold,—and, finally, satisfied with his investigation, proceeded to mingle another draught.

11   "I know not Lethe nor Nepenthe," remarked he; "but I have learned many new secrets in the wilderness, and here is one of them,—a recipe that an Indian taught me, in requital of some lessons of my own, that were as old as Paracelsus. Drink it! It may be less soothing than a sinless conscience. That I cannot give thee. But it will calm the swell and heaving of thy passion, like oil thrown on the waves of a tempestuous sea."

12   He presented the cup to Hester, who received it with a slow, earnest look into his face; not precisely a look of fear, yet full of doubt and questioning, as to what his purposes might be. She looked also at her slumbering child.

13   "I have thought of death," she said,—"have wished for it,—would even have prayed for it, were it fit that such as I should pray for any thing. Yet, if death be in this cup, I bid thee think again, ere thou beholdest me quaff it. See! It is even now at my lips."

14   "Drink, then," replied he, still with the same cold composure. "Dost thou know me so little, Hester Prynne? Are my purposes wont to be so shallow? Even if I imagine a scheme of vengeance, what could I do better for my object than to let thee live,—than to give thee medicines against all harm and peril of life,—so that this burning shame may still blaze upon thy bosom?"—As he spoke, he laid his long forefinger on the scarlet letter, which forthwith seemed to scorch into Hester's breast, as if it had been red-hot. He noticed her involuntary gesture, and smiled.—"Live, therefore, and bear about thy doom with thee, in the eyes of men and women,—in the eyes of him whom thou didst call thy husband,—in the eyes of yonder child! And, that thou mayest live, take off this draught."

15   Without further expostulation or delay, Hester Prynne drained the cup, and, at the motion of the man of skill, seated herself on the bed where the child was sleeping; while he drew the only chair which the room afforded, and took his own seat beside her. She could not but tremble at these preparations; for she felt that—having now done all that humanity, or principle, or, if so it were, a refined cruelty, impelled him to do, for the relief of physical suffering—he was next to treat with her as the man whom she had most deeply and irreparably injured.

16   "Hester," said he, "I ask not wherefore, nor how, thou hast fallen into the pit, or say rather, thou hast ascended to the pedestal of infamy, on which I found thee. The reason is not far to seek. It was my folly, and thy weakness. I,—a man of thought,—the book worm of great libraries,—a man already in decay, having given my best years to feed the hungry dream of knowledge,—what had I to do with youth and beauty like thine own! Misshapen from my birth-hour, how could I delude myself with the idea that intellectual gifts might veil physical deformity in a young girl's fantasy! Men call me wise. If sages were ever wise in their own behoof, I might have foreseen all this. I might have known that, as

I came out of the vast and dismal forest, and entered this settlement of Christian men, the very first object to meet my eyes would be thyself, Hester Prynne, standing up, a statue of ignominy, before the people. Nay, from the moment when we came down the old church-steps together, a married pair, I might have beheld the bale-fire of that scarlet letter blazing at the end of our path!"

17 "Thou knowest," said Hester,—for, depressed as she was, she could not endure this last quiet stab at the token of her shame,—"thou knowest that I was frank with thee. I felt no love, nor feigned any."

18 "True!" replied he. "It was my folly! I have said it. But, up to that epoch of my life, I had lived in vain. The world had been so cheerless! My heart was a habitation large enough for many guests, but lonely and chill, and without a household fire. I longed to kindle one! It seemed not so wild a dream,—old as I was, and sombre as I was, and misshapen as I was,—that the simple bliss, which is scattered far and wide, for all mankind to gather up, might yet be mine. And so, Hester, I drew thee into my heart, into its innermost chamber, and sought to warm thee by the warmth which thy presence made there!"

19 "I have greatly wronged thee," murmured Hester.

20 "We have wronged each other," answered he. "Mine was the first wrong, when I betrayed thy budding youth into a false and unnatural relation with my decay. Therefore, as a man who has not thought and philosophized in vain, I seek no vengeance, plot no evil against thee. Between thee and me, the scale hangs fairly balanced. But, Hester, the man lives who has wronged us both! Who is he?"

21 "Ask me not!" replied Hester Prynne, looking firmly into his face. "That thou shalt never know!"

22 "Never, sayest thou?" rejoined he, with a smile of dark and self-relying intelligence. "Never know him! Believe me, Hester, there are few things,—whether in the outward world, or, to a certain depth, in the invisible sphere of thought,—few things hidden from the man, who devotes himself earnestly and unreservedly to the solution of a mystery. Thou mayest cover up thy secret from the prying multitude. Thou mayest conceal it, too, from the ministers and magistrates, even as thou didst this day, when they sought to wrench the name out of thy heart, and give thee a partner on thy pedestal. But, as for me, I come to the inquest with other senses than they possess. I shall seek this man, as I have sought truth in books; as I have sought gold in alchemy. There is a sympathy that will make me conscious of him. I shall see him tremble. I shall feel myself shudder, suddenly and unawares. Sooner or later, he must needs be mine!"

23 The eyes of the wrinkled scholar glowed so intensely upon her, that Hester Prynne clasped her hands over her heart, dreading lest he should read the secret there at once.

24 "Thou wilt not reveal his name? Not the less he is mine," resumed he, with a look of confidence, as if destiny were at one with him. "He bears no letter of infamy wrought into his garment, as thou dost; but I shall read it on his heart. Yet fear not for him! Think not that I shall interfere with Heaven's own method of retribution, or, to my own loss, betray him to the gripe of human law. Neither

do thou imagine that I shall contrive aught against his life; no, nor against his fame, if, as I judge, he be a man of fair repute. Let him live! Let him hide himself in outward honor, if he may! Not the less he shall be mine!"

25   "Thy acts are like mercy," said Hester, bewildered and appalled. "But thy words interpret thee as a terror!"

26   "One thing, thou that wast my wife, I would enjoin upon thee," continued the scholar. "Thou hast kept the secret of thy paramour. Keep, likewise, mine! There are none in this land that know me. Breathe not, to any human soul, that thou didst ever call me husband! Here, on this wild outskirt of the earth, I shall pitch my tent; for, elsewhere a wanderer, and isolated from human interests, I find here a woman, a man, a child amongst whom and myself there exist the closest ligaments. No matter whether of love or hate; no matter whether of right or wrong! Thou and thine, Hester Prynne, belong to me. My home is where thou art, and where he is. But betray me not!"

27   "Wherefore dost thou desire it?" inquired Hester, shrinking, she hardly knew why, from this secret bond. "Why not announce thyself openly, and cast me off at once?"

28   "It may be," he replied, "because I will not encounter the dishonor that besmirches the husband of a faithless woman. It may be for other reasons. Enough, it is my purpose to live and die unknown. Let, therefore, thy husband be to the world as one already dead, and of whom no tidings shall ever come. Recognize me not, by word, by sign, by look! Breathe not the secret, above all, to the man thou wottest of. Shouldst thou fail me in this, beware! His fame, his position, his life, will be in my hands. Beware!"

29   "I will keep thy secret, as I have his," said Hester.

30   "Swear it!" rejoined he.

31   And she took the oath.

32   "And now, Mistress Prynne," said old Roger Chillingworth, as he was hereafter to be named, "I leave thee alone; alone with thy infant, and the scarlet letter! How is it, Hester? Doth thy sentence bind thee to wear the token in thy sleep? Art thou not afraid of nightmares and hideous dreams?"

33   "Why dost thou smile so at me?" inquired Hester, troubled at the expression of his eyes. "Art thou like the Black Man that haunts the forest round about us? Hast thou enticed me into a bond that will prove the ruin of my soul?"

34   "Not thy soul," he answered, with another smile. "No, not thine!"

CHAPTER 4

JOURNAL

1. **MLA Works Cited** *Using this model, record this book.*
   Author's Last Name, First Name. The Scarlet Letter. 1850. Title of This Book.
      Ed. First Name Last Name. City: Publisher, year.
2. **Main Character(s)** *Describe each main character and explain why you think each is a main character.*

3. **Supporting Characters** *Describe each supporting character and explain why you think each is a supporting character.*
4. **Setting** *Describe the setting(s) and any relevant prop(s).*
5. **Sequence** *Outline the events in this chapter in order.*
6. **Plot** *Summarize this chapter's events in no more than two sentences.*
7. **Conflicts** *Identify and explain all conflicts involved in this chapter.*
8. **Significant Quotations** *Explain the importance of each of these quotations. Record the page number in the parentheses.*
   a. "As night approached, it proving impossible to quell her insubordination by rebuke or threats of punishment, Master Brackett, the jailer, thought fit to introduce a physician [. . .]" (   ).
   b. "He was lodged in the prison, not as suspected of any offence, but as the most convenient and suitable mode of disposing of him, until the magistrates should have conferred with the Indian sagamores respecting his ransom. His name was announced as Roger Chillingworth [. . .]" (   ).
   c. "'Here, woman! The child is yours,—she is none of mine,—neither will she recognize my voice or aspect as a father's. Administer this draught, therefore, with thine own hand'" (   ).
   d. "'Dost thou know me so little, Hester Prynne? Are my purposes wont to be so shallow? [. . .]'" (   ).
   e. "'I have greatly wronged thee,' murmured Hester.
   'We have wronged each other,' answered he [. . .]" (   ).
9. **Recap** *Summarize what has happened so far from the beginning of the book through this chapter.*

FOLLOW-UP QUESTIONS

6 SHORT QUESTIONS

*Select the **best** answer for each.*

_____ 1. The interview in the prison cell takes place between
   a. Hester and her husband.
   b. Hester and the baby's father.
   c. the baby's father and Hester's husband.

_____ 2. Until he finds his own lodgings, Roger Chillingworth is staying in
   a. the hotel.
   b. the market place.
   c. the prison.

_____ 3. At the beginning of the interview, Hester is
   a. upset and fearful.
   b. happy to see the physician.
   c. quiet and subdued.

_____ 4. Roger Chillingworth gives Hester a cup of
   a. water.
   b. medicine.
   c. poison.

____ 5. Roger Chillingworth is
a. the jailer.
b. a magistrate.
c. a physician.

____ 6. Roger Chillingworth asks
Hester Prynne not to
a. leave Boston.
b. reveal his true name.
c. reveal the baby's father.

5 SIGNIFICANT QUOTATIONS

Explain the importance of each of these quotations.

1. "'Wouldst thou avenge thyself on the innocent babe?' whispered she."
2. "'The medicine is potent for good; and were it my child,—yea, mine own, as well as thine!—I could do no better for it.'"
3. "'It was my folly, and thy weakness [. . .]. Misshapen from my birth-hour, how could I delude myself with the idea that intellectual gifts might veil physical deformity in a young girl's fantasy! Men call me wise. If sages were ever wise in their own behoof, I might have foreseen all this [. . .].'"
4. "'Mine was the first wrong, when I betrayed thy budding youth into a false and unnatural relation with my decay. Therefore, as a man who has not thought and philosophized in vain, I seek no vengeance, plot no evil against thee. Between thee and me, the scale hangs fairly balanced. But, Hester, the man lives who has wronged us both! Who is he?'"
5. "'Thy acts are like mercy,' said Hester, bewildered and appalled. 'But thy words interpret thee as a terror!'"

2 COMPREHENSION ESSAY QUESTIONS

Use specific details and information from the chapter to answer these questions as completely as possible.

1. As if things aren't bad enough already, Hester must face the stranger. Why is this a difficult interview? Use specific details and information from the chapter to explain.
2. Hester makes a promise to Roger Chillingworth that makes her uneasy. This is an example of foreshadowing, a technique by which an author hints at future actions. What do you think might happen as a result of this promise? Use specific details and information from the chapter to predict.

DISCUSSION QUESTIONS

Be prepared to discuss these questions in class.

1. What is the relationship between Hester Prynne and Roger Chillingworth?
2. Is Roger Chillingworth evil? On whom does he want revenge?

CHAPTERS 1–4

JOURNAL

1. **MLA Works Cited** *Using this model, record this book.*
   Author's Last Name, First Name. The Scarlet Letter. 1850. Title of This Book.
   Ed. First Name Last Name. City: Publisher, year.
2. **Main Character(s)** *Describe each main character and explain why you think each is a main character.*
3. **Supporting Characters** *Describe each supporting character and explain why you think each is a supporting character.*
4. **Setting** *Describe the setting(s) and any relevant prop(s).*
5. **Sequence** *Outline the events in these chapters in order.*
6. **Plot** *Summarize these chapters' events in no more than five sentences.*
7. **Conflicts** *Identify and explain all conflicts involved in these chapters.*
8. **Significant Quotations** *Explain the importance of each of these quotations. Record the page number in the parentheses.*
   a. "But, on one side of the portal, and rooted almost at the threshold, was a wild rose-bush, covered, in this month of June, with its delicate gems, which might be imagined to offer their fragrance and fragile beauty to the prisoner as he went in, and to the condemned criminal as he came forth to his doom, in token that the deep heart of Nature could pity and be kind to him" (   ).
   b. "'Goodwives,' said a hard-featured dame of fifty, 'I'll tell ye a piece of my mind. It would be greatly for the public behoof, if we women, being of mature age and church-members in good repute, should have the handling of such malefactresses as this Hester Prynne. [. . .] If the hussy stood up for judgement before us five, that are now here in a knot together, would she come off with such a sentence as the worshipful magistrates have awarded? [. . .]'" (   ).
   c. "'People say,' said another, 'that the Reverend Master Dimmesdale, her godly pastor, takes it very grievously to heart that such a scandal should have come upon his congregation'" (   ).
   d. "[O]n the threshold of the prison-door, she repelled [the town beadle], by an action marked with natural dignity and force of character, and stepped into the open air, as if by her own free-will. She bore in her arms a child, a baby of some three months old, who winked and turned aside its little face from the too vivid light of day; because its existence, heretofore, had brought it acquainted only with the gray twilight of a dungeon, or other darksome apartment of the prison" (   ).
   e. "In a moment, however, wisely judging that one token of her shame would but poorly serve to hide another, she took the baby on her arm, and, with a burning blush, and yet with a haughty smile, and a glance that would not be abashed, looked around at her townspeople and neighbors [. . .]" (   ).

f. "On the breast of her gown, in fine red cloth, surrounded with an elaborate embroidery and fantastic flourishes of gold thread, appeared the
letter A [. . .]" (   ).

g. "From this intense consciousness of being the object of severe and universal observation, the wearer of the scarlet letter was at length relieved by
discerning, on the outskirts of the crowd, a figure which irresistibly took
possession of her thoughts, [. . .]. By the Indian's side, and evidently
sustaining a companionship with him, stood a white man, clad in a
strange disarray of civilized and savage costume" (   ).

h. "'She will not speak!' murmured Mr. Dimmesdale, who, leaning over the
balcony, with his hand upon his heart, had awaited the result of his
appeal, [. . .]. 'Wondrous strength and generosity of a woman's heart!
She will not speak!'" (   ).

i. "'[T]hou knowest that I was frank with thee. I felt no love, nor feigned
any'" (   ).

j. "'I shall seek this man, as I have sought truth in books; as I have sought
gold in alchemy. There is a sympathy that will make me conscious of him.
I shall see him tremble. I shall feel myself shudder, suddenly and unawares.
Sooner or later, he must needs be mine!'" (   ).

9. **Recap** *Summarize what has happened so far, from the beginning of the novel
through these chapters.*

FOLLOW-UP QUESTIONS

20 SHORT QUESTIONS

Select the <u>best</u> answer for each.

____ 1. This new Puritan colony is
located in
   a. Salem.
   b. Utopia.
   c. Boston.

____ 2. Growing outside the prison
door are weeds and
   a. oak trees.
   b. vegetables.
   c. roses.

____ 3. The story begins in the season of
   a. winter.
   b. summer.
   c. fall.

____ 4. Hester Prynne is guilty of the
sin of
   a. adultery.
   b. witchcraft.
   c. theft.

____ 5. This new colony is about
   a. seventy years old.
   b. twenty years old.
   c. three years old.

____ 6. The colonists originally come
from
   a. England.
   b. France.
   c. Germany.

____ 7. On the scaffold, Hester Pyrnne
is holding
a. a book.
b. a baby.
c. a bottle.

____ 8. In the crowd, most women
a. are sympathetic to
Hester's plight.
b. say nothing at all about
Hester.
c. think Hester's punish-
ment is not harsh enough.

____ 9. As punishment, Hester must
a. wear a red letter A.
b. leave the colony.
c. beg for forgiveness.

____ 10. Standing on the scaffold,
Hester
a. remembers the past.
b. cries and shakes.
c. asks to get down.

____ 11. Hester Prynne
a. is not married.
b. has left her husband for
another man.
c. has had a child by a man
other than her husband.

____ 12. Hester Prynne's punishment
is to
a. wear the scarlet letter
for three hours.
b. stand alone on the scaffold
before the crowd for three
hours.
c. wear the scarlet letter
for life and stand on the
scaffold for three hours.

____ 13. John Wilson is
a. a young clergyman.
b. an old clergyman.
c. a stranger to the colony.

____ 14. The baby
a. cries sadly for the entire
time.
b. cries from time to time.
c. is silent the entire time.

____ 15. The stranger at the edge of
the crowd has
a. been in Indian captivity.
b. just gotten off a ship.
c. been in prison.

____ 16. In the prison, Hester meets
with
a. the baby's father.
b. her husband.
c. her minister.

____ 17. Hester's husband's name is
a. John Wilson.
b. Arthur Dimmesdale.
c. Roger Chillingworth.

____ 18. Roger Chillingworth is
a. the jailer.
b. a physician.
c. a minister.

____ 19. Hester promises to
a. conceal her husband's
identity.
b. leave the colony.
c. reveal the name of the
baby's father.

____ 20. Roger Chillingworth
a. is young and strong.
b. is old and misshapen.
c. is young and learned.

10 SIGNIFICANT QUOTATIONS

Explain the importance of each of these quotations.

1. "A throng of bearded men, in sad-colored garments and gray, steeple-crowned
hats, intermixed with women, some wearing hoods, and others bareheaded,

was assembled in front of a wooden edifice, the door of which was heavily
timbered with oak, and studded with iron spikes."

2. "Certain it is, that, some fifteen or twenty years after the settlement of the
town, the wooden jail was already marked with weather-stains and other
indications of age, which gave a yet darker aspect to its beetle-browed and
gloomy front. The rust on the ponderous ironwork of its oaken door looked
more antique than anything else in the new world. Like all that pertains to
crime, it seemed never to have known a youthful era [. . .]."

3. "'At the very least, they should have put the brand of a hot iron on Hester
Prynne's forehead. Madam Hester would have winced at that, I warrant me.
But she,—the naughty baggage,—little will she care what they put upon
the bodice of her gown! Why, look you, she may cover it with a brooch, or
such like heathenish adornment, and so walk the streets as brave as ever!'"

4. "It was no great distance, in those days, from the prison-door to the market-
place. Measured by the prisoner's experience, however, it might be reckoned
a journey of some length; for, haughty as her demeanor was, she perchance
underwent an agony from every footstep of those that thronged to see her, as
if her heart had been flung into the street for them all to spurn and trample
upon [. . .]."

5. "Accordingly, the crowd was sombre and grave. The unhappy culprit sustained herself as best a woman might, under the heavy weight of a thousand
unrelenting eyes, all fastened upon her, and concentrated at her bosom.
It was almost intolerable to be borne [. . .]."

6. "Although, by a seemingly careless arrangement of his heterogeneous garb,
he had endeavored to conceal or abate the peculiarity, it was sufficiently evident to Hester Prynne, that one of this man's shoulders rose higher than the
other. Again, at the first instant of perceiving that thin visage, and the slight
deformity of the figure, she pressed her infant to her bosom, with so convulsive a force that the poor babe uttered another cry of pain [. . .]."

7. "'[. . .] I am a stranger, and have been a wanderer, sorely against my will.
I have met with grievous mishaps by sea and land, and have been long held
in bonds among the heathen-folk, to the southward; and am now brought
hither by this Indian, to be redeemed out of my captivity [. . .]'"

8. "'The penalty thereof is death. But, in their great mercy and tenderness of
heart, they have doomed Mistress Prynne to stand only a space of three hours
on the platform of the pillory, and then and thereafter, for the remainder of
her natural life, to wear a mark of shame upon her bosom.'"

9. "[. . .] [Master Brackett] described him as a man of skill in all Christian
modes of physical science, and likewise familiar with whatever the savage
people could teach, in respect to medicinal herbs and roots that grew in the
forest [. . .]."

10. "'Thou hast kept the secret of thy paramour. Keep, likewise, mine! [. . .].
No matter whether of love or hate; no matter whether of right or wrong!
Thou and thine, Hester Prynne, belong to me. My home is where thou art,
and where he is. But betray me not!'"

2 COMPREHENSION ESSAY QUESTIONS

Use specific details and information from these chapters to answer these questions as completely as possible.

1. Part of following a novel is keeping track of the characters. Which characters do you feel are important at this point?
2. Part of following a novel is also keeping track of events. What has happened so far?

DISCUSSION QUESTIONS

Be prepared to discuss these questions in class.

1. What is the relationship between Hester Prynne and Roger Chillingworth?
2. How would you describe Hester Prynne? Do you like her? Why or why not?
3. What do you think of the scarlet letter that Hester makes? What does it show about her nature?

WRITING

Use each of these ideas to write an essay.

1. The type of clothing worn by the Puritans reveals much about their lifestyle, customs and beliefs. What does your style of clothing—or that of someone you know or have observed—reveal about you and/or your culture?
2. Religious beliefs and civil laws coincide in The Scarlet Letter. To what degree do religion and law overlap in contemporary American culture? Use one of more examples in your essay.
3. The Puritans in the story believe they are setting up a new society, one that will root out and repel evil. If you were setting up a new society, what three things would be important to you?
4. How might you describe the kind of language Hawthorne uses to tell the story? Use examples from the first four chapters to illustrate Hawthorne's style of syntax, diction, vocabulary, and punctuation.

FURTHER WRITING

1. Does severe punishment deter crime? Research the arguments for and against the death penalty or use of torture in contemporary society.
2. Write a description of your school or town in the style of the novel's narrator. Add dialogue, as needed.
3. The Puritans settled in New England centuries ago and have left lasting influences on the American culture. Research the beliefs and cultural characteristics of the Puritans.

4. The Puritans believed that laws should be strict and that punishment should be severe to deter criminals. The penalty for adultery, for example, was often death. Are there any laws that you feel are too severe or perhaps penalties that are too harsh? Conversely, are there any laws that you feel should be stronger? Research the history of these laws.

5. Hester's marriage to Roger was apparently an arranged marriage, a common occurrence in many societies then and now. What cultures believe in arranged marriages? What are the advantages and disadvantages of such unions? Research marriage traditions in another culture(s).

CHAPTER 5

HESTER AT HER NEEDLE

Use context clues to define these words before reading. Use a dictionary as needed.

1. Ian's artwork is considered *morbid* because it focuses on dead bodies and decaying buildings. *Morbid* means _____
   _____.

2. Since the clothesline had no *tension* when it was full of wet clothes, it sagged low to the ground. *Tension* means _____
   _____.

3. People who exercise regularly and *vigorously* are often energetic and strong. *Vigorous* means _____
   _____.

4. The *ignominy* of his crime embarrassed him for the rest of his life. *Ignominy* means _____
   _____.

5. On the night of the Hollywood awards ceremony, actresses wear *gorgeous* gowns, one more beautiful than the other. *Gorgeous* means _____
   _____.

6. The ancient Egyptian symbols on the tomb were *inscrutable* until an archeologist figured out the code. *Inscrutable* means _____
   _____.

7. The old tree was so weak and broken that it was *inevitable* the tree would fall in the next storm. *Inevitable* means _____
   _____.

8. Watching the sun set over the mountains, we *lingered* for two hours over coffee, taking our time to enjoy the view. *Linger* means _____
   _____.

9. Aiden's *conscience* bothered him after he got away with robbing the convenience store. *Conscience* means _____
_____.

10. Many girls wear ribbons and bows as *adornments* in their hair. *Adornment* means _____.

11. Carrying six heavy textbooks to class every day can be a *burden*. *Burden* means _____.

12. The newly engaged couple spent many hours in *contemplation*, thinking about their future together. *Contemplation* means _____
_____.

13. The cook *seared* the meat on both sides on high heat before lowering the heat to slowly cook it the rest of the way. *Seared* means _____
_____.

14. Mother *banished* the kitten from the living room after it tore up the furniture. *Banish* means _____
_____.

15. Rodney waited for the tomatoes to ripen and turn bright *crimson* before he picked them. *Crimson* means _____
_____.

16. Alone in the desert, I felt quite *solitary*. *Solitary* means _____
_____.

17. In the twentieth century, science developed vaccines *potent* enough to eliminate polio and other diseases almost entirely. *Potent* means _____
_____.

18. Andrew Carnegie improved social conditions when he *endowed* New York City with enough money to create the public library system. *Endowed* means
_____.

19. The witness *averred* that he had seen a ghost in his hotel room, but no one wanted to believe him. *Averred* means _____
_____.

20. After living in a city all his life, Peter couldn't wait to move to a *remote* little town in the middle of woods. *Remote* means _____
_____.

PRE-READING VOCABULARY
STRUCTURAL ATTACK

Define these words by solving the parts. Use the Glossary or a dictionary as needed.

1. embody	11. tortured	21. fatality
2. sustain	12. unnatural	22. tinged
3. thither	13. combative	23. tempted
4. compel	14. customary	24. peninsula
5. self-delusion	15. toiled	25. infrequently
6. vicinity	16. rural	26. preacher
7. sufficed	17. grievous	27. perceive
8. intangible	18. purged	28. infernal
9. exquisite	19. individuality	29. red-hot
10. confinement	20. condemnation	30. eternal

PRE-READING QUESTIONS

Try answering these questions as you read.

Where does Hester live?
How does Hester's punishment change as she resumes her daily life?
How does Hester make a living for herself and her child?
Why doesn't she leave Boston?

CHAPTER 5

HESTER AT HER NEEDLE

1 Hester Prynne's term of confinement was now at an end. Her prison-door was thrown open, and she came forth into the sunshine, which, falling on all alike, seemed, to her sick and morbid heart, as if meant for no other purpose than to reveal the scarlet letter on her breast. Perhaps there was a more real torture in her first unattended footsteps from the threshold of the prison, than even in the procession and spectacle that have been described, where she was made the common infamy, at which all mankind was summoned to point its finger. Then, she was supported by an unnatural tension of the nerves, and by all the combative energy of her character, which enabled her to convert the scene into a kind of lurid triumph. It was, moreover, a separate and insulated event, to occur but once in her lifetime, and to meet which, therefore, reckless of economy, she might call up the vital strength that would have sufficed for many quiet years. The very law that condemned her—a giant of stern features, but with vigor to support, as well as to annihilate, in his iron arm—had held her up, through the terrible ordeal of her

ignominy. But now, with this unattended walk from her prison-door, began the daily custom, and she must either sustain and carry it forward by the ordinary resources of her nature, or sink beneath it. She could no longer borrow from the future, to help her through the present grief. To-morrow would bring its own trial with it; so would the next day, and so would the next; each its own trial, and yet the very same that was now so unutterably grievous to be borne. The days of the far-off future would toil onward, still with the same burden for her to take up, and bear along with her, but never to fling down; for the accumulating days, and added years, would pile up their misery upon the heap of shame. Throughout them all, giving up her individuality, she would become the general symbol at which the preacher and moralist might point, and in which they might vivify and embody their images of women's frailty and sinful passion. Thus the young and pure would be taught to look at her, with the scarlet letter flaming on her breast,—at her, the child of honorable parents,—at her, the mother of a babe, that would hereafter be a woman,—at her, who had once been innocent,—as the figure, the body, the reality of sin. And over her grave, the infamy that she must carry thither would be her only monument.

2   It may seem marvellous, that, with the world before her,—kept by no restrictive clause of her condemnation within the limits of the Puritan settlement, so remote and so obscure,—free to return to her birthplace, or to any other European land, and there hide her character and identity under a new exterior, as completely as if emerging into another state of being,—and having also the passes of the dark, inscrutable forest open to her, where the wildness of her nature might assimilate itself with a people whose customs and life were alien from the law that had condemned her,—it may seem marvellous, that this woman should still call that place her home, where, and where only, she must needs be the type of shame. But there is a fatality, a feeling so irresistible and inevitable that it has the force of doom, which almost invariably compels human beings to linger around and haunt, ghost-like, the spot where some great and marked event has given the color to their lifetime; and still the more irresistibly, the darker the tinge that saddens it. Her sin, her ignominy, were the roots which she had struck into the soil. It was as if a new birth, with stronger assimilations than the first, had converted the forest-land, still so uncongenial to every other pilgrim and wanderer, into Hester Prynne's wild and dreary, but lifelong home. All other scenes of earth—even that village of rural. England, where happy infancy and stainless maidenhood seemed yet to be in her mother's keeping, like garments put off long ago—were foreign to her, in comparison. The chain that bound her here was of iron links, and galling to her inmost soul, but never could be broken.

3   It might be, too,—doubtless it was so, although she hid the secret from herself, and grew pale whenever it struggled out of her heart, like a serpent from its hole,—it might be that another feeling kept her within the scene and pathway that had been so fatal. There dwelt, there trode the feet of one with whom she deemed herself connected in a union, that, unrecognized on earth, would bring them together before the bar of final judgment, and make that their marriage-altar, for a joint futurity of endless retribution. Over and over again, the temper of souls had thrust this idea upon Hester's contemplation, and laughed at the passionate and desperate joy with which she seized, and then strove to cast it from her. She barely looked the idea in the face, and hastened to bar it in its dungeon. What she compelled herself to believe,—what, finally, she reasoned upon, as her motive for continuing a resident, of New England,—was half a truth, and half a self-delusion. Here, she said to herself, had been the scene of her guilt, and here should be the scene of her earthly punishment; and so, perchance, the torture of her daily shame would at length purge her soul, and work out another purity than that which she had lost; more saint-like, because the result of martyrdom.

4   Hester Prynne, therefore, did not flee. On the outskirts of the town, within the verge of the peninsula, but not in close vicinity to any other habitation, there was a small thatched cottage. It had been built by an earlier settler, and abandoned, because the soil about it was too sterile for cultivation, while its comparative remoteness put it out of the sphere of that social activity which already marked the habits of the emigrants. It stood on the shore, looking across a basin of the sea at the forest-covered hills, towards the west. A clump of scrubby trees,

such as alone grew on the peninsula, did not so much conceal the cottage from view, as seem to denote that here was some object which would fain have been, or at least ought to be, concealed. In this little, lonesome dwelling, with some slender means that she possessed, and by the license of the magistrates, who still kept an inquisitorial watch over her, Hester established herself, with her infant child. A mystic shadow of suspicion immediately attached itself to the spot. Children, too young to comprehend wherefore this woman should be shut out from the sphere of human charities, would creep nigh enough to behold her plying her needle at the cottage-window, or standing in the door-way, or laboring in her little garden, or coming forth along the pathway that led townward; and, discerning the scarlet letter on her breast, would scamper off, with a strange, contagious fear.

5   Lonely as was Hester's situation, and without a friend on earth who dared to show himself, she, however, incurred no risk of want. She possessed an art that sufficed, even in a land that afforded comparatively little scope for its exercise, to supply food for her thriving infant and herself. It was the art—then, as now, almost the only one within a woman's grasp—of needle-work. She bore on her breast, in the curiously embroidered letter, a specimen of her delicate and imaginative skill, of which the dames of a court might gladly have availed themselves, to add the richer and more spiritual adornment of human ingenuity to their fabrics of silk and gold. Here, indeed, in the sable simplicity that generally characterized the Puritanic modes of dress, there might be an infrequent call for the finer productions of her handiwork. Yet the taste of the age, demanding whatever was elaborate in compositions of this kind, did not fail to extend its influence over our stern progenitors, who had cast behind them so many fashions which it might seem harder to dispense with. Public ceremonies, such as ordinations, the installations of magistrates, and all that could give majesty to the forms in which a new government manifested itself to the people, were, as a matter of policy, marked by a stately and well-conducted ceremonial, and a sombre, but yet a studied magnificence. Deep ruffs, painfully wrought bands, and gorgeously embroidered gloves, were all deemed necessary to the official state of men assuming the reins of power; and were readily allowed to individuals dignified by rank or wealth, even while sumptuary laws forbade these and similar extravagances to the plebeian order. In the array of funerals, too,—whether for the apparel of the dead body, or to typify, by manifold emblematic devices of sable cloth and snowy lawn, the sorrow of the survivors,—there was a frequent and characteristic demand for such labor as Hester Prynne could supply. Baby-linen—for babies then wore robes of state—afforded still another possibility of toil and emolument.

6   By degrees, nor very slowly, her handiwork became what would now be termed the fashion. Whether from commiseration for a woman of so miserable a destiny; or from the morbid curiosity that gives a fictitious value even to common or worthless things; or by whatever other intangible circumstance was then,

as now, sufficient to bestow, on some persons, what others might seek in vain; or because Hester really filled a gap which must otherwise have remained vacant; it is certain that she had ready and fairly requited employment for as many hours as she saw fit to occupy with her needle. Vanity, it may be, chose to mortify itself, by putting on, for ceremonials of pomp and state, the garments that had been wrought by her sinful hands. Her needle-work was seen on the ruff of the Governor; military men wore it on their scarfs, and the minister on his band; it decked the baby's little cap; it was shut up, to be mildewed and moulder away, in the coffins of the dead. But it is not recorded that, in a single instance, her skill was called in aid to embroider the white veil which was to cover the pure blushes of a bride. The exception indicated the ever relentless vigor with which society frowned upon her sin.

7   Hester sought not to acquire any thing beyond a subsistence, of the plainest and most ascetic description, for herself, and a simple abundance for her child. Her own dress was of the coarsest materials and the most sombre hue; with only that one ornament,—the scarlet letter,—which it was her doom to wear. The child's attire, on the other hand, was distinguished by a fanciful, or, we might rather say, a fantastic ingenuity, which served, indeed, to heighten the airy charm that early began to develop itself in the little girl, but which appeared to have also a deeper meaning. We may speak further of it hereafter. Except for that small expenditure in the decoration of her infant, Hester bestowed all her superfluous means in charity, on wretches less miserable than herself, and who not unfrequently insulted the hand that fed them. Much of the time, which she might readily have applied to the better efforts of her art, she employed in making coarse garments for the poor. It is probable that there was an idea of penance in this mode of occupation, and that she offered up a real sacrifice of enjoyment, in devoting so many hours to such rude handiwork. She had in her nature a rich, voluptuous, Oriental characteristic,—a taste for the gorgeously beautiful, which, save in the exquisite productions of her needle, found nothing else, in all the possibilities of her life, to exercise itself upon. Women derive a pleasure, incomprehensible to the other sex, from the delicate toil of the needle. To Hester Prynne it might have been a mode of expressing, and therefore soothing, the passion of her life. Like all other joys, she rejected it as sin. This morbid meddling of conscience with an immaterial matter betokened, it is to be feared, no genuine and stedfast penitence, but something doubtful, something that might be deeply wrong, beneath.

8   In this manner, Hester Prynne came to have a part to perform in the world. With her native energy of character, and rare capacity, it could not entirely cast her off, although it had set a mark upon her, more intolerable to a woman's heart than that which branded the brow of Cain. In all her intercourse with society, however, there was nothing that made her feel as if she belonged to it. Every gesture, every word, and even the silence of those with whom she came in contact, implied, and often expressed, that she was banished, and as much alone as if she inhabited another

sphere, or communicated with the common nature by other organs and senses than the rest of human kind. She stood apart from mortal interests, yet close beside them, like a ghost that revisits the familiar fireside, and can no longer make itself seen or felt; no more smile with the household joy, nor mourn with the kindred sorrow; or, should it succeed in manifesting its forbidden sympathy, awakening only terror and horrible repugnance. These emotions, in fact, and its bitterest scorn besides, seemed to be the sole portion that she retained in the universal heart. It was not an age of delicacy; and her position, although she understood it well, and was in little danger of forgetting it, was often brought before her vivid self-perception, like a new anguish, by the rudest touch upon the tenderest spot. The poor, as we have already said, whom she sought out to be the objects of her bounty, often reviled the hand that was stretched forth to succor them. Dames of elevated rank, likewise, whose doors she entered in the way of her occupation, were accustomed to distil drops of bitterness into her heart; sometimes through that alchemy of quiet malice, by which women can concoct a subtile poison from ordinary trifles; and sometimes, also, by a coarser expression, that fell upon the sufferer's defenceless breast like a rough blow upon an ulcerated wound. Hester had schooled herself long and well; she never responded to these attacks, save by a flush of crimson that rose irrepressibly over her pale cheek, and again subsided into the depths of her bosom. She was patient,—a martyr, indeed,—but she forbore to pray for her enemies; lest, in spite of her forgiving aspirations, the words of the blessing should stubbornly twist themselves into a curse.

9   Continually, and in a thousand other ways, did she feel the innumerable throbs of anguish that had been so cunningly contrived for her by the undying, the ever-active sentence of the Puritan tribunal. Clergymen paused in the street to address words of exhortation, that brought a crowd, with its mingled grin and frown, around the poor, sinful woman. If she entered a church, trusting to share the Sabbath smile of the Universal Father, it was often her mishap to find herself the text of the discourse. She grew to have a dread of children; for they had imbibed from their parents a vague idea of something horrible in this dreary woman, gliding silently through the town, with never any companion but one only child. Therefore, first allowing her to pass, they pursued her at a distance with shrill cries, and the utterance of a word that had no distinct purport to their own minds, but was none the less terrible to her, as proceeding from lips that babbled it unconsciously. It seemed to argue so wide a diffusion of her shame, that all nature knew of it; it could have caused her no deeper pang, had the leaves of the trees whispered the dark story among themselves,—had the summer breeze murmured about it,—had the wintry blast shrieked it aloud! Another peculiar torture was felt in the gaze of a new eye. When strangers looked curiously at the scarlet letter,—and none ever failed to do so,—they branded it afresh into Hester's soul; so that, oftentimes, she could scarcely refrain, yet always did refrain, from covering the symbol with her hand. But then, again, an accustomed eye had like-wise its own anguish to inflict. Its cool stare of familiarity was intolerable. From

first to last, in short, Hester Prynne had always this dreadful agony in feeling a human eye upon the token; the spot never grew callous; it seemed, on the contrary, to grow more sensitive with daily torture.

10   But sometimes, once in many days, or perchance in many months, she felt an eye—a human eye—upon the ignominious brand, that seemed to give a momentary relief, as if half of her agony were shared. The next instant, back it all rushed again, with still a deeper throb of pain; for, in that brief interval, she had sinned anew. Had Hester sinned alone?

11   Her imagination was somewhat affected, and, had she been of a softer moral and intellectual fibre, would have been still more so, by the strange and solitary anguish of her life. Walking to and fro, with those lonely footsteps, in the little world with which she was outwardly connected, it now and then appeared to Hester,—if altogether fancy, it was nevertheless to potent to be resisted,—she felt or fancied, then, that the scarlet letter had endowed her with a new sense. She shuddered to believe, yet could not help believing, that it gave her a sympathetic knowledge of the hidden sin in other hearts. She was terror-stricken by the revelations that were thus made. What were they? Could they be other than the insidious whispers of the bad angel, who would fain have persuaded the struggling woman, as yet only half his victim, that the outward guise of purity was but a lie, and that, if truth were everywhere to be shown, a scarlet letter would blaze forth on many a bosom besides Hester Prynne's? Or, must she receive those intimations—so obscure, yet so distinct—as truth? In all her miserable experience, there was nothing else so awful and so loathsome as this sense. It perplexed, as well as shocked her, by the irreverent inopportuneness of the occasions that brought it into vivid action. Sometimes, the red infamy upon her breast would give a sympathetic throb, as she passed near a venerable minister or magistrate, the model of piety and justice, to whom that age of antique reverence looked up, as to a mortal man in fellowship with angels. "What evil thing is at hand?" would Hester say to herself. Lifting her reluctant eyes, there would be nothing human within the scope of view, save the form of this earthly saint! Again, a mystic sisterhood would contumaciously assert itself, as she met the sanctified frown of some matron, who, according to the rumor of all tongues, had kept cold snow within her bosom throughout life. That unsunned snow in the matron's bosom, and the burning shame on Hester Prynne's—what had the two in common? Or, once more, the electric thrill would give her warning,—"Behold, Hester, here is a companion!"—and, looking up, she would detect the eyes of a young maiden glancing at the scarlet letter, shyly and aside, and quickly averted, with a faint, chill crimson in her cheeks; as if her purity were somewhat sullied by that momentary glance. O Fiend, whose talisman was that fatal symbol, wouldst thou leave nothing, whether in youth or age, for this poor sinner to revere?—Such loss of faith is ever one of the saddest results of sin. Be it accepted as a proof that all was not corrupt in this poor victim of her own frailty, and man's hard law, that Hester Prynne yet struggled to believe that no fellow–mortal was guilty like herself.

12   The vulgar, who, in those dreary old times, were always contributing a
grotesque horror to what interested their imaginations, had a story about the
scarlet letter which we might readily work up into a terrific legend. They
averred, that the symbol was not mere scarlet cloth, tinged in an earthly dye-pot,
but was red-hot with infernal fire, and could be seen glowing all alight, whenever Hester Prynne walked abroad in the night-time. And we must needs say, it
seared Hester's bosom so deeply, that perhaps there was more truth in the rumor
than our modern incredulity may be inclined to admit.

CHAPTER 5

JOURNAL

1. **MLA Works Cited** *Using this model, record this book.*
   Author's Last Name, First Name. The Scarlet Letter. 1850. Title of This Book.
      Ed. First Name Last Name. City: Publisher, year.
2. **Main Character(s)** *Describe each main character and explain why you think each
   is a main character.*
3. **Supporting Characters** *Describe each supporting character and explain why you
   think each is a supporting character.*
4. **Setting** *Describe the setting(s) and any relevant prop(s).*
5. **Sequence** *Outline the events in this chapter in order.*
6. **Plot** *Summarize this chapter's events in no more than two sentences.*
7. **Conflicts** *Identify and explain all conflicts involved in this chapter.*
8. **Significant Quotations** *Explain the importance of each of these quotations. Record
   the page number in the parentheses.*
   a. "Hester Prynne's term of confinement was now at an end" (   ).
   b. "Here, she said to herself, had been the scene of her guilt, and here should
      be the scene of her earthly punishment; and so, perchance, the torture of her
      daily shame would at length purge her soul [. . .]" (   ).
   c. "She possessed an art that sufficed, even in a land that afforded compara-
      tively little scope for its exercise, to supply food for her thriving infant and
      herself. It was that art—then, as now, almost the only one within a woman's
      grasp—of needle-work [. . .]" (   ).
   d. "She grew to have a dread of children; for they had imbibed from their
      parents a vague idea of something horrible in this dreary woman, glid-
      ing silently through the town, with never any companion but one only
      child [. . .]" (   ).
   e. "Such loss of faith is ever one of the saddest results of sin. Be it accepted as a
      proof that all was not corrupt in this poor victim of her own frailty, and
      man's hard law, that Hester Prynne yet struggled to believe that no fellow-
      mortal was guilty like herself" (   ).
9. **Recap** *Summarize what has happened so far, from the beginning of the book through
   this chapter.*

FOLLOW-UP QUESTIONS

6 SHORT QUESTIONS

Select the <u>best</u> answer for each.

____ 1. Hester makes her living by
  a. nursing.
  b. sewing.
  c. farming.

____ 2. Hester does not leave Boston because
  a. she is not allowed.
  b. she doesn't have enough money.
  c. she still loves the baby's father.

____ 3. Hester and her child live
  a. on a lonely peninsula.
  b. near the jail.
  c. in town.

____ 4. Ceremonial clothes worn by the Puritans are
  a. highly embroidered.
  b. dull and somber.
  c. ordinary and practical.

____ 5. When Hester has extra earnings, she
  a. buries the money in the ground.
  b. gives the money to charity.
  c. donates the money to Master Dimmesdale's church.

____ 6. Hester sometimes feels that the scarlet letter gives her
  a. courage to go on.
  b. pride in living in Boston.
  c. knowledge of sin in other hearts.

5 SIGNIFICANT QUESTIONS

Explain the importance of each of these quotations.

1. "To-morrow would bring its own trial with it; so would the next day, and so would the next; each with its own trial, and yet the very same that was now so unutterably grievous to be borne [. . .]."

2. "It might be, too,—doubtless it was so, although she hid the secret from herself, and grew pale whenever it struggled out of her heart, like a serpent from its hole,—it might be that another feeling kept her within the scene and pathway that had been so fatal. There dwelt, there trode the feet of one with whom she deemed herself connected in a union [. . .]."

3. "By degrees, nor very slowly, her handiwork became what would now be termed the fashion [. . .]."

4. "When strangers looked curiously at the scarlet letter,—and none ever failed to do so,—they branded it afresh into Hester's soul; so that, oftentimes, she could scarcely refrain, yet always did refrain, from covering the symbol with her hand [. . .]."

5. "They averred, that the symbol was not mere scarlet cloth, tinged in an earthly dye-pot, but was red-hot with infernal fire, and could be seen glowing all alight, whenever Hester Prynne walked abroad in the night-time [. . .]."

2 COMPREHENSION ESSAY QUESTIONS

Use specific details and information from the chapter to answer these questions as completely as possible.

1. The Puritans, though stern and somber, attended and participated in many ceremonies. What is the importance of ceremony in the Puritan community? Use specific details and information from the chapter.
2. This chapter shows how Hester Prynne supports herself and her child. In today's society, we would call her "a single mother." How does Hester manage to survive? Use specific details and information from the chapter to support your answer.

DISCUSSION QUESTIONS

Be prepared to discuss these questions in class.

1. How does Hester spend her time once her prison sentence is over?
2. What unexpected torments and side effects of the punishment does Hester suffer? Why does she stay in Boston? What would you do, if you were in Hester's predicament?

CHAPTER 6

PEARL

Use context clues to define these words before reading. Use a dictionary as needed.

1. Creatures that never die, like vampires and ghosts, are said to be *immortal*. *Immortal* means _____
   _____.

2. After I added good soil and compost, my garden had a *luxuriance* of flowers. *Luxuriance* means _____
   _____.

3. Coffee, with its jolt of caffeine, is quite *efficacious* in helping me wake up in the morning. *Efficacious* means _____
   _____.

4. For the wedding ceremony, the bride was *arrayed* in a beautiful gown and matching veil while the groom wore his best suit. *Array* means _____
   _____.

5. Phyllis has the most *peculiar* laugh and no one else in the world can laugh the way she does. *Peculiar* means _____
   _____.

6. Steven and Ann felt *despondent* after their home burned down, destroying all their family mementos. *Despondent* means _____
   _____.

7. The diamond and emerald bracelet was so *dear* that I could not afford to buy it. *Dear* means _____
   _____.

8. To improve his heart health, Tom keeps to a strict *regimen* of daily exercise and a low-fat diet. *Regimen* means _____
   _____.

9. In a moment of *caprice*, Renee picked up and moved to Denver with her friends, almost overnight. *Caprice* means _____ _____.

10. The homeowner *pleaded* with the builder to finish the new deck before summer. *Plead* means _____ _____.

11. Just to be *perverse*, Mrs. Brennan refused to participate in the annual block party with all the rest of her neighbors. *Perverse* means _____ _____.

12. A person not accepted by the society is considered an *outcast*. *Outcast* means _____ _____.

13. With no money and no job, Gene thought the future looked *dismal*. *Dismal* means _____ _____.

14. The *unearthly* glow in the sky following the explosion was like nothing that Maleka had ever seen. *Unearthly* means _____ _____.

15. Residing away from town on a lonely peninsula, Hester and Pearl live in *seclusion*. *Seclusion* means _____ _____.

16. Fixated on his own beliefs, Vincent was *intolerant* of other people's opinions. *Intolerant* means _____ _____.

17. After his girlfriend called off the wedding, Christopher was so *melancholy* that his friends became worried and tried to cheer him up. *Melancholy* means _____ _____.

18. Gert carefully *uprooted* the weeds that had grown among the flowers in her garden. *Uprooted* means _____ _____.

19. Being attacked from all sides, the wrestler *smote* the second wrestler with a folding chair; then he turned to *smite* another one. *Smote* and *smite* mean _____ _____.

20. Because his mouth was swollen after his dental work, Denny's remarks were *incoherent. Incoherent* means _____

_____.

PRE-READING VOCABULARY
STRUCTURAL ATTACK

Define these words by solving the parts. Use the Glossary or a dictionary as needed.

1. preternatural	13. transformation	25. rankled
2. undue	14. dexterity	26. elvish
3. severity	15. rustic	27. impish
4. gesticulate	16. co-exist	28. query
5. thwarted	17. radiance	29. labyrinth
6. phantasmagoric	18. mutability	30. epoch
7. emblem	19. disorder	31. detect
8. enmity	20. perpetuate	32. procure
9. brooding	21. solely	33. shameful
10. relentless	22. evoke	34. enable
11. outlandish	23. acquaintance	
12. instinctive	24. anathema	

PRE-READING QUESTIONS

Try answering these questions as you read.

Who is Pearl?
Why is she named Pearl?
What problems does Hester face as a single mother?
How does Pearl react to the townspeople?
How is Pearl dressed?

CHAPTER 6

PEARL

1   We have as yet hardly spoken of the infant; that little creature, whose innocent life had sprung, by the inscrutable decree of Providence, a lovely and immortal flower, out of the rank luxuriance of a guilty passion. How strange it seemed to the sad woman, as she watched the growth, and the beauty that became every day more brilliant, and the intelligence that threw its quivering sunshine over the tiny features of this child! Her Pearl!—For so had Hester called her; not as a name

expressive of her aspect, which had nothing of the calm, white, unimpassioned lustre that would be indicated by the comparison. But she named the infant "Pearl," as being of great price,—purchased with all she had,—her mother's only treasure! How strange, indeed! Man had marked this woman's sin by a scarlet letter, which had such potent and disastrous efficacy that no human sympathy could reach her, save it were sinful like herself. God, as a direct consequence of the sin which man thus punished, had given her a lovely child, whose place was on that same dishonored bosom, to connect her parent for ever with the race and descent of mortals, and to be finally a blessed soul in heaven! Yet these thoughts affected Hester Prynne less with hope than apprehension. She knew that her deed had been evil; she could have no faith, therefore, that its result would be for good. Day after day, she looked fearfully into the child's expanding nature; ever dreading to detect some dark and wild peculiarity, that should correspond with the guiltiness to which she owed her being.

2   Certainly, there was no physical defect. By its perfect shape, its vigor, and its natural dexterity in the use of all its untried limbs, the infant was worthy to have been brought forth in Eden; worthy to have been left there, to be the plaything of the angels, after the world's first parents were driven out. The child had a native grace which does not invariably coexist with faultless beauty; its attire, however simple, always impressed the beholder as if it were the very garb that precisely became it best. But little Pearl was not clad in rustic weeds. Her mother, with a morbid purpose that may be better understood hereafter, had bought the richest tissues that could be procured, and allowed her imaginative faculty its full play in the arrangement and decoration of the dresses which the child wore, before the public eye. So magnificent was the small figure, when thus arrayed, and such was the splendor of Pearl's own proper beauty, shining through the gorgeous robes which might have extinguished a paler loveliness, that there was an absolute circle of radiance around her, on the darksome cottage-floor. And yet a russet gown, torn and soiled with the child's rude play, made a picture of her just as perfect. Pearl's aspect was imbued with a spell of infinite variety; in this one child there were many children, comprehending the full scope between the wild-flower prettiness of a peasant-baby, and the pomp, in little, of an infant princess. Throughout all, however, there was a trait of passion, a certain depth of hue, which she never lost; and if, in any of her changes, she had grown fainter or paler, she would have ceased to be herself;—it would have been no longer Pearl!

3   This outward mutability indicated, and did not more than fairly express, the various properties of her inner life. Her nature appeared to possess depth, too, as well as variety; but—or else Hester's fears deceived her—it lacked reference and adaptation to the world into which she was born. The child could not be made amenable to rules. In giving her existence, a great law had been broken; and the result was a being, whose elements were perhaps beautiful and brilliant, but all in disorder; or with an order peculiar to themselves, amidst which the point of variety and arrangement was difficult or impossible to be discovered. Hester could only account for the child's character—and even then, most vaguely and

imperfectly—by recalling what she herself had been, during that momentous period while Pearl was imbibing her soul from the spiritual world, and her bodily frame from its material of earth. The mother's impassioned state had been the medium through which were transmitted to the unborn infant the rays of its moral life; and, however white and clear originally, they had taken the deep stains of crimson and gold, the fiery lustre, the black shadow, and the untempered light, of the intervening substance. Above all, the warfare of Hester's spirit, at that epoch, was perpetuated in Pearl. She could recognize her wild, desperate, defiant mood, the flightiness of her temper, and even some of the very cloud-shapes of gloom and despondency that had brooded in her heart. They were now illuminated by the morning radiance of a young child's disposition, but, later in the day of earthly existence, might be prolific of the storm and whirlwind.

4   The discipline of the family, in those days, was of a far more rigid kind than now. The frown, the harsh rebuke, the frequent application of the rod, enjoined by Scriptural authority, were used, not merely in the way of punishment for actual offences, but as a wholesome regimen for the growth and promotion of all childish virtues. Hester Prynne, nevertheless, the lonely mother of this one child, ran little risk of erring on the side of undue severity. Mindful, however, of her own errors and misfortunes, she early sought to impose a tender, but strict, control over the infant immortality that was committed to her charge. But the task was beyond her skill. After testing both smiles and frowns, and proving that neither mode of treatment possessed any calculable influence, Hester was ultimately compelled to stand aside, and permit the child to be swayed by her own impulses. Physical compulsion or restraint was effectual, of course, while it lasted. As to any other kind of discipline, whether addressed to her mind or heart, little Pearl might or might not be within its reach, in accordance with the caprice that ruled the moment. Her mother, while Pearl was yet an infant, grew acquainted with a certain peculiar look, that warned her when it would be labor thrown away to insist, persuade, or plead. It was a look so intelligent, yet inexplicable, so perverse, sometimes so malicious, but generally accompanied by a wild flow of spirits, that Hester could not help questioning, at such moments, whether Pearl was a human child. She seemed rather an airy sprite, which, after playing its fantastic sports for a little while upon the cottage-floor, would flit away with a mocking smile. Whenever that look appeared in her wild, bright, deeply black eyes, it invested her with a strange remoteness and intangibility; it was as if she were hovering in the air and might vanish, like a glimmering light that comes we know not whence, and goes we know not whither. Beholding it, Hester was constrained to rush towards the child,—to pursue the little elf in the flight which she invariably began,—to snatch her to her bosom, with a close pressure and earnest kisses,—not so much from overflowing love, as to assure herself that Pearl was flesh and blood, and not utterly delusive. But Pearl's laugh, when she was caught, though full of merriment and music, made her mother more doubtful than before.

5   Heart-smitten at this bewildering and baffling spell, that so often came between herself and her sole treasure, whom she had bought so dear, and who was all her world, Hester sometimes burst into passionate tears. Then, perhaps,—for there was no foreseeing how it might affect her,—Pearl would frown, and clench her little fist, and harden her small features into a stern, unsympathizing look of discontent. Not seldom, she would laugh anew, and louder than before, like a thing incapable and unintelligent of human sorrow. Or—but this more rarely happened—she would be convulsed with a rage of grief, and sob out her love for her mother, in broken words, and seem intent on proving that she had a heart, by breaking it. Yet Hester was hardly safe in confiding herself to that gusty tenderness; it passed, as suddenly as it came. Brooding over all these matters, the mother felt like one who has evoked a spirit, but, by some irregularity in the process of conjuration, has failed to win the master-word that should control this new and incomprehensible intelligence. Her only real comfort was when the child lay in the placidity of sleep. Then she was sure of her, and tasted hours of quiet, sad, delicious happiness; until—perhaps with that perverse expression glimmering from beneath her opening lids—little Pearl awoke!

6   How soon—with what strange rapidity, indeed!—did Pearl arrive at an age that was capable of social intercourse, beyond the mother's ever-ready smile and nonsense-words! And then what a happiness would it have been, could Hester Prynne have heard her clear, bird-like voice mingling with the uproar of other childish voices, and have distinguished and unravelled her own darling's tones, amid all the entangled outcry of a group of sportive children! But this could never be. Pearl was a born outcast of the infantile world. An imp of evil, emblem and product of sin, she had no right among christened infants. Nothing was more remarkable than the instinct, as it seemed, with which the child comprehended her loneliness; the destiny that had drawn an inviolable circle round about her; the whole peculiarity, in short, of her position in respect to other children. Never, since her release from prison, had Hester met the public gaze without her. In all her walks about the town, Pearl, too, was there; first as the babe in arms, and afterwards as the little girl, small companion of her mother, holding a forefinger with her whole grasp, and tripping along at the rate of three or four footsteps to one of Hester's. She saw the children of the settlement, on the grassy margin of the street, or at the domestic thresholds, disporting themselves in such grim fashion as the Puritanic nurture would permit; playing at going to church, perchance; or at scourging Quakers; or taking scalps in a sham-fight with the Indians; or scaring one another with freaks of imitative witchcraft. Pearl saw, and gazed intently, but never sought to make acquaintance. If spoken to, she would not speak again. If the children gathered about her, as they sometimes did, Pearl would grow positively terrible in her puny wrath, snatching up stones to fling at them, with shrill, incoherent exclamations that made her mother tremble, because they had so much the sound of a witch's anathemas in some unknown tongue.

7   The truth was, that the little Puritans, being of the most intolerant brood that ever lived, had got a vague idea of something outlandish, unearthly, or at

variance with ordinary fashions, in the mother and child; and therefore scorned them in their hearts, and not unfrequently reviled them with their tongues. Pearl felt the sentiments, and requited it with the bitterest hatred that can be supposed to rankle in a childish bosom. These outbreaks of a fierce temper had a kind of value, and even comfort, for her mother; because there was at least an intelligible earnestness in the mood, instead of the fitful caprice that so often thwarted her in the child's manifestations. It appalled her, nevertheless, to discern here, again, a shadowy reflection of the evil that had existed in herself. All this enmity and passion had Pearl inherited, by inalienable right, out of Hester's heart. Mother and daughter stood together in the same circle of seclusion from human society; and in the nature of the child seemed to be perpetuated those unquiet elements that had distracted Hester Prynne before Pearl's birth, but had since begun to be soothed away by the softening influences of maternity.

8   At home, within and around her mother's cottage, Pearl wanted not a wide and various circle of acquaintance. The spell of life went forth from her ever creative spirit, and communicated itself to a thousand objects, as a torch kindles a flame wherever it may be applied. The unlikeliest materials, a stick, a bunch of rags, a flower, were the puppets of Pearl's witchcraft, and, without undergoing any outward change, became spiritually adapted to whatever drama occupied the stage of her inner world. Her one baby-voice served a multitude of imaginary personages, old and young, to talk withal. The pine-trees, aged, black, and solemn, and flinging groans and other melancholy utterances on the breeze, needed little transformation to figure as Puritan elders, the ugliest weeds of the garden were their children, whom Pearl smote down and uprooted, most unmercifully. It was wonderful, the vast variety of forms into which she threw her intellect, with no continuity, indeed, but darting up and dancing, always in a state of preternatural activity,—soon sinking down, as if exhausted by so rapid and feverish a tide of life,—and succeeded by other shapes of a similar wild energy. It was like nothing so much as the phantasmagoric play of the northern lights. In the mere exercise of the fancy, however, and the sportiveness of a growing mind, there might be little more than was observable in other children of bright faculties; except as Pearl, in the dearth of human playmates, was thrown more upon the visionary throng which she created. The singularity lay in the hostile feelings with which the child regarded all these offspring of her own heart and mind. She never created a friend, but seemed always to be sowing broadcast the dragon's teeth, whence sprung a harvest of armed enemies, against whom she rushed to battle. It was inexpressibly sad— then what depth of sorrow to a mother, who felt in her own heart the cause!—to observe, in one so young, this constant recognition of an adverse world, and so fierce a training of the energies that were to make good her cause, in the contest that must ensue.

9   Gazing at Pearl, Hester Prynne often dropped her work upon her knees, and cried out, with an agony which she would fain have hidden, but which made utterance for itself, betwixt speech and a groan,—"O Father in Heaven,—if Thou art still my Father,—what is this being which I have brought into the world!"

And Pearl, overhearing the ejaculation, or aware, through some more subtle channel, of those throbs of anguish, would turn her vivid and beautiful little face upon her mother, smile with sprite-like intelligence, and resume her play.

10   One peculiarity of the child's deportment remains yet to be told. The very first thing which she had noticed, in her life, was—what?—not the mother's smile, responding to it, as other babies do, by that faint, embryo smile of the little mouth, remembered so doubtfully afterwards, and with such fond discussion whether it were indeed a smile. By no means. But that first object of which Pearl seemed to become aware was—shall we say it?—the scarlet letter on Hester's bosom! One day, as her mother stooped over the cradle, the infant's eyes had been caught by the glimmering of the gold embroidery about the letter; and, putting up her little hand, she grasped at it, smiling, not doubtfully, but with a decided gleam that gave her face the look of a much older child. Then, gasping for breath, did Hester Prynne clutch the fatal token, instinctively endeavouring to tear it away; so infinite was the torture inflicted by the intelligent touch of Pearl's baby-hand. Again, as if her mother's agonized gesture were meant only to make sport for her, did little Pearl look into her eyes, and smile! From that epoch, except when the child was asleep, Hester had never felt a moment's safety; not a moment's calm enjoyment of her. Weeks, it is true, would sometimes elapse, during which Pearl's gaze might never once be fixed upon the scarlet letter; but then, again, it would come at unawares, like the stroke of sudden death, and always with that peculiar smile, and odd expression of the eyes.

11   Once, this freakish, elfish cast came into the child's eyes, while Hester was looking at her own image in them, as mothers are fond of doing; and, suddenly,— for women in solitude, and with troubled hearts, are pestered with unaccountable delusions,—she fancied that she beheld, not her own miniature portrait, but another face in the small black mirror of Pearl's eye. It was a face, fiend-like, full of smiling malice, yet bearing the semblance of features that she had known full well, though seldom with a smile, and never with malice, in them. It was as if an evil spirit possessed the child, and had just then peeped forth in mockery. Many a time afterwards had Hester been tortured, though less vividly, by the same illusion.

12   In the afternoon of a certain summer's day, after Pearl grew big enough to run about, she amused herself with gathering handfuls of wild-flowers, and flinging them, one by one, at her mother's bosom; dancing up and down, like a little elf, whenever she hit the scarlet letter. Hester's first motion had been to cover her bosom with her clasped hands. But, whether from pride or resignation, or a feeling that her penance might best be wrought out by this unutterable pain, she resisted the impulse, and sat erect, pale as death, looking sadly into little Pearl's wild eyes. Still came the battery of flowers, almost invariably hitting the mark, and covering her mother's breast with hurts for which she could find no balm in this world, nor knew how to seek it in another. At last, her shot being all expended, the child stood still and gazed at Hester, with that little, laughing image of a fiend peeping out—or, whether it peeped or no, her mother so imagined it—from the unsearchable abyss of her black eyes.

13   "Child, what art thou?" cried the mother.

14   "Oh, I am your little Pearl!" answered the child.

15   But, while she said it, Pearl laughed and began to dance up and down, with the humorsome gesticulation of a little imp, whose next freak might be to fly up the chimney.

16   "Art thou my child, in very truth?" asked Hester.

17   Nor did she put the question altogether idly, but, for the moment, with a portion of genuine earnestness; for, such was Pearl's wonderful intelligence, that her mother half doubted whether she were not acquainted with the secret spell of her existence, and might not now reveal herself.

18   "Yes; I am little Pearl!" repeated the child, continuing her antics.

19   "Thou art not my child! Thou art no Pearl of mine!" said the mother, half playfully; for it was often the case that a sportive impulse came over her, in the midst of her deepest suffering. "Tell me, then, what thou art, and who sent thee hither?"

20   "Tell me, mother!" said the child, seriously, coming up to Hester, and pressing herself close to her knees. "Do thou tell me!"

21   "Thy Heavenly Father sent thee!" answered Hester Prynne.

22   But she said it with a hesitation that did not escape the acuteness of the child. Whether moved only by her ordinary freakishness, or because an evil spirit prompted her, she put up her small forefinger, and touched the scarlet letter.

23   "He did not send me!" cried she, positively. "I have no Heavenly Father!"

24   "Hush, Pearl, hush! Thou must not talk so!" answered the mother, suppressing a groan. "He sent us all into this world. He sent even me, thy mother. Then, much more, thee! Or, if not, thou strange and elfish child, whence didst thou come?"

25   "Tell me! Tell me!" repeated Pearl, no longer seriously, but laughing, and capering about the floor. "It is thou that must tell me!"

26   But Hester could not resolve the query, being herself in a dismal labyrinth of doubt. She remembered—betwixt a smile and a shudder—the talk of the neighbouring townspeople; who, seeking vainly elsewhere for the child's paternity, and observing some of her odd attributes, had given out that poor little Pearl was a demon offspring; such as, ever since old Catholic times, had occasionally been seen on earth, through the agency of their mothers' sin, and to promote some foul and wicked purpose. Luther, according to the scandal of his monkish enemies, was a brat of that hellish breed; nor was Pearl the only child to whom this inauspicious origin was assigned, among the New England Puritans.

CHAPTER 6

JOURNAL

1. **MLA Works Cited** *Using this model, record this book.*
   Author's Last Name, First Name. The Scarlet Letter. 1850. Title of This Book.
   Ed. First Name Last Name. City: Publisher, year.

2. **Main Character(s)** *Describe each main character and explain why you think each is a main character.*

3. **Supporting Characters** *Describe each supporting character and explain why you think each is a supporting character.*
4. **Setting** *Describe the setting(s) and any relevant prop(s).*
5. **Sequence** *Outline the events in this chapter in order.*
6. **Plot** *Summarize this chapter's events in no more than two sentences.*
7. **Conflicts** *Identify and explain all conflicts involved in this chapter.*
8. **Significant Quotations** *Explain the importance of each of these quotations. Record the page number in the parentheses.*
   a. "But she named the infant 'Pearl' as being of great price,—purchased with all she had,—her mother's only treasure! [. . .]" (　).
   b. "Certainly, there was no physical defect. By its perfect shape, its vigor, and its natural dexterity in the use of all its untried limbs, the infant was worthy to have been brought forth in Eden; worthy to have been left there, to be the plaything of the angels, after the world's first parents were driven out [. . .]" (　).
   c. "[. . .] Pearl was a born outcast of the infantile world. An imp of evil, emblem and product of sin, she had no right among christened infants. Nothing was more remarkable that the instinct, as it seemed, with which the child comprehended her loneliness; [. . .]" (　).
   d. "The pine trees, aged, black, and solemn, and flinging groans and other melancholy utterances on the breeze, needed little transformation to figure as Puritan elders; the ugliest weeds in the garden were their children, whom Pearl smote down and uprooted, most unmercifully [. . .]" (　).
   e. "'Child, what are thou?' cried the mother" (　).
9. **Recap** *Summarize what has happened so far, from the beginning of the book through this chapter.*

FOLLOW-UP QUESTIONS

6 SHORT QUESTIONS

Select the __best__ answer for each.

____ 1. Hester names her child Pearl because
   a. they live near the sea.
   b. her skin looks like pearls.
   c. a pearl is an expensive treasure.

____ 2. Pearl's clothing is
   a. old and tattered.
   b. gray and somber.
   c. gorgeous and splendid.

____ 3. As a small child, Pearl
   a. obeys her mother.
   b. is impulsive and creative.
   c. walks and speaks quietly.

____ 4. The Puritan children
   a. say unkind things to Pearl.
   b. welcome Pearl to play with them.
   c. completely ignore Pearl.

_____ 5. One day, at the scarlet letter   _____ 6. Hester worries that Pearl is
on Hester's dress Pearl throws   a. the devil's child.
a. stones.   b. too quiet.
b. wild-flowers.   c. not healthy in body.
c. scraps of cloth.

5 SIGNIFICANT QUOTATIONS

Explain the importance of each of these quotations.

1. "Day after day, she looked fearfully into the child's expanding nature; ever dreading to detect some dark and wild peculiarity, that should correspond with the guiltiness to which she owed her being."
2. "The child could not be made amenable to rules. In giving her existence, a great law had been broken; and the result was a being whose elements were perhaps beautiful and brilliant, but all in disorder; [. . .]."
3. "After testing both smiles and frowns, and proving that neither mode of treatment possessed any calculable influence, Hester was ultimately compelled to stand aside, and permit the child to be swayed by her own impulses [. . .]."
4. "The truth was, that the little Puritans, being of the most intolerant brood that ever lived, had got a vague idea of something outlandish, unearthly, or at variance with ordinary fashions, in the mother and child; and therefore scorned them in their hearts, and not unfrequently reviled them with their tongues [. . .]."
5. "In the afternoon of a certain summer's day, after Pearl grew big enough to run about, she amused herself with gathering handfuls of wild-flowers, and flinging them, one by one, at her mother's bosom; dancing up and down like a little elf, whenever she hit the scarlet letter [. . .]."

2 COMPREHENSION ESSAY QUESTIONS

Use specific details and information from the chapter to answer these questions as completely as possible.

1. How would you describe Pearl's personality and appearance? Using specific details and information from the chapter in your essay, discuss Pearl as a character.
2. How do the townspeople treat Hester and Pearl when they walk through town? Use specific details and information from the chapter in your explanation.

DISCUSSION QUESTIONS

Be prepared to discuss these questions in class.

1. What kind of relationship is developing between Pearl and Hester? Is Hester a good mother?
2. How does Hawthorne present the Puritans to the reader in this chapter?

CHAPTER 7

THE GOVERNOR'S HALL

PRE-READING VOCABULARY
CONTEXT

Use context clues to define these words before reading. Use a dictionary as needed.

1. Ceil loves to sew and often *embroiders* flowers with colorful thread on her clothing. *Embroider* means _____
_____.

2. After shopping upstairs at the mall, we *descended* to the lower level by using the elevator. *Descend* means _____
_____.

3. The early *inhabitants* of New England faced many difficulties when they first arrived. *Inhabitants* means _____
_____.

4. When his wife would not let him have dessert because he was overweight, Johnny felt *deprived. Deprived* means _____
_____.

5. Knowing the difference between right and wrong and acting accordingly are the marks of a *moral* person. *Moral* means _____
_____.

6. Some people seek *salvation* and atonement for their sins by helping others less fortunate. *Salvation* means _____
_____.

7. The mischievous children behaved like *imps*, laughing loudly and playing silly games. *Imps* means _____
_____.

8. The firefighters *dauntlessly* climbed tall ladders and entered smoky floors as they fought to control the blazing fire in the fifty-story building. *Dauntless* means _____.

9. Some people dislike walking in a cemetery at night because they fear that *demons* and evil spirits will frighten them. *Demon* means _____

   _____.

10. Using the Internet, we can now trace our *lineage*, or family ancestry, back five or six generations. *Lineage* means _____

   _____.

11. When Brenda got married, Grandmother gave her some *heirloom* jewelry that had belonged to her great-grandmother. *Heirloom* means _____

   _____.

12. The playful children *capered* and jumped about, making us all laugh. *Caper* means _____.

13. Because she was fussy, Grandfather rocked Baby Julia and sang songs to calm and *pacify* her. *Pacify* means _____

   _____.

14. When guests arrived on short notice, Mother was able to *contrive* a delicious meal out of the supplies in the cabinet. *Contrive* means _____

   _____.

15. The staff at the weapons museum carefully polished the *gleaming armor* worn by knights centuries ago. *Gleaming armor* means _____

   _____.

16. Puritan leaders in the seventeenth and eighteenth centuries often wore *ruffs*, stiffly starched circular collars, on their clothing. *Ruffs* means _____

   _____.

17. The roots of the flowers became so *intermixed* with those of weeds in the garden that it was very difficult for us to separate them. *Intermixed* means

   _____.

18. The *wayfarers* traveled the roads and hiked the trails to see the Rocky Mountains. *Wayfarers* means _____

   _____.

19. A good education and profession can raise your *rank*, or standing, in society. *Rank* means _____

   _____.

20. The extremely large wave was *gigantic in* size. *Gigantic* means _____

   _____.

PRE-READING VOCABULARY
STRUCTURAL ATTACK

Define these words by solving the parts. Use the Glossary or a dictionary as needed.

1. intrinsic	13. habitation	25. prominent
2. imperious	14. mansion	26. hitherto
3. impel	15. influential	27. opposition
4. wanly	16. ludicrous	28. gestured
5. pallid	17. token	29. exaggerate
6. extant	18. pestilence	30. deliberation
7. yea	19. godly	31. grinning
8. forsooth	20. leeched	32. heaved
9. decaying	21. subsistence	33. advance
10. moss-grown	22. welfare	34. reproach
11. singular	23. pristine	35. sighed
12. cottage	24. legislator	

PRE-READING QUESTIONS

Try answering these questions as you read.

Why does Hester go to the governor's mansion?
What kind of place is the governor's mansion?
How does Pearl behave at the governor's mansion?
How old is Pearl now?

CHAPTER 7
THE GOVERNOR'S HALL

1   Hester Prynne went, one day, to the mansion of Governor Bellingham, with a pair of gloves, which she had fringed and embroidered to his order, and which were to be worn on some great occasion of state; for, though the chances of a popular election had caused this former ruler to descend a step or two from the highest rank, he still held an honorable and influential place among the colonial magistracy.

2   Another and far more important reason than the delivery of a pair of embroidered gloves impelled Hester, at this time, to seek an interview with a personage of so much power and activity in the affairs of the settlement. It had reached her ears, that there was a design on the part of some of the leading inhabitants, cherishing the more rigid order of principles in religion and government, to deprive her of her child. On the supposition that Pearl, as already hinted, was of demon origin, these good people not unreasonably argued that a Christian interest in

the mother's soul required them to remove such a stumbling-block from her path. If the child, on the other hand, were really capable of moral and religious growth, and possessed the elements of ultimate salvation, then, surely, it would enjoy all the fairer prospect of these advantages by being transferred to wiser and better guardianship than Hester Prynne's. Among those who promoted the design, Governor Bellingham was said to be one of the most busy. It may appear singular, and, indeed, not a little ludicrous, that an affair of this kind, which, in later days, would have been referred to no higher jurisdiction than that of the selectmen of the town, should then have been a question publicly discussed, and on which statesmen of eminence took sides. At that epoch of pristine simplicity, however, matters of even slighter public interest, and of far less intrinsic weight than the welfare of Hester and her child, were strangely mixed up with the deliberations of legislators and acts of state. The period was hardly, if at all, earlier than that of our story, when a dispute concerning the right of property in a pig, not only caused a fierce and bitter contest in the legislative body of the colony, but resulted in an important modification of the framework itself of the legislature.

3   Full of concern, therefore,—but so conscious of her own right, that it seemed scarcely an unequal match between the public, on the one side, and a lonely woman, backed by the sympathies of nature, on the other,—Hester Prynne set forth from her solitary cottage. Little Pearl, of course, was her companion. She was now of an age to run lightly along by her mother's side, and, constantly in motion from morn till sunset, could have accomplished a much longer journey than that before her. Often, nevertheless, more from caprice than necessity, she demanded to be taken up in arms, but was soon as imperious to be set down again, and frisked onward before Hester on the grassy pathway, with many a harmless trip and tumble. We have spoken of Pearl's rich and luxuriant beauty; a beauty that shone with deep and vivid tints; a bright complexion, eyes possessing intensity both of depth and glow, and hair already of a deep, glossy brown, and which, in after years, would be nearly akin to black. There was fire in her and throughout her; she seemed the unpremeditated offshoot of a passionate moment. Her mother, in contriving the child's garb, had allowed the gorgeous tendencies of her imagination their full play; arraying her in a crimson velvet tunic, of a peculiar cut, abundantly embroidered with fantasies and flourishes of gold thread. So much strength of coloring, which must have given a wan and pallid aspect to cheeks of a fainter bloom, was admirably adapted to Pearl's beauty, and made her the very brightest little jet of flame that ever danced upon the earth.

4   But it was a remarkable attribute of this garb, and, indeed, of the child's whole appearance, that it irresistibly and inevitably reminded the beholder of the token which Hester Prynne was doomed to wear upon her bosom. It was the scarlet letter in another form; the scarlet letter endowed with life! The mother herself—as if the red ignominy were so deeply scorched into her brain, that all her conceptions assumed its form—had carefully wrought out the similitude; lavishing many hours of morbid ingenuity, to create an analogy between the object of her affection, and the emblem of her guilt and torture. But, in truth,

Pearl was the one, as well as the other; and only in consequence of that identity had Hester contrived so perfectly to represent the scarlet letter in her appearance.

5   As the two wayfarers came within the precincts of the town, the children of the Puritans looked up from their play,—or what passed for play with those sombre little urchins,—and spake gravely one to another:—

6   "Behold, verily, there is the woman of the scarlet letter; and, of a truth, moreover, there is the likeness of the scarlet letter running along by her side! Come, therefore, and let us fling mud at them!"

7   But Pearl, who was a dauntless child, after frowning, stamping her foot, and shaking her little hand with a variety of threatening gestures, suddenly made a rush at the knot of her enemies, and put them all to flight. She resembled, in her fierce pursuit of them, an infant pestilence,—the scarlet fever, or some such half-fledged angel of judgment,—whose mission was to punish the sins of the rising generation. She screamed and shouted, too, with a terrific volume of sound, which doubtless caused the hearts of the fugitives to quake within them. The victory accomplished, Pearl returned quietly to her mother, and looked up smiling into her face.

8   Without further adventure, they reached the dwelling of Governor Bellingham. This was a large wooden house, built in a fashion of which there are specimens still extant in the streets of our elder towns; now moss-grown, crumbling to decay, and melancholy at heart with the many sorrowful or joyful occurrences, remembered or forgotten, that have happened, and passed away, within their dusky chambers. Then, however, there was the freshness of the passing year on its exterior, and the cheerfulness, gleaming forth from the sunny windows, of a human habitation into which death had never entered. It had indeed a very cheery aspect; the walls being overspread with a kind of stucco, in which fragments of broken glass were plentifully intermixed; so that, when the sunshine fell aslant-wise over the front of the edifice, it glittered and sparkled as if diamonds had been flung against it by the double handful. The brilliancy might have befitted Aladdin's palace, rather than the mansion of a grave old Puritan ruler. It was further decorated with strange and seemingly cabalistic figures and diagrams, suitable to the quaint taste of the age, which had been drawn in the stucco when newly laid on, and had now grown hard and durable, for the admiration of after times.

9   Pearl, looking at this bright wonder of a house, began to caper and dance, and imperatively required that the whole breadth of sunshine should be stripped off its front, and given her to play with.

10   "No, my little Pearl!" said her mother. "Thou must gather thine own sunshine. I have none to give thee!"

11   They approached the door; which was of an arched form, and flanked on each side by a narrow tower or projection of the edifice, in both of which were lattice-windows, with wooden shutters to close over them at need. Lifting the iron hammer that hung at the portal, Hester Prynne gave a summons, which was answered by one of the Governor's bond-servants; a free-born Englishman, but now a seven years' slave. During that term he was to be the property of his master, and as

much a commodity of bargain and sale as an ox, or a joint-stool. The serf wore the blue coat, which was the customary garb of serving-men at that period, and long before, in the old hereditary halls of England.

12 "Is the worshipful Governor Bellingham within?" inquired Hester.

13 "Yea, forsooth," replied the bond-servant, staring with wide-open eyes at the scarlet letter, which, being a newcomer in the country, he had never before seen. "Yea, his honorable worship is within. But he hath a godly minister or two with him, and likewise a leech. Ye may not see his worship now."

14 "Nevertheless, I will enter," answered Hester Prynne; and the bond-servant, perhaps judging from the decision of her air and the glittering symbol in her bosom, that she was a great lady in the land, offered no opposition.

15 So the mother and little Pearl were admitted into the hall of entrance. With many variations, suggested by the nature of his building-materials, diversity of climate, and a different mode of social life, Governor Bellingham had planned his new habitation after the residences of gentlemen of fair estate in his native land. Here, then, was a wide and reasonably lofty hall, extending through the whole depth of the house, and forming a medium of general communication, more or less directly, with all the other apartments. At one extremity, this spacious room was lighted by the windows of the two towers, which formed a small recess on either side of the portal. At the other end, though partly muffled by a curtain, it was more powerfully illuminated by one of those embowed hall-windows which we read of in old books, and which was provided with a deep and cushioned seat. Here, on the cushion, lay a folio tome, probably of the Chronicles of England, or other such substantial literature; even as, in our own days, we scatter gilded volumes on the centre-table, to be turned over by the casual guest. The furniture of the hall consisted of some ponderous chairs, the backs of which were elaborately carved with wreaths of oaken flowers; and likewise a table in the same taste; the whole being of the Elizabethan age, or perhaps earlier, and heirlooms, transferred hither from the Governor's paternal home. On the table—in token that the sentiment of old English hospitality had not been left behind—stood a large pewter tankard, at the bottom of which, had Hester or Pearl peeped into it, they might have seen the frothy remnant of a recent draught of ale.

16 On the wall hung a row of portraits, representing the forefathers of the Bellingham lineage, some with armour on their breasts, and others with stately ruffs and robes of peace. All were characterized by the sternness and severity which old portraits so invariably put on; as if they were the ghosts, rather than the pictures, of departed worthies, and were gazing with harsh and intolerant criticism at the pursuits and enjoyments of living men.

17 At about the centre of the oaken panels, that lined the hall, was suspended a suit of mail, not, like the pictures, an ancestral relic, but of the most modern date; for it had been manufactured by a skilful armorer in London, the same year in which Governor Bellingham came over to New England. There was a steel head-piece, a cuirass, a gorget, and greaves, with a pair of gauntlets and a sword hanging beneath; all, and especially the helmet and breastplate, so highly

burnished as to glow with white radiance, and scatter an illumination every-where about upon the floor. This bright panoply was not meant for mere idle show, but had been worn by the Governor on many a solemn muster and training field, and had glittered, moreover, at the head of a regiment in the Pequod war. For, though bred a lawyer, and accustomed to speak of Bacon, Coke, Noye, and Finch, as his professional associates, the exigencies of this new country had trans-formed Governor Bellingham into a soldier, as well as a statesman and ruler.

18   Little Pearl—who was as greatly pleased with the gleaming armour as she had been with the glittering frontispiece of the house—spent some time looking into the polished mirror of the breastplate.

19   "Mother," cried she, "I see you here, Look! Look!"

20   Hester looked, by way of humoring the child; and she saw that, owing to the peculiar effect of this convex mirror, the scarlet letter was represented in exagger-ated and gigantic proportions, so as to be greatly the most prominent feature of her appearance. In truth, she seemed absolutely hidden behind it. Pearl pointed upward, also, at a similar picture in the head-piece; smiling at her mother, with the elfish intelligence that was so familiar an expression on her small physiog-nomy. That look of naughty merriment was likewise reflected in the mirror, with so much breadth and intensity of effect, that it made Hester Prynne feel as if it could not be the image of her own child, but of an imp who was seeking to mould itself into Pearl's shape.

21   "Come along, Pearl!" said she, drawing her away. "Come and look into this fair garden. It may be, we shall see flowers there; more beautiful ones than we find in the woods."

22   Pearl, accordingly, ran to the bow-window, at the farther end of the hall, and looked along the vista of a garden-walk, carpeted with closely shaven grass, and bordered with some rude and immature attempt at shrubbery. But the proprietor appeared already to have relinquished, as hopeless, the effort to perpetuate on this side of the Atlantic, in a hard soil and amid the close struggle for subsistence, the native English taste for ornamental gardening. Cabbages grew in plain sight; and a pumpkin vine, rooted at some distance, had run across the intervening space, and deposited one of its gigantic products directly beneath the hall-window; as if to warn the Governor that this great lump of vegetable gold was as rich an orna-ment as New England earth would offer him. There were a few rose-bushes, how-ever, and a number of apple-trees, probably the descendants of those planted by the Reverend Mr. Blackstone, the first settler of the peninsula; that half mytho-logical personage who rides through our early annals, seated on the back of a bull.

23   Pearl, seeing the rose-bushes, began to cry for a red rose, and would not be pacified.

24   "Hush, child, hush!" said her mother earnestly. "Do not cry, dear little Pearl! I hear voices in the garden. The Governor is coming, and gentlemen along with him!"

25   In fact, down the vista of the garden-avenue, a number of persons were seen approaching towards the house. Pearl, in utter scorn of her mother's attempt to

quiet her, gave an eldritch scream, and then became silent; not from any notion of obedience, but because the quick and mobile curiosity of her disposition was excited by the appearance of these new personages.

CHAPTER 7

JOURNAL

1. **MLA Works Cited** *Using this model, record this book.*
   Author's Last Name, First Name. The Scarlet Letter. *1850.* Title of This Book. *Ed. First Name Last Name. City: Publisher, year.*
2. **Main Character(s)** *Describe each main character and explain why you think each is a main character.*
3. **Supporting Characters** *Describe each supporting character and explain why you think each is a supporting character.*
4. **Setting** *Describe the setting(s) and any relevant prop(s).*
5. **Sequence** *Outline the events in this chapter in order.*
6. **Plot** *Summarize this chapter's events in no more than two sentences.*
7. **Conflicts** *Identify and explain all conflicts involved in this chapter.*
8. **Significant Quotations** *Explain the importance of each of these quotations. Record the page number in the parentheses.*
   a. "It had reached her ears, that there was a design on the part of some of the leading inhabitants, cherishing the more rigid order of principles in religion and government, to deprive her of her child [. . .]" (   ).
   b. "Full of concern, therefore,—but so conscious of her own right, that it seemed scarcely an unequal match between the public, on the one side, and a lonely woman, backed by the sympathies of nature, on the other,—Hester Prynne set forth from her solitary cottage. Little Pearl, of course, was her companion [. . .]" (   ).
   c. "But Pearl, who was a dauntless child, after frowning, stamping her foot, and shaking her little hand with a variety of threatening gestures, suddenly made a rush at the knot of her enemies, and put them all to flight [. . .]. She screamed and shouted, too, with a terrific volume of sound, which doubtless caused the hearts of the fugitives to quake within them. The victory accomplished, Pearl returned quietly to her mother, and looked up smiling into her face" (   ).
   d. " 'Yea, his honorable worship is within. But he hath a godly minister or two with him, and likewise a leech. Ye may not see his worship now' " (   ).
   e. " 'Nevertheless, I will enter,' answered Hester Prynne; and the broad-servant, perhaps judging from the decision of her air and the glittering symbol in her bosom, that she was a great lady in the land, offered no opposition" (   ).
9. **Recap** *Summarize what has happened so far, from the beginning of the book through this chapter.*

FOLLOW-UP QUESTIONS

6 SHORT QUESTIONS

Select the <u>best</u> answer for each.

____ 1. Hester goes to Governor Bellingham's mansion to deliver
a. an embroidered robe.
b. a pair of gloves.
c. money for charity.

____ 2. Hester also goes to Governor Bellingham's mansion to
a. look at the gardens.
b. give up her child for adoption.
c. keep custody of Pearl.

____ 3. Hester has heard that some townspeople
a. want Hester and Pearl to leave town.
b. believe Pearl is a demon child.
c. want Pearl also to wear a scarlet letter.

____ 4. The servant at the mansion
a. does not know Hester.
b. does know Hester.
c. does not answer the door.

____ 5. Pearl's character is
a. brave.
b. quiet.
c. weak.

____ 6. The governor's mansion does not have
a. armor.
b. portraits.
c. fancy gardens.

5 SIGNIFICANT QUOTATIONS

Explain the importance of each of these quotations.

1. "At that epoch of pristine simplicity, however, matters of even slighter public interest, and of far less intrinsic weight than the welfare of Hester and her child, were strangely mixed up with the deliberations of legislators and acts of state [. . .]."
2. "She was now of an age to run lightly along by her mother's side, and, constantly in motion from morn till sunset, could have accomplished a much longer journey than that before her. Often, nevertheless, more from caprice than necessity, she demanded to be taken up in arms, but was soon as imperious to be set down again, and frisked onward before Hester on the grassy pathway, with many a harmless trip and tumble [. . .]."
3. "'No, my little Pearl!' said her mother. 'Thou must gather thine own sunshine. I have none to give thee.'"
4. "Hester looked, by way of humoring the child; and she saw that, owing to the peculiar effect of this convex mirror, the scarlet letter was represented in

exaggerated and gigantic proportions, so as to be greatly the most prominent feature of her appearance [. . .]."

5. " 'Hush, child, hush!' said her mother earnestly. 'Do not cry, dear little Pearl!
I hear voices in the garden. The governor is coming, and gentlemen along
with him!' "

2 COMPREHENSION ESSAY QUESTIONS

*Use specific details and information from the chapter to answer these questions
as completely as possible.*

1. Hester Prynne visits the governor's mansion for two reasons. What are her
reasons? Use specific information and details from the chapter to support
your answers.
2. The setting in a story can help to reveal the thoughts and values of the
people who live there. What do the mansion and the things that are in it tell
us about the governor and the Puritan people who settled in New England
at this time? Use specific details and information from the chapter to support your answer.

DISCUSSION QUESTIONS

Be prepared to discuss these questions in class.

1. What kind of child is Pearl? What are her positive and negative qualities?
2. What do we learn about Hester Prynne in this chapter?

CHAPTER 8

THE ELF-CHILD AND THE MINISTER

Use context clues to define these words before reading. Use a dictionary as needed.

1. In her *autumnal* years, Mrs. Markham plans to retire from her job and move to Nevada to be near her grandchildren. *Autumnal* means _____ _____.

2. The learned wisdom and great dignity of the judge made her a *venerable* person. *Venerable* means _____ _____.

3. *Clad* in her green exercise suit and matching running shoes, Jane was off to the gym for a workout. *Clad* means _____ _____.

4. Tina Marie *nurtures* her plants by adding compost and nutrients to the soil so that they will grow strong and healthy. *Nurtures* means _____ _____.

5. The *pious* woman prays every night and attends church faithfully. *Pious* means _____.

6. The Puritans believed that rules and strict punishment would keep good people from evil and *depravity*. *Depravity* means _____ _____.

7. The town expected the new factory to be a *boon* to the local economy by adding jobs with benefits and good wages. *Boon* means _____ _____.

8. Santi is a *vehement* speaker: he speaks forcefully, with strong emotion. *Vehement* means _____ _____.

9. Many Christians learn their *creed*, or set of religious beliefs, by memorizing the questions and answers from a book called a *catechism*. *Creed* and *catechism* mean _____.

10. When Estelle dislocated her shoulder, she thought the pain was sheer *torture*. *Torture* means _____
_____.

11. Rose tried on seven sweaters to find just the right *hue* of blue to match the color of her eyes. *Hue* means _____
_____.

12. When Camille heard that she had a serious illness, she prayed to *Providence* for help and strength. *Providence* means _____
_____.

13. Frogs lay thousands of eggs to ensure that many *offspring* will survive. *Offspring* means _____
_____.

14. After the legislator illegally used state money to enrich his friends, he had to leave office because of the resulting *scandal*. *Scandal* means _____
_____.

15. Evelyn's cheerful *aspect* changed from smiles to frowns when she didn't get a raise in pay. *Aspect* means _____
_____.

16. Seven days a week, Aunt Irene is *wont* to visit the local diner for her daily breakfast. *Wont* means _____
_____.

17. Peter *tread* lightly on the forest path so there was no evidence of his passing. *Tread* means _____
_____.

18. In some religions, the devil, also known as *Satan* and *the Black Man,* is the major spirit or figure of evil and the enemy of good. *Satan* and *the Black Man* mean _____.

19. On an *impulse*, Michaela bought one hundred dollars worth of lottery tickets, surprising us all. *Impulse* means _____
_____.

20. Lying, cheating, and stealing are all examples of *sinful* behavior. *Sinful* means _____
_____.

PRE-READING VOCABULARY
STRUCTURAL ATTACK

Define these words by solving the parts. Use the Glossary or a dictionary as needed.

1. albeit	13. domestic	25. influence
2. disgrace	14. elf-child	26. stumbles
3. insomuch	15. utmost	27. pitfalls
4. forthwith	16. caressed	28. guidance
5. eternity	17. behest	29. temporal
6. methinks	18. physic	30. tarrying
7. constrain	19. prithee	31. tenfold
8. righteousness	20. ailing	32. inopportune
9. flourish	21. ruby	33. startled
10. reluctant	22. coral	34. perceive
11. ill-omened	23. shrewdly	35. emerge
12. latticed	24. authority	

PRE-READING QUESTIONS

Try answering these questions as you read.

Will Hester be allowed to keep Pearl?
What arguments are made for and against Hester's keeping Pearl?
What will Hester do if she loses her child?

CHAPTER 8

THE ELF-CHILD AND THE MINISTER

1 Governor Bellingham, in a loose gown and easy cap,—such as elderly gentlemen love to indue themselves with, in their domestic privacy,—walked foremost, and appeared to be showing off his estate, and expatiating on his projected improvements. The wide circumference of an elaborate ruff, beneath his gray beard, in the antiquated fashion of King James's reign, caused his head to look not a little like that of John the Baptist in a charger. The impression made by his aspect, so rigid and severe, and frost-bitten with more than autumnal age, was hardly in keeping with the appliances of worldly enjoyment wherewith he had evidently done his utmost to surround himself. But it is an error to suppose that our grave forefathers—though accustomed to speak and think of human existence as a state merely of trial and warfare, and though unfeignedly prepared to sacrifice goods and life at the behest of duty—made it a matter of conscience to reject such means of comfort or even luxury, as lay fairly within their grasp. This creed was never taught, for

instance, by the venerable pastor, John Wilson, whose beard, white as a snow-drift, was seen over Governor Bellingham's shoulder; while its wearer suggested that pears and peaches might yet be naturalized in the New England climate, and that purple grapes might possibly be compelled to flourish, against the sunny garden-wall. The old clergyman, nurtured at the rich bosom of the English Church, had a long established and legitimate taste for all good and comfortable things; and however stern he might show himself in the pulpit, or in his public reproof of such transgressions as that of Hester Prynne, still, the genial benevolence of his private life had won him warmer affection than was accorded to any of his professional contemporaries.

2   Behind the Governor and Mr. Wilson came two other guests: one, the Reverend Arthur Dimmesdale, whom the reader may remember, as having taken a brief and reluctant part in the scene of Hester Prynne's disgrace; and, in close companionship with him, old Roger Chillingworth, a person of great skill in physic, who, for two or three years past, had been settled in the town. It was understood that this learned man was the physician as well as friend of the young minister, whose health had severely suffered, of late, by his too unreserved self-sacrifice to the labors and duties of the pastoral relation.

3   The Governor, in advance of his visitors, ascended one or two steps, and, throwing open the leaves of the great hall-window, found himself close to little Pearl. The shadow of the curtain fell on Hester Prynne, and partially concealed her.

4   "What have we here?" said Governor Bellingham, looking with surprise at the scarlet little figure before him. "I profess, I have never seen the like, since my days of vanity, in old King James's time, when I was wont to esteem it a high favor to be admitted to a court mask! There used to be a swarm of these small apparitions, in holiday-time; and we called them children of the Lord of Misrule. But how gat such a guest into my hall?"

5   "Ay, indeed!" cried good old Mr. Wilson. "What little bird of scarlet plumage may this be? Methinks I have seen just such figures, when the sun has been shining through a richly painted window, and tracing out the golden and crimson images across the floor. But that was in the old land. Prithee, young one, who art thou, and what has ailed thy mother to bedizen thee in this strange fashion? Art thou a Christian child,—ha? Dost know thy catechism? Or art thou one of those naughty elfs or fairies, whom we thought to have left behind us, with other relics of Papistry, in merry old England?"

6   "I am mother's child," answered the scarlet vision, "and my name is Pearl!"

7   "Pearl?—Ruby, rather!—or Coral!—or Red Rose, at the very least, judging from thy hue!" responded the old minister, putting forth his hand in a vain attempt to pat little Pearl on the cheek. "But where is this mother of thine? Ah! I see," he added; and, turning to Governor Bellingham, whispered,—"This is the self-same child of whom we have held speech together; and behold here the unhappy woman, Hester Prynne, her mother!"

8   "Sayest thou so?" cried the Governor. "Nay, we might have judged that such a child's mother must needs be a scarlet woman, and a worthy type of her of Babylon! But she comes at a good time; and we will look into this matter forthwith."

9   Governor Bellingham stepped through the window into the hall, followed by his three guests.

10   "Hester Prynne," said he, fixing his naturally stern regard on the wearer of the scarlet letter, "there hath been much question concerning thee, of late. The point hath been weightily discussed, whether we, that are of authority and influence, do well discharge our consciences by trusting an immortal soul, such as there is in yonder child, to the guidance of one who hath stumbled and fallen, amid the pitfalls of this world. Speak thou, the child's own mother! Were it not, thinkest thou, for thy little one's temporal and eternal welfare, that she be taken out of thy charge, and clad soberly, and disciplined strictly, and instructed in the truths of heaven and earth? What canst thou do for the child, in this kind?"

11   "I can teach my little Pearl what I have learned from this!" answered Hester Prynne, laying her finger on the red token.

12   "Woman, it is thy badge of shame!" replied the stern magistrate. "It is because of the stain which that letter indicates, that we would transfer thy child to other hands."

13   "Nevertheless," said the mother calmly, though growing more pale, "this badge hath taught me,—it daily teaches me,—it is teaching me at this moment,—lessons whereof my child may be the wiser and better, albeit they can profit nothing to myself."

14   "We will judge warily," said Bellingham, "and look well what we are about to do. Good Master Wilson, I pray you, examine this Pearl,—since that is her name,—and see whether she hath had such Christian nurture as befits a child of her age."

15   The old minister seated himself in an arm-chair, and made an effort to draw Pearl betwixt his knees. But the child, unaccustomed to the touch or familiarity of any but her mother, escaped through the open window and stood on the upper step, looking like a wild, tropical bird, of rich plumage, ready to take flight into the upper air. Mr. Wilson, not a little astonished at this outbreak,—for he was a grandfatherly sort of personage, and usually a vast favorite with children,—essayed, however, to proceed with the examination.

16   "Pearl," said he, with great solemnity, "thou must take heed to instruction, that so, in due season, thou mayest wear in thy bosom the pearl of great price. Canst thou tell me, my child, who made thee?"

17   Now Pearl knew well enough who made her; for Hester Prynne, the daughter of a pious home, very soon after her talk with the child about her Heavenly Father, had begun to inform her of those truths which the human spirit, at whatever stage of immaturity, imbibes with such eager interest. Pearl, therefore, so large were the attainments of her three years' lifetime, could have borne a fair examination in the New England Primer, or the first column of the Westminster Catechism, although unacquainted with the outward form of either of those celebrated works. But that perversity, which all children have more or less of, and of which little Pearl had a tenfold portion, now, at the most inopportune moment, took thorough possession of her, and closed her lips, or impelled her to speak

words amiss. After putting her finger in her mouth, with many ungracious refusals to answer good Mr. Wilson's question, the child finally announced that she had not been made at all, but had been plucked by her mother off the bush of wild roses, that grew by the prison-door.

18   This fantasy was probably suggested by the near proximity of the Governor's red roses, as Pearl stood outside of the window; together with her recollection of the prison rose-bush, which she had passed in coming hither.

19   Old Roger Chillingworth, with a smile on his face, whispered something in the young clergyman's ear. Hester Prynne looked at the man of skill, and even then, with her fate hanging in the balance, was startled to perceive what a change had come over his features,—how much uglier they were,—how his dark complexion seemed to have grown duskier, and his figure more misshapen,—since the days when she had familiarly known him. She met his eyes for an instant, but was immediately constrained to give all her attention to the scene now going forward.

20   "This is awful!" cried the Governor, slowly recovering from the astonishment into which Pearl's response had thrown him. "Here is a child of three years old, and she cannot tell who made her! Without question, she is equally in the dark as to her soul, its present depravity, and future destiny! Methinks, gentlemen, we need inquire no further."

21   Hester caught hold of Pearl, and drew her forcibly into her arms, confronting the old Puritan magistrate with almost a fierce expression. Alone in the world, cast off by it, and with this sole treasure to keep her heart alive, she felt that she possessed indefeasible rights against the world, and was ready to defend them to the death.

22   "God gave me the child!" cried she. "He gave her, in requital of all things else, which ye had taken from me. She is my happiness!—she is my torture, none the less! Pearl keeps me here in life! Pearl punishes me too! See ye not, she is the scarlet letter, only capable of being loved, and so endowed with a million-fold the power of retribution for my sin? Ye shall not take her! I will die first!"

23   "My poor woman," said the not unkind old minister, "the child shall be well cared for!—far better than thou canst do it."

24   "God gave her into my keeping," repeated Hester Prynne, raising her voice almost to a shriek. "I will not give her up!"—And here, by a sudden impulse, she turned to the young clergyman, Mr. Dimmesdale, at whom, up to this moment, she had seemed hardly so much as once to direct her eyes.—"Speak thou for me!" cried she. "Thou wast my pastor, and hadst charge of my soul, and knowest me better than these men can. I will not lose the child. Speak for me! Thou knowest,—for thou hast sympathies which these men lack!—thou knowest what is in my heart, and what are a mother's rights, and how much the stronger they are, when that mother has but her child and the scarlet letter! Look thou to it! I will not lose the child! Look to it!"

25   At this wild and singular appeal, which indicated that Hester Prynne's situation had provoked her to little less than madness, the young minister at once came forward, pale, and holding his hand over his heart, as was his custom whenever

his peculiarly nervous temperament was thrown into agitation. He looked now more careworn and emaciated than as we described him at the scene of Hester's public ignominy; and whether it were his falling health, or whatever the cause might be, his large dark eyes had a world of pain in their troubled and melancholy depth.

26   "There is truth in what she says," began the minister, with a voice sweet, tremuloùs, but powerful, insomuch that the hall reëchoed, and the hollow armour rang with it,—"truth in what Hester says, and in the feeling which inspires her! God gave her the child, and gave her, too, an instinctive knowledge of its nature and requirements,—both seemingly so peculiar,—which no other mortal being can possess. And, moreover, is there not a quality of awful sacredness in the relation between this mother and this child?"

27   "Ay!—how is that, good Master Dimmesdale?" interrupted the Governor. "Make that plain, I pray you!"

28   "It must be even so," resumed the minister. "For, if we deem it otherwise, do we not thereby say that the Heavenly Father, the Creator of all flesh, hath lightly recognized a deed of sin, and made of no account the distinction between unhallowed lust and holy love? This child of its father's guilt and its mother's shame hath come from the hand of God, to work in many ways upon her heart, who pleads so earnestly, and with such bitterness of spirit, the right to keep her. It was meant for a blessing; for the one blessing of her life! It was meant, doubtless, as the mother herself hath told us, for a retribution too; a torture, to be felt at many an unthought of moment; a pang, a sting, an ever-recurring agony, in the midst of a troubled joy! Hath she not expressed this thought in the garb of the poor child, so forcibly reminding us of that red symbol which sears her bosom?"

29   "Well said, again!" cried good Mr. Wilson. "I feared the woman had no better thought than to make a mountebank of her child!"

30   "O, not so!—not so!" continued Mr. Dimmesdale. "She recognizes, believe me, the solemn miracle which God hath wrought, in the existence of that child. And may she feel, too,—what, methinks, is the very truth,—that this boon was meant, above all things else, to keep the mother's soul alive, and to preserve her from blacker depths of sin into which Satan might else have sought to plunge her! Therefore it is good for this poor, sinful woman that she hath an infant immortality, a being capable of eternal joy or sorrow, confided to her care,—to be trained up by her to righteousness,—to remind her, at every moment, of her fall,—but yet to teach her, as it were by the Creator's sacred pledge, that, if she bring the child to heaven, the child also will bring its parent thither! Herein is the sinful mother happier than the sinful father. For Hester Prynne's sake, then, and no less for the poor child's sake, let us leave them as Providence hath seen fit to place them!"

31   "You speak, my friend, with a strange earnestness," said old Roger Chillingworth, smiling at him.

32   "And there is weighty import in what my young brother hath spoken," added the Reverend Mr. Wilson. "What say you, worshipful Master Bellingham? Hath he not pleaded well for the poor woman?"

33   "Indeed hath he," answered the magistrate, "and hath adduced such arguments, that we will even leave the matter as it now stands; so long, at least, as there shall be no further scandal in the woman. Care must be had, nevertheless, to put the child to due and stated examination in the catechism at thy hands or Master Dimmesdale's. Moreover, at a proper season, the tithing-men must take heed that she go both to school and to meeting."

34   The young minister, on ceasing to speak, had withdrawn a few steps from the group, and stood with his face partially concealed in the heavy folds of the window-curtain; while the shadow of his figure, which the sunlight cast upon the floor, was tremulous with the vehemence of his appeal. Pearl, that wild and flighty little elf, stole softly towards him, and, taking his hand in the grasp of both her own, laid her cheek against it; a caress so tender, and withal so unobtrusive, that her mother, who was looking on, asked herself,—"Is that my Pearl?" Yet she knew that there was love in the child's heart, although it mostly revealed itself in passion, and hardly twice in her lifetime had been softened by such gentleness as now. The minister,—for, save the long-sought regards of woman, nothing is sweeter than these marks of childish preference, accorded spontaneously by a spiritual instinct, and therefore seeming to imply in us something truly worthy to be loved,—the minister looked round, laid his hand on the child's head, hesitated an instant, and then kissed her brow. Little Pearl's unwonted mood of sentiment lasted no longer; she laughed, and went capering down the hall, so airily, that old Mr. Wilson raised a question whether even her tiptoes touched the floor.

35   "The little baggage hath witchcraft in her, I profess," said he to Mr. Dimmesdale. "She needs no old woman's broomstick to fly withal!"

36   "A strange child!" remarked old Roger Chillingworth. "It is easy to see the mother's part in her. Would it be beyond a philosopher's research, think ye, gentlemen, to analyze that child's nature, and, from its make and mould, to give a shrewd guess at the father?"

37   "Nay; it would be sinful, in such a question, to follow the clew of profane philosophy," said Mr. Wilson. "Better to fast and pray upon it; and still better, it may be, to leave the mystery as we find it, unless Providence reveal it of its own accord. Thereby, every good Christian man hath a title to show a father's kindness towards the poor, deserted babe."

38   The affair being so satisfactorily concluded, Hester Prynne, with Pearl, departed from the house. As they descended the steps, it is averred that the lattice of a chamber-window was thrown open, and forth into the sunny day was thrust the face of Mistress Hibbins, Governor Bellingham's bitter-tempered sister, and the same who, a few years later, was executed as a witch.

39   "Hist, hist!" said she, while her ill-omened physiognomy seemed to cast a shadow over the cheerful newness of the house. "Wilt thou go with us to-night? There will be a merry company in the forest; and I wellnigh promised the Black Man that comely Hester Prynne should make one."

40   "Make my excuse to him, so please you!" answered Hester, with a triumphant smile. "I must tarry at home, and keep watch over my little Pearl. Had they

taken her from me, I would willingly have gone with thee into the forest, and
signed my name in the Black Man's book too, and that with mine own blood!"

41   "We shall have thee there anon!" said the witch-lady, frowning, as she drew
back her head.

42   But here—if we suppose this interview betwixt Mistress Hibbins and Hester
Prynne to be authentic, and not a parable—was already an illustration of the young
minister's argument against sundering the relation of a fallen mother to the offspring of her frailty. Even thus early had the child saved her from Satan's snare.

CHAPTER 8

JOURNAL

1. **MLA Works Cited** *Using this model, record this book.*
   Author's Last Name, First Name. The Scarlet Letter. *1850.* Title of This Book.
       Ed. First Name Last Name. City: Publisher, year.
2. **Main Character(s)** *Describe each main character and explain why you think each
   is a main character.*
3. **Supporting Characters** *Describe each supporting character and explain why you
   think each is a supporting character.*
4. **Setting** *Describe the setting(s) and any relevant prop(s).*
5. **Sequence** *Outline the events in this chapter in order.*
6. **Plot** *Summarize this chapter's events in no more than two sentences.*
7. **Conflicts** *Identify and explain all conflicts involved in this chapter.*
8. **Significant Quotations** *Explain the importance of each of these quotations. Record
   the page number in the parentheses.*
   a. "It was understood that this learned man was the physician as well as friend
      of the young minister, whose health had severely suffered, of late, by his too
      unreserved self-sacrifice to the labors and duties of the pastoral relation" (   ).
   b. "'Prithee, young one, who art thou, and what has ailed thy mother to bedi-
      zen thee in this strange fashion? Art thou a Christian child,—ha? Dost know
      thy catechism? Or art thou one of those naughty elfs or fairies [. . .]'" (   ).
   c. "Hester caught hold of Pearl, and drew her forcibly into her arms, con-
      fronting the old Puritan magistrate with almost a fierce expression. Alone
      in the world, cast off by it, and with this sole treasure to keep her heart
      alive, she felt that she possessed indefeasible rights against the world, and
      was ready to defend them to the death" (   ).
   d. "'Speak thou for me!' cried she. 'Thou wast my pastor, and hadst charge of
      my soul, and knowest me better than these men can. I will not lose the
      child! Speak for me! Thou knowest,—for thou hast sympathies which these
      men lack!—thou knowest what is in my heart [. . .]'" (   ).
   e. "[T]he minister looked round, laid his hand on the child's head, hesitated
      an instant, and then kissed her brow" (   ).

9. **Recap** *Summarize what has happened so far, from the beginning of the book through this chapter.*

FOLLOW-UP QUESTIONS

6 SHORT QUESTIONS

Select the <u>best</u> answer for each.

_____ 1. Hester Prynne is not asked to embroider
   a. baby linens.
   b. funeral garments.
   c. bridal veils.

_____ 2. Governor Bellingham keeps a
   a. cold and bare home.
   b. comfortable and tasteful home.
   c. practical and empty home.

_____ 3. Since Hester endured her punishment on the scaffold, it has been about
   a. three weeks.
   b. three months.
   c. three years.

_____ 4. Pearl wears
   a. colorful clothing.
   b. typical Puritan garb.
   c. dull, homemade attire.

_____ 5. Mr. Wilson asks Pearl about
   a. her mother.
   b. her Christian knowledge.
   c. the flowers in the garden.

_____ 6. Arthur Dimmesdale argues that
   a. Hester should give up Pearl for adoption.
   b. Hester should keep Pearl.
   c. the ministers should fast and pray about this issue.

5 SIGNIFICANT QUOTATIONS

Explain the importance of each of these quotations.

1. "'Pearl?—Ruby, rather!—or Coral!—or Red Rose, at the very least, judging from thy hue!' responded the old minister, putting forth his hand in a vain attempt to pat little Pearl on the cheek. "But where is this mother of thine? [. . .].'"

2. "[. . .] Hester Prynne looked at [Roger Chillingworth], and even then, with her fate hanging in the balance, was startled to perceive what a change had come over his features,—how much uglier they were,—how his dark complexion seemed to have grown duskier, and his figure more misshapen,—since the days when she had familiarly known him [. . .]."

3. "'God gave me the child!' cried she. 'He gave her, in requital of all things else, which ye had taken from me. She is my happiness!—she is my torture, none the less! Pearl keeps me here in life! Pearl punishes me too! See ye not, she is the scarlet letter, only capable of being loved, and so endowed with a

million-fold the power of retribution for my sin? Ye shall not take her! I will die first!'"

4. "[. . .] Pearl, that wild and flighty little elf, stole softly towards him, and, taking his hand in the grasp of both her own, laid her cheek against it; a caress so tender, and withal so unobtrusive, that her mother, who was look-ing on, asked herself,—'Is that my Pearl?' [. . .]."

5. "'Make my excuse to him, so please you!' answered Hester, with a triumphant smile. 'I must tarry at home, and keep watch over my little Pearl. Had they taken her from me, I would willingly have gone with thee into the forest, and signed my name in the Black Man's book too, and that with mine own blood!'"

2 COMPREHENSION ESSAY QUESTIONS

Use specific details and information from the chapter to answer these questions as completely as possible.

1. The name of a character can sometimes reveal important character traits. From their names, what do you think that Hawthorne wants us to know about Roger Chillingworth and Arthur Dimmesdale? Use specific details and information from the recent chapters in your explanation.
2. We learn a great deal about characters by their actions, thoughts, and words. How would you explain the characters' actions, using specific details and information from this chapter?

DISCUSSION QUESTIONS

Be prepared to discues these questions in class.

1. What are the arguments in favor of Hester being allowed to keep Pearl?
2. What are the arguments against Hester being allowed to keep Pearl?
3. Do you feel sympathy for Hester? Do you feel sympathy for little Pearl?

CHAPTERS 5–8

JOURNAL

1. **MLA Works Cited** *Using this model, record this book.*
   Author's Last Name, First Name. <u>The Scarlet Letter</u>. 1850. <u>Title of This Book</u>.
   Ed. First Name Last Name. City: Publisher, year.
2. **Main Character(s)** *Describe each main character and explain why you think each is a main character.*
3. **Supporting Characters** *Describe each supporting character and explain why you think each is a supporting character.*
4. **Setting** *Describe the setting(s) and any relevant prop(s).*
5. **Sequence** *Outline the events in these chapters in order.*
6. **Plot** *Summarize these chapters' events in no more than five sentences.*
7. **Conflicts** *Identify and explain all conflicts involved in these chapters.*
8. **Significant Quotations** *Explain the importance of each of these quotations. Record the page number in the parentheses.*
   a. "Hester Prynne's term of confinement was now at an end. Her prison-door was thrown open, and she came forth into the sunshine, which, falling on all alike, seemed, to her sick and morbid heart, as if meant for no other purpose than to reveal the scarlet letter on her breast [. . .]" ( ).
   b. "Clergymen paused in the street to address words of exhortation, that brought a crowd, with its mingled grin and frown, around the poor, sinful woman. If she entered a church, [. . .] it was often her mishap to find herself the text of the discourse [. . .]" ( ).
   c. "But little Pearl was not clad in rustic weeds. Her mother [. . .] had bought the richest tissues that could be procured, and allowed her imaginative faculty its full play in the arrangement and decoration of the dresses which the child wore, before the public eye. So magnificent was the small figure, when thus arrayed, and such was the splendor of Pearl's own proper beauty [. . .] that there was an absolute circle of radiance around her, on the darksome cottage-floor [. . .]" ( ).
   d. "Never, since her release from prison, had Hester met the public gaze without her. In all her walks about the town, Pearl, too, was there; first as the babe in arms, and afterwards as the little girl, small companion of her mother, holding a forefinger with her whole grasp, and tripping along at the rate of three or four footsteps to one of Hester's [. . .]" ( ).
   e. "'No, my little Pearl!'" said her mother. 'Thou must gather thine own sunshine. I have none to give thee!'" ( ).
   f. "'Come along, Pearl!' said she, drawing her away. 'Come and look into this fair garden. It may be, we shall see flowers there; more beautiful ones than we find in the woods'" ( ).
   g. "'Speak thou, the child's own mother! Were it not, thinkest thou, for thy little one's temporal and eternal welfare, that she be taken out of thy charge, and clad soberly, and disciplined strictly, and instructed in the

truths of heaven and earth? What canst thou do for the child, in this kind?'" (   ).

h. "'Nevertheless,' said the mother calmly, though growing more pale, 'this badge hath taught me,—it daily teaches me,—it is teaching me at this moment,—lessons whereof my child may be the wiser and better, albeit they can profit nothing to myself'" (   ).

i. "'Speak thou for me!' cried she. 'Thou wast my pastor, and hadst charge of my soul, and knowest me better than these men can. I will not lose the child! Speak for me! Thou knowest,—for thou hast sympathies which these men lack!—thou knowest what is in my heart, and what are a mother's rights, and how much the stronger they are, when that mother has but her child and the scarlet letter! Look thou to it! I will not lose the child! Look to it!'" (   ).

j. "'For Hester Prynne's sake, then, and no less for the poor child's sake, let us leave them as Providence hath seen fit to place them!'" (   ).

9. **Recap** *Summarize what has happened so far, from the beginning of the novel, through these chapters.*

FOLLOW-UP QUESTIONS

20 SHORT QUESTIONS

Select the <u>best</u> answer for each.

____ 1. Released from prison, Hester makes her living by
   a. collecting plants and roots in the woods.
   b. nursing the sick and infirm.
   c. sewing and embroidery.

____ 2. Hester remains in the colony because
   a. she is not allowed to leave Boston.
   b. she loves the baby's father.
   c. she does not have enough money to leave.

____ 3. Hester lives in an abandoned cottage
   a. in town.
   b. next to the prison.
   c. on a peninsula.

____ 4. Hester Prynne sometimes feels that the scarlet letter
   a. gives her knowledge of sin in other people's hearts.
   b. protects her from the townspeople's curiosity.
   c. makes her feel proud.

____ 5. Some townspeople believe that the scarlet letter
   a. glows all night with fire.
   b. is an unfair punishment.
   c. will fall off when the punishment ends.

____ 6. Hester gives her extra money to
   a. Mistress Hibbins.
   b. the church.
   c. the poor.

____ 7. Hester names the baby Pearl because
   a. it is a pretty name and the baby is pretty.
   b. a pearl is an expensive and rare treasure.
   c. they live near the sea.

____ 8. Hester dresses Pearl in
   a. somber, gray clothes.
   b. old, torn clothing.
   c. colorful, beautiful clothing.

____ 9. Little Pearl is
   a. quiet and obedient.
   b. a model Puritan child.
   c. impulsive and wilful.

____ 10. The Puritan children
   a. feel rejected by Pearl.
   b. say hurtful things to Pearl.
   c. want to play with Pearl.

____ 11. Hester finds that Pearl is
   a. not easy to manage.
   b. often sick.
   c. too quiet.

____ 12. Hester learns that some magistrates want
   a. to take Pearl away from her.
   b. Hester and Pearl to leave the colony.
   c. Pearl to wear a scarlet letter.

____ 13. Hester goes to the governor's mansion to
   a. measure the governor for a new robe.
   b. deliver a pair of gloves.
   c. ask for money.

____ 14. The servant who answers the door at the mansion
   a. recognizes Hester and lets her in.
   b. does not recognize Hester or the scarlet letter.
   c. will not let her enter the mansion.

____ 15. The governor's mansion is
   a. decorated with armor and portraits.
   b. bare and gloomy.
   c. used only for official business and is not lived in.

____ 16. The governor's name is
   a. Wilson.
   b. Dimmesdale.
   c. Bellingham.

____ 17. The governor is
   a. young and handsome.
   b. elderly and stern.
   c. elderly and deformed.

____ 18. Pearl wrongly answers questions about
   a. her mother.
   b. her religion.
   c. plants in the garden and forest.

____ 19. To support her position, Hester asks for help from
   a. Roger Chillingworth.
   b. John Wilson.
   c. Arthur Dimmesdale.

____ 20. The Reverend Arthur Dimmesdale says that
   a. Hester should keep Pearl.
   b. Hester has no control over Pearl.
   c. Pearl should be given to a Christian family for adoption.

10 SIGNIFICANT QUOTATIONS

Explain the importance of each of these quotations.

1. "To-morrow would bring its own trial with it; so would the next day, and so would the next; each its own trial, and yet the very same that was now so unutterably grievous to be borne. The days of the far-off future would toil onward, still with the same burden for her to take up, and bear along with her, but never to fling down; for the accumulating days, and added years, would pile up their misery upon the heap of shame [. . .]."

2. "But there is a fatality, a feeling so irresistible and inevitable that it has the force of doom, which almost invariably compels human beings to linger around and haunt, ghost-like, the spot where some great and marked event has given the color to their lifetime; and still the more irresistibly, the darker the tinge that saddens it. Her sin, her ignominy, were the roots which she had struck into the soil [. . .]."

3. "But it is not recorded that, in a single instance, her skill was called in aid to embroider the white veil which was to cover the pure blushes of a bride. The exception indicated the ever relentless vigor with which society frowned upon her sin."

4. "The truth was, that the little Puritans, being of the most intolerant brood that ever lived, had got a vague idea of something outlandish, unearthly, or at variance with ordinary fashions, in the mother and child; and therefore scorned them in their hearts, and not unfrequently reviled them with their tongues. Pearl felt the sentiment and requited it with the bitterest hatred that can be supposed to rankle in a childish bosom [. . .]."

5. "But that first object of which Pearl seemed to become aware was—shall we say it?—the scarlet letter on Hester's bosom! [. . .]."

6. "In the afternoon of a certain summer's day, after Pearl grew big enough to run about, she amused herself with gathering handfuls of wild-flowers, and flinging them, one by one, at her mother's bosom; dancing up and down, like a little elf, whenever she hit the scarlet letter [. . .]."

7. "If the child, on the other hand, were really capable of moral and religious growth, and possessed the elements of ultimate salvation, then, surely, it would enjoy all the fairer prospect of these advantages by being transferred to wiser and better guardianship than Hester Prynne's [. . .]."

8. "Behind the Governor and Mr. Wilson came two other guests; one, the Reverend Arthur Dimmesdale, [. . .] and, in close companionship with him, old Roger Chillingworth, a person of great skill in physic, who, for two or three years past, had been settled in the town [. . .]."

9. "'God gave her into my keeping,' repeated Hester Prynne, raising her voice almost to a shriek. 'I will not give her up! [. . .].'"

10. "'This child of its father's guilt and its mother's shame hath come from the hand of God, to work in many ways upon her heart, who pleads so earnestly,

and with such bitterness of spirit, the right to keep her. It was meant for a blessing; for the one blessing of her life! [. . .].'"

2 COMPREHENSION ESSAY QUESTIONS

Use specific details and information from these chapters to answer these questions as completely as possible.

1. Hester is condemned to wear the scarlet letter as punishment. Beyond that, how else is Hester punished by members of the community? How do she and Pearl handle this?
2. As if things are not bad enough, some of the magistrates and townspeople want to take Pearl away from Hester. What are the arguments for and against this idea?

DISCUSSION QUESTIONS

Be prepared to discuss these questions in class.

1. Is Hester a good mother? Is Pearl a difficult child?
2. Who are these men at the governor's mansion considering Pearl's fate? What do you think of their arguments? Why does Hester ask Arthur to speak for her?

WRITING

Use each of these ideas to write an essay.

1. Describe a punishment that you or someone you know had to endure. Explain the circumstances. Was the punishment fair or unfair? What did the experience teach?
2. Hester Prynne and Arthur Dimmesdale respond to guilt in different ways. What effects does guilt have on a person's life? Describe a time when you felt guilty. How did your behavior change? What did you do to relieve your guilt?
3. The Puritans wore simple, plain clothing, yet the magistrates wore highly embroidered garments. Was this a luxury or a reflection of rank? Write an essay in which you consider at what point something becomes a luxury. For example, is it a luxury to pay extra for a particular ring on your cell phone?

FURTHER WRITING

1. The Puritans believed in strict punishments and enforcement of their moral code. Many people today think some of their rules were too harsh. Is there a

law that you feel is unfair or too harsh? Research the law and its punishment and explain your position in an argument essay.

2. Sometimes, the government removes children from their parents in cases of abuse and neglect. Research the factors involved in these removals and how these children fare in foster care.

3. What makes a good parent? Research three traits that are necessary for good parenting.

4. Who was Anne Hutchinson and why was she banished from the Puritan colony? Research her life, beliefs, and influence on women in religion.

5. The magistrates ordered Hester Prynne to wear the letter A as punishment. Hester, however, embroiders the symbol with elaborate stitchery, with red and gold flourishes. She dresses Pearl in gorgeous red clothing. What does this show about Hester as an individual within a strict society? Use specific citations from the story to support your points.

CHAPTER 9

THE LEECH

Use context clues to define these words before reading. Use a dictionary as needed.

1. *Leeches*, bloodsucking worms that live in water, have been used worldwide by doctors to bleed patients with toxic illnesses. The term *leech* once meant a physician, but has also come to mean someone who sucks the life of another person. *Leech* means _____

    _____ .

2. Healthcare workers wash their hands before and after treating each patient to avoid spreading disease or *contagion*. *Contagion* means _____

    _____ .

3. The old house was in a state of *decay*, with rotting floorboards and decomposing walls. *Decay* means _____

    _____ .

4. My dog Dakota loves to *pursue* squirrels and birds, chasing them all around our yard. *Pursue* means _____

    _____ .

5. Doctor Romano is a fine *physician* and has been practicing medicine for over twenty years. *Physician* means _____

    _____ .

6. *Apothecary* is an old-fashioned term for druggist or pharmacist, referring to someone who formulates and fills prescriptions. *Apothecary* means _____

    _____ .

7. A doctor's *sphere* of business is medicine while a banker's sphere of business is money. *Sphere* means _____

    _____ .

8. Jody and Frank finally *acquired* a house of their own after saving money for a down payment for over ten years. *Acquire* means _____
_____.

9. The Christian religions observe the *Sabbath*, or Sunday, as a day of rest and worship. *Sabbath* means _____
_____.

10. Teddy is an *exemplary* student, getting A's and commendations from his professors. *Exemplary* means _____
_____.

11. In this competitive era, many companies *scrutinize* an applicant's resume and credentials, looking very carefully for the best candidate. *Scrutinize* means
_____.

12. Henry is very curious and always *delving* into other people's business and other people's affairs. *Delve* means _____
_____.

13. *Cultivating* a friendship requires time and effort to see friends, talk on the telephone, and go places together. *Cultivate* means _____
_____.

14. The couple's *intimacy* was very deep, and they shared all their thoughts and time together. *Intimacy* means _____
_____.

15. Albert spends all of his time studying, doing research, and writing articles; he is a true *scholar*. *Scholar* means _____
_____.

16. People who study extensively and delve deeply into their studies achieve *erudition*. *Erudition* means _____
_____.

17. Ian's paintings sometimes focus on *diabolical* images—devils and demons are pictured with pitchforks and fire. *Diabolical* means _____
_____.

18. According to a King Arthur legend, Sir Galahad went on a long and arduous journey in his *quest* to find the Holy Grail. *Quest* means _____
_____.

19. David likes to visit his childhood *abode,* the house he lived in as a little boy, whenever he returns to his hometown. *Abode* means _____ _____.

20. When Mother offered us either vanilla or chocolate ice cream, Thomas took the *latter* because he loves chocolate. *Latter* means _____ _____.

PRE-READING VOCABULARY
STRUCTURAL ATTACK

Define these words by solving the parts. Use the Glossary or a dictionary as needed.

1. travel-worn	12. vindicate	23. infirmity
2. perilous	13. orbit	24. striven
3. kindred	14. decline	25. probed
4. pedestal	15. ground-work	26. unaware
5. vanished	16. pathway	27. benevolent
6. untutored	17. intellect	28. paternal
7. savagely	18. uglier	29. guises
8. aught	19. piety	30. undergone
9. deacon	20. deemed	31. victory
10. accustomed	21. diffused	32. secured
11. attribute	22. emissary	33. acquainted

PRE-READING QUESTIONS

Try answering these questions as you read.

What kind of person is Roger Chillingworth?

What is Roger Chillingworth searching for?

What kind of relationship develops between Arthur Dimmesdale and Roger Chillingworth?

Where does Roger Chillingworth live?

How is Arthur Dimmesdale's health?

CHAPTER 9

THE LEECH

1 Under the appellation of Roger Chillingworth, the reader will remember, was hidden another name, which its former wearer had resolved should never more be spoken. It has been related, how, in the crowd that witnessed Hester Prynne's ignominious exposure, stood a man, elderly, travel-worn, who, just emerging from

the perilous wilderness, beheld the woman, in whom he hoped to find embodied the warmth and cheerfulness of home, set up as a type of sin before the people. Her matronly fame was trodden under all men's feet. Infamy was babbling around her in the public market-place. For her kindred, should the tidings ever reach them, and for the companions of her unspotted life, there remained nothing but the contagion of her dishonor; which would not fail to be distributed in strict accordance and proportion with the intimacy and sacredness of their previous relationship. Then why—since the choice was with himself—should the individual, whose connection with the fallen woman had been the most intimate and sacred of them all, come forward to vindicate his claim to an inheritance so little desirable? He resolved not to be pilloried beside her on her pedestal of shame. Unknown to all but Hester Prynne, and possessing the lock and key of her silence, he chose to withdraw his name from the roll of mankind, and as regarded his former ties and interests, to vanish out of life as completely as if he indeed lay at the bottom of the ocean, whither rumor had long ago consigned him. This purpose once effected, new interests would immediately spring up, and likewise a new purpose; dark, it is true, if not guilty, but of force enough to engage the full strength of his faculties.

2   In pursuance of this resolve, he took up his residence in the Puritan town, as Roger Chillingworth, without other introduction than the learning and intelligence of which he possessed more than a common measure. As his studies, at a previous period of his life, had made him extensively acquainted with the medical science of the day, it was as a physician that he presented himself, and as such was cordially received. Skilful men, of the medical and chirurgical profession, were of rare occurrence in the colony. They seldom, it would appear, partook of the religious zeal that brought other emigrants across the Atlantic. In their researches into the human frame, it may be that the higher and more subtile faculties of such men were materialized, and that they lost the spiritual view of existence amid the intricacies of that wondrous mechanism, which seemed to involve art enough to comprise all of life within itself. At all events, the health of the good town of Boston, so far as medicine had aught to do with it, had hitherto lain in the guardianship of an aged deacon and apothecary, whose piety and godly deportment were stronger testimonials in his favor, than any that he could have produced in the shape of a diploma. The only surgeon was one who combined the occasional exercise of that noble art with the daily and habitual flourish of a razor. To such a professional body Roger Chillingworth was a brilliant acquisition. He soon manifested his familiarity with the ponderous and imposing machinery of

antique physic; in which every remedy contained a multitude of far-fetched and heterogeneous ingredients, as elaborately compounded as if the proposed result had been the Elixir of Life. In his Indian captivity, moreover, he had gained much knowledge of the properties of native herbs and roots; nor did he conceal from his patients, that these simple medicines, Nature's boon to the untutored savage, had quite as large a share of his own confidence as the European pharmacopœia, which so many learned doctors had spent centuries in elaborating.

3   This learned stranger was exemplary, as regarded at least the outward forms of a religious life, and, early after his arrival, had chosen for his spiritual guide the Reverend Mr. Dimmesdale. The young divine, whose scholar-like renown still lived in Oxford, was considered by his more fervent admirers as little less than a heaven-ordained apostle, destined, should he live and labor for the ordinary term of life, to do as great deeds for the now feeble New England Church, as the early Fathers had achieved for the infancy of the Christian faith. About this period, however, the health of Mr. Dimmesdale had evidently begun to fail. By those best acquainted with his habits, the paleness of the young minister's cheek was accounted for by his too earnest devotion to study, his scrupulous fulfillment of parochial duty, and, more than all, by the fasts and vigils of which he made a frequent practice, in order to keep the grossness of this earthly state from clogging and obscuring his spiritual lamp. Some declared, that, if Mr. Dimmesdale were really going to die, it was cause enough, that the world was not worthy to be any longer trodden by his feet. He himself, on the other hand, with characteristic humility, avowed his belief, that, if Providence should see fit to remove him, it would be because of his own unworthiness to perform its humblest mission here on earth. With all this difference of opinion as to the cause of his decline, there could be no question of the fact. His form grew emaciated; his voice, though still rich and sweet, had a certain melancholy prophecy of decay in it; he was often observed, on any slight alarm or other sudden accident, to put his hand over his heart, with first a flush and then a paleness, indicative of pain.

4   Such was the young clergyman's condition, and so imminent the prospect that his dawning light would be extinguished, all untimely, when Roger Chillingworth made his advent to the town. His first entry on the scene, few people could tell whence, dropping down, as it were, out of the sky, or starting from the nether earth, had an aspect of mystery, which was easily heightened to the miraculous. He was now known to be a man of skill; it was observed that he gathered herbs, and the blossoms of wild-flowers, and dug up roots and plucked off twigs from the forest-trees, like one acquainted with hidden virtues in what was valueless to common eyes. He was heard to speak of Sir Kenelm Digby, and other famous men,—whose scientific attainments were esteemed hardly less than supernatural,—as having been his correspondents or associates. Why, with such rank in the learned world, had he come hither? What could he, whose sphere was in great cities, be seeking in the wilderness? In answer to this query, a rumor gained ground,—and, however absurd, was entertained by some very sensible people,—that Heaven had wrought an absolute miracle, by transporting an

eminent Doctor of Physic, from a German university, bodily through the air, and setting him down at the door of Mr. Dimmesdale's study! Individuals of wiser faith, indeed, who knew that Heaven promotes its purposes without aiming at the stage-effect of what is called miraculous interposition, were inclined to see a providential hand in Roger Chillingworth's so opportune arrival.

5   This idea was countenanced by the strong interest which the physician ever manifested in the young clergyman; he attached himself to him as a parishioner, and sought to win a friendly regard and confidence from his naturally reserved sensibility. He expressed great alarm at his pastor's state of health, but was anxious to attempt the cure, and, if early undertaken, seemed not despondent of a favorable result. The elders, the deacons, the motherly dames, and the young and fair maidens, of Mr. Dimmesdale's flock, were alike importunate that he should make trial of the physician's frankly offered skill. Mr. Dimmesdale gently repelled their entreaties.

6   "I need no medicine," said he.

7   But how could the young minister say so, when, with every successive Sabbath, his cheek was paler and thinner, and his voice more tremulous than before,—when it had now become a constant habit, rather than a casual gesture, to press his hand over his heart? Was he weary of his labors? Did he wish to die? These questions were solemnly propounded to Mr. Dimmesdale by the elder ministers of Boston and the deacons of his church, who, to use their own phrase, "dealt with him" on the sin of rejecting the aid which Providence so manifestly held out. He listened in silence, and finally promised to confer with the physician.

8   "Were it God's will," said the Reverend Mr. Dimmesdale, when, in fulfilment of this pledge, he requested old Roger Chillingworth's professional advice, "I could be well content, that my labors, and my sorrows, and my sins, and my pains, should shortly end with me, and what is earthly of them be buried in my grave, and the spiritual go with me to my eternal state, rather than that you should put your skill to the proof in my behalf."

9   "Ah," replied Roger Chillingworth, with that quietness which, whether imposed or natural, marked all his department, "it is thus that a young clergyman is apt to speak. Youthful men, not having taken a deep root, give up their hold of life so easily! And saintly men, who walk with God on earth, would fain be away, to walk with him on the golden pavements of the New Jerusalem."

10   "Nay," rejoined the young minister, putting his hand to his heart, with a flush of pain flitting over his brow, "were I worthier to walk there, I could be better content to toil here."

11   "Good men ever interpret themselves too meanly," said the physician.

12   In this manner, the mysterious old Roger Chillingworth became the medical adviser of the Reverend Mr. Dimmesdale. As not only the disease interested the physician, but he was strongly moved to look into the character and qualities of the patient, these two men, so different in age, came gradually to spend much

time together. For the sake of the minister's health, and to enable the leech to gather plants with healing balm in them, they took long walks on the seashore, or in the forest; mingling various talk with the plash and murmur of the waves, and the solemn wind-anthem among the tree-tops. Often, likewise, one was the guest of the other, in his place of study and retirement. There was a fascination for the minister in the company of the man of science, in whom he recognized an intellectual cultivation of no moderate depth or scope; together with a range and freedom of ideas, that he would have vainly looked for among the members of his own profession. In truth, he was startled, if not shocked, to find this attribute in the physician. Mr. Dimmesdale was a true priest, a true religionist, with the reverential sentiment largely developed, and an order of mind that impelled itself powerfully along the track of a creed, and wore its passage continually deeper with the lapse of time. In no state of society would he have been what is called a man of liberal views; it would always be essential to his peace to feel the pressure of a faith about him, supporting, while it confined him within its iron framework. Not the less, however, though with a tremulous enjoyment, did he feel the occasional relief of looking at the universe through the medium of another kind of intellect than those with which he habitually held converse. It was as if a window were thrown open, admitting a freer atmosphere into the close and stifled study, where his life was wasting itself away, amid lamp-light, or obstructed daybeams, and the musty fragrance, be it sensual or moral, that exhales from books. But the air was too fresh and chill to be long breathed, with comfort. So the minister, and the physician with him, withdrew again within the limits of what their church defined as orthodox.

13   Thus Roger Chillingworth scrutinized his patient carefully, both as he saw him in his ordinary life, keeping an accustomed pathway in the range of thoughts familiar to him, and as he appeared when thrown amidst other moral scenery, the novelty of which might call out something new to the surface of his character. He deemed it essential, it would seem, to know the man, before attempting to do him good. Wherever there is a heart and an intellect, the diseases of the physical frame are tinged with the peculiarities of these. In Arthur Dimmesdale, thought and imagination were so active, and sensibility so intense, that the bodily infirmity would be likely to have its groundwork there. So Roger Chillingworth— the man of skill, the kind and friendly physician—strove to go deep into his patient's bosom, delving among his principles, prying into his recollections, and probing every thing with a cautious touch, like a treasure-seeker in a dark cavern. Few secrets can escape an investigator, who has opportunity and license to undertake such a quest, and skill to follow it up. A man burdened with a secret should especially avoid the intimacy of his physician. If the latter possess native sagacity, and a nameless something more,—let us call it intuition; if he show no intrusive egotism, nor disagreeably prominent characteristics of his own; if he have the power, which must be born with him, to bring his mind into such affinity with his patient's, that this last shall unawares have spoken what he imagines

himself only to have thought; if such revelations be received without tumult, and acknowledged not so often by an uttered sympathy, as by silence, an inarticulate breath, and here and there a word, to indicate that all is understood; if, to these qualifications of a confidant be joined the advantages afforded by his recognized character as a physician;—then, at some inevitable moment, will the soul of the sufferer be dissolved, and flow forth in a dark, but transparent stream, bringing all its mysteries into the daylight.

14 Roger Chillingworth possessed all, or most, of the attributes above enumerated. Nevertheless, time went on; a kind of intimacy, as we have said, grew up between these two cultivated minds, which had as wide a field as the whole sphere of human thought and study, to meet upon; they discussed every topic of ethics and religion, of public affairs, and private character; they talked much, on both sides, of matters that seemed personal to themselves; and yet no secret, such as the physician fancied must exist there, ever stole out of the minister's consciousness into his companion's ear. The latter had his suspicions, indeed, that even the nature of Mr. Dimmesdale's bodily disease had never fairly been revealed to him. It was a strange reserve!

15 After a time, at a hint from Roger Chillingworth, the friends of Mr. Dimmesdale effected an arrangement by which the two were lodged in the same house; so that every ebb and flow of the minister's life-tide might pass under the eye of his anxious and attached physician. There was much joy throughout the town, when this greatly desirable object was attained. It was held to be the best possible measure for the young clergyman's welfare; unless, indeed, as often urged by such as felt authorized to do so, he had selected some one of the many blooming damsels, spiritually devoted to him, to become his devoted wife. This latter step, however, there was no present prospect that Arthur Dimmesdale would be prevailed upon to take; he rejected all suggestions of the kind, as if priestly celibacy were one of his articles of church-discipline Doomed by his own choice, therefore, as Mr. Dimmesdale so evidently was, to eat his unsavory morsel always at another's board, and endure the life-long chill which must be his lot who seeks to warm himself only at another's fireside, it truly seemed that this sagacious, experienced, benevolent, old physician, with his concord of paternal and reverential love for the young pastor, was the very man, of all mankind, to be constantly within reach of his voice.

16 The new abode of the two friends was with a pious widow, of good social rank, who dwelt in a house covering pretty nearly the site on which the venerable structure of King's Chapel has since been built. It had the grave-yard, originally Isaac Johnson's home-field, on one side, and so was well adapted to call up serious reflections, suited to their respective employments, in both minister and man of physic. The motherly care of the good widow assigned to Mr. Dimmesdale a front apartment, with a sunny exposure, and heavy window-curtains to create a noontide shadow, when desirable. The walls were hung round with tapestry, said to be from the Gobelin looms, and, at all events, representing the Scriptural story of David and Bathsheba, and Nathan the Prophet, in colors still unfaded, but

which made the fair woman of the scene almost as grimly picturesque as the woe-denouncing seer. Here, the pale clergyman piled up his library, rich with parchment-bound folios of the Fathers, and the lore of Rabbis, and monkish erudition, of which the Protestant divines, even while they vilified and decried that class of writers, were yet constrained often to avail themselves. On the other side of the house, old Roger Chillingworth arranged his study and laboratory; not such as a modern man of science would reckon even tolerably complete, but provided with a distilling apparatus, and the means of compounding drugs and chemicals, which the practised alchemist knew well how to turn to purpose. With such commodiousness of situation, these two learned persons sat themselves down, each in his own domain, yet familiarly passing from one apartment to the other, and bestowing a mutual and not incurious inspection into one another's business.

17   And the Reverend Arthur Dimmesdale's best discerning friends, as we have intimated, very reasonably imagined that the hand of Providence had done all this, for the purpose—besought in so many public, and domestic, and secret prayers—of restoring the young minister to health. But—it must now be said— another portion of the community had latterly begun to take its own view of the relation betwixt Mr. Dimmesdale and the mysterious old physician. When an uninstructed multitude attempts to see with its eyes, it is exceedingly apt to be deceived. When, however, it forms its judgment, as it usually does, on the intuitions of its great and warm heart, the conclusions thus attained are often so profound and so unerring, as to possess the character of truths supernaturally revealed. The people, in the case of which we speak, could justify its prejudice against Roger Chillingworth by no fact or argument worthy of serious refutation. There was an aged handicraftsman, it is true, who had been a citizen of London at the period of Sir Thomas Overbury's murder, now some thirty years agone; he testified to having seen the physician, under some other name, which the narrator of the story had now forgotten, in company with Doctor Forman, the famous old conjurer, who was implicated in the affair of Overbury. Two or three individuals hinted, that the man of skill, during his Indian captivity, had enlarged his medical attainments by joining in the incantations of the savage priests; who were universally acknowledged to be powerful enchanters, often performing seemingly miraculous cures by their skill in the black art A large number—and many of these were persons of such sober sense and practical observation, that their opinions would have been valuable, in other matters— affirmed that Roger Chillingworth's aspect had undergone a remarkable change while he had dwelt in town, and especially since his abode with Mr. Dimmesdale. At first, his expression had been calm, meditative, scholar-like. Now, there was something ugly and evil in his face, which they had not previously noticed, and which grew still the more obvious to sight, the oftener they looked upon him. According to the vulgar idea, the fire in his laboratory had been brought from the lower regions, and was fed with infernal fuel; and so, as might be expected, his visage was getting sooty with the smoke.

18   To sum up the matter it grew to be a widely diffused opinion, that the
Reverend Arthur Dimmesdale, like many other personages of especial sanctity,
in all ages of the Christian world, was haunted either by Satan himself, or Satan's
emissary, in the guise of old Roger Chillingworth. This diabolical agent had the
Divine permission, for a season, to burrow into the clergyman's intimacy, and
plot against his soul. No sensible man, it was confessed, could doubt on which
side the victory would turn. The people looked, with an unshaken hope, to see
the minister come forth out of the conflict, transfigured with the glory which
he would unquestionably win. Meanwhile, nevertheless, it was sad to think
of the perchance mortal agony through which he must struggle towards his
triumph.

19   'Alas, to judge from the gloom and terror in the depths of the poor minister's
eyes, the battle was a sore one, and the victory any thing but secure!

CHAPTER 9

JOURNAL

1. **MLA Works Cited** *Using this model, record this book.*
   Author's Last Name, First Name. The Scarlet Letter. 1850. Title of This Book.
      Ed. First Name Last Name. City: Publisher, year.
2. **Main Character(s)** *Describe each main character and explain why you think each
   is a main character.*
3. **Supporting Characters** *Describe each supporting character and explain why you
   think each is a supporting character.*
4. **Setting** *Describe the setting(s) and any relevant prop(s).*
5. **Sequence** *Outline the events in this chapter in order.*
6. **Plot** *Summarize this chapter's events in no more than two sentences.*
7. **Conflicts** *Identify and explain all conflicts involved in this chapter.*
8. **Significant Quotations** *Explain the importance of each of these quotations. Record
   the page number in the parentheses.*
   a. "As his studies, at a previous period of his life, had made him exten-
      sively acquainted with the medical science of the day, it was as a physician
      that he presented himself, and as such was cordially received. Skill-
      ful men, of the medical [. . .] profession, were of rare occurrence in the
      colony [. . .]" (   ).
   b. "His form grew emaciated; his voice, though still rich and sweet, had a cer-
      tain melancholy prophecy of decay in it; he was often observed, on any
      slight alarm or other sudden accident, to put his hand over his heart, with
      first a flush and then a paleness, indicative of pain" (   ).
   c. "In this manner, the mysterious old Roger Chillingworth became the
      medical advisor of the Reverend Mr. Dimmesdale. As not only the disease
      interested the physician, but he was strongly moved to look into the

character and qualities of the patient, these two men, so different in age, came gradually to spend much time together [. . .]" ( ).

   d. "Few secrets can escape an investigator, who has opportunity and license to undertake such a quest, and skill to follow it up. A man burdened with a secret should especially avoid the intimacy of his physician [. . .]" ( ).

   e. "To sum up the matter, it grew to be a widely diffused opinion, that the Reverend Arthur Dimmesdale, like many other personages of especial sanctity, in all ages of the Christian world, was haunted either by Satan himself, or Satan's emissary, in the guise of old Roger Chillingworth [. . .]" ( ).

9. **Recap** *Summarize what has happened so far, from the beginning of the book through this chapter.*

FOLLOW-UP QUESTIONS

6 SHORT QUESTIONS

Select the <u>best</u> answer for each.

____ 1. Roger Chillingworth has
   a. never married.
   b. changed his name.
   c. told the townspeople that Hester is his wife.

____ 2. Roger Chillingworth becomes very close friends with
   a. Arthur Dimmesdale.
   b. Hester Prynne.
   c. Mistress Hibbins.

____ 3. Roger Chillingworth's face becomes
   a. sterner.
   b. paler.
   c. uglier.

____ 4. Roger Chillingworth and Arthur Dimmesdale
   a. have many topics to talk about.
   b. do not talk much to each other.
   c. talk only about religion.

____ 5. Arthur Dimmesdale's health
   a. worsens.
   b. improves.
   c. stays the same.

____ 6. Arthur Dimmesdale often puts his hand
   a. in his pocket.
   b. on his holy book.
   c. over his heart.

5 SIGNIFICANT QUOTATIONS

Explain the importance of each of these quotations.

1. "He was now known to be a man of skill; it was observed that he gathered herbs, and the blossoms of wild-flowers, and dug up roots and plucked off twigs from the forest-trees, like one acquainted with hidden virtues in what was valueless to common eyes [. . .]."

2. "[W]ith every successive Sabbath, his cheek was paler and thinner, and his voice more tremulous than before,—when it had now become a constant habit, rather than a casual gesture, to press his hand over his heart [. . .]."

3. "Nevertheless, time went on; a kind of intimacy, as we have said, grew up between these two cultivated minds, which had as wide a field as the whole sphere of human thought and study, to meet upon; they discussed every topic of ethics and religion, of public affairs, and private character; they talked much, on both sides, of matters that seemed personal to themselves; and yet no secret, such as the physician fancied must exist there, ever stole out of the minister's consciousness into his companion's ear [. . .]."

4. "A large number [of townspeople] affirmed that Roger Chillingworth's aspect had undergone a remarkable change while he had dwelt in town, and especially since his abode with Mr. Dimmesdale. At first, his expression had been calm, meditative, scholar-like. Now there was something ugly and evil in his face, which they had not previously noticed, and which grew still the more obvious to sight, the oftener they looked upon him [. . .]."

5. "Alas, to judge from the gloom and terror in the depths of the poor minister's eyes, the battle was a sore one, and the victory any thing but secure!"

2 COMPREHENSION ESSAY QUESTIONS

Use specific details and information from the chapter to answer these questions as completely as possible.

1. How does the chapter's title, "The Leech," relate to the story so far? What does the term *"leech"*, both literally and figuratively, suggest or reveal about Roger Chillingworth? Use specific details and information from the chapter in your explanation.

2. What are the ironies in this chapter, particularly in regards to the developing relationship between Arthur Dimmesdale and Roger Chillingworth? Use specific details and information from this chapter and previous chapters in your explanation.

DISCUSSION QUESTIONS

Be prepared to discuss these questions in class.

1. What does this chapter tell us about the nature of friendship?
2. For which character do you feel the most sympathy? The least?

CHAPTER 10

THE LEECH AND HIS PATIENT

PRE-READING VOCABULARY
CONTEXT

Use context clues to define these words before reading. Use a dictionary as needed.

1. *Upright* citizens are moral and honorable and provide good models for others. *Upright* means _____
   _____.

2. Because we live in a state of *mortality*, meaning that we all must die someday, we are called *mortals*. *Mortality* and *mortals* mean _____
   _____.

3. The congressman who accepted bribes was found guilty of *corruption*. *Corruption* means _____
   _____.

4. Once caught, individuals who have broken laws and committed crimes will be found *guilty* in a court of law. *Guilty* means _____
   _____.

5. Steven and Ann were very *reluctant* to hire the same contractor after he took too long to finish their house and charged them too much money. *Reluctant* means _____
   _____.

6. Otto is very nosy and is always snooping and *prying* into other people's personal affairs. *Prying* means _____
   _____.

7. Not wanting anyone to know that she was going off her diet, Cindy walked *stealthily* into the kitchen for some cookies. *Stealthily* means _____
   _____.

8. The runway model followed such a strict diet that she lost too much weight and looked *emaciated*. *Emaciated* means _____
   _____.

9. When the used car dealer offered too good a deal, Doreen became *wary* and called the Better Business Bureau. *Wary* means _____.

10. Some things are too deep or painful to be put into words, so these feelings are *unutterable*. *Unutterable* means _____.

11. A mistake could be life-threatening, so let us *err* on the side of caution. *Err* means _____.

12. Richelle felt absolutely *wretched* after losing her house and belongings in a fire. *Wretched* means _____.

13. Marla liked to *torment* her younger sister by ordering her around and calling her "a little pain." *Torment* means _____.

14. Unfortunately, this world has bad people who do sick things, and this is often referred to as the state of human *iniquity*. *Iniquity* means _____.

15. Amar was in *ecstasy* when he learned that he had won the lottery. *Ecstasy* means _____.

16. Soap operas often show nosy characters who ask lots of questions and *meddle* in other peoples' business. *Meddle* means _____.

17. When he went camping at the lake, Jorge brought all the necessary supplies *save* a flashlight, which meant he was unable to see the path at night. *Save* means _____.

18. At the awards ceremony, the president *bestowed* the medal of honor on the courageous soldier. *Bestow* means _____.

19. Honesty is a *trait*, or characteristic, that we should encourage in our children. *Trait* means _____.

20. After walking through the field of weeds going to seed, we had to comb several *burrs* out of the dog's fur. *Burrs* means _____
_____.

PRE-READING VOCABULARY
STRUCTURAL ATTACK

Define these words by solving the parts. Use the Glossary or a dictionary as needed.

1. bygone	13. flings	25. missile
2. disorder	14. forth	26. frisking
3. feeble	15. commanded	27. fantastically
4. alas	16. entreaty	28. akin
5. apple of one's eye	17. inclosure	29. sexton
6. premeditated	18. traverse	30. demerits
7. rustled	19. graveyard	31. suffering
8. ghastly	20. tenacious	32. conjoined
9. intercourse	21. adhere	33. integrity
10. solace	22. mirthful	34. aspiration
11. sought	23. nervous	
12. ere	24. dreaded	

PRE-READING QUESTIONS

Try answering these questions as you read.

What does Roger Chillingworth do to Arthur Dimmesdale?
What does Roger Chillingworth say about Arthur Dimmesdale's health?
What does Pearl throw at her mother and at Arthur Dimmesdale?
What does Roger Chillingworth find out?

CHAPTER 10
THE LEECH AND HIS PATIENT

1 Old Roger Chillingworth, throughout life, had been calm in temperament, kindly, though not of warm affections, but ever, and in all his relations with the world, a pure and upright man. He had begun an investigation, as he imagined, with the severe and equal integrity of a judge, desirous only of truth, even as if the question involved no more than the air-drawn lines and figures of a geometrical problem, instead of human passions, and wrongs inflicted on himself. But, as he proceeded, a terrible fascination, a kind of fierce, though still calm, necessity seized the old man

within its gripe, and never set him free again, until he had done all its bidding. He now dug into the poor clergyman's heart, like a miner searching for gold; or, rather, like a sexton delving into a grave, possibly in quest of a jewel that had been buried on the dead man's bosom, but likely to find nothing save mortality and corruption. Alas for his own soul, if these were what he sought.

2   Sometimes, a light glimmered out of the physician's eyes, burning blue and ominous, like the reflection of a furnace, or, let us say, like one of those gleams of ghastly fire that darted from Bunyan's awful door-way in the hill-side, and quivered on the pilgrim's face. The soil where this dark miner was working had perchance shown indications that encouraged him.

3   "This man," said he, at one such moment, to himself, "pure as they deem him,—all spiritual as he seems,—hath inherited a strong animal nature from his father or his mother. Let us dig a little farther in the direction of this vein!"

4   Then, after long search into the minister's dim interior, and turning over many precious materials, in the shape of high aspirations for the welfare of his race, warm love of souls, pure sentiments, natural piety, strengthened by thought and study, and illuminated by revelation,—all of which invaluable gold was perhaps no better than rubbish to the seeker,—he would turn back, discouraged, and begin his quest towards another point. He groped along as stealthily, with as cautious a tread, and as wary an outlook, as a thief entering a chamber where a man lies only half asleep,—or, it may be, broad awake,—with purpose to steal the very treasure which this man guards as the apple of his eye. In spite of his premeditated carefulness, the floor would now and then creak; his garments would rustle; the shadow of his presence, in a forbidden proximity, would be thrown across his victim. In other words, Mr. Dimmesdale, whose sensibility of nerve often produced the effect of spiritual intuition, would become vaguely aware that something inimical to his peace had thrust itself into relation with him. But old Roger Chillingworth, too, had perceptions that were almost intuitive; and when the minister threw his startled eyes towards him, there the physician sat; his kind, watchful, sympathizing, but never intrusive friend.

5   Yet Mr. Dimmesdale would perhaps have seen this individual's character more perfectly, if a certain morbidness, to which sick hearts are liable, had not rendered him suspicious of all mankind. Trusting no man as his friend, he could not recognize his enemy when the latter actually appeared. He therefore still kept up a familiar intercourse with him, daily receiving the old physician in his study; or visiting the laboratory, and, for recreation's sake, watching the process by which weeds were converted into drugs of potency.

6   One day, leaning his forehead on his hand, and his elbow on the sill of the open window, that looked towards the grave-yard, he talked with Roger Chillingworth, while the old man was examining a bundle of unsightly plants.

7   "Where," asked he, with a look askance at them,—for it was the clergyman's peculiarity that he seldom, now-a-days, looked straightforth at any subject, whether human or inanimate,—"where, my kind doctor, did you gather those herbs, with such a dark, flabby leaf?"

8 "Even in the grave-yard, here at hand," answered the physician, continuing his employment. "They are new to me. I found them growing on a grave, which bore no tombstone, nor other memorial of the dead man, save these ugly weeds that have taken upon themselves to keep him in remembrance. They grew out of his heart, and typify, it may be, some hideous secret that was buried with him, and which he had done better to confess during his lifetime."

9 "Perchance," said Mr. Dimmesdale, "he earnestly desired it, but could not."

10 "And wherefore?" rejoined the physician. "Wherefore not; since all the powers of nature call so earnestly for the confession of sin, that these black weeds have sprung up out of a buried heart, to make manifest an unspoken crime?"

11 "That, good Sir, is but a fantasy of yours," replied the minister. "There can be, if I forebode aright, no power, short of the Divine mercy, to disclose, whether by uttered words, or by type or emblem, the secrets that may be buried with a human heart. The heart, making itself guilty of such secrets, must perforce hold them, until the day when all hidden things shall be revealed. Nor have I so read or interpreted Holy Writ, as to understand that the disclosure of human thoughts and deeds, then to be made, is intended as a part of the retribution. That, surely, were a shallow view of it. No; these revelations, unless I greatly err, are meant merely to promote the intellectual satisfaction of all intelligent beings, who will stand waiting, on that day, to see the dark problem of this life made plain. A knowledge of men's hearts will be needful to the completest solution of that problem. And I conceive, moreover, that the hearts holding such miserable secrets as you speak of will yield them up, at that last day, not with reluctance, but with a joy unutterable."

12 "Then why not reveal them here?" asked Roger Chillingworth, glancing quietly aside at the minister. "Why should not the guilty ones sooner avail themselves of this unutterable solace?"

13 "They mostly do," said the clergyman, griping hard at his breast, as if afflicted with an importunate throb of pain. "Many, many a poor soul hath given its confidence to me, not only on the death-bed, but while strong in life, and fair in reputation. And ever, after such an outpouring, O, what a relief have I witnessed in those sinful brethren! even as in one who at last draws free air, after long stifling with his own polluted breath. How can it be otherwise? Why should a wretched man, guilty, we will say, of murder, prefer to keep the dead corpse buried in his own heart, rather than fling it forth at once, and let the universe take care of it!"

14 "Yet some men bury their secrets thus," observed the calm physician.

15 "True; there are such men," answered Mr. Dimmesdale. "But, not to suggest more obvious reasons, it may be that they are kept silent by the very constitution of their nature. Or,—can we not suppose it?—guilty as they may be, retaining, nevertheless, a zeal for God's glory and man's welfare, they shrink from displaying themselves black and filthy in the view of men; because, thenceforward, no good can be achieved by them; no evil of the past be redeemed by better service. So, to their own unutterable torment, they go about among their fellow-creatures, looking pure as new-fallen snow; while their hearts are all speckled and spotted with iniquity of which they cannot rid themselves."

16   "These men deceive themselves," said Roger Chillingworth, with somewhat more emphasis than usual, and making a slight gesture with his forefinger. "They fear to take up the shame that rightfully belongs to them. Their love for man, their zeal for God's service,—these holy impulses may or may not coexist in their hearts with the evil inmates to which their guilt has unbarred the door, and which must needs propagate a hellish breed within them. But, if they seek to glorify God, let them not lift heavenward their unclean hands! If they would serve their fellow-men, let them do it by making manifest the power and reality of conscience, in constraining them to penitential self-abasement! Wouldst thou have me to believe, O wise and pious friend, that a false show can be better—can be more for God's glory, or man's welfare—than God's own truth? Trust me, such men deceive themselves!"

17   "It may be so," said the young clergyman indifferently, as waiving a discussion that he considered irrelevant or unseasonable. He had a ready faculty, indeed, of escaping from any topic that agitated his too sensitive and nervous temperament.—"But, now, I would ask of my well-skilled physician, whether, in good sooth, he deems me to have profited by his kindly care of this weak frame of mine?"

18   Before Roger Chillingworth could answer, they heard the clear, wild laughter of a young child's voice, proceeding from the adjacent burial-ground. Looking instinctively from the open window,—for it was summer-time,—the minister beheld Hester Prynne and little Pearl passing along the footpath that traversed the inclosure. Pearl looked as beautiful as the day, but was in one of those moods of perverse merriment which, whenever they occurred, seemed to remove her entirely out of the sphere of sympathy or human contact. She now skipped irreverently from one grave to another; until, coming to the broad, flat, armorial tombstone of a departed worthy,—perhaps of Isaac Johnson himself,—she began to dance upon it. In reply to her mother's command and entreaty that she would behave more decorously, little Pearl paused to gather the prickly burrs from a tall burdock, which grew beside the tomb. Taking a handful of these, she arranged them along the lines of the scarlet letter that decorated the maternal bosom, to which the burrs, as their nature was, tenaciously adhered. Hester did not pluck them off.

19   Roger Chillingworth had by this time approached the window, and smiled grimly down.

20   "There is no law, nor reverence for authority, no regard for human ordinances or opinions, right or wrong, mixed up with that child's composition," remarked he, as much to himself as to his companion. "I saw her, the other day, bespatter the Governor himself with water, at the cattle trough in Spring Lane. What, in Heaven's name, is she? Is the imp altogether evil? Hath she affections? Hath she any discoverable principle of being?"

21   "None,—save the freedom of a broken law," answered Mr. Dimmesdale, in a quiet way, as if he had been discussing the point within himself. "Whether capable of good, I know not."

22   The child probably overheard their voices; for, looking up to the window, with a bright, but naughty smile of mirth and intelligence, she threw one of the prickly

burrs at the Reverend. Mr. Dimmesdale. The sensitive clergyman shrunk, with nervous dread, from the light missile. Detecting his emotion, Pearl clapped her little hands in the most extravagant ecstasy. Hester Prynne, likewise, had involuntarily looked up; and all these four persons, old and young, regarded one another in silence, till the child laughed aloud, and shouted,—"Come away, mother! Come away, or yonder old Black Man will catch you! He hath got hold of the minister already. Come away, mother, or he will catch you! But he cannot catch little Pearl!"

23   So she drew her mother away, skipping, dancing, and frisking fantastically among the hillocks of the dead people, like a creature that had nothing in common with a bygone and buried generation, nor owned herself akin to it. It was as if she had been made afresh, out of new elements, and must perforce be permitted to live her own life, and be a law unto herself, without her eccentricities being reckoned to her for a crime.

24   "There goes a woman," resumed Roger Chillingworth, after a pause, "who, be her demerits what they may, hath none of that mystery of hidden sinfulness which you deem so grievous to be borne. Is Hester Prynne the less miserable, think you, for that scarlet letter on her breast?"

25   "I do verily believe it," answered the clergyman. "Nevertheless, I cannot answer for her. There was a look of pain in her face, which I would gladly have been spared the sight of. But still, methinks, it must needs be better for the sufferer to be free to show his pain, as this poor woman Hester is, than to cover it all up in his heart."

26   There was another pause; and the physician began anew to examine and arrange the plants which he had gathered.

27   "You inquired of me, a little time agone," said he, at length, "my judgment as touching your health."

28   "I did," answered the clergyman, "and would gladly learn it. Speak frankly, I pray you, be it for life or death."

29   "Freely, then, and plainly," said the physician, still busy with his plants, but keeping a wary eye on Mr. Dimmesdale, "the disorder is a strange one; not so much in itself, nor as outwardly manifested,—in so far, at least, as the symptoms have been laid open to my observation. Looking daily at you, my good Sir, and watching the tokens of your aspect, now for months gone by, I should deem you a man sore sick, it may be, yet not so sick but that an instructed and watchful physician might well hope to cure you. But—I know not what to say—the disease is what I seem to know, yet know it not."

30   "You speak in riddles, learned Sir," said the pale minister, glancing aside out of the window.

31   "Then, to speak more plainly," continued the physician, "and I crave pardon, Sir,—should it seem to require pardon,—for this needful plainness of my speech. Let me ask,—as your friend,—as one having charge, under Providence, of your life and physical well-being,—hath all the operation of this disorder been fairly laid open and recounted to me?"

32   "How can you question it?" asked the minister. "Surely, it were child's play to call in a physician, and then hide the sore!"

33   "You would tell me, then, that I know all?" said Roger Chillingworth, deliberately, and fixing an eye, bright with intense and concentrated intelligence, on
the minister's face. "Be it so! But, again! He to whom only the outward and
physical evil is laid open knoweth, oftentimes, but half the evil which he is called
upon to cure. A bodily disease, which we look upon as whole and entire within
itself, may, after all, be but a symptom of some ailment in the spiritual part.
Your pardon, once again, good Sir, if my speech give the shadow of offence.
You, Sir, of all men whom I have known, are he whose body is the closest conjoined, and imbued, and identified, so to speak, with, the spirit whereof it is the
instrument."

34   "Then I need ask no further," said the clergyman, somewhat hastily rising
from his chair. "You deal not, I take it, in medicine for the soul!"

35   "Thus, a sickness," continued Roger Chillingworth, going on, in an unal-
tered tone, without heeding the interruption,—but standing up, and confronting the emaciated and white-cheeked minister with his low, dark, and
misshapen figure,—"a sickness, a sore place, if we may so call it, in your spirit,
hath immediately its appropriate manifestation in your bodily frame. Would
you, therefore, that your physician heal the bodily evil? How may this be, unless
you first lay open to him the wound or trouble in your soul?"

36   "No!—not to thee!—not to an earthly physician!" cried Mr. Dimmesdale,
passionately, and turning his eyes, full and bright, and with a kind of fierceness,
on old Roger Chillingworth. "Not to thee! But, if it be the soul's disease, then do
I commit myself to the one Physician of the soul! He, if it stand with his good
pleasure, can cure; or he can kill! Let him do with me as, in his justice and wisdom, he shall see good. But who art thou, that meddlest in this matter?—that
dares thrust himself between the sufferer and his God?"

37   With a frantic gesture, he rushed out of the room.

38   "It is as well to have made this step," said Roger Chilling worth to himself,
looking after the minister with a grave smile. "There is nothing lost. We shall be
friends again anon. But see, now, how passion takes hold upon this man, and hurri-
eth him out of himself! As with one passion, so with another! He hath done a wild
thing ere now, this pious Master Dimmesdale, in the hot passion of his heart!"

39   It proved not difficult to reëstablish the intimacy of the two companions, on
the same footing and in the same degree as heretofore. The young clergyman,
after a few hours of privacy, was sensible that the disorder of his nerves had hurried him into an unseemly outbreak of temper, which there had been nothing in
the physician's words to excuse or palliate. He marvelled, indeed, at the violence
with which he had thrust back the kind old man, when merely proffering the
advice which it was his duty to bestow, and which the minister himself had
expressly sought. With these remorseful feelings, he lost no time in making the
amplest apologies, and besought his friend still to continue the care, which, if
not successful in restoring him to health, had, in all probability, been the means
of prolonging his feeble existence to that hour. Roger Chillingworth readily
assented, and went on with his medical supervision of the minister; doing his

best for him, in all good faith, but always quitting the patient's apartment, at the close of a professional interview, with a mysterious and puzzled smile upon his lips. This expression was invisible in Mr. Dimmesdale's presence, but grew strongly evident as the physician crossed the threshold.

40 "A rare case!" he muttered. "I must needs look deeper into it. A strange sympathy betwixt soul and body! Were it only for the art's sake, I must search this matter to the bottom!"

41 It came to pass, not long after the scene above recorded, that the Reverend Mr. Dimmesdale, at noonday, and entirely unawares, fell into a deep, deep slumber, sitting in his chair, with a large black-letter volume open before him on the table. It must have been a work of vast ability in the somniferous school of literature. The profound depth of the minister's repose was the more remarkable; inasmuch as he was one of those persons whose sleep, ordinarily, is as light, as fitful, and as easily scared away, as a small bird hopping on a twig. To such an unwonted remoteness, however, had his spirit now withdrawn into itself, that he stirred not in his chair, when old Roger Chillingworth, without any extraordinary precaution, came into the room. The physician advanced directly in front of his patient, laid his hand upon his bosom, and thrust aside the vestment, that, hitherto, had always covered it even from the professional eye.

42 Then, indeed, Mr. Dimmesdale shuddered, and slightly stirred.

43 After a brief pause, the physician turned away.

44 But with what a wild look of wonder, joy, and horror! With what a ghastly rapture, as it were, too mighty to be expressed only by the eye and features, and therefore bursting forth through the whole ugliness of his figure, and making itself even riotously manifest by the extravagant gestures with which he threw up his arms towards the ceiling, and stamped his foot upon the floor! Had a man seen old Roger Chillingworth, at that moment of his ecstasy, he would have had no need to ask how Satan comports himself, when a precious human soul is lost to heaven, and won into his kingdom.

45 But what distinguished the physician's ecstasy from Satan's was the trait of wonder in it!

CHAPTER 10

JOURNAL

1. **MLA Works Cited** *Using this model, record this book.*
   Author's Last Name, First Name. The Scarlet Letter. 1850. Title of This Book.
   Ed. First Name Last Name. City: Publisher, year.
2. **Main Character(s)** *Describe each main character and explain why you think each is a main character.*
3. **Supporting Characters** *Describe each supporting character and explain why you think each is a supporting character.*

4. **Setting** *Describe the setting(s) and any relevant prop(s).*

5. **Sequence** *Outline the events in this chapter in order.*

6. **Plot** *Summarize this chapter's events in no more than two sentences.*

7. **Conflicts** *Identify and explain all conflicts involved in this chapter.*

8. **Significant Quotations** *Explain the importance of each of these quotations. Record the page number in the parentheses.*

    a. "Old Roger Chillingworth, throughout life, had been calm in temperament, kindly, though not of warm affections, but ever, and in all his relations with the world, a pure and upright man [. . .]" ( ).

    b. "Trusting no man as his friend, he could not recognize his enemy when the latter actually appeared [. . .]" ( ).

    c. "'I found [these weeds] growing on a grave, which bore no tombstone [. . .]. They grew out of his heart, and typify, it may be, some hideous secret that was buried with him, and which he had done better to confess during his lifetime'" ( ).

    d. "'The heart, making itself guilty of such secrets, must perforce hold them, until the day when all hidden things shall be revealed [. . .]'" ( ).

    e. "'As with one passion, so with another! He hath done a wild thing ere now, this pious Master Dimmesdale, in the hot passion of his heart!'" ( ).

9. **Recap** *Summarize what has happened so far, from the beginning of the book through this chapter.*

FOLLOW-UP QUESTIONS

6 SHORT QUESTIONS

Select the <u>best</u> answer for each.

____ 1. Before coming to Boston, Roger Chillingworth had always been
    a. ugly and evil-hearted.
    b. kindly and pure in heart.
    c. strict but careless.

____ 2. Roger Chillingworth has become very focused on
    a. starting a medical school.
    b. prying into Arthur Dimmesdale's life.
    c. becoming a minister.

____ 3. Arthur Dimmesdale does not
    a. want Roger Chillingworth's friendship.
    b. want Hester Prynne to become friends with Roger Chillingworth.
    c. recognize Roger Chillingworth as his enemy.

____ 4. Roger Chillingworth tells Arthur Dimmesdale that Arthur's illness
    a. does not exist.
    b. is of a spiritual nature.
    c. is of a bodily nature.

____ 5. While Arthur Dimmesdale is asleep, Roger Chillingworth looks inside
  a. Arthur's shirt.
  b. Arthur's books.
  c. Arthur's closet.

____ 6. In the graveyard, Pearl throws burrs at
  a. Hester's scarlet letter.
  b. Hester's scarlet letter and Roger Chillingworth.
  c. Hester's scarlet letter and Arthur Dimmesdale.

5 SIGNIFICANT QUOTATIONS

Explain the importance of each of these quotations.

1. "He now dug into the poor clergyman's heart, like a miner searching for gold; or, rather, like a sexton delving into a grave, possibly in quest of a jewel that had been buried on the dead man's bosom, but likely to find nothing save mortality and corruption. Alas for his own soul, if these were what he sought!"
2. "'And I conceive, moreover, that the hearts holding such miserable secrets as you speak of will yield them up, at that last day, not with reluctance, but with a joy unutterable.'"
3. "Hester Prynne, likewise, had involuntarily looked up; and all these four persons, old and young, regarded one another in silence, till the child laughed aloud, and shouted,—'Come away, mother! Come away, or yonder old Black Man will catch you! He hath got hold of the minister already. Come away, mother, or he will catch you! But he cannot catch little Pearl!'"
4. "'A rare case!' he muttered. 'I must needs look deeper into it. A strange sympathy betwixt soul and body! Were it only for the art's sake, I must search this matter to the bottom!'"
5. "The physician advanced directly in front of his patient, laid his hand upon his bosom, and thrust aside the vestment, that, hitherto, had always covered it even from the professional eye."

2 COMPREHENSION ESSAY QUESTIONS

Use specific details and information from the chapter to answer these questions as completely as possible.

1. Which two characters interest you? Choose two of the main characters and discuss their relationships to and with each other. Use specific details and information from this chapter and previous chapters in your explanation.
2. Which character in the novel so far seems to be suffering the most? The least? Use specific details and information from this chapter and previous chapters in your explanation.

DISCUSSION QUESTIONS

Be prepared to discuss these questions in class.

1. How has the relationship between Roger Chillingworth and Arthur Dimmesdale changed?
2. What does Roger Chillingworth discover about Arthur Dimmesdale? What do you think will happen next?

CHAPTER 11

THE INTERIOR OF A HEART

PRE-READING VOCABULARY
CONTEXT

Use context clues to define these words before reading. Use a dictionary as needed.

1. Barbara did not like living on the seacoast, so she moved inland to the *interior* of the country. *Interior* means _____
   _____.

2. During our *intercourse* with the insurance company, we wrote letters and made many phone calls back and forth to the agent. *Intercourse* means _____
   _____.

3. After Heath left Elena for another girl, Elena felt much *malice* towards Heath. *Malice* means _____
   _____.

4. A simple blood test can reveal whether one has a *latent* infection, one that has not yet shown its symptoms. *Latent* means _____
   _____.

5. Because they lost the World Series, the following season the Yankees wanted to *wreak revenge* against the Red Sox. *Wreak revenge* means _____
   _____.

6. After running over a squirrel with her car, Angela, a devoted animal lover, felt such *remorse* that she would not drive for a month. *Remorse* means _____
   _____.

7. The bully was *pitiless* as he took the hungry child's lunch away from him. *Pitiless* means _____
   _____.

8. When Billy apologized for breaking the window and offered to pay for a new one, our neighbors decided to *forgive* him. *Forgive* means _____
   _____.

9. Melissa's headache *throbbed* so violently it felt like someone pounding a drum in her head. *Throb* means _____
_____.

10. Joanna took another dose of painkiller to relieve the *agony* of her sprained ankle. *Agony* means _____
_____.

11. The preacher walked up to the *pulpit*, a raised platform that allowed everyone in church to see her, and delivered her sermon. *Pulpit* means _____
_____.

12. Every time Bob walked in the woods or fields, he came down with poison ivy and so he developed an *abhorrence* for the outdoors. *Abhorrence* means _____
_____.

13. The coffee, leftover from yesterday morning and reheated today, tasted so *vile* that I dumped it into the sink. *Vile* means _____
_____.

14. Gert *loathes* eggplant no matter how it is prepared and she groaned when she saw that it was for dinner. *Loathe* means _____
_____.

15. In medieval Europe, a whip used to inflict severe punishment was called a *scourge*, and criminals were often *scourged* publicly as an example and deterrent to others. *Scourge* and *scourged* mean _____
_____.

16. Samuel's parents had taught him that telling *falsehoods* was wrong, and he prided himself on always telling the truth. *Falsehood* means _____
_____.

17. To clean the kitchen and bathroom, Rosemary *purifies* the water with a few drops of bleach. *Purifies* means _____
_____.

18. The guard kept his *vigil* as he watched over the sleeping town. *Vigil* means
_____.

19. In some religions, asking for forgiveness is a way of doing *penance* for one's sins. *Penance* means _____
_____.

20. It is common for teenagers to practice *introspection*—a deep self-examination of their inner thoughts and feelings. *Introspection* means _____
_____.

PRE-READING VOCABULARY
STRUCTURAL ATTACK

Define these words by solving the parts. Use the Glossary or a dictionary as needed.

1. external	12. antipathy	23. gnawed
2. spectator	13. presentiment	24. bitterly
3. ceased	14. forlorn	25. likewise
4. impalpable	15. machinations	26. looking-glass
5. balking	16. eminent	27. expelled
6. lavishly	17. sanctity	28. odious
7. pardons	18. confide	29. perceive
8. celestial	19. avenger	30. townspeople
9. subsequent	20. gesture	31. unison
10. phantom	21. gaits	32. staircase
11. dimly	22. garments	

PRE-READING QUESTIONS

Try answering these questions as you read.

How does Arthur Dimmesdale feel about himself?
What does Arthur Dimmesdale do at night?
How do the townspeople feel about Arthur Dimmesdale?

CHAPTER 11

THE INTERIOR OF A HEART

1 After the incident last described, the intercourse between the clergyman and the physician, though externally the same, was really of another character than it had previously been. The intellect of Roger Chillingworth had now a sufficiently plain path before it. It was not, indeed, precisely that which he had laid out for himself to tread. Calm, gentle, passionless, as he appeared, there was yet, we fear, a quiet depth of malice, hitherto latent, but active now, in this unfortunate old man, which led him to imagine a more intimate revenge than any mortal had ever wreaked upon an enemy. To make himself the one trusted friend, to whom should be confided all the fear, the remorse, the agony, the ineffectual repentance,

the backward rush of sinful thoughts, expelled in vain! All that guilty sorrow, hidden from the world, whose great heart would have pitied and forgiven, to be revealed to him, the Pitiless, to him, the Unforgiving! All that dark treasure to be lavished on the very man, to whom nothing else could so adequately pay the debt of vengeance!

2   The clergyman's shy and sensitive reserve had balked this scheme. Roger Chillingworth, however, was inclined to be hardly, if at all, less satisfied with the aspect of affairs, which Providence—using the avenger and his victim for its own purposes, and, perchance, pardoning, where it seemed most to punish—had substituted for his black devices. A revelation, he could almost say, had been granted to him. It mattered little, for his object, whether celestial, or from what other region. By its aid, in all the subsequent relations betwixt him and Mr. Dimmesdale, not merely the external presence, but the very inmost soul of the latter seemed to be brought out before his eyes, so that he could see and comprehend its every movement. He became, thenceforth, not a spectator only, but a chief actor, in the poor minister's interior world. He could play upon him as he chose. Would he arouse him with a throb of agony? The victim was for ever on the rack; it needed only to know the spring that controlled the engine;—and the physician knew it well! Would he startle him with sudden fear? As at the waving of a magician's wand, uprose a grisly phantom,—uprose a thousand phantoms,—in many shapes, of death, or more awful shame, all flocking roundabout the clergyman, and pointing with their fingers at his breast!

3   All this was accomplished with a subtlety so perfect, that the minister, though he had constantly a dim perception of some evil influence watching over him, could never gain a knowledge of its actual nature. True, he looked doubt-fully, fearfully,—even, at times, with horror and the bitterness of hatred,—at the formed figure of the old physician. His gestures, his gait, his grizzled beard, his slightest and most indifferent acts, the very fashion of his garments, were odious in the clergyman's sight; a token, implicitly to be relied on, of a deeper antipathy in the breast of the latter than he was willing to acknowledge to himself. For, as it was impossible to assign a reason for such distrust and abhorrence, so Mr. Dimmesdale, conscious that the poison of one morbid spot was infecting his heart's entire substance, attributed all his presentiments to no other cause. He took himself to task for his bad sympathies in reference to Roger Chillingworth, disregarded the lesson that he should have drawn from them, and did his best to root them out. Unable to accomplish this, he nevertheless, as a matter of principle, continued his habits of social familiarity with the old man, and thus gave him constant opportunities for perfecting the purpose to which—poor, forlorn creature that he was, and more wretched than his victim—the avenger had devoted himself.

4   While thus suffering under bodily disease, and gnawed and tortured by some black trouble of the soul, and given over to the machinations of his deadliest enemy, the Reverend Mr. Dimmesdale had achieved a brilliant popularity in his sacred office. He won it, indeed, in great part, by his sorrows. His intellectual

gifts, his moral perceptions, his power of experiencing and communicating emotion, were kept in a state of preternatural activity by the prick and anguish of his daily life. His fame, though still on its upward slope, already overshadowed the soberer reputations of his fellow-clergymen, eminent as several of them were. There were scholars among them, who had spent more years in acquiring abstruse lore, connected with the divine profession, than Mr. Dimmesdale had lived; and who might well, therefore, be more profoundly versed in such solid and valuable attainments than their youthful brother. There were men, too, of a sturdier texture of mind than his, and endowed with a far greater share of shrewd, hard, iron or granite understanding; which, duly mingled with a fair proportion of doctrinal ingredient, constitutes a highly respectable, efficacious, and unamiable variety of the clerical species. There were others, again, true saintly fathers, whose faculties had been elaborated by weary toil among their books, and by patient thought, and etherealized, moreover, by spiritual communications with the better world, into which their purity of life had almost introduced these holy personages, with their garments of mortality still clinging to them. All that they lacked was the gift that descended upon the chosen disciples, at Pentecost, in tongues of flame; symbolizing, it would seem, not the power of speech in foreign and unknown languages, but that of addressing the whole human brotherhood in the heart's native language. These fathers, otherwise so apostolic, lacked Heaven's last and rarest attestation of their office, the Tongue of Flame. They would have vainly sought—had they ever dreamed of seeking—to express the highest truths through the humblest medium of familiar words and images. Their voices came down, afar and indistinctly, from the upper heights where they habitually dwelt.

5   Not improbably, it was to this latter class of men that Mr. Dimmesdale, by many of his traits of character, naturally belonged. To their high mountain-peaks of faith and sanctity he would have climbed, had not the tendency been thwarted by the burden, whatever it might be, of crime or anguish, beneath which it was his doom to totter. It kept him down, on a level with the lowest; him, the man of ethereal attributes, whose voice the angels might else have listened to and answered! But this very burden it was, that gave him sympathies so intimate with the sinful brotherhood of mankind; so that his heart vibrated in unison with theirs, and received their pain into itself, and sent its own throb of pain through a thousand other hearts, in gushes of sad, persuasive eloquence. Oftenest persuasive, but sometimes terrible! The people knew not the power that moved them thus. They deemed the young clergyman a miracle of holiness. They fancied him the mouth-piece of Heaven's messages of wisdom, and rebuke, and love. In their eyes, the very ground on which he trod was sanctified. The virgins of his church grew pale around him, victims of a passion so imbued with religious sentiment that they imagined it to be all religion, and brought it openly, in their white bosoms, as their most acceptable sacrifice before the altar. The aged members of his flock, beholding Mr. Dimmesdale's frame so feeble, while they were themselves so rugged in their infirmity, believed that he would go heavenward

before them, and enjoined it upon their children, that their old bones should be buried close to their young pastor's holy grave. And, all this time, perchance, when poor Mr. Dimmesdale was thinking of his grave, he questioned with himself whether the grass would ever grow on it, because an accursed thing must there be buried!

6   It is inconceivable, the agony with which this public veneration tortured him! It was his genuine impulse to adore the truth, and to reckon all things shadow-like, and utterly devoid of weight or value, that had not its divine essence as the life within their life. Then, what was he?—a substance?—or the dimmest of all shadows? He longed to speak out, from his own pulpit, at the full height of his voice, and tell the people what he was. "I, whom you behold in these black garments of the priesthood,—I, who ascend the sacred desk, and turn my pale face heavenward, taking upon myself to hold communion, in your behalf, with the Most High Omniscience,—I, in whose daily life you discern the sanctity of Enoch,—I, whose footsteps, as you suppose, leave a gleam along my earthly track, whereby the pilgrims that shall come after me may be guided to the regions of the blest,—I, who have laid the hand of baptism upon your children,—I, who have breathed the parting prayer over your dying friends, to whom the Amen sounded faintly from a world which they had quitted,—I, your pastor, whom you so reverence and trust, am utterly a pollution and a lie!"

7   More than once, Mr. Dimmesdale had gone into the pulpit, with a purpose never to come down its steps, until he should have spoken words like the above. More than once, he had cleared his throat, and drawn in the long, deep, and tremulous breath, which, when sent forth again, would come burdened with the black secret of his soul. More than once—nay, more than a hundred times—he had actually spoken! Spoken! But how? He had told his hearers that he was altogether vile, a viler companion of the vilest, the worst of sinners, an abomination, a thing of unimaginable iniquity; and that the only wonder was, that they did not see his wretched body shrivelled up before their eyes, by the burning wrath of the Almighty! Could there be plainer speech than this? Would not the people start up in their seats, by a simultaneous impulse, and tear him down out of the pulpit which he defiled? Not so, indeed! They heard it all, and did but reverence him the more. They little guessed what deadly purport lurked in those self-condemning words. "The godly youth!" said they among themselves. "The saint on earth! Alas, if he discern such sinfulness in his own white soul, what horrid spectacle would he behold in thine or mine!" The minister well knew—subtle, but remorseful hypocrite that he was!—the light in which his vague confession would be viewed. He had striven to put a cheat upon himself by making the avowal of a guilty conscience, but had gained only one other sin, and a self-acknowledged shame, without the momentary relief of being self-deceived. He had spoken the very truth, and transformed it into the veriest falsehood. And yet, by the constitution of his nature, he loved the truth, and loathed the lie, as few men ever did. Therefore, above all things else, he loathed his miserable self!

8   His inward trouble drove him to practices, more in accordance with the old, corrupted faith of Rome, than with the better light of the church in which he had been born and bred. In Mr. Dimmesdale's secret closet, under lock and key, there was a bloody scourge. Oftentimes, this Protestant and Puritan divine had plied it on his own shoulders; laughing bitterly at himself the while, and smiting so much the more pitilessly, because of that bitter laugh. It was his custom, too, as it has been that of many other pious Puritans, to fast,—not, however, like them, in order to purify the body and render it the fitter medium of celestial illumination,—but rigorously, and until his knees trembled beneath him, as an act of penance. He kept vigils, likewise, night after night, sometimes in utter darkness; sometimes with a glimmering lamp; and sometimes, viewing his own face in a looking-glass, by the most powerful light which he could throw upon it. He thus typified the constant introspection wherewith he tortured, but could not purify, himself. In these lengthened vigils, his brain often reeled, and visions seemed to flit before him; perhaps seen doubtfully, and by a faint light of their own, in the remote dimness of the chamber, or more vividly, and close beside him, within the looking-glass. Now it was a herd of diabolic shapes, that grinned and mocked at the pale minister, and beckoned him away with them; now a group of shining angels, who flew upward heavily, as sorrow-laden, but grew more ethereal as they rose. Now came the dead friends of his youth, and his white-bearded father, with a saint-like frown, and his mother, turning her face away as she passed by. Ghost of a mother,—thinnest fantasy of a mother,—methinks she might yet have thrown a pitying glance towards her son! And now, through the chamber which these spectral thoughts had made so ghastly, glided Hester Prynne, leading along little Pearl, in her scarlet garb, and pointing her forefinger, first, at the scarlet letter on her bosom, and then at the clergyman's own breast.

9   None of these visions ever quite deluded him. At any moment, by an effort of his will, he could discern substances through their misty lack of substance, and convince himself that they were not solid in their nature, like yonder table of carved oak, or that big, square, leathern-bound and brazen-clasped volume of divinity. But, for all that, they were, in one sense, the truest and most substantial things which the poor minister now dealt with. It is the unspeakable misery of a life so false as his, that it steals the pith and substance out of whatever realities there are around us, and which were meant by Heaven to be the spirit's joy and nutriment. To the untrue man, the whole universe is false,—it is impalpable,—it shrinks to nothing within his grasp. And he himself, in so far as he shows himself in a false light, becomes a shadow, or, indeed, ceases to exist. The only truth, that continued to give Mr. Dimmesdale a real existence on this earth, was the anguish in his inmost soul, and the undissembled expression of it in his aspect. Had he once found power to smile, and wear a face of gayety, there would have been no such man!

10   On one of those ugly nights, which we have faintly hinted at, but forborne to picture forth, the minister started from his chair. A new thought had struck him.

There might be a moment's peace in it. Attiring himself with as much care as if it had been for public worship, and precisely in the same manner, he stole softly down the staircase, undid the door, and issued forth.

CHAPTER 11

JOURNAL

1. **MLA Works Cited** *Using this model, record this book.*
   Author's Last Name, First Name. The Scarlet Letter. 1850. Title of This Book. Ed. First Name Last Name. City: Publisher, year.
2. **Main Character(s)** *Describe each main character and explain why you think each is a main character.*
3. **Supporting Characters** *Describe each supporting character and explain why you think each is a supporting character.*
4. **Setting** *Describe the setting(s) and any relevant prop(s).*
5. **Sequence** *Outline the events in this chapter in order.*
6. **Plot** *Summarize this chapter's events in no more than two sentences.*
7. **Conflicts** *Identify and explain all conflicts involved in this chapter.*
8. **Significant Quotations** *Explain the importance of each of these quotations. Record the page number in the parentheses.*
   a. "Calm, gentle, passionless, as he appeared, there was yet, we fear, a quiet depth of malice, hitherto latent, but active now, in this unfortunate old man, which led him to imagine a more intimate revenge than any mortal had ever wreaked upon an enemy. To make himself the one trusted friend, to whom should be confided all the fear, the remorse, the agony, the ineffectual repentance, the backward rush of sinful thoughts, expelled in vain! [. . .]" (   ).
   b. "While thus suffering under bodily disease, and gnawed and tortured by some black trouble of the soul, and given over to the machinations of his deadliest enemy, the Reverend Mr. Dimmesdale had achieved a brilliant popularity in his sacred office [. . .]" (   ).
   c. "It is inconceivable, the agony with which this public veneration tortured him! It was his genuine impulse to adore the truth [. . .]" (   ).
   d. "In Mr. Dimmesdale's secret closet, under lock and key, there was a bloody scourge. Oftentimes, [he] had plied it on his own shoulders; laughing bitterly at himself the while, and smiting so much the more pitilessly, because of that bitter laugh [. . .]" (   ).
   e. "Attiring himself with as much care as if it had been for public worship, and precisely in the same manner, he stole softly down the staircase, undid the door, and issued forth" (   ).
9. **Recap** *Summarize what has happened so far, from the beginning of the book through this chapter.*

FOLLOW-UP QUESTIONS

6 SHORT QUESTIONS

Select the <u>best</u> answer for each.

_____ 1. Within the town and church,
Arthur Dimmesdale is
a. barely known.
b. feared and distrusted.
c. more popular than ever.

_____ 2. Arthur Dimmesdale
a. loathes himself.
b. always tells the truth.
c. keeps no secrets.

_____ 3. Arthur Dimmesdale suffers
from
a. a guilty conscience.
b. living a lonely life by
himself on the peninsula.
c. jealousy of Roger
Chillingworth's
accomplishments.

_____ 4. Arthur Dimmesdale punishes
himself by
a. overeating.
b. scourging himself.
c. confiding in Roger
Chillingworth.

_____ 5. As a speaker, Arthur Dimmesdale is
a. unclear.
b. persuasive.
c. unsympathetic.

_____ 6. The people feel that Arthur
Dimmesdale
a. understands sin.
b. does not understand sin.
c. does not forgive sin.

5 SIGNIFICANT QUOTATIONS

Explain the importance of each of these quotations.

1. "He became, thenceforth, not a spectator only, but a chief actor, in the poor minister's interior world. He could play upon him as he chose. Would he arouse him with a throb of agony? The victim was for ever on the rack; it needed only to know the spring that controlled the engine;—and the physician knew it well! [. . .]."

2. "True, he looked doubtfully, fearfully,—even at times, with horror and the bitterness of hatred,—at the deformed figure of the old physician. His gestures, his gait, his grizzled beard, his slightest and most indifferent acts, the very fashion of his garments, were odious in the clergyman's sight [. . .]."

3. "But this very burden it was, that gave him sympathies so intimate with the sinful brotherhood of mankind; so that his heart vibrated in unison with theirs, and received their pain into itself, and sent its own throb of pain through a thousand other hearts, in gushes of sad, persuasive eloquence [. . .]. The people knew not the power that moved them thus. They deemed the young clergyman a miracle of holiness [. . .]."

4. "He kept vigils, likewise, night after night, sometimes in utter darkness; sometimes with a glimmering lamp; and sometimes, viewing his own face

in a looking-glass, by the most powerful light which he could throw upon it. He thus typified the constant introspection wherewith he tortured, but could not purify, himself [. . .]."

5. "To the untrue man, the whole universe is false,—it is impalpable,—it shrinks to nothing with in his grasp. And he himself, in so far as he shows himself in a false light, becomes a shadow, or indeed, ceases to exist [. . .]."

2 COMPREHENSION ESSAY QUESTIONS

Use specific details and information from the chapter to answer these questions as completely as possible.

1. Honesty is an important value in our personal relationships. We expect others to be honest and we feel betrayed when we are deceived. How is honesty—or the lack of honesty—portrayed in the characters of Arthur Dimmesdale and Roger Chillingworth? Use specific details and information from the chapter in your explanation.
2. Explain Arthur Dimmesdale's actions. How does he feel about himself? Use specific details and information from the chapter in your explanation.

DISCUSSION QUESTIONS

Be prepared to discuss these questions in class.

1. How and why does Arthur Dimmesdale punish himself?
2. How do you feel now about Arthur Dimmesdale?

CHAPTER 12

THE MINISTER'S VIGIL

PRE-READING VOCABULARY
CONTEXT

Use context clues to define these words before reading. Use a dictionary as needed.

1. Walking in your sleep and not remembering it is called *somnambulism*. *Somnambulism* means _____
   _____.

2. Ernest *ascended* the stairs of the speakers' platform above the audience to give the opening remarks. *Ascend* means _____
   _____.

3. Dwayne *rejoiced* when he received a promotion over seven other candidates and he held a party to celebrate his happiness. *Rejoice* means _____
   _____.

4. When the batter struck out and lost the game, he faced the *mockery* and boos of the jeering crowd. *Mockery* means _____
   _____.

5. The *Cowardly* Lion in <u>The Wizard of Oz</u> overcomes his *cowardice* at the end of the story when he is finally able to face scary situations without running away. *Cowardly* and *cowardice* mean _____
   _____.

6. The Puritans believed that *fiends*, or evil spirits sent by Satan, try to turn good people into bad people. *Fiends* means _____
   _____.

7. We watched the carpenter *wield* his hammer as he worked on the new building. *Wield* means _____
   _____.

8. The young people who painted graffiti on the walls will *expiate* their crime by cleaning the walls and repainting them. *Expiate* means _____
   _____.

9. Ghosts, vampires, and other nightmarish creatures were just some of the *grotesque* Halloween costumes we saw at the party. *Grotesque* means _____
_____.

10. The noise of the thunder *reverberated* through the valley, echoing from side to side. *Reverberate* means _____
_____.

11. Shawn did not want to appear bored and offend his co-workers, so he tried to *suppress* his yawns during the long meeting. *Suppress* means _____
_____.

12. At the toy store, the spoiled child *beseeched* his mother to buy him the latest video game, begging repeatedly at every aisle. *Beseech* means _____
_____.

13. Hurricane Katrina's *intense* winds and heavy rainfall caused terrible damage to the great city of New Orleans. *Intense* means _____
_____.

14. When the Yankees won the series, the crowd was *tumultuous* as fans yelled loudly, threw hats and papers into the air, and ran onto the playing field. *Tumultuous* means _____
_____.

15. After several days of heavy rain, the small stream became a *torrent* and flooded its banks. *Torrent* means _____
_____.

16. Parents should *restrain* their children from running and screaming in supermarkets and other public places. *Restrain* means _____
_____.

17. Rainbows, lightning, and other natural *phenomena* are remarkable and often unexpected events. *Phenomena* means _____
_____.

18. Lorraine turned on all the lights to *illuminate* the dark classroom. *Illuminate* means _____
_____.

19. Eating healthful foods and getting enough exercise is *vital* to good health. *Vital* means _____
_____.

20. Natural phenomena such as shooting stars and rainbows are sometimes seen as *portents*, or signs, that something momentous is about to happen. *Portents* means _____

_____.

PRE-READING VOCABULARY
STRUCTURAL ATTACK

Define these words by solving the parts. Use the Glossary or a dictionary as needed.

1. obscure	11. shriek	21. densely
2. palls	12. outcry	22. trifles
3. muffled	13. supernatural	23. teeming
4. perils	14. meteoric	24. credibility
5. discovery	15. settlement	25. luridly
6. unvaried	16. to and fro	26. symptom
7. arch-fiend	17. bandy	27. attribute
8. dank	18. torpid	28. zenith
9. catarrh	19. noontide	29. scurrilous
10. iron-nerved	20. radiance	30. endure

PRE-READING QUESTIONS

Try answering these questions as you read.

Where does Arthur Dimmesdale go?
What is the nature of Arthur Dimmesdale's vigil?
Who joins Dimmesdale in his vigil?
What happens in the sky?

CHAPTER 12
THE MINISTER'S VIGIL

1 Walking in the shadow of a dream, as it were, and perhaps actually under the influence of a species of somnambulism, Mr. Dimmesdale reached the spot, where, now so long since, Hester Prynne had lived through her first hour of public ignominy. The same platform or scaffold, black and weather-stained with the storm or sunshine of seven long years, and foot-worn, too, with the tread of many culprits who had since ascended it, remained standing beneath the balcony of the meeting-house. The minister went up the steps.

2 It was an obscure night of early May. An unvaried pall of cloud muffled the whole expanse of sky from zenith to horizon. If the same multitude which had

stood as eyewitnesses while Hester Prynne sustained her punishment could now have been summoned forth, they would have discerned no face above the platform, nor hardly the outline of a human shape, in the dark gray of the midnight. But the town was all asleep. There was no peril of discovery. The minister might stand there, if it so pleased him, until morning should redden in the east, without other risk than that the dank and chill night-air would creep into his frame, and stiffen his joints with rheumatism, and clog his throat with catarrh and cough; thereby defrauding the expectant audience of to-morrow's prayer and sermon. No eye could see him, save that ever-wakeful one which had seen him in his closet, wielding the bloody scourge. Why, then, had he come hither? Was it but the mockery of penitence? A mockery, indeed, but in which his soul trifled with itself! A mockery at which angels blushed and wept, while fiends rejoiced, with jeering laughter! He had been driven hither by the impulse of that Remorse which dogged him everywhere, and whose own sister and closely linked companion was that Cowardice which invariably drew him back, with her tremulous gripe, just when the other impulse had hurried him to the verge of a disclosure. Poor, miserable man! what right had infirmity like his to burden itself with crime? Crime is for the iron-nerved, who have their choice either to endure it, or, if it press too hard, to exert their fierce and savage strength for a good purpose, and fling it off at once! This feeble and most sensitive of spirits could do neither, yet continually did one thing or another, which intertwined, in the same inextricable knot, the agony of heaven-defying guilt and vain repentance.

3   And thus, while standing on the scaffold, in this vain show of expiation, Mr. Dimmesdale was overcome with a great horror of mind, as if the universe were gazing at a scarlet token on his naked breast, right over his heart. On that spot, in very truth, there was, and there had long been, the gnawing and poisonous tooth of bodily pain. Without any effort of his will, or power to restrain himself, he shrieked aloud; an outcry that went pealing through the night, and was beaten back from one house to another, and reverberated from the hills in the background; as if a company of devils, detecting so much misery and terror in it, had made a plaything of the sound, and were bandying it to and fro.

4   "It is done!" muttered the minister, covering his face with his hands. "The whole town will awake, and hurry forth, and find me here!"

5   But it was not so. The shriek had perhaps sounded with a far greater power, to his own startled ears, than it actually possessed. The town did not awake; or, if it did, the drowsy slumberers mistook the cry either for something frightful in a dream, or for the noise of witches; whose voices, at that period, were often heard to pass over the settlements or lonely cottages, as they rode with Satan through the air. The clergyman, therefore, hearing no symptoms of disturbance, uncovered his eyes and looked about him. At one of the chamber-windows of Governor Bellingham's mansion, which stood at some distance, on the line of another street, he beheld the appearance of the old magistrate himself, with a lamp in his hand, a white night-cap on his head, and a long white gown enveloping his figure. He looked like a ghost, evoked unseasonably from the grave. The cry had

evidently startled him. At another window of the same house, moreover, appeared old Mistress Hibbins, the Governor's sister, also with a lamp, which, even thus far off, revealed the expression of her sour and discontented face. She thrust forth her head from the lattice, and looked anxiously upward. Beyond the shadow of a doubt, this venerable witch-lady had heard Mr. Dimmesdale's outcry, and interpreted it, with its multitudinous echoes and reverberations, as the clamor of the fiends and nighthags, with whom she was well known to make excursions into the forest.

6   Detecting the gleam of Governor Bellingham's lamp, the old lady quickly extinguished her own, and vanished. Possibly, she went up among the clouds. The minister saw nothing further of her motions. The magistrate, after a wary observation of the darkness—into which, nevertheless, he could see but little farther than he might into a millstone—retired from the window.

7   The minister grew comparatively calm. His eyes, however, were soon greeted by a little, glimmering light, which, at first a long way off, was approaching up the street. It threw a gleam of recognition on here a post, and there a garden-fence, and here a latticed window-pane, and there a pump, with its full trough of water, and here, again, an arched door of oak, with an iron knocker, and a rough log for the door-step. The Reverend Mr. Dimmesdale noted all these minute particulars, even while firmly convinced that the doom of his existence was stealing onward, in the footsteps which he now heard; and that the gleam of the lantern would fall upon him, in a few moments more, and reveal his long-hidden secret. As the light drew nearer, he beheld, within its illuminated circle, his brother clergyman,—or, to speak more accurately, his professional father, as well as highly valued friend,—the Reverend Mr. Wilson; who, as Mr. Dimmesdale now conjectured, had been praying at the bedside of some dying man. And so he had. The good old minister came freshly from the death-chamber of Governor Winthrop, who had passed from earth to heaven within that very hour. And now, surrounded, like the saint-like personages of olden times, with a radiant halo, that glorified him amid this gloomy night of sin,—as if the departed Governor had left him an inheritance of his glory, or as if he had caught upon himself the distant shine of the celestial city, while looking thitherward to see the triumphant pilgrim pass within its gates,—now, in short, good Father Wilson was moving homeward, aiding his footsteps with a lighted lantern! The glimmer of this luminary suggested the above conceits to Mr. Dimmesdale, who smiled,— nay, almost laughed at them,—and then wondered if he were going mad.

8   As the Reverend Mr. Wilson passed beside the scaffold, closely muffling his Geneva cloak about him with one arm, and holding the lantern before his breast with the other, the minister could hardly restrain himself from speaking.

9   "A good evening to you, venerable Father Wilson! Come up hither, I pray you, and pass a pleasant hour with me!"

10   Good heavens! Had Mr. Dimmesdale actually spoken? For one instant, he believed that these words had passed his lips. But they were uttered only within his imagination. The venerable Father Wilson continued to step slowly onward,

looking carefully at the muddy pathway before his feet, and never once turning his head towards the guilty platform. When the light of the glimmering lantern had faded quite away, the minister discovered, by the faintness which came over him, that the last few moments had been a crisis of terrible anxiety; although his mind had made an involuntary effort to relieve itself by a kind of lurid playfulness.

11   Shortly afterwards, the like grisly sense of the humorous again stole in among the solemn phantoms of his thought. He felt his limbs growing stiff with the unaccustomed chilliness of the night, and doubted whether he should be able to descend the steps of the scaffold. Morning would break, and find him there. The neighbourhood would begin to rouse itself. The earliest riser, coming forth in the dim twilight, would perceive a vaguely defined figure aloft on the place of shame; and, half crazed betwixt alarm and curiosity, would go, knocking from door to door, summoning all the people to behold the ghost—as he needs must think it—of some defunct transgressor. A dusky tumult would flap its wings from one house to another. Then—the morning light still waxing stronger—old patriarchs would rise up in great haste, each in his flannel gown, and matronly dames, without pausing to put off their night-gear. The whole tribe of decorous personages, who had never heretofore been seen with a single hair of their heads awry, would start into public view, with the disorder of a nightmare in their aspects. Old Governor Bellingham would come grimly forth, with his King James's ruff fastened askew; and Mistress Hibbins, with some twigs of the forest clinging to her skirts, and looking sourer than ever, as having hardly got a wink of sleep after her night ride; and good Father Wilson, too, after spending half the night at a death-bed, and liking ill to be disturbed, thus early, out of his dreams about the glorified saints. Hither, likewise, would come the elders and deacons of Mr. Dimmesdale's church, and the young virgins who so idolized their minister, and had made a shrine for him in their white bosoms; which, now, by the by, in their hurry and confusion, they would scantly have given themselves time to cover with their kerchiefs. All people, in a word, would come stumbling over their thresholds, and turning up their amazed and horror-stricken visages around the scaffold. Whom would they discern there, with the red eastern light upon his brow? Whom, but the Reverend Arthur Dimmesdale, half frozen to death, over-whelmed with shame, and standing where Hester Prynne had stood!

12   Carried away by the grotesque horror of this picture, the minister, unawares, and to his own infinite alarm, burst into a great peal of laughter. It was immedi-ately responded to by a light, airy, childish laugh, in which, with a thrill of the heart,—but he knew not whether of exquisite pain, or pleasure as acute,—he recognized the tones of little Pearl.

13   "Pearl! Little Pearl!" cried he, after a moment's pause; then, suppressing his voice,—"Hester! Hester Prynne! Are you there?"

14   "Yes; it is Hester Prynne!" she replied, in a tone of surprise; and the minister heard her footsteps approaching from the sidewalk, along which she had been passing.—"It is I, and my little Pearl."

15   "Whence come you, Hester?" asked the minister. "What sent you hither?"

16   "I have been watching at a death-bed," answered Hester Prynne;—"at Governor Winthrop's death-bed, and have taken his measure for a robe, and am now going homeward to my dwelling."

17   "Come up hither, Hester, thou and little Pearl," said the Reverend Mr. Dimmesdale. "Ye have both been here before, but I was not with you. Come up hither once again, and we will stand all three together!"

18   She silently ascended the steps and stood on the platform, holding little Pearl by the hand. The minister felt for the child's other hand, and took it. The moment that he did so, there came what seemed a tumultuous rush of new life, other life than his own, pouring like a torrent into his heart, and hurrying through all his veins, as if the mother and the child were communicating their vital warmth to his half-torpid system. The three formed an electric chain.

19   "Minister!" whispered little Pearl.

20   "What wouldst thou say, child?" asked Mr. Dimmesdale.

21   "Wilt thou stand here with mother and me, to-morrow noontide?" inquired Pearl.

22   "Nay; not so, my little Pearl!" answered the minister; for, with the new energy of the moment, all the dread of public exposure, that had so long been the anguish of his life, had returned upon him; and he was already trembling at the conjunction in which—with a strange joy, nevertheless—he now found himself. "Not so, my child. I shall, indeed, stand with thy mother and thee one other day, but not to-morrow!"

23   Pearl laughed, and attempted to pull away her hand. But the minister held it fast.

24   "A moment longer, my child!" said he.

25   "But wilt thou promise," asked Pearl, "to take my hand, and mother's hand, to-morrow noontide?"

26   "Not then, Pearl," said the minister, "but another time!"

27   "And what other time?" persisted the child.

28   "At the great judgment day!" whispered the minister,—and, strangely enough, the sense that he was a professional teacher of the truth impelled him to answer the child so. "Then, and there, before the judgment-seat, thy mother, and thou, and I, must stand together! But the daylight of this world shall not see our meeting!"

29   Pearl laughed again.

30   But, before Mr. Dimmesdale had done speaking, a light gleamed far and wide over all the muffled sky. It was doubtless caused by one of those meteors, which the night-watcher may so often observe burning out to waste, in the vacant regions of the atmosphere. So powerful was its radiance, that it thoroughly illuminated the dense medium of cloud betwixt the sky and earth. The great vault brightened, like the dome of an immense lamp. It showed the familiar scene of the street, with the distinctness of midday, but also with the awfulness that is always imparted to familiar objects by an unaccustomed light. The wooden houses, with their jutting stories and quaint gable-peaks; the doorsteps

and thresholds, with the early grass springing up about them; the garden-plots, black with freshly turned earth; the wheel-track, little worn, and, even in the marketplace, margined with green on either side;—all were visible, but with a singularity of aspect that seemed to give another moral interpretation to the things of this world than they had ever borne before. And there stood the minister, with his hand over his heart; and Hester Prynne, with the embroidered letter glimmering on her bosom; and little Pearl, herself a symbol, and the connecting link between those two. They stood in the noon of that strange and solemn splendor, as if it were the light that is to reveal all secrets, and the daybreak that shall unite all who belong to one another.

31   There was witchcraft in little Pearl's eyes; and her face, as she glanced upward at the minister, wore that naughty smile which made its expression frequently so elfish. She withdrew her hand from Mr. Dimmesdale's, and pointed across the street. But he clasped both his hands over his breast, and cast his eyes towards the zenith.

32   Nothing was more common, in those days, than to interpret all meteoric appearances, and other natural phenomena, that occurred with less regularity than the rise and set of sun and moon, as so many revelations from a supernatural source. Thus, a blazing spear, a sword of flame, a bow, or a sheaf of arrows, seen in the midnight sky, prefigured Indian warfare. Pestilence was known to have been foreboded by a shower of crimson light. We doubt whether any marked event, for good or evil, ever befell New England, from its settlement down to Revolutionary times, of which the inhabitants had not been previously warned by some spectacle of this nature. Not seldom, it had been seen by multitudes. Oftener, however, its credibility rested on the faith of some lonely eyewitness, who beheld the wonder through the colored, magnifying, and distorting medium of his imagination, and shaped it more distinctly in his afterthought. It was, indeed, a majestic idea, that the destiny of nations should be revealed, in these awful hieroglyphics, on the cope of heaven. A scroll so wide might not be deemed too expansive for Providence to write a people's doom upon. The belief was a favorite one with our forefathers, as betokening that their infant commonwealth was under a celestial guardianship of peculiar intimacy and strictness. But what shall we say, when an individual discovers a revelation, addressed to himself alone, on the same vast sheet of record! In such a case, it could only be the symptom of a highly disordered mental state, when a man, rendered morbidly self-contemplative by long, intense, and secret pain, had extended his egotism over the whole expanse of nature, until the firmament itself should appear no more than a fitting page for his soul's history and fate.

33   We impute it, therefore, solely to the disease in his own eye and heart, that the minister, looking upward to the zenith, beheld there the appearance of an immense letter,—the letter A,—marked out in lines of dull red light. Not but the meteor may have shown itself at that point, burning duskily through a veil of cloud; but with no such shape as his guilty imagination gave it; or, at least, with so little definiteness, that another's guilt might have seen another symbol in it.

34   There was a singular circumstance that characterized Mr. Dimmesdale's psychological state, at this moment. All the time that he gazed upward to the zenith, he was, nevertheless, perfectly aware that little Pearl was pointing her finger towards old Roger Chillingworth, who stood at no great distance from the scaffold. The minister appeared to see him, with the same glance that discerned the miraculous letter. To his features, as to all other objects, the meteoric light imparted a new expression; or it might well be that the physician was not careful then, as at all other times, to hide the malevolence with which he looked upon his victim. Certainly, if the meteor kindled up the sky, and disclosed the earth, with an awfulness that admonished Hester Prynne and the clergyman of the day of judgment, then might Roger Chillingworth have passed with them for the arch-fiend, standing there, with a smile and scowl, to claim his own. So vivid was the expression, or so intense the minister's perception of it, that it seemed still to remain painted on the darkness, after the meteor had vanished, with an effect as if the street and all things else were at once annihilated.

35   "Who is that man, Hester?" gasped Mr. Dimmesdale, overcome with terror. "I shiver at him! Dost thou know the man? hate him, Hester!"

36   She remembered her oath, and was silent.

37   "I tell thee, my soul shivers at him," muttered the minister again. "Who is he? Who is he? Canst thou do nothing for me? I have a nameless horror of the man."

38   "Minister," said little Pearl, "I can tell thee who he is!"

39   "Quickly, then, child!" said the minister, bending his ear close to her lips. "Quickly!—and as low as thou canst whisper."

40   Pearl mumbled something into his ear, that sounded, indeed, like human language, but was only such gibberish as children may be heard amusing themselves with, by the hour together. At all events, if it involved any secret information in regard to old Roger Chillingworth, it was in a tongue unknown to the erudite clergyman, and did but increase the bewilderment of his mind. The elfish child then laughed aloud.

41   "Dost thou mock me now?" said the minister.

42   "Thou wast not bold!—thou wast not true!" answered the child. "Thou wouldst not promise to take my hand, and mother's hand, to-morrow noontide!"

43   "Worthy Sir," said the physician, who had now advanced to the foot of the platform. "Pious Master Dimmesdale! can this be you? Well, well, indeed! We men of study, whose heads are in our books, have need to be straitly looked after! We dream in our waking moments, and walk in our sleep. Come, good Sir, and my dear friend, I pray you, let me lead you home!"

44   "How knewest thou that I was here?" asked the minister, fearfully.

45   "Verily, and in good faith," answered Roger Chillingworth, "I knew nothing of the matter. I had spent the better part of the night at the bedside of the worshipful Governor Winthrop, doing what my poor skill might to give him ease. He was going home to a better world, I, likewise, was on my way homeward, when this strange light shone out. Come with me, I beseech you, Reverend Sir; else you will

be poorly able to do Sabbath duty to-morrow. Aha! see now, how they trouble the brain,—these books!—these books! You should study less, good Sir, and take a little pastime; or these night-whimseys will grow upon you!"

46   "I will go home with you," said Mr. Dimmesdale.

47   With a chill despondency, like one awaking, all nerveless, from an ugly dream, he yielded himself to the physician, and was led away.

48   The next day, however, being the Sabbath, he preached a discourse which was held to be the richest and most powerful, and the most replete with heavenly influences, that had ever proceeded from his lips. Souls, it is said, more souls than one, were brought to the truth by the efficacy of that sermon, and vowed within themselves to cherish a holy gratitude towards Mr. Dimmesdale throughout the long hereafter. But, as he came down the pulpit-steps, the gray-bearded sexton met him, holding up a black glove, which the minister recognized as his own.

49   "It was found," said the sexton, "this morning, on the scaffold, where evil-doers are set up to public shame. Satan dropped it there, I take it, intending a scurrilous jest against your reverence. But, indeed, he was blind and foolish, as he ever and always is. A pure hand needs no glove to cover it!"

50   "Thank you, my good friend," said the minister gravely, but startled at heart; for, so confused was his remembrance, that he had almost brought himself to look at the events of the past night as visionary. "Yes, it seems to be my glove indeed!"

51   "And, since Satan saw fit to steal it, your reverence must needs handle him without gloves, henceforward," remarked the old sexton, grimly smiling. "But did your reverence hear of the portent that was seen last night? A great red letter in the sky,—the letter A,—which we interpret to stand for Angel. For, as our good Governor Winthrop was made an angel this past night, it was doubtless held fit that there should be some notice thereof!"

52   "No," answered the minister. "I had not heard of it."

CHAPTER 12

JOURNAL

1. **MLA Works Cited** *Using this model, record this book.*
   Author's Last Name, First Name. The Scarlet Letter. 1850. Title of This Book. Ed. First Name Last Name. City: Publisher, year.
2. **Main Character(s)** *Describe each main character and explain why you think each is a main character.*
3. **Supporting Characters** *Describe each supporting character and explain why you think each is a supporting character.*
4. **Setting** *Describe the setting(s) and any relevant prop(s).*
5. **Sequence** *Outline the events in this chapter in order.*

6. **Plot** *Summarize this chapter's events in no more than two sentences.*

7. **Conflicts** *Identify and explain all conflicts involved in this chapter.*

8. **Significant Quotations** *Explain the importance of each of these quotations. Record the page number in the parentheses.*

   a. "'Come up hither, Hester, thou and little Pearl,' said the Reverend Mr. Dimmesdale. 'Ye have both been here before, but I was not with you. Come up hither once again, and we will stand all three together!'" (   ).

   b. "Nothing was more common, in those days, than to interpret all meteoric appearances, and other natural phenomena, that occurred with less regularity than the rise and set of the sun and moon, as so many revelations from a supernatural source [. . .]" (   ).

   c. "'Who is that man, Hester?' gasped Mr. Dimmesdale, overcome with terror. 'I shiver at him! Dost thou know the man? I hate him, Hester!'" (   ).

   d. "'Thou wast not bold!—thou wast not true!' answered the child. 'Thou wouldst not promise to take my hand, and mother's hand, to-morrow at noontide!' " (   ).

   e. "'But did your reverence hear of the portent that was seen last night? A great red letter in the sky,—the letter A,—which we interpret to stand for Angel [. . .]'" (   ).

9. **Recap** *Summarize what has happened so far, from the beginning of the book through this chapter.*

FOLLOW-UP QUESTIONS

6 SHORT QUESTIONS

Select the <u>best</u> answer for each.

_____ 1. When Arthur Dimmesdale laughs out loud on the scaffold, he is answered by
   a. Rev. Wilson.
   b. Roger Chillingworth.
   c. Pearl.

_____ 2. Appearing in the sky is
   a. a blazing spear.
   b. a large red letter A.
   c. a sheaf of arrows.

_____ 3. On the scaffold, Arthur Dimmesdale holds hands with
   a. Rev. Wilson.
   b. Roger Chillingworth.
   c. Hester Prynne and Pearl.

_____ 4. Arthur Dimmesdale tells Hester that he
   a. hates Roger Chillingworth.
   b. is best friends with Roger Chillingworth.
   c. wants Roger Chillingworth to become a minister.

_____ 5. Pearl asks Arthur Dimmes-   _____ 6. Arthur Dimmesdale goes
     dale to   home with
     a. stand with her and Hester   a. Hester Prynne.
       on the scaffold the next day.   b. Rev. Wilson.
     b. come down from the   c. Roger Chillingworth.
       scaffold.
     c. pray with her.

5 SIGNIFICANT QUOTATIONS

Explain the importance of each of these quotations.

1. "Why, then, had he come hither? Was it but the mockery of penitence? A mockery, indeed, but in which his soul trifled with itself! A mockery at which angels blushed and wept, while fiends rejoiced, with jeering laughter! [. . .]."

2. "Without any effort of his will, or power to restrain himself, he shrieked aloud; an outcry that went pealing through the night, and was beaten back from one house to another, and reverberated from the hills in the background; as if a company of devils, detecting so much misery and terror, had made a plaything of the sound, and were bandying it to and fro."

3. "Carried away by the grotesque horror of this picture, the minister, unawares, and to his own infinite alarm, burst into a great peal of laughter. It was immediately responded to by a light, airy, childish laugh, in which, with a thrill of the heart,—but he knew not whether of exquisite pain, or pleasure as acute,—he recognized the tones of little Pearl."

4. "The minister felt for the child's other hand, and took it. The moment that he did so, there came what seemed a tumultuous rush of new life, other life than his own, pouring like a torrent into his heart, and hurrying through all his veins, as if the mother and the child were communicating their vital warmth to his half-torpid system. The three formed an electric chain."

5. "'[. . .] Pious Master Dimmesdale! can this be you? Well, well, indeed! We men of study, whose heads are in our books, have need to be straitly looked after! We dream in our waking moments, and walk in our sleep. Come, good Sir, and my dear friend, I pray you, let me lead you home!'"

2 COMPREHENSION ESSAY QUESTIONS

Use specific details and information from the chapter to answer these questions as completely as possible.

1. Characters sometimes look to their surroundings for clues to understand their lives. How do characters in this chapter try to interpret signs and events? Use specific details and information from the chapter to support your answer.

2. Whether old or young, one often has to face something feared. How does Arthur Dimmesdale face his fears? Use specific details and information from the chapter for your explanation.

DISCUSSION QUESTIONS

Be prepared to discuss these questions in class.

1. How and why does Arthur Dimmesdale keep a vigil on the scaffold?
2. Do you think Arthur Dimmesdale is sane? Why or why not? What do you predict will happen to him?

CHAPTERS 9–12

JOURNAL

1. **MLA Works Cited** *Using this model, record this book.*
   Author's Last Name, First Name. The Scarlet letter. 1850. Title of This Book.
   Ed. First Name Last Name. City: Publisher, year.
2. **Main Character(s)** *Describe each main character and explain why you think each is a main character.*
3. **Supporting Characters** *Describe each supporting character and explain why you think each is a supporting character.*
4. **Setting** *Describe the setting(s) and any relevant prop(s).*
5. **Sequence** *Outline the events in these chapters in order.*
6. **Plot** *Summarize these chapters' events in no more than five sentences.*
7. **Conflicts** *Identify and explain all conflicts involved in these chapters.*
8. **Significant Quotations** *Explain the importance of each of these quotations. Record the page number in the parentheses.*
   a. "He resolved not to be pilloried beside her on her pedestal of shame. Unknown to all but Hester Prynne, and possessing the lock and key of her silence, he chose to withdraw his name from the roll of mankind, and, as regarded his former ties and interests, to vanish out of life as completely as if he indeed lay at the bottom of the ocean, whither rumor had long ago consigned him [. . .]" (   ).
   b. "Thus Roger Chillingworth scrutinized his patient carefully [. . .]. He deemed it essential [. . .] to know the man, before attempting to do him good. Wherever there is a heart and an intellect, the diseases of the physical frame are tinged with the peculiarities of these [. . .]" (   ).
   c. "Doomed by his own choice, therefore, as Mr. Dimmesdale so evidently was, to eat his unsavory morsel always at another's board, and endure the life-long chill which must be his lot who seeks to warm himself only at another's fireside, it truly seemed that this sagacious, experienced, benevolent, old physician, with his concord of paternal and reverential love for the young pastor, was the very man, of all mankind, to be constantly within reach of his voice" (   ).
   d. "But with what a wild look of wonder, joy, and horror! With what a ghastly rapture, as it were, too mighty to be expressed only by the eye and features, and therefore bursting forth through the whole ugliness of his figure, and making itself even riotously manifest by the extravagant gestures with which he threw up his arms towards the ceiling, and stamped his foot upon the floor! [. . .]" (   ).
   e. "Would he startle him with sudden fear? As at the waving of a magician's wand, uprose a grisly phantom,—uprose a thousand phantoms,—in many shapes, of death, or more awful shame, all flocking roundabout the clergyman, and pointing with their fingers at his breast!" (   ).
   f. "For, as it was impossible to assign a reason for such distrust and abhorrence, so Mr. Dimmesdale, conscious that the poison of one morbid spot

was infecting his heart's entire substance, attributed all his presentiments to no other cause. He took himself to task for his bad sympathies in reference to Roger Chillingworth, disregarded the lesson that he should have drawn from them, and did his best to root them out [. . .]" (   ).

g. "Walking in the shadow of a dream, as it were, and perhaps actually under the influence of a species of somnambulism, Mr. Dimmesdale reached the spot, where, now so long since, Hester Prynne had lived through her first hour of public ignominy. [. . .]. The minister went up the steps" (   ).

h. "But, before Mr. Dimmesdale had done speaking, a light gleamed far and wide over all the muffled sky. [. . .]. So powerful was its radiance, that it thoroughly illuminated the dense medium of cloud betwixt the sky and earth. [. . .]. And there stood the minister, with his hand over his heart; and Hester Prynne, with the embroidered letter glimmering on her bosom; and little Pearl, herself a symbol, and the connecting link between those two [. . .]" (   ).

i. "All the time that he gazed upward to the zenith, he was, nevertheless, perfectly aware that little Pearl was pointing her finger towards old Roger Chillingworth, who stood at no great distance from the scaffold [. . .]" (   ).

j. "'But did your reverence hear of the portent that was seen last night? A great red letter in the sky,—the letter A,—which we interpret to stand for Angel [. . .]'" (   ).

9. **Recap** *Summarize what has happened so far, from the beginning of the novel through these chapters.*

FOLLOW-UP QUESTIONS

2 0 SHORT QUESTIONS

Select the <u>best</u> answer for each.

____ 1. Roger Chillingworth is a
   a. physician.
   b. minister.
   c. sexton.

____ 2. Roger Chillingworth
   a. tells the townspeople that Hester Prynne is his wife.
   b. has never been married.
   c. changed his name when he came to Boston.

____ 3. Roger Chillingworth moves into the same house as
   a. Governor Bellingham.
   b. Master Brackett.
   c. Arthur Dimmesdale.

____ 4. As time goes by, Roger Chillingworth's face
   a. becomes ugly.
   b. turns very pale.
   c. looks friendlier.

____ 5. As time goes by, Arthur Dimmesdale's
   a. voice strengthens.
   b. popularity declines.
   c. health worsens.

____ 6. The character who always has a hand over the heart is
   a. Mistress Hibbins.
   b. Arthur Dimmesdale.
   c. Hester Prynne.

____ 7. When Roger Chillingworth lived in England, he was
   a. evil-hearted and unkind.
   b. good-hearted and kind.
   c. ugly and evil-hearted.

____ 8. Arthur Dimmesdale
   a. recognizes Roger Chillingworth as his enemy.
   b. has nothing to say to Roger Chillingworth.
   c. thinks Roger Chillingworth is his friend.

____ 9. Roger Chillingworth, as his physician, tells Arthur Dimmesdale that
   a. Arthur's illness is caused by bodily disease.
   b. Arthur is physically healthy.
   c. Arthur's illness is of a spiritual nature.

____ 10. While Arthur Dimmesdale is asleep, Roger Chillingworth looks inside
   a. Arthur's books.
   b. Arthur's shirt.
   c. Arthur's closet.

____ 11. In his closet, Arthur Dimmesdale secretly keeps
   a. a scourge.
   b. a scarlet letter.
   c. letters from Hester Prynne.

____ 12. Roger Chillingworth is obsessed with
   a. seeing that Pearl is raised in a Christian family.
   b. making Hester Prynne pay for her mistakes.
   c. making Arthur Dimmesdale suffer.

____ 13. At night, Arthur Dimmesdale
   a. punishes himself.
   b. goes to the woods with Mistress Hibbins.
   c. sleeps.

____ 14. One particular night, Arthur Dimmesdale keeps a vigil
   a. on the scaffold.
   b. in the pillory.
   c. in the church.

____ 15. Arthur Dimmesdale's wild laugh is answered by
   a. Hester's soft voice.
   b. Pearl's airy, childish laughter.
   c. Chillingworth's stern command.

____ 16. Arthur Dimmesdale is joined in his vigil by
   a. Roger Chillingworth, Hester Prynne, and Pearl.
   b. Rev. John Wilson, Mistress Hibbins, and Hester Prynne.
   c. Roger Chillingworth, Governor Bellingham, and Rev. John Wilson.

____ 17. Arthur Dimmesdale is invigorated by
   a. keeping vigils.
   b. holding hands with Hester and Pearl.
   c. shrieking aloud.

____ 18. In the night sky appears
   a. an angel.
   b. a sword of flame.
   c. an immense letter A.

____ 19. Arthur Dimmesdale tells
Hester that he hates
a. her.
b. Roger Chillingworth.
c. her and Roger
Chillingworth.

____ 20. Arthur's glove is found by
a. Roger Chillingworth.
b. the jailor.
c. the sexton.

10 SIGNIFICANT QUOTATIONS

Explain the importance of each of these quotations.

1. "Then why—since the choice was with himself—should the individual, whose connection with the fallen woman had been the most intimate and sacred of all, come forward to vindicate his claim to an inheritance so little desirable? [. . .]."

2. "[H]e took up his residence in the Puritan town, as Roger Chillingworth, without other introduction than the learning and intelligence of which he possessed more than a common measure [. . .]."

3. "About this period, however, the health of Mr. Dimmesdale had evidently begun to fail. By those best acquainted with his habits, the paleness of the young minister's cheek was accounted for by his too earnest devotion to study, his scrupulous fulfillment of parochial duty, and, more than all, by the fasts and vigils of which he made a frequent practice [. . .]."

4. "Trusting no man as his friend, he could not recognize his enemy when the latter actually appeared [. . .]."

5. "It came to pass [. . .] that the Reverend Mr. Dimmesdale, at noonday, and entirely unawares, fell into a deep, deep slumber, sitting in his chair, with a large black-letter volume open before him on the table [. . .]."

6. "In Mr. Dimmesdale's secret closet, under lock and key, there was a bloody scourge. Oftentimes [he] had plied it on his own shoulders; laughing bitterly at himself the while, and smiting so much the more pitilessly, because of that bitter laugh [. . .]."

7. "To the untrue man, the whole universe is false,—it is impalpable,—it shrinks to nothing within his grasp. And he himself, in so far as he shows himself in a false light, becomes a shadow, or, indeed, ceases to exist [. . .]."

8. "The minister felt for the child's other hand, and took it. The moment that he did so, there came what seemed a tumultuous rush of new life, other life than his own, pouring like a torrent into his heart, and hurrying through all his veins, as if the mother and the child were communicating their vital warmth to his half-torpid system. The three formed an electric chain."

9. "'Wilt thou stand here with mother and me, to-morrow noon-tide?' inquired Pearl."

10. "With a chill despondency, like one awaking, all nerveless, from an ugly dream, he yielded himself to the physician, and was led away."

2 COMPREHENSION ESSAY QUESTIONS

Use specific details and information from these chapters to answer these questions as completely as possible.

1. What do Roger Chillingworth and Arthur Dimmesdale have in common? Describe their developing relationship using specific details and information from these chapters.
2. How perceptive is Pearl? What does she notice about the main characters? Use specific details and information from these chapters in your explanation.

DISCUSSION QUESTIONS

Be prepared to discuss these questions in class.

1. What has Roger Chillingworth lost by changing his identity? What has he gained?
2. Why does the talented and beloved Arthur Dimmesdale feel like a "'false man'"?

WRITING

Use each of these ideas to write an essay.

1. Natural phenomena like thunderstorms or comet sightings catch our attention. Some people find them scientifically interesting, while the Puritans and other cultures have viewed them as religious or supernatural signs. Have you ever been strongly affected by something in nature—a storm, a sunset, the night sky, a waterfall, for example? Describe this natural phenomenon and the effect(s) it had upon you.
2. Hester Prynne has grown in strength and stamina while Arthur Dimmesdale has weakened in both body and mind. Using examples from these four chapters, explain why these characters have reacted so differently to their situations. Would it have been better for Arthur Dimmesdale if Hester had named him as the baby's father seven years earlier?
3. Hester has conformed to the Puritan code of dress and behavior, except in the way she dresses Pearl. In what ways does our society demand that we conform? Do we have the freedom to choose?
4. Places, objects, events, and settings can be symbolic in a novel. Discuss one or two symbolic aspects of <u>The Scarlet Letter</u>. Explain what is being symbolized.

FURTHER WRITING

1. The government of the Puritan colony was a form of theocracy—a system in which the religious laws are the same as the civil laws. What countries today

are theocracies? Research one contemporary theocratic society and the types of laws and freedoms it has. Is a true separation of church and state possible? Why or why not?

2. Recent psychological studies have shown that people who forgive those who hurt them live longer than those who hold grudges, like Roger Chillingworth. Research the relationship between forgiveness and physical and/or psychological health.

3. Is it true that there is a fine line between genius and insanity? Poets, artists, and other creative people have sometimes succumbed to mental illness. Research to find out how, in some cases, genius or a high level of creativity may be linked to insanity.

4. Nathaniel Hawthorne's contemporaries include Bronson Alcott, Susan Fenimore Cooper, Ralph Waldo Emerson, Washington Irving, Henry Wadsworth Longfellow, Herman Melville, Franklin Pierce, Edgar Allan Poe, and Harriet Beecher Stowe. Research the significant achievements of one or more of these individuals and discuss their roles in history or society.

CHAPTER 13

ANOTHER VIEW OF HESTER

PRE-READING VOCABULARY
CONTEXT

Use context clues to define these words before reading. Use a dictionary as needed.

1. Joseph felt quite degraded when the boss *abased* him for his unfinished report in front of other employees. *Abased* means _____
_____.

2. When Carlos pointed at the chewed-up shoe on the floor, the puppy *groveled* guiltily at his feet, crawling across the floor with his eyes averted. *Grovel* means
_____.

3. After the snow fell, the streets looked clean, white, and *pristine*. *Pristine* means
_____.

4. When the comedian told bad jokes that were not funny, the crowd jeered and *gibed* at him. *Gibed* means _____
_____.

5. After a month in the dry desert, Leah thirstily *imbibed* the rain and mist. *Imbibe* means _____
_____.

6. Mary has the most *irksome* habit of repeating what she says at least two times. *Irksome* means _____
_____.

7. The irate customer *accosted* the manager to complain about conditions in the store. *Accosted* means _____
_____.

8. Bodybuilders work out at the gym, take vitamins, and drink special protein shakes to *fortify* their muscles and bones. *Fortify* means _____
_____.

9. Hard-working people have a *propensity* towards performing many tasks and tend to do a good job every time. *Propensity* means _____
_____.

10. In the fall, the *foliage* of many trees turns from green to yellow, orange, or red, creating quite a colorful forest covering. *Foliage* means _____
    _____.

11. During the war, the soldiers' quarters were quite *austere*: bare walls, simple beds with blankets, and plain shades on the windows. *Austere* means _____
    _____.

12. After the Morgans paid off their mortgage and all their bills, they felt *emancipated* from debt, free to spend money on whatever they wanted. *Emancipated* means _____
    _____.

13. Looking at the *labyrinth* of offices, Yvonne felt as if she had entered a confusing and complicated maze with no clear path. *Labyrinth* means _____
    _____.

14. After climbing the mountain, Helena stood on the edge *of the precipice* and looked down the steep sides into the distant valley. *Precipice* means _____
    _____.

15. After the earthquake, a deep *chasm* opened in the earth and we could not get across. *Chasm* means _____
    _____.

16. Howard *attained* at least two of his goals when he graduated from law school and received a position at a good law firm. *Attain* means _____
    _____.

17. Someone suffering from a mental disorder may act strangely and show signs of *lunacy*, or insanity. *Lunacy* means _____
    _____.

18. As an emergency room nurse, Toni has learned to face every *calamity*, from accidents to disease, with calm efficiency. *Calamity* means _____
    _____.

19. The rumble of thunder in the distance and the darkening sky can *forebode* the coming of a storm. *Forebode* means _____
    _____.

20. Cape Cod in Massachusetts is a well-known *peninsula*, a long, narrow piece of land that projects out into the ocean. *Peninsula* means _____
    _____.

PRE-READING VOCABULARY
STRUCTURAL ATTACK

Define these words by solving the parts. Use the Glossary or a dictionary as needed.

1. legitimate	13. tapered	25. monarch
2. repose	14. wither	26. expel
3. singular	15. strenuous	27. venomous
4. infer	16. impede	28. lonesome
5. responsibility	17. acquiesce	29. avails
6. linked	18. submit	30. repulsive
8. bitter-hearted	19. stigmatize	31. stooped
8. pauper	20. hostile	32. inadequate
9. reckon	21. prophetess	33. confront
10. utmost	22. exertion	34. tampered
11. suffice	23. pestilence	35. humblest
12. wretched	24. benevolence	

PRE-READING QUESTIONS

Try answering these questions as you read.

How old is Pearl?

What does Hester notice about Arthur Dimmesdale? What does she think is the
   cause?

What does Hester decide to do?

How do the townspeople regard Hester these days?

How has Hester changed?

CHAPTER 13

ANOTHER VIEW OF HESTER

1   In her late singular interview with Mr. Dimmesdale, Hester Prynne was shocked
at the condition to which she found the clergyman reduced. His nerve seemed
absolutely destroyed. His moral force was abased into more than childish weakness. It grovelled helpless on the ground, even while his intellectual faculties
retained their pristine strength, or had perhaps acquired a morbid energy, which
disease only could have given them. With her knowledge of a train of circumstances hidden from all others, she could readily infer, that, besides the legitimate action of his own conscience, a terrible machinery had been brought to
bear, and was still operating, on Mr. Dimmesdale's well-being and repose.
Knowing what this poor, fallen man had once been, her whole soul was moved by

the shuddering terror with which he had appealed to her,—the outcast woman,—for support against his instinctively discovered enemy. She decided, moreover, that he had a right to her utmost aid. Little accustomed, in her long seclusion from society, to measure her ideas of right and wrong by any standard external to herself, Hester saw—or seemed to see—that there lay a responsibility upon her, in reference to the clergyman, which she owed to no other, nor to the whole world besides. The links that united her to the rest of human kind—links of flowers, or silk, or gold, or whatever the material—had all been broken. Here was the iron link of mutual crime, which neither he nor she could break. Like all other ties, it brought along with it its obligations.

2   Hester Prynne did not now occupy precisely the same position in which we beheld her during the earlier periods of her ignominy. Years had come, and gone. Pearl was now seven years old. Her mother, with the scarlet letter on her breast, glittering in its fantastic embroidery, had long been a familiar object to the townspeople. As is apt to be the case when a person stands out in any prominence before the community, and, at the same time, interferes neither with public nor individual interests and convenience, a species of general regard had ultimately grown up in reference to Hester Prynne. It is to the credit of human nature, that, except where its selfishness is brought into play, it loves more readily than it hates. Hatred, by a gradual and quiet process, will even be transformed to love, unless the change be impeded by a continually new irritation of the original feeling of hostility. In this matter of Hester Prynne, there was neither irritation nor irksomeness. She never battled with the public, but submitted uncomplainingly to its worst usage; she made no claim upon it, in requital for what she suffered; she did not weigh upon its sympathies. Then, also, the blameless purity of her life, during all these years in which she had been set apart to infamy, was reckoned largely in her favor. With nothing now to lose, in the sight of mankind, and with no hope, and seemingly no wish, of gaining any thing, it could only be a genuine regard for virtue that had brought back the poor wanderer to its paths.

3   It was perceived, too, that, while Hester never put forward even the humblest title to share in the world's privileges,—farther than to breathe the common air, and earn daily bread for little Pearl and herself by the faithful labor of her hands,—she was quick to acknowledge her sisterhood with the race of man, whenever benefits were to be conferred. None so ready as she to give of her little substance to every demand of poverty; even though the bitter-hearted pauper threw back a gibe in requital of the food brought regularly to his door, or the garments wrought for him by the fingers that could have embroidered a monarch's robe. None so self-devoted as Hester, when pestilence stalked through the town. In all seasons of calamity, indeed, whether general or of individuals, the outcast of society at once found her place. She came, not as a guest, but as a rightful inmate, into the household that was darkened by trouble; as if its gloomy twilight were a medium in which she was entitled to hold intercourse with her fellow-creatures. There glimmered the embroidered letter, with comfort in its unearthly ray. Elsewhere the token of sin, it was the taper of the sick-chamber. It had even thrown its gleam, in the sufferer's hard extremity, across the verge of time. It had shown him where to set his foot, while the light of earth was fast becoming dim, and ere the light of futurity could reach him. In such emergencies, Hester's nature showed itself warm and rich; a well-spring of human tenderness, unfailing to every real demand, and inexhaustible by the largest. Her breast, with its badge of shame, was but the softer pillow for the head that needed one. She was self-ordained a Sister of Mercy; or, we may rather say, the world's heavy hand had so ordained her, when neither the world nor she looked forward to this result. The letter was the symbol of her calling. Such helpfulness was found in her,—so much power to do, and power to sympathize,—that many people refused to interpret the scarlet A by its original signification. They said that it meant Able; so strong was Hester Prynne, with a woman's strength.

4   It was only the darkened house that could contain her. When sunshine came again, she was not there. Her shadow had faded across the threshold. The helpful inmate had departed, without one backward glance to gather up the mead of gratitude, if any were in the hearts of those whom she had served so zealously. Meeting them in the street, she never raised her head to receive their greeting. If they were resolute to accost her, she laid her finger on the scarlet letter, and passed on. This might be pride, but was so like humility, that it produced all the softening influence of the latter quality on the public mind. The public is despotic in its temper; it is capable of denying common justice, when too strenuously demanded as a right; but quite as frequently it awards more than justice, when the appeal is made, as despots love to have it made, entirely to its generosity. Interpreting Hester Prynne's deportment as an appeal of this nature, society was inclined to show its former victim a more benign countenance than she cared to be favored with, or, perchance, than she deserved.

5   The rulers, and the wise and learned men of the community, were longer in acknowledging the influence of Hester's good qualities than the people. The prejudices which they shared in common with the latter were fortified in themselves by

an iron framework of reasoning, that made it a far tougher labor to expel them. Day by day, nevertheless, their sour and rigid wrinkles were relaxing into something which, in the due course of years, might grow to be an expression of almost benevolence. Thus it was with the men of rank, on whom their eminent position imposed the guardianship of the public morals. Individuals in private life, meanwhile, had quite forgiven Hester Prynne for her frailty; nay, more, they had begun to look upon the scarlet letter as the token, not of that one sin, for which she had borne so long and dreary a penance, but of her many good deeds since. "Do you see that woman with the embroidered badge?" they would say to strangers. "It is our Hester,—the town's own Hester,—who is so kind to the poor, so helpful to the sick, so comfortable to the afflicted!" Then, it is true, the propensity of human nature to tell the very worst of itself, when embodied in the person of another, would constrain them to whisper the black scandal of bygone years. It was none the less a fact, however, that, in the eyes of the very men who spoke thus, the scarlet letter had the effect of the cross on a nun's bosom. It imparted to the wearer a kind of sacredness, which enabled her to walk securely amid all peril. Had she fallen among thieves, it would have kept her safe. It was reported, and believed by many, that an Indian had drawn his arrow against the badge, and that the missile struck it, but fell harmless to the ground.

6   The effect of the symbol—or rather, of the position in respect to society that was indicated by it—on the mind of Hester Prynne herself, was powerful and peculiar. All the light and graceful foliage of her character had been withered up by this red-hot brand, and had long ago fallen away, leaving a bare and harsh outline, which might have been repulsive, had she possessed friends or companions to be repelled by it. Even the attractiveness of her person had undergone a similar change. It might be partly owing to the studied austerity of her dress, and partly to the lack of demonstration in her manners. It was a sad transformation, too, that her rich and luxuriant hair had either been cut off, or was so completely hidden by a cap, that not a shining lock of it ever once gushed into the sunshine. It was due in part to all these causes, but still more to something else, that there seemed to be no longer any thing in Hester's face for Love to dwell upon; nothing in Hester's form, though majestic and statue-like, that Passion would ever dream of clasping in its embrace; nothing in Hester's bosom, to make it ever again the pillow of Affection. Some attribute had departed from her, the permanence of which had been essential to keep her a woman. Such is frequently the fate, and such the stern development, of the feminine character and person, when the woman has encountered, and lived through, an experience of peculiar severity. If she be all tenderness, she will die. If she survive, the tenderness will either be crushed out of her, or—and the outward semblance is the same—crushed so deeply into her heart that it can never show itself more. The latter is perhaps the truest theory. She who has once been woman, and ceased to be so, might at any moment become a woman again, if there were only the magic touch to effect the transfiguration. We shall see whether Hester Prynne were ever afterwards so touched, and so transfigured.

7   Much of the marble coldness of Hester's impression was to be attributed to
the circumstance that her life had turned, in a great measure, from passion and
feeling, to thought. Standing alone in the world,—alone, as to any dependence
on society, and with little Pearl to be guided and protected,—alone, and hopeless
of retrieving her position, even had she not scorned to consider it desirable,—she
cast away the fragments of a broken chain. The world's law was no law for her
mind. It was an age in which the human intellect, newly emancipated, had taken
a more active and a wider range than for many centuries before. Men of the sword
had overthrown nobles and kings. Men bolder than these had overthrown and
rearranged—not actually, but within the sphere of theory, which was their most
real abode—the whole system of ancient prejudice, wherewith was linked much
of ancient principle. Hester Prynne imbibed this spirit. She assumed a freedom
of speculation, then common enough on the other side of the Atlantic, but which
our forefathers, had they known of it, would have held to be a deadlier crime
than that stigmatized by the scarlet letter. In her lonesome cottage, by the sea-
shore, thoughts visited her, such as dared to enter no other dwelling in New
England; shadowy guests, that would have been as perilous as demons to their
entertainer, could they have been seen so much as knocking at her door.

8   It is remarkable, that persons who speculate the most boldly often conform
with the most perfect quietude to the external regulations of society. The
thought suffices them, without investing itself in the flesh and blood of action.
So it seemed to be with Hester. Yet, had little Pearl never come to her from the
spiritual world, it might have been far otherwise. Then, she might have come
down to us in history, hand in hand with Ann Hutchinson, as the foundress of a
religious sect. She might, in one of her phases, have been a prophetess. She
might, and not improbably would, have suffered death from the stern tribunals
of the period, for attempting to undermine the foundations of the Puritan estab-
lishment. But, in the education of her child, the mother's enthusiasm of thought
had something to wreak itself upon. Providence, in the person of this little girl,
had assigned to Hester's charge the germ and blossom of womanhood, to be cherished and developed amid a host of difficulties. Every thing was against her. The
world was hostile. The child's own nature had something wrong in it, which continually betokened that she had been born amiss,—the effluence of her mother's
lawless passion,—and often impelled Hester to ask, in bitterness of heart,
whether it were for ill or good that the poor little creature had been born at all.

9   Indeed, the same dark question often rose into her mind, with reference to the
whole race of womanhood. Was existence worth accepting, even to the happiest
among them? As concerned her own individual existence, she had long ago
decided in the negative, and dismissed the point as settled. A tendency to speculation, though it may keep woman quiet, as it does man, yet makes her sad. She dis-
cerns, it may be, such a hopeless task before her. As a first step, the whole system
of society is to be torn down, and built up anew. Then, the very nature of the
opposite sex, or its long hereditary habit, which has become like nature, is to be
essentially modified, before woman can be allowed to assume what seems a fair

and suitable position. Finally, all other difficulties being obviated, woman cannot take advantage of these preliminary reforms, until she herself shall have undergone a still mightier change; in which, perhaps, the ethereal essence, wherein she has her truest life, will be found to have evaporated. A woman never overcomes these problems by any exercise of thought. They are not to be solved, or only in one way. If her heart chance to come uppermost, they vanish. Thus, Hester Prynne, whose heart had lost its regular and healthy throb, wandered without a clew in the dark labyrinth of mind; now turned aside by an insurmountable precipice; now starting back from a deep chasm. There was wild and ghastly scenery all around her, and a home and comfort nowhere. At times, a fearful doubt strove to possess her soul, whether it were not better to send Pearl at once to heaven, and go herself to such futurity as Eternal Justice should provide.

10   The scarlet letter had not done its office.

11   Now, however, her interview with the Reverend Mr. Dimmesdale, on the night of his vigil, had given her a new theme of reflection, and held up to her an object that appeared worthy of any exertion and sacrifice for its attainment. She had witnessed the intense misery beneath which the minister struggled, or, to speak more accurately, had ceased to struggle. She saw that he stood on the verge of lunacy, if he had not already stepped across it. It was impossible to doubt, that, whatever painful efficacy there might be in the secret sting of remorse, a deadlier venom had been infused into it by the hand that proffered relief. A secret enemy had been continually by his side, under the semblance of a friend and helper, and had availed himself of the opportunities thus afforded for tampering with the delicate springs of Mr. Dimmesdale's nature. Hester could not but ask herself, whether there had not originally been a defect of truth, courage, and loyalty, on her own part, in allowing the minister to be thrown into a position where so much evil was to be foreboded, and nothing auspicious to be hoped. Her only justification lay in the fact, that she had been able to discern no method of rescuing him from a blacker ruin than had overwhelmed herself, except by acquiescing in Roger Chillingworth's scheme of disguise. Under that impulse, she had made her choice, and had chosen, as it now appeared, the more wretched alternative of the two. She determined to redeem her error, so far as it might yet be possible. Strengthened by years of hard and solemn trial, she felt herself no longer so inadequate to cope with Roger Chillingworth as on that night, abased by sin, and half maddened by the ignominy that was still new, when they had talked together in the prison-chamber. She had climbed her way, since then, to a higher point. The old man, on the other hand, had brought himself nearer to her level, or perhaps below it, by the revenge which he had stooped for.

12   In fine, Hester Prynne resolved to meet her former husband, and do what might be in her power for the rescue of the victim on whom he had so evidently set his gripe. The occasion was not long to seek. One afternoon, walking with Pearl in a retired part of the peninsula, she beheld the old physician, with a basket on one arm, and a staff in the other hand, stooping along the ground, in quest of roots and herbs to concoct his medicines withal.

CHAPTER 13

JOURNAL

1. **MLA Works Cited** *Using this model, record this book.*
   Author's Last Name, First Name. The Scarlet Letter. 1850. Title of This Book.
   Ed. First Name Last Name. City: Publisher, year.
2. **Main Character(s)** *Describe each main character and explain why you think each is a main character.*
3. **Supporting Characters** *Describe each supporting character and explain why you think each is a supporting character.*
4. **Setting** *Describe the setting(s) and any relevant prop(s).*
5. **Sequence** *Outline the events in this chapter in order.*
6. **Plot** *Summarize this chapter's events in no more than two sentences.*
7. **Conflicts** *Identify and explain all conflicts involved in this chapter.*
8. **Significant Quotations** *Explain the importance of each of these quotations. Record the page number in the parentheses.*
   a. "In her late singular interview with Mr. Dimmesdale, Hester Prynne was shocked at the condition to which she found the clergyman reduced [. . .]" ( ).
   b. "With her knowledge of a train of circumstances hidden from all others, she could readily infer, that, besides the legitimate action of his own con-science, a terrible machinery had been brought to bear, and was still operat-ing, on Mr. Dimmesdale's well-being and repose [. . .]" ( ).
   c. "The letter was the symbol of her calling. Such helpfulness was found in her,—so much power to do, and power to sympathize,—that many people refused to interpret the scarlet A by its original signification. They said that it meant Able; so strong was Hester Prynne, with a woman's strength" ( ).
   d. "All the light and graceful foliage of her character had been withered up by this red-hot brand, and had long ago fallen away, leaving a bare and harsh outline, which might have been repulsive, had she possessed friends or companions to be repelled by it [. . .]" ( ).
   e. "Strengthened by years of hard and solemn trial, she felt herself no longer inadequate to cope with Roger Chillingworth as on that night, abased by sin, and half maddened by the ignominy that was still new, when they had talked together in the prison-chamber [. . .]" ( ).
9. **Recap** *Summarize what has happened so far, from the beginning of the book through this chapter.*

FOLLOW-UP QUESTIONS

6 SHORT QUESTIONS

Select the __best__ answer for each.

_____ 1. Hester is shocked by
   a. the way the townspeople treat her.
   b. Pearl's behavior.
   c. Arthur Dimmesdale's misery.

_____ 2. Hester thinks that
   a. Roger Chillingworth is responsible for the minister's condition.
   b. Arthur Dimmesdale is beyond help.
   c. she should reveal the name of Pearl's father.

_____ 3. Hester's letter A, to some people, means
   a. Angel.
   b. Able.
   c. Agreeable.

_____ 4. Hester's appearance has become
   a. very feminine.
   b. quite severe.
   c. rather colorful.

_____ 5. Hester fears that
   a. Arthur Dimmesadle has lost his sanity.
   b. Arthur Dimmesdale will confide in Roger Chillingworth.
   c. Arthur Dimmesdale is becoming too scholarly.

_____ 6. Hester decides to
   a. avoid Roger Chillingworth.
   b. avoid Arthur Dimmesdale.
   c. confront Roger Chillingworth.

5 SIGNIFICANT QUOTATIONS

Explain the importance of each of these quotations.

1. "Knowing what this poor, fallen man had once been, her whole soul was moved by the shuddering terror with which he had appealed to her,—the outcast woman,—for support against his instinctively discovered enemy. She decided, moreover, that he had a right to her utmost aid [. . .]."
2. "In all seasons of calamity, indeed, whether general or of individuals, the outcast of society at once found her place. She came, not as a guest, but as a rightful inmate, into the household that was darkened by trouble [. . .]."
3. "She had witnessed the intense misery beneath which the minister struggled, or, to speak more accurately, had ceased to struggle. She saw that he stood on the verge of lunacy, if he had not already stepped across it [. . .]."
4. "A secret enemy had been continually by his side, under the semblance of a friend and helper, and had availed himself of the opportunities thus afforded for tampering with the delicate springs of Mr. Dimmesdale's nature [. . .]."
5. "She had climbed her way, since then, to a higher point. The old man, on the other hand, had brought himself nearer to her level, or perhaps below it, by the revenge which he had stooped for."

2 COMPREHENSION ESSAY QUESTIONS

Use specific details and information from the chapter to answer these questions as completely as possible.

1. The narrator of the book is a fictional character who tells us the story. The narrator does not always represent the author's opinions and beliefs but instead presents his own feelings and attitudes. Using specific details and information from this chapter and other parts of the novel, how would you describe the narrator of The Scarlet Letter?
2. Living a lonely life as a social outcast, Hester has sometimes felt quite sad. How has she handled this loneliness? Use specific details and information from the chapter in your explanation.

DISCUSSION QUESTIONS

Be prepared to discuss these questions in class.

1. Why is Hester Prynne so concerned about Arthur Dimmesdale? Is she right to be so concerned?
2. What does Hester Prynne decide to do?

CHAPTER 14

HESTER AND THE PHYSICIAN

Use context clues to define these words before reading. Use a dictionary as needed.

1. At the gas station, when Jennifer asked for instructions to the turnpike, the mechanic pointed to the distance and said, "Turn left just before *yonder* hills." *Yonder* means _____
   _____.

2. Shirley *beckoned* with her hand for us to follow her to the dean's office. *Beckoned* means _____
   _____.

3. Every time it storms, Tyler, who is afraid of thunder and lightning, becomes *agitated* and needs us to calm him down. *Agitated* means _____
   _____.

4. A dishonest businessman *extorts* money from clients with false promises of future wealth. *Extorts* means _____
   _____.

5. Even though Pamela finds writing term papers a challenge, she is determined to do her best and would never *stoop* to buying one off the Internet and handing it in as her own. *Stoop* means _____
   _____.

6. After the wildfire swept through his home town, Rodney frantically waited for *tidings* of his family and friends. *Tidings* means _____
   _____.

7. On Halloween, children in costumes may come to the door, asking, "Trick or treat!" This is, in reality, an *entreaty* for candy. *Entreaty* means _____
   _____.

8. With the touch of her magic wand, the fairy godmother *transformed* Cinderella's rags into a beautiful gown so she could attend the Prince's ball. *Transformed* means _____

_____.

9. After the student lied about why she was late to school every day, the professor had *misgivings* about believing her excuses for missing the final exam. *Misgivings* means _____

_____.

10. When Jonathan lost his job, he was so unhappy that he was *miserable*. *Miserable* means _____

_____.

11. To find nuts and seeds, a squirrel will often *burrow* under the soil, leaving holes all over the yard. *Burrow* means _____

_____.

12. Shocked by the horrifying crash she had witnessed, Carol kept telling us the *lurid* details of the mangled cars and the injuries of the victims. *Lurid* means

_____

_____.

13. Sallie and Georgiana are *confidants*: they tell each other every thought and secret. *Confidant* means _____

_____.

14. When taking prescription medicines, it is necessary to maintain the appropriate *interval* of time between doses. *Interval* means _____

_____.

15. Losing her car and home to the devastating tsunami made Su-Li want to *weep*. *Weep* means _____

_____.

16. Gambling addiction can be the *bane* of a family's existence and many have lost their homes and savings to pay off the gambler's debts. *Bane* means

_____

_____.

17. Kim is very *disciplined*: she exercises each day for an hour, eats the right foods, and does all her school work on time. *Disciplined* means _____

_____.

18. Some religions believe that by confessing your sins, you can *purge* your soul of evil and be pure again. *Purge* means _____
_____ .

19. When the guests arrived unexpectedly as she was sweeping off the dusty sidewalk, Gail said, "Please *pardon* my appearance. I did not know that you were coming today." *Pardon* means _____
_____ .

20. Wondering about her future, Roseann consulted a fortuneteller to see if it was her *fate* to marry Patrick. *Fate* means _____
_____ .

PRE-READING VOCABULARY
STRUCTURAL ATTACK

Define these words by solving the parts. Use the Glossary or a dictionary as needed.

1. margins
2. gatherer
3. playmate
4. yester-eve
5. weal
6. debated
7. anon
8. rejoin
9. impel
10. propinquity
11. deriving

12. patter
13. fragment
14. purport
15. wiry
16. flickering
17. smouldered
18. evidence
19. proceed
20. gloated
21. usurp
22. hatred

23. undertake
24. horrors
25. benefit
26. strewn
27. studious
28. secrecy
29. earnest
30. clutched
31. gallows
32. aiding

PRE-READING QUESTIONS

Try answering these questions as you read.

Why does Hester Prynne intend to speak to Roger Chillingworth after all these years?
How does Roger Chillingworth respond?
How does Roger Chillingworth's appearance change?
Where does this conversation take place and what is Chillingworth doing there?
What does Hester decide to do next?

CHAPTER 14

HESTER AND THE PHYSICIAN

1 Hester bade little Pearl run down to the margin of the water, and play with the shells and tangled seaweed, until she should have talked awhile with yonder gatherer of herbs. So the child flew away like a bird, and, making bare her small white feet, went pattering along the moist margin of the sea. Here and there, she came to a full stop, and peeped curiously into a pool, left by the retiring tide as a mirror for Pearl to see her face in. Forth peeped at her, out of the pool, with dark, glistening curls around her head, and an elf-smile in her eyes, the image of a little maid, whom Pearl, having no other playmate, invited to take her hand and run a race with her. But the visionary little maid, on her part, beckoned likewise, as if to say,—"This is a better place! Come thou into the pool!" And Pearl, stepping in, mid-leg deep, beheld her own white feet at the bottom; while, out of a still lower depth, came the gleam of a kind of fragmentary smile, floating to and fro in the agitated water.

2 Meanwhile, her mother had accosted the physician.

3 "I would speak a word with you," said she,—"a word that concerns us much."

4 "Aha! And is it Mistress Hester that has a word for old Roger Chillingworth?" answered he, raising himself from his stooping posture. "With all my heart! Why, Mistress, I hear good things of you on all hands! No longer ago than yester-eve, a magistrate, a wise and godly man, was discoursing of your affairs, Mistress Hester, and whispered me that there had been question concerning you in the council. It was debated whether or no, with safety to the common weal, yonder scarlet letter might be taken off your bosom. On my life, Hester, I made my entreaty to the worshipful magistrate that it might be done forthwith!"

5 "It lies not in the pleasure of the magistrates to take off this badge," calmly replied Hester. "Were I worthy to be quit of it, it would fall away of its own nature or be transformed into something that should speak a different purport."

6 "Nay, then, wear it, if it suit you better," rejoined he. "A woman must needs follow her own fancy, touching the adornment of her person. The letter is gayly embroidered, and shows right bravely on your bosom!"

7 All this while, Hester had been looking steadily at the old man, and was shocked, as well as wonder-smitten, to discern what a change had been wrought upon him within the past seven years. It was not so much that he had grown older; for though the traces of advancing life were visible, he bore his age well, and seemed to retain a wiry vigor and alertness. But the former aspect of an intellectual and studious man, calm and quiet, which was what she best remembered in him, had altogether vanished, and been succeeded by an eager, searching, almost fierce, yet carefully guarded look. It seemed to be his wish and purpose to mask this expression with a smile; but the latter played him false, and flickered over his visage so derisively, that the spectator could see his blackness all the better for it. Ever and anon, too, there came a glare of red light out of his eyes; as if

the old man's soul were on fire, and kept on smouldering duskily within his breast, until, by some casual puff of passion, it was blown into a momentary flame. This he repressed as speedily as possible, and strove to look as if nothing of the kind had happened.

8 In a word, old Roger Chillingworth was a striking evidence of man's faculty of transforming himself into a devil, if he will only, for a reasonable space of time, undertake a devil's office. This unhappy person had effected such a transformation by devoting himself, for seven years, to the constant analysis of a heart full of torture, and deriving his enjoyment thence, and adding fuel to those fiery tortures which he analyzed and gloated over.

9 The scarlet letter burned on Hester Prynne's bosom. Here was another ruin, the responsibility of which came partly home to her.

10 "What see you in my face," asked the physician, "that you look at it so earnestly?"

11 "Something that would make me weep, if there were any tears bitter enough for it," answered she. "But let it pass! It is of yonder miserable man that I would speak."

12 "And what of him?" cried Roger Chillingworth eagerly, as if he loved the topic, and were glad of an opportunity to discuss it with the only person of whom he could make a confidant. "Not to hide the truth, Mistress Hester, my thoughts happen just now to be busy with the gentleman. So speak freely; and I will make answer."

13 "When we last spake together," said Hester, "now seven years ago, it was your pleasure to extort a promise of secrecy, as touching the former relation betwixt yourself and me. As the life and good fame of yonder man were in your hands, there seemed no choice to me, save to be silent, in accordance with your behest. Yet it was not without heavy misgivings that I thus bound myself; for, having cast off all duty towards other human beings, there remained a duty towards him; and something whispered me that I was betraying it, in pledging myself to keep your counsel. Since that day, no man is so near to him as you. You tread behind his every footstep. You are beside him, sleeping and waking. You search his thoughts. You burrow and rankle in his heart! Your clutch is on his life, and you cause him to die daily a living death; and still he knows you not. In permitting this, I have surely acted a false part by the only man to whom the power was left me to be true!"

14 "What choice had you?" asked Roger Chillingworth. "My finger, pointed at this man, would have hurled him from his pulpit into a dungeon,—thence, peradventure, to the gallows!"

15 "It had been better so!" said Hester Prynne.

16 "What evil have I done the man?" asked Roger Chillingworth again. "I tell thee, Hester Prynne, the richest fee that ever physician earned from monarch could not have bought such care as I have wasted on this miserable priest! But for my aid, his life would have burned away in torments, within the first two years after the perpetration of his crime and thine. For, Hester, his spirit lacked the

strength that could have borne up, as thine has, beneath a burden like thy scarlet letter. O, I could reveal a goodly secret! But enough! What art can do, I have exhausted on him. That he now breathes, and creeps about on earth, is owing all to me!"

17   "Better he had died at once!" said Hester Prynne.

18   "Yea woman, thou sayest truly!" cried old Roger Chillingworth, letting the lurid fire of his heart blaze out before her eyes. "Better had he died at once! Never did mortal suffer what this man has suffered. And all, all, in the sight of his worst enemy! He has been conscious of me. He has felt an influence dwelling always upon him like a curse. He knew, by some spiritual sense,—for the Creator never made another being so sensitive as this,—he knew that no friendly hand was pulling at his heartstrings, and that an eye was looking curiously into him, which sought only evil, and found it. But he knew not that the eye and hand were mine! With the superstition common to his brotherhood, he fancied himself given over to a fiend, to be tortured with frightful dreams, and desperate thoughts, the sting of remorse, and despair of pardon; as a foretaste of what awaits him beyond the grave. But it was the constant shadow of my presence!— the closest propinquity of the man whom he had most vilely wronged!—and who had grown to exist only by this perpetual poison of the direst revenge! Yea, indeed!—he did not err!—there was a fiend at his elbow! A mortal man, with once a human heart, has become a fiend for his especial torment!"

19   The unfortunate physician, while uttering these words, lifted his hands with a look of horror, as if he had beheld some frightful shape, which he could not recognize, usurping the place of his own image in a glass. It was one of those moments—which sometimes occur only at the interval of years—when a man's moral aspect is faithfully revealed to his mind's eye. Not improbably, he had never before viewed himself as he did now.

20   "Hast thou not tortured him enough?" said Hester, noticing the old man's look. "Has he not paid thee all?"

21   "No!—no!—He has but increased the debt!" answered the physician; and, as he proceeded, his manner lost its fiercer characteristics, and subsided into gloom. "Dost thou remember me, Hester, as I was nine years agone? Even then, I was in the autumn of my days, nor was it the early autumn. But all my life had been made up of earnest, studious, thoughtful, quiet years, bestowed faithfully for the increase of mine own knowledge, and faithfully, too, though this latter object was but casual to the other,—faithfully for the advancement of human welfare. No life had been more peaceful and innocent than mine; few lives so rich with benefits conferred. Dost thou remember me? Was I not, though you might deem me cold, nevertheless a man thoughtful for others, craving little for himself,— kind, true, just, and of constant, if not warm affections? Was I not all this?"

22   "All this, and more," said Hester.

23   "And what am I now?" demanded he, looking into her face, and permitting the whole evil within him to be written on his features. "I have already told thee what I am! A fiend! Who made me so?"

24   "It was myself!" cried Hester, shuddering. "It was I, not less than he. Why hast thou not avenged thyself on me?"

25   "I have left thee to the scarlet letter," replied Roger Chillingworth. "If that have not avenged me, I can do no more!"

26   He laid his finger on it, with a smile.

27   "It has avenged thee!" answered Hester Prynne.

28   "I judged no less," said the physician. "And now, what wouldst thou with me touching this man?"

29   "I must reveal the secret," answered Hester, firmly. "He must discern thee in thy true character. What may be the result, I know not. But this long debt of confidence, due from me to him, whose bane and ruin I have been, shall at length be paid. So far as concerns the overthrow or preservation of his fair fame and his earthly state, and perchance his life, he is in thy hands. Nor do I,—whom the scarlet letter has disciplined to truth, though it be the truth of red-hot iron, entering into the soul,—nor do I perceive such advantage in his living any longer a life of ghastly emptiness, that I shall stoop to implore thy mercy. Do with him as thou wilt! There is no good for him,—no good for me,—no good for thee! There is no good for little Pearl! There is no path to guide us out of this dismal maze!"

30   "Woman, I could wellnigh pity thee!" said Roger Chillingworth, unable to restrain a thrill of admiration too; for there was a quality almost majestic in the despair which she expressed. "Thou hadst great elements. Peradventure, hadst thou met earlier with a better love than mine, this evil had not been. I pity thee, for the good that has been wasted in thy nature!"

31   "And I thee," answered Hester Prynne, "for the hatred that has transformed a wise and just man to a fiend. Wilt thou yet purge it out of thee, and be once more human? If not for his sake, then doubly for thine own! Forgive, and leave his further retribution to the Power that claims it! I said, but now, that there could be no good event for him, or thee, or me, who are here wandering together in this gloomy maze of evil, and stumbling, at every step, over the guilt where-with we have strewn our path. It is not so! There might be good for thee, and thee alone, since thou hast been deeply wronged, and hast it at thy will to pardon. Wilt thou give up that only privilege? Wilt thou reject that priceless benefit?"

32   "Peace, Hester, peace!" replied the old man, with gloomy sternness. "It is not granted me to pardon. I have no such power as thou tellest me of. My old faith, long forgotten, comes back to me, and explains all that we do, and all we suffer. By thy first step awry, thou didst plant the germ of evil; but, since that moment, it has all been a dark necessity. Ye that have wronged me are not sinful, save in a kind of typical illusion; neither am I fiend-like, who have snatched a fiend's office from his hands. It is our fate. Let the black flower blossom as it may! Now go thy ways, and deal as thou wilt with yonder man."

33   He waved his hand, and betook himself again to his employment of gathering herbs.

CHAPTER 14

JOURNAL

1. **MLA Works Cited** *Using this model, record this book.*
   Author's Last Name, First Name. The Scarlet Letter. *1850.* Title of This Book.
   Ed. First Name Last Name. City: Publisher, year.
2. **Main Character(s)** *Describe each main character and explain why you think each is a main character.*
3. **Supporting Characters** *Describe each supporting character and explain why you think each is a supporting character.*
4. **Setting** *Describe the setting(s) and any relevant prop(s).*
5. **Sequence** *Outline the events in this chapter in order.*
6. **Plot** *Summarize this chapter's events in no more than two sentences.*
7. **Conflicts** *Identify and explain all conflicts involved in this chapter.*
8. **Significant Quotations** *Explain the importance of each of these quotations. Record the page number in the parentheses.*
   a. "'Were I worthy to be quit of [this badge], it would fall away of its own nature, or be transformed into something that should speak a different purport'" ( ).
   b. "In a word, old Roger Chillingworth was a striking evidence of man's faculty of transforming himself into a devil, if he will only, for a reasonable space of time, undertake a devil's office [. . .]" ( ).
   c. "'What art can do, I have exhausted on him. That he now breathes, and creeps about on earth, is owing all to me!'" ( ).
   d. "'No life had been more peaceful and innocent than mine; few lives so rich with benefits conferred. Dost thou remember me? Was I not, though you might deem me cold, nevertheless a man thoughtful for others, craving little for himself,—kind, true, just, and of constant, if not warm affections? Was I not all this?'" ( ).
   e. "'[. . .] I have already told thee what I am! A fiend! Who made me so?'" ( ).
9. **Recap** *Summarize what has happened so far, from the beginning of the book through this chapter.*

FOLLOW-UP QUESTIONS

6 SHORT QUESTIONS

Select the best answer for each.

____ 1. Hester Prynne speaks to Roger
Chillingworth
    a. in the prison.
    b. on the beach.
    c. in the forest.

____ 2. When Hester speaks to Roger
Chillingworth, he is
    a. gathering herbs.
    b. treating sick people.
    c. looking for Arthur
Dimmesdale.

____ 3. Hester asks Roger Chillingworth
    a. to heal Arthur Dimmes-
dale.
    b. to leave Arthur
Dimmesdale alone.
    c. to leave Boston.

____ 4. Hester accuses Roger Chillingworth of
    a. adultery.
    b. practicing medicine
without a license.
    c. revenge.

____ 5. Roger Chillingworth realizes
that
    a. he is not punishing
Arthur Dimmesdale.
    b. he should move out of
Boston.
    c. he has become evil.

____ 6. Hester begs Roger Chillingworth to
    a. forgive Arthur Dimmes-
dale.
    b. pray for guidance.
    c. save Arthur Dimmesdale's
health.

5 SIGNIFICANT QUOTATIONS

Explain the importance of each of these quotations.

1. "Ever and anon, too, there came a glare of red light out of his eyes; as if the old man's soul were on fire, and kept on smouldering duskily within his breast, until, by some casual puff of passion, it was blown into a momentary flame. This he repressed as speedily as possible, and strove to look as if nothing of the kind had happened."

2. "'Since that day, no man is so near to him as you. You tread behind his every footstep. You are beside him, sleeping and waking. You search his thoughts. You burrow and rankle in his heart! Your clutch is on his life, and you cause him to die daily a living death; and still he knows you not. In permitting this, I have surely acted a false part by the only man to whom the power was left me to be true!'"

3. "'What choice had you?' asked Roger Chillingworth. 'My finger, pointed at this man, would have hurled him from his pulpit into a dungeon,—thence, peradventure, to the gallows!'"

4. "The unfortunate physician, while uttering these words, lifted his hands with a look of horror, as if he had beheld some frightful shape, which he could not recognize, usurping the place of his own image in a glass."

5. "'I must reveal the secret,' answered Hester, firmly. 'He must discern thee in thy true character. What may be the result, I know not. But this long debt of confidence, due from me to him, whose bane and ruin I have been, shall at length be paid [. . .].'"

2 COMPREHENSION ESSAY QUESTIONS

Use specific details and information from the chapter to answer these questions as completely as possible.

1. "What does not kill you can make you stronger." Suffering can affect individuals in different ways. What effect(s) has suffering had on one of the major characters? Use specific details and information from the story to support your explanation.
2. Betrayal is a major theme in this story. How has one of the major characters betrayed or been betrayed by another character? Use specific details and information from the story to support you explanation.

DISCUSSION QUESTIONS

Be prepared to discuss these questions in class.

1. How does Roger Chillingworth react to Hester's request?
2. How does Roger Chillingworth see himself? How do you see him?

CHAPTER 15

HESTER AND PEARL

Use context clues to define these words before reading. Use a dictionary as needed.

1. Children who do not receive enough nutrients in their diet may develop *deformities* in their bones and skeletal systems. *Deformity* means _____
   _____.

2. The park rangers noted with concern how many trees on the mountainside had died from an unknown *blight*. *Blight* means _____
   _____.

3. During the dry season when there is no rain, the plants and ground become very *sere*. *Sere* means _____
   _____.

4. Because she likes to have plenty of food on hand, Susan buys enough groceries to *suffice* for a family three times the size of hers. *Suffice* means _____
   _____.

5. Nutritionists recommend that we consume at least five to eight servings a day of fruits and vegetables for a *wholesome* and healthful diet. *Wholesome* means
   _____.

6. Smoking cigarettes can have a *deleterious* effect on a person's lungs and breathing passages. *Deleterious* means _____
   _____.

7. Many scientists are predicting *ominous* consequences of global warning if the world does not take action to stop polluting the air and environment. *Ominous* means _____
   _____.

8. The professor was angry and *upbraided* the class for not having the projects completed on time. *Upbraid* means _____
   _____.

9. After watching a science fiction thriller, Loretta *marveled* at how realistic special effects have become in movies. *Marvel* means _____
_____.

10. Gloria likes to keep track of who sends her holiday and birthday cards so that she can *reciprocate* by sending them cards in return. *Reciprocate* means _____
_____.

11. Betraying the confidence of a trusting friend is a *foul* thing to do. *Foul* means
_____.

12. A child who can read and write at the early age of three shows much *precocity*. *Precocity* means _____
_____.

13. Lawyers and other professionals who must think on their feet need to have mental *acuteness* and sharp instincts. *Acuteness* means _____
_____.

14. A *malignant* growth in the body is cancerous and deadly to an individual, whereas a benign growth is not harmful. *Malignant* means _____
_____.

15. <u>*Phantom of the Opera*</u> is a play about a character with *hideous* scars from a fire, who hides in an opera house so as not to be seen and pitied. *Hideous* means
_____.

16. Absolutely nothing will grow in the *barren* ground near the abandoned chemical factory. *Barren* means _____
_____.

17. After winning her first case in court, Mary Beth gained many new clients and began a *flourishing* career as a defense attorney. *Flourish* means _____
_____.

18. Stefanie felt *betrayed* when Gina told her secrets to everyone at the party. *Betray* means _____
_____.

19. Evelyn kissed and *caressed* her baby daughter, Kristin. *Caress* means _____
_____.

20. After asking the children twice to clean up the playroom, the babysitter spoke with some *asperity* the third time. *Asperity* means _____
_____.

PRE-READING VOCABULARY
STRUCTURAL ATTACK

Define these words by solving the parts. Use the Glossary or a dictionary as needed.

1. naughty	11. wavered	21. purport
2. dexterity	12. reproach	22. inquiry
3. devise	13. seclusion	23. subsequent
4. drapery	14. eventide	24. sedulous
5. vivacity	15. impart	25. grubbed
6. acrid	16. repentance	26. ventured
7. sterling	17. lukewarm	27. hovered
8. absurdly	18. talisman	28. innate
9. incongruity	19. enigma	29. unflinching
10. grieve	20. flits	30. climates

PRE-READING QUESTIONS

Try answering these questions as you read.

How does Hester feel about Roger Chillingworth and his actions?
Why does Hester want to talk with the minister?
How does Pearl occupy herself at the beach?
What does Pearl ask her mother?

CHAPTER 15

HESTER AND PEARL

1 So Roger Chillingworth—a deformed old figure, with a face that haunted men's memories longer than they liked—took leave of Hester Prynne, and went stooping away along the earth. He gathered here and there an herb, or grubbed up a root, and put it into the basket on his arm. His gray beard almost touched the ground, as he crept onward. Hester gazed after him a little while, looking with a half-fantastic curiosity to see whether the tender grass of early spring would not be blighted beneath him, and show the wavering track of his footsteps, sere and brown, across its cheerful verdure. She wondered what sort of herbs they were, which the old man was so sedulous to gather. Would not the earth, quickened to an evil purpose by the sympathy of his eye, greet him with poisonous shrubs, of species hitherto unknown, that would start up under his fingers? Or might it suffice him, that every wholesome growth should be converted into something deleterious and malignant at his touch? Did the sun, which shone so brightly everywhere else, really fall upon him? Or was there, as it rather seemed, a circle

of ominous shadow moving along with his deformity, whichever way he turned himself? And whither was he now going? Would he not suddenly sink into the earth, leaving a barren and blasted spot, where, in due course of time, would be seen deadly nightshade, dogwood, henbane, and whatever else of vegetable wickedness the climate could produce, all flourishing with hideous luxuriance? Or would he spread bat's wings and flee away, looking so much the uglier, the higher he rose towards heaven?

2   "Be it sin or no," said Hester Prynne bitterly, as she still gazed after him, "I hate the man!"

3   She upbraided herself for the sentiment, but could not overcome or lessen it. Attempting to do so, she thought of those long-past days, in a distant land, when he used to emerge at eventide from the seclusion of his study, and sit down in the fire-light of their home, and in the light of her nuptial smile. He needed to bask himself in that smile, he said, in order that the chill of so many lonely hours among his books might be taken off the scholar's heart. Such scenes had once appeared not otherwise than happy, but now, as viewed through the dismal medium of her subsequent life, they classed themselves among her ugliest remembrances. She marvelled how such scenes could have been! She marvelled how she could ever have been wrought upon to marry him! She deemed it her crime most to be repented of, that she had ever endured, and reciprocated, the lukewarm grasp of his hand, and had suffered the smile of her lips and eyes to mingle and melt into his own. And it seemed a fouler offence committed by Roger Chillingworth, than any which had since been done him, that, in the time when her heart knew no better, he had persuaded her to fancy herself happy by his side.

4   "Yes, I hate him!" repeated Hester, more bitterly than before. "He betrayed me! He has done me worse wrong than I did him!"

5   Let men tremble to win the hand of woman, unless they win along with it the utmost passion of her heart! Else it may be their miserable fortune, as it was Roger Chillingworth's, when some mightier touch than their own may have awakened all her sensibilities, to be reproached even for the calm content, the marble image of happiness, which they will have imposed upon her as the warm reality. But Hester ought long ago to have done with this injustice. What did it betoken? Had seven long years, under the torture of the scarlet letter, inflicted so much of misery, and wrought out no repentance?

6   The emotions of that brief space, while she stood gazing after the crooked figure of old Roger Chillingworth, threw a dark light on Hester's state of mind, revealing much that she might not otherwise have acknowledged to herself.

7   He being gone, she summoned back her child.

8   "Pearl, Little Pearl! Where are you?"

9   Pearl, whose activity of spirit never flagged, had been at no loss for amusement while her mother talked with the old gatherer of herbs. At first, as already told, she had flirted fancifully with her own image in a pool of water, beckoning the phantom forth, and—as it declined to venture—seeking a passage for herself

into its sphere of impalpable earth and unattainable sky. Soon finding, however, that either she or the image was unreal, she turned elsewhere for better pastime. She made little boats out of birch-bark, and freighted them with snail-shells, and sent out more ventures on the mighty deep than any merchant in New England; but the larger part of them foundered near the shore. She seized a live horseshoe by the tail, and made prize of several five-fingers, and laid out a jelly-fish to melt in the warm sun. Then she took up the white foam, that streaked the line of the advancing tide, and threw it upon the breeze, scampering after it with winged footsteps, to catch the great snow-flakes ere they fell. Perceiving a flock of beach-birds, that fed and fluttered along the shore, the naughty child picked up her apron full of pebbles, and, creeping from rock to rock after these small sea-fowl, displayed remarkable dexterity in pelting them. One little gray bird, with a white breast, Pearl was almost sure, had been hit by a pebble, and fluttered away with a broken wing. But then the elf-child sighed, and gave up her sport; because it grieved her to have done harm to a little being that was as wild as the sea-breeze, or as wild as Pearl herself.

10 Her final employment was to gather sea-weed, of various kinds, and make herself a scarf, or mantle, and a headdress, and thus assume the aspect of a little mermaid. She inherited her mother's gift for devising drapery and costume. As the last touch to her mermaid's garb, Pearl took some eel-grass, and imitated, as best she could, on her own bosom, the decoration with which she was so familiar on her mother's. A letter,—the letter A,—but freshly green, instead of scarlet! The child bent her chin upon her breast, and contemplated this device with strange interest; even as if the one only thing for which she had been sent into the world was to make out its hidden import.

11 "I wonder if mother will ask me what it means!" thought Pearl.

12 Just then, she heard her mother's voice, and, flitting along as lightly as one of the little sea-birds, appeared before Hester Prynne, dancing, laughing, and pointing her finger to the ornament upon her bosom.

13 "My little Pearl," said Hester, after a moment's silence, "the green letter, and on thy childish bosom, has no purport. But dost thou know, my child, what this letter means which thy mother is doomed to wear?"

14 "Yes, mother," said the child. "It is the great letter A. Thou hast taught it me in the horn-book."

15 Hester looked steadily into her little face; but, though there was that singular expression which she had so often remarked in her black eyes, she could not satisfy herself whether Pearl really attached any meaning to the symbol. She felt a morbid desire to ascertain the point.

16 "Dost thou know, child, wherefore thy mother wears this letter?"

17 "Truly do I!" answered Pearl, looking brightly into her mother's face. "It is for the same reason that the minister keeps his hand over his heart!"

18 "And what reason is that?" asked Hester, half smiling at the absurd incongruity of the child's observation; but, on second thoughts, turning pale. "What has the letter to do with any heart, save mine?"

19   "Nay, mother, I have told all I know," said Pearl, more seriously than she was wont to speak. "Ask yonder old man whom thou hast been talking with! It may be he can tell. But in good earnest now, mother dear, what does this scarlet letter mean?—and why dost thou wear it on thy bosom?—and why does the minister keep his hand over his heart?"

20   She took her mother's hand in both her own, and gazed into her eyes with an earnestness that was seldom seen in her wild and capricious character. The thought occurred to Hester, that the child might really be seeking to approach her with childlike confidence, and doing what she could, and as intelligently as she knew how, to establish a meeting-point of sympathy. It showed Pearl in an unwonted aspect. Heretofore, the mother, while loving her child with the intensity of a sole affection, had schooled herself to hope for little other return than the waywardness of an April breeze; which spends its time in airy sport, and has its gusts of inexplicable passion, and is petulant in its best of moods, and chills oftener than caresses you, when you take it to your bosom; in requital of which misdemeanours, it will sometimes, of its own vague purpose, kiss your cheek with a kind of doubtful tenderness, and play gently with your hair, and then begone about its other idle business, leaving a dreamy pleasure at your heart. And this, moreover, was a mother's estimate of the child's disposition. Any other observer might have seen few but unamiable traits, and have given them a far darker coloring. But now the idea came strongly into Hester's mind, that Pearl, with her remarkable precocity and acuteness, might already have approached the age when she could be made a friend, and intrusted with as much of her mother's sorrows as could be imparted, without irreverence either to the parent or the child. In the little chaos of Pearl's character, there might be seen emerging—and could have been, from the very first—the stedfast principles of an unflinching courage,—an uncontrollable will,—a sturdy pride, which might be disciplined into self-respect,—and a bitter scorn of many things which, when examined, might be found to have the taint of falsehood in them. She possessed affections, too, though hitherto acrid and disagreeable, as are the richest flavors of unripe fruit. With all these sterling attributes, thought Hester, the evil which she inherited from her mother must be great indeed, if a noble woman do not grow out of this elfish child.

21   Pearl's inevitable tendency to hover about the enigma of the scarlet letter seemed an innate quality of her being. From the earliest epoch of her conscious life, she had entered upon this as her appointed mission. Hester had often fancied that Providence had a design of justice and retribution, in endowing the child with this marked propensity; but never, until now, had she bethought herself to ask, whether, linked with that design, there might not likewise be a purpose of mercy and beneficence. If little Pearl were entertained with faith and trust, as a spirit-messenger no less than an earthly child, might it not be her errand to soothe away the sorrow that lay cold in her mother's heart, and converted it into a tomb?—and to help her to overcome the passion, once so wild, and even yet neither dead nor asleep, but only imprisoned within the same tomb-like heart?

22   Such were some of the thoughts that now stirred in Hester's mind, with as much vivacity of impression as if they had actually been whispered into her ear. And there was little Pearl, all this while, holding her mother's hand in both her own, and turning her face upward, while she put these searching questions, once, and again, and still a third time.

23   "What does the letter mean, mother?—and why dost thou wear it?—and why does the minister keep his hand over his heart?"

24   "What shall I say?" thought Hester to herself.—"No! If this be the price of the child's sympathy, I cannot pay it!"

25   Then she spoke aloud.

26   "Silly Pearl," said she, "what questions are these? There are many things in this world that a child must not ask about. What know I of the minister's heart? And as for the scarlet letter, I wear it for the sake of its gold thread!"

27   In all the seven bygone years, Hester Prynne had never before been false to the symbol on her bosom. It may be that it was the talisman of a stern and severe, but yet a guardian spirit, who now forsook her; as recognizing that, in spite of his strict watch over her heart, some new evil had crept into it, or some old one had never been expelled. As for little Pearl, the earnestness soon passed out of her face.

28   But the child did not see fit to let the matter drop. Two or three times, as her mother and she went homeward, and as often at supper-time, and while Hester was putting her to bed, and once after she seemed to be fairly asleep, Pearl looked up, with mischief gleaming in her black eyes.

29   "Mother," said she, "what does the scarlet letter mean?"

30   And the next morning, the first indication the child gave of being awake was by popping up her head from the pillow, and making that other inquiry, which she had so unaccountably connected with her investigations about the scarlet letter:—

31   "Mother!—Mother!—Why does the minister keep his hand over his heart?"

32   "Hold thy tongue, naughty child!" answered her mother, with an asperity that she had never permitted to herself before. "Do not tease me; else I shall shut thee into the dark closet!"

CHAPTER 15

JOURNAL

1. **MLA Works Cited** *Using this model, record this book.*
   Author's Last Name, First Name. The Scarlet Letter. 1850. Title of This Book.
   Ed. First Name Last Name. City: Publisher, year.
2. **Main Character(s)** *Describe each main character and explain why you think each is a main character.*
3. **Supporting Characters** *Describe each supporting character and explain why you think each is a supporting character.*
4. **Setting** *Describe the setting(s) and any relevant prop(s).*

5. **Sequence** *Outline the events in this chapter in order.*
6. **Plot** *Summarize this chapter's events in no more than two sentences.*
7. **Conflicts** *Identify and explain all conflicts involved in this chapter.*
8. **Significant Quotations** *Explain the importance of each of these quotations. Record the page number in the parentheses.*
   a. "So Roger Chillingworth—a deformed old figure, with a face that haunted men's memories longer than they liked—took leave of Hester Prynne, and went stooping away along the earth. He gathered here and there an herb, or grubbed up a root, and put it into the basket on his arm. His gray beard almost touched the ground, as he crept onward [. . .]" (   ).
   b. " 'Be it sin or no,' said Hester Prynne bitterly, as she still gazed after him, 'I hate the man!' " (   ).
   c. "And it seemed a fouler offence committed by Roger Chillingworth, than any which had since been done him, that, in the time when her heart knew no better, he had persuaded her to fancy herself happy by his side" (   ).
   d. "As the last touch to her mermaid's garb, Pearl took some eel-grass, and imitated, as best she could, on her own bosom, the decoration with which she was so familiar on her mother's. A letter,—the letter A,—but freshly green, instead of scarlet! [. . .]" (   ).
   e. " 'Hold thy tongue, naughty child!' answered her mother, with an asperity that she had never permitted to herself before. 'Do not tease me; else I shall shut thee into the dark closet!' " (   ).
9. **Recap** *Summarize what has happened so far, from the beginning of the book through this chapter.*

FOLLOW-UP QUESTIONS

6 SHORT QUESTIONS

Select the best answer for each.

____ 1. As Roger Chillingworth walks away from Hester, she wonders if
   a. the grass might wither away under his feet.
   b. angels would bear him away.
   c. he were on the edge of madness.

____ 2. Roger Chillingworth continues
   a. arguing with Hester Prynne.
   b. praying for forgiveness.
   c. gathering plants.

____ 3. Hester decides that
   a. she hates Roger Chillingworth.
   b. she hates Arthur Dimmesdale.
   c. she should forgive Arthur Dimmesdale.

____ 4. Out of eel-grass, Pearl makes
     a. a mermaid costume.
     b. a green letter A.
     c. a doll with a letter A.

____ 5. Hester considers
     a. leaving New England.
     b. killing Roger Chilling-
       worth.
     c. confiding in Pearl as a
       friend.

____ 6. When Pearl asks Hester why
     she wears the scarlet letter,
     a. Hester refuses to answer
       at all.
     b. Hester tells Pearl a lie.
     c. Hester tells Pearl the
       truth.

5 SIGNIFICANT QUOTATIONS

Explain the importance of each of these quotations.

1. "Would he not suddenly sink into the earth, leaving a barren and blasted spot, where, in due course of time, would be seen deadly nightshade, dogwood, henbane, and whatever else of vegetable wickedness the climate could produce, all flourishing with hideous luxuriance? Or would he spread bat's wings and flee away, looking so much the uglier, the higher he rose towards heaven?"

2. "'Yes, I hate him!' repeated Hester, more bitterly than before. 'He betrayed me! He has done me worse than I did him!'"

3. "Let men tremble to win the hand of woman, unless they win along with it the utmost passion of her heart! Else it may be their miserable fortune, as it was Roger Chillingworth's, when some mightier touch than their own may have awakened all her sensibilities, to be reproached even for the calm content, the marble image of happiness, which they will have imposed upon her as the warm reality [. . .]."

4. "'What does the letter mean, mother?—and why dost thou wear it?—and why does the minister keep his hand over his heart?'"

5. "'Silly Pearl,' said she, 'what questions are these? There are many things in this world that a child must not ask about. What know I of the minister's heart? And as for the scarlet letter, I wear it for the sake of its gold thread!'"

2 COMPREHENSION ESSAY QUESTIONS

Use specific details and information from the chapter to answer these questions as completely as possible.

1. Children often imitate their parents. How does Pearl imitate Hester and how does Hester react? Use specific details and information from the story to support your explanation.

2. Many characters feel guilty about their actions in <u>The Scarlet Letter</u>. Why does Hester Prynne feel guilty at this time and what does she do about it? Use specific details and information from this chapter and elsewhere in the novel in your explanation.

DISCUSSION QUESTIONS

Be prepared to discuss these questions in class.

1. How does Hester Prynne feel about Roger Chillingworth? Is she right to feel this way?
2. How does Pearl keep herself busy at the beach?

CHAPTER 16

A FOREST WALK

Use context clues to define these words before reading. Use a dictionary as needed.

1. On their wedding day, Monica and Billy declared their love would be true and *constant*, for all the days of their lives. *Constant* means _____
   _____.

2. At the beginning of the new school year, Brian always feels a new *resolve* to study harder and learn even more than last year. *Resolve* means _____
   _____.

3. Although Tracy said she came to the party to celebrate the holiday, we suspect she had the *ulterior* motive of seeing her old boyfriend. *Ulterior* means
   _____.

4. Driving near large electrical substations often causes *interference* on my car radio, sometimes blocking the signal, at other times, creating an irritating noise. *Interference* means _____
   _____.

5. From the hushed conversations and the odd phone calls, Jill had a strong *suspicion* that her family was planning a surprise party for her birthday. *Suspicion* means _____
   _____.

6. The fog was so *dense* on the road that I could not see more than two feet in front of me. *Dense* means _____
   _____.

7. Being very *superstitious*, Wilson always carries a shiny new penny in his pocket when a test or big game is coming up. *Superstitious* means _____
   _____.

8. Randy wanted *privacy* when he proposed to Jami, so he brought her to the beach at midnight so they could be alone. *Privacy* means _____
   _____.

9. Walking at a fast and even *pace* burns more calories and is better for your heart than walking slowly. *Pace* means _____
_____.

10. After the hurricane, the town did not allow anyone to go swimming for fear that strong ocean *currents* would carry swimmers out to sea. *Current* means
_____.

11. The ketchup *gushed* all over the table when Aimee squeezed the plastic bottle too hard. *Gushed* means _____
_____.

12. During the prehistoric *epoch*, dinosaurs roamed the earth. *Epoch* means
_____.

13. While hiking through the woods, Gert and Peter stopped for lunch at a shady *dell*, a small wooded hollow off the trail. *Dell* means _____
_____.

14. When Iris won the lottery, she became so excited she could hardly speak, *babbling* nonsense instead. *Babble* means _____
_____.

15. Whether reading a poem or singing a song, the orator's *cadence* was elegant and rhythmic. *Cadence* means _____
_____.

16. Dirt, large rocks, and huge *boulders* roared down the mountainside during the avalanche. *Boulders* means _____
_____.

17. After working overtime for three nights in a row, Hassan looked *haggard* and tired. *Haggard* means _____
_____.

18. When my normally very active son is *listless* and has no energy, I check to see if he has a fever. *Listless* means _____
_____.

19. After a bout with the flu, Greg felt rather weak and *feeble*, too unsteady to leave his bed. *Feeble* means _____
_____.

20. After knocking over the table and breaking all the glasses, Terry was so *penitent* that he immediately began to clean up the mess and offered to buy a new set of glasses. *Penitent* means _____
_____.

PRE-READING VOCABULARY
STRUCTURAL ATTACK

Define these words by solving the parts. Use the Glossary or a dictionary as needed.

1. vainly	8. strayed	15. impart
2. meditative	9. rapidly	16. loquacity
3. amiss	10. aloft	17. staffs
4. convert	11. impute	18. seclusion
5. vivacity	12. inconvenient	19. scintillate
6. lamentation	13. impending	20. accumulate
7. eddies	14. lingering	21. prattled

PRE-READING QUESTIONS

Try answering these questions as you read.

Why does Hester want to meet with Arthur Dimmesdale? Why does she choose
the forest?
Where does Pearl play?
What does Pearl ask her mother about?

CHAPTER 16

A FOREST WALK

1 Hester Prynne remained constant in her resolve to make known to Mr. Dimmesdale, at whatever risk of present pain or ulterior consequences, the true character of the man who had crept into his intimacy. For several days, however, she vainly sought an opportunity of addressing him in some of the meditative walks which she knew him to be in the habit of taking, along the shores of the peninsula, or on the wooded hills of the neighbouring country. There would have been no scandal, indeed, nor peril to the holy whiteness of the clergyman's good fame, had she visited him in his own study; where many a penitent, ere now, had confessed sins of perhaps as deep a dye as the one betokened by the scarlet letter. But, partly that she dreaded the secret or undisguised interference of old Roger Chillingworth, and partly that her conscious heart imputed suspicion where

none could have been felt, and partly that both the minister and she would need the whole wide world to breathe in, while they talked together,—for all these reasons, Hester never thought of meeting him in any narrower privacy than beneath the open sky.

2　　At last, while attending in a sick-chamber, whither the Reverend Mr. Dimmesdale had been summoned to make a prayer, she learnt that he had gone, the day before, to visit the Apostle Eliot, among his Indian converts. He would probably return, by a certain hour, in the afternoon of the morrow. Betimes, therefore, the next day, Hester took little Pearl,—who was necessarily the companion of all her mother's expeditions, however inconvenient her presence,—and set forth.

3　　The road, after the two wayfarers had crossed from the peninsula to the mainland, was no other than a footpath. It straggled onward into the mystery of the primeval forest. This hemmed it in so narrowly, and stood so black and dense on either side, and disclosed such imperfect glimpses of the sky above, that, to Hester's mind, it imaged not amiss the moral wilderness in which she had so long been wandering. The day was chill and sombre. Overhead was a gray expanse of cloud, slightly stirred, however, by a breeze; so that a gleam of flickering sunshine might now and then be seen at its solitary play along the path. This flitting cheerfulness was always at the farther extremity of some long vista through the forest. The sportive sunlight—feebly sportive, at best, in the predominant pensiveness of the day and scene—withdrew itself as they came nigh, and left the spots where it had danced the drearier, because they had hoped to find them bright.

4　　"Mother," said little Pearl, "the sunshine does not love you. It runs away and hides itself, because it is afraid of something on your bosom. Now, see! There it is, playing, a good way off. Stand you here, and let me run and catch it. I am but a child. It will not flee from me; for I wear nothing on my bosom yet!"

5　　"Nor ever will, my child, I hope," said Hester.

6　　"And why not, mother?" asked Pearl, stopping short, just at the beginning of her race. "Will not it come of its own accord, when I am a woman grown?"

7　　"Run away, child," answered her mother, "and catch the sunshine! It will soon be gone."

8　　Pearl set forth, at a great pace, and, as Hester smiled to perceive, did actually catch the sunshine, and stood laughing in the midst of it, all brightened by its splendor, and scintillating with the vivacity excited by rapid motion. The light lingered about the lonely child, as if glad of such a playmate, until her mother had drawn almost nigh enough to step into the magic circle too.

9　　"It will go now!" said Pearl, shaking her head.

10　　"See!" answered Hester, smiling. "Now I can stretch out my hand, and grasp some of it."

11　　As she attempted to do so, the sunshine vanished; or, to judge from the bright expression that was dancing on Pearl's features, her mother could have fancied that the child had absorbed it into herself, and would give it forth again, with a gleam about her path, as they should plunge into some gloomier shade.

There was no other attribute that so much impressed her with a sense of new and untransmitted vigor in Pearl's nature, as this never-failing vivacity of spirits; she had not the disease of sadness, which almost all children, in these latter days, inherit, with the scrofula, from the troubles of their ancestors. Perhaps this too was a disease, and but the reflex of the wild energy with which Hester had fought against her sorrows, before Pearl's birth. It was certainly a doubtful charm, imparting a hard, metallic luster to the child's character. She wanted—what some people want throughout life—a grief that should deeply touch her, and thus humanize and make her capable of sympathy. But there was time enough yet for little Pearl!

12   "Come, my child!" said Hester, looking about her, from the spot where Pearl had stood still in the sunshine. "We will sit down a little way within the wood, and rest ourselves."

13   "I am not aweary, mother," replied the little girl. "But you may sit down, if you will tell me a story meanwhile."

14   "A story, child!" said Hester. "And about what?"

15   "O, a story about the Black Man!" answered Pearl, taking hold of her mother's gown, and looking up, half earnestly, half mischievously, into her face. "How he haunts this forest, and carries a book with him,—a big, heavy book, with iron clasps; and how this ugly Black Man offers his book and an iron pen to every body that meets him here among the trees; and they are to write their names with their own blood. And then he sets his mark on their bosoms! Didst thou ever meet the Black Man, mother?"

16   "And who told you this story, Pearl?" asked her mother, recognizing a common superstition of the period.

17   "It was the old dame in the chimney-corner, at the house where you watched last night," said the child. "But she fancied me asleep while she was talking of it. She said that a thousand and a thousand people had met him here, and had written in his book, and have his mark on them. And that ugly-tempered lady, old Mistress Hibbins, was one. And, mother, the old dame said that this scarlet letter was the Black Man's mark on thee, and that it glows like a red flame when thou meetest him at midnight, here in the dark wood. Is it true, mother? And dost thou go to meet him in the night-time?"

18   "Didst thou ever awake, and find thy mother gone?" asked Hester.

19   "Not that I remember," said the child. "If thou fearest to leave me in our cottage, thou mightest take me along with thee. I would very gladly go! But, mother, tell me now! Is there such a Black Man? And didst thou ever meet him? And is this his mark?"

20   "Wilt thou let me be at peace, if I once tell thee?" asked her mother.

21   "Yes, if thou tellest me all," answered Pearl.

22   "Once in my life I met the Black Man!" said her mother. "This scarlet letter is his mark!"

23   Thus conversing, they entered sufficiently deep into the wood to secure themselves from the observation of any casual passenger along the forest-track.

Here they sat down on a luxuriant heap of moss; which, at some epoch of the preceding century, had been a gigantic pine, with its roots and trunk in the darksome shade, and its head aloft in the upper atmosphere. It was a little dell where they had seated themselves, with a leaf-strewn bank rising gently on either side, and a brook flowing through the midst, over a bed of fallen and drowned leaves. The trees impending over it had flung down great branches, from time to time, which choked up the current, and compelled it to form eddies and black depths at some points; while, in its swifter and livelier passages, there appeared a channel way of pebbles, and brown, sparkling sand. Letting the eyes follow along the course of the stream, they could catch the reflected light from its water, at some short distance within the forest, but soon lost all traces of it amid the bewilderment of tree-trunks and underbrush, and here and there a huge rock, covered over with gray lichens. All these giant trees and boulders of granite seemed intent on making a mystery of the course of this small brook; fearing, perhaps, that, with its never-ceasing loquacity, it should whisper tales out of the heart of the old forest whence it flowed, or mirror its revelations on the smooth surface of a pool. Continually, indeed, as it stole onward, the streamlet kept up a babble, kind, quiet, soothing, but melancholy, like the voice of a young child that was spending its infancy without playfulness, and knew not how to be merry among sad acquaintance and events of sombre hue.

24   "O brook! O foolish and tiresome little brook!" cried Pearl, after listening awhile to its talk. "Why art thou so sad? Pluck up a spirit, and do not be all the time sighing and murmuring!"

25   But the brook, in the course of its little lifetime among the forest-trees, had gone through so solemn an experience that it could not help talking about it, and seemed to have nothing else to say. Pearl resembled the brook, inasmuch as the current of her life gushed from a well-spring as mysterious, and had flowed through scenes shadowed as heavily with gloom. But, unlike the little stream, she danced and sparkled, and prattled airily along her course.

26   "What does this sad little brook say, mother?" inquired she.

27   "If thou hadst a sorrow of thine own, the brook might tell thee of it," answered her mother, "even as it is telling me of mine! But now, Pearl, I hear a footstep along the path, and the noise of one putting aside the branches. I would have thee betake thyself to play, and leave me to speak with him that comes yonder."

28   "Is it the Black Man?" asked Pearl.

29   "Wilt thou go and play, child?" repeated her mother. "But do not stray far into the wood. And take heed that thou come at my first call."

30   "Yes, mother," answered Pearl. "But, if it be the Black Man, wilt thou not let me stay a moment, and look at him, with his big book under his arm?"

31   "Go, silly child!" said her mother, impatiently. "It is no Black Man! Thou canst see him now through the trees. It is the minister!"

32   "And so it is!" said the child. "And, mother, he has his hand over his heart! Is it because, when the minister wrote his name in the book, the Black Man set his

mark in that place? But why does he not wear it outside his bosom, as thou dost, mother?"

33   "Go now, child, and thou shalt tease me as thou wilt another time!" cried Hester Prynne. "But do not stray far. Keep where thou canst hear the babble of the brook."

34   The child went singing away, following up the current of the brook, and striving to mingle a more lightsome cadence with its melancholy voice. But the little stream would not be comforted, and still kept telling its unintelligible secret of some very mournful mystery that had happened—or making a prophetic lamentation about something that was yet to happen—within the verge of the dismal forest. So Pearl, who had enough of shadow in her own little life, chose to break off all acquaintance with this repining brook. She set herself, therefore, to gathering violets and wood-anemones, and some scarlet columbines that she found growing in the crevices of a high rock.

35   When her elf-child had departed, Hester Prynne made a step or two towards the track that led through the forest, but still remained under the deep shadow of the trees. She beheld the minister advancing along the path, entirely alone, and leaning on a staff which he had cut by the way-side. He looked haggard and feeble, and betrayed a nerveless despondency in his air, which had never so remarkably characterized him in his walks about the settlement, nor in any other situation where he deemed himself liable to notice. Here it was wofully visible, in this intense seclusion of the forest, which of itself would have been a heavy trial to the spirits. There was a listlessness in his gait; as if he saw no reason for taking one step farther, nor felt any desire to do so, but would have been glad, could he be glad of any thing, to fling himself down at the root of the nearest tree, and lie there passive for evermore. The leaves might bestrew him, and the soil gradually accumulate and form a little hillock over his frame, no matter whether there were life in it or no. Death was too definite an object to be wished for, or avoided.

36   To Hester's eye, the Reverend Mr. Dimmesdale exhibited no symptom of positive and vivacious suffering, except that, as little Pearl had remarked, he kept his hand over his heart.

CHAPTER 16

JOURNAL

1. **MLA Works Cited** *Using this model, record this book.*
   Author's Last Name, First Name. The Scarlet Letter. *1850.* Title of This Book.
   Ed. First Name Last Name. City: Publisher, year.
2. **Main Character(s)** *Describe each main character and explain why you think each is a main character.*
3. **Supporting Characters** *Describe each supporting character and explain why you think each is a supporting character.*
4. **Setting** *Describe the setting(s) and any relevant prop(s).*

5. **Sequence** *Outline the events in this chapter in order.*
6. **Plot** *Summarize this chapter's events in no more than two sentences.*
7. **Conflicts** *Identify and explain all conflicts involved in this chapter.*
8. **Significant Quotations** *Explain the importance of each of these quotations. Record the page number in the parentheses.*

   a. "But, partly that she dreaded the secret or undisguised interference of old Roger Chillingworth, and partly that her conscious heart imputed suspicion where none could have been felt, and partly that both the minister and she would need the whole wide world to breathe in, while they talked together,—for all these reasons, Hester never thought of meeting him in any narrower privacy than beneath the open sky" (   ).

   b. " 'Mother,' said little Pearl, 'the sunshine does not love you. It runs away and hides itself, because it is afraid of something on your bosom. Now, see! There it is, playing, a good way off. Stand you here, and let me run and catch it. I am but a child. It will not flee from me; for I wear nothing on my bosom yet!' " (   ).

   c. " 'Once in my life I met the Black Man!' said her mother. 'This scarlet letter is his mark!' " (   ).

   d. "Pearl resembled the brook, inasmuch as the current of her life gushed from a well-spring as mysterious, and had flowed through scenes shadowed as heavily with gloom. But, unlike the little stream, she danced and sparkled, and prattled airily along her course" (   ).

   e. "She beheld the minister advancing along the path, entirely alone, and leaning on a staff which he had cut by the way-side. He looked haggard and feeble, and betrayed a nerveless despondency in his air [. . .]" (   ).

9. **Recap** *Summarize what has happened so far, from the beginning of the book through this chapter.*

FOLLOW-UP QUESTIONS

6 SHORT QUESTIONS

Select the <u>best</u> answer for each.

____ 1. Hester resolves to
    a. confront Roger Chillingworth.
    b. tell Arthur Dimmesdale the truth about Roger Chillingworth.
    c. keep Roger Chillingworth's secret.

____ 2. Hester waits for Arthur
    a. at the beach.
    b. in Arthur's study.
    c. in the forest.

____ 3. Arthur Dimmesdale returns from visiting
    a. the Apostle Eliot and the Indians.
    b. old John Wilson.
    c. sick Puritans.

____ 4. Pearl plays
    a. in the shade.
    b. in the sunshine.
    c. in the rain.

____ 5. Pearl asks for a story about
    a. Mistress Hibbins.
    b. the Black Man's book.
    c. Arthur Dimmesdale.

____ 6. When Arthur approaches Hester, his appearance is
    a. weak.
    b. young.
    c. strong.

5 SIGNIFICANT QUOTATIONS

Explain the importance of each of these quotations.

1. "Hester Prynne remained constant in her resolve to make known to Mr. Dimmesdale, at whatever risk of present pain or ulterior consequences, the true character of the man who had crept into his intimacy [. . .]."

2. "Pearl set forth, at a great pace, and, as Hester smiled to perceive, did actually catch the sunshine, and stood laughing in the midst of it, all brightened by its splendor, and scintillating with the vivacity excited by rapid motion. The light lingered about the lonely child, as if glad of such a playmate, until her mother had drawn almost nigh enough to step into the magic circle too."

3. "'And, mother, the old dame said that this scarlet letter was the Black Man's mark on thee, and that it glows like a red flame when thou meetest him at midnight, here in the dark wood. Is it true, mother? And dost thou go to meet him in the night-time?'"

4. "'And, mother, he has his hand over his heart! It is because, when the minister wrote his name in the book, the Black Man set his mark in that place? But why does he not wear it outside his bosom, as thou dost, mother?'"

5. "There was a listlessness in his gait; as if he saw no reason for taking one step farther, nor felt any desire to do so, but would have been glad, could he be glad of any thing, to fling himself down at the root of the nearest tree, and lie there passive for evermore [. . .]."

2 COMPREHENSION ESSAY QUESTIONS

Use specific details and information from the chapter to answer these questions as completely as possible.

1. Pearl is old enough to have heard some legends and superstitions. What superstition does she ask her mother about? Why is this important to her? Use specific details and information from the story to support your explanation.

2. Darkness and sunshine are part of the setting in this chapter. How does the sunshine highlight or reveal Pearl's character? What does the absence of sunshine show about Hester Prynne? Use specific details and information from the chapter in your explanation.

DISCUSSION QUESTIONS

Be prepared to discuss these questions in class.

1. What does Pearl ask her mother about?
2. What is the forest like and why does Hester go there?

CHAPTERS 13–16

JOURNAL

1. **MLA Works Cited** *Using this model, record this book.*
   Author's Last Name, First Name. The Scarlet Letter. *1850.* Title of This Book.
   Ed. First Name Last Name. City: Publisher, year.
2. **Main Character(s)** *Describe each main character and explain why you think each is a main character.*
3. **Supporting Characters** *Describe each supporting character and explain why you think each is a supporting character.*
4. **Setting** *Describe the setting(s) and any relevant prop(s).*
5. **Sequence** *Outline the events in these chapters in order.*
6. **Plot** *Summarize these chapters' events in no more than five sentences.*
7. **Conflicts** *Identify and explain all conflicts involved in these chapters.*
8. **Significant Quotations** *Explain the importance of each of these quotations. Record the page number in the parentheses.*
   a. "His nerve seemed absolutely destroyed. His moral force was abased into more than childish weakness. It grovelled helpless on the ground, even while his intellectual faculties retained their pristine strength [. . .]" (   ).
   b. "She never battled with the public, but submitted uncomplainingly to its worst usage; she made no claim upon it, in requital for what she suffered; she did not weigh upon its sympathies. Then, also, the blameless purity of her life, during all these years in which she had been set apart to infamy, was reckoned largely in her favor [. . .]" (   ).
   c. "In fine, Hester Prynne resolved to meet her former husband, and do what might be in her power for the rescue of the victim on whom he had so evidently set his gripe [. . .]" (   ).
   d. "This unhappy person had effected such a transformation by devoting himself, for seven years, to the constant analysis of a heart full of torture, and deriving his enjoyment thence, and adding fuel to those fiery tortures which he analyzed and gloated over" (   ).
   e. "'But for my aid, his life would have burned away in torments, within the first two years after the perpetration of his crime and thine. For, Hester, his spirit lacked the strength that could have borne up, as thine has, beneath a burden like thy scarlet letter'" (   ).
   f. "'No life had been more peaceful and innocent than mine; few lives so rich with benefits conferred. Dost thou remember me? [. . .]'" (   ).
   g. "'I must reveal the secret,' answered Hester, firmly. 'He must discern thee in thy true character. What may be the result, I know not [. . .]'" (   ).
   h. "'And I [pity] thee,' answered Hester Prynne, 'for the hatred that has transformed a wise and just man to a fiend! Wilt thou yet purge it out of thee, and be once more human? [. . .]'" (   ).
   i. "Let men tremble to win the hand of woman, unless they win along with it the utmost passion of her heart! [. . .]" (   ).

j. "'Mother,' said little Pearl, 'the sunshine does not love you. It runs away and hides itself, because it is afraid of something on your bosom. [. . .] I am but a child. It will not flee from me; for I wear nothing on my bosom yet!'" (   ).

9. **Recap** *Summarize what has happened so far, from the beginning of the novel through these chapters.*

FOLLOW-UP QUESTIONS

20 SHORT QUESTIONS

Select the <u>best</u> answer for each.

_____ 1. Since Hester Prynne first stood with her infant on the scaffold
    a. three years have passed.
    b. seven years have passed.
    c. ten years have passed.

_____ 2. Hester is shocked at
    a. Arthur's deteriorated condition.
    b. Roger's success as a physician.
    c. Pearl's behavior.

_____ 3. The townspeople now
    a. fear Hester Prynne.
    b. treat Hester Prynne the same as they always have.
    c. respect Hester Prynne.

_____ 4. Hester's appearance
    a. is very feminine.
    b. is repressed and severe.
    c. is colorful and defiant.

_____ 5. Hester feels guilty about the changes in
    a. Arthur.
    b. Roger.
    c. Arthur and Roger.

_____ 6. Chillingworth gloats that
    a. he has kept Arthur Dimmesdale alive to make him suffer.
    b. he is in great health and will live for a long time.
    c. he is on good terms with the magistrates and governor.

_____ 7. Hester thinks that
    a. she should give Pearl up for adoption.
    b. Arthur Dimmesdale is too popular with the townspeople.
    c. Roger Chillingworth is responsible for the minister's weakened state.

_____ 8. Roger Chillingworth is obsessed with
    a. adultery.
    b. revenge.
    c. spiritual growth.

_____ 9. Roger Chillingworth realizes
    a. that he has become evil but will not change his behavior.
    b. that he wants to return to the Old World.
    c. that Hester is weak and cannot stand up for herself.

____ 10. Hester says she hates
    a. Arthur Dimmesdale.
    b. Roger Chillingworth.
    c. Governor Winthrop.

____ 11. Hester's letter A, to some
people, now means
    a. able.
    b. angel.
    c. artistic.

____ 12. Hester worries that Arthur
Dimmesdale
    a. has no friends.
    b. has lost his sanity.
    c. will confront Roger
       Chillingworth.

____ 13. The sunshine seems to follow
    a. Roger Chillingworth.
    b. Hester Prynne.
    c. Pearl.

____ 14. When Pearl asks Hester why
she wears the scarlet letter,
    a. Hester gives no answer.
    b. Hester lies to Pearl.
    c. Hester tells Pearl the
       truth.

____ 15. Hester Prynne confronts
Roger Chillingworth
    a. at the prison.
    b. in the forest.
    c. on the beach.

____ 16. Roger Chillingworth has a
basket of
    a. berries.
    b. roots and herbs.
    c. clothes.

____ 17. Hester asks Roger Chillingworth
    a. to stop hurting Arthur
       Dimmesdale.
    b. to leave Boston and return
       to the Old World.
    c. to heal Arthur Dimmes-
       dale's illness.

____ 18. Pearl makes a letter A out of
    a. nuts and berries.
    b. eel-grass.
    c. burrs.

____ 19. When Pearl asks Hester about
the Black Man, Hester
    a. tells her to stop listening
       to old ladies' stories.
    b. tells her to ask the
       minister.
    c. tells her that the scarlet
       letter is his mark.

____ 20. Arthur walks through the
forest
    a. leaning on a staff.
    b. gathering herbs and roots.
    c. practicing his sermon.

10 SIGNIFICANT QUOTATIONS

Explain the importance of each of these quotations.

1. "None [were] so self-devoted as Hester, when pestilence stalked through the town. In all seasons of calamity, indeed, whether general or of individuals, the outcast of society at once found her place [. . .]."
2. "Meeting them in the street, she never raised her head to receive their greeting. If they were resolute to accost her, she laid her finger on the scarlet letter, and passed on [. . .]."
3. "It was a sad transformation, too, that her rich and luxuriant hair had either been cut off, or was so completely hidden by a cap, that not a shining lock of it ever once gushed into the sunshine [. . .]."

4. "She had witnessed the intense misery beneath which the minister struggled, or, to speak more accurately, had ceased to struggle. She saw that he stood on the verge of lunacy, if he had not already stepped across it [. . .]."
5. " 'Hast thou not tortured him enough?' said Hester [. . .]. 'Has he not paid thee all?' "
6. " 'Thou hadst great elements. Peradventure, hadst thou met earlier with a better love than mine, this evil had not been. I pity thee, for the good that has been wasted in thy nature!' "
7. "So Roger Chillingworth—a deformed old figure, with a face that haunted men's memories longer than they liked—took leave of Hester Prynne, and went stooping away along the earth. He gathered here and there an herb, or grubbed up a root, and put it into the basket on his arm [. . .]."
8. " 'But in good earnest now, mother dear, what does this scarlet letter mean?— and why dost thou wear it on thy bosom?—and why does the minister keep his hand over his heart?' "
9. " 'Once in my life I met the Black Man!' said her mother. 'This scarlet letter is his mark!' "
10. "She beheld the minister advancing along the path, entirely alone, and leaning on a staff which he had cut by the way-side. He looked haggard and feeble, and betrayed a nerveless despondency in his air [. . .]."

2 COMPREHENSION ESSAY QUESTIONS

Use specific details and information from these chapters to answer these questions as completely as possible.

1. Guilt and shame are strong influences in the story. Choose one character and explain how she or he has dealt with guilt and shame. Has the character become weaker or stronger? Use specific details and information from these chapters and the rest of the novel to support your explanation.
2. Readers get to know characters by what they say, by how they act, and by how others react to them. Compare Arthur Dimmesdale's actions to those of old Roger Chillingworth. Whose actions are more unacceptable? Use specific details and information from these chapters and the rest of the novel to support your explanation.

DISCUSSION QUESTIONS

Be prepared to discuss these questions in class.

1. How does Roger Chillingworth's appearance change? How does Hester react to Chillingworth?
2. What are Arthur Dimmesdale's good qualities?

WRITING

Use each of these ideas to write an essay.

1. In literature, writers often use colors or objects to represent larger ideas or themes. Choose a color or an object that you feel has significant meaning to you. What does it symbolize or mean to you? Give specific examples to support your essay.
2. Like Hester and Roger, many of us have found ourselves locked in bad relationships. Describe an unhealthy relationship that you have been in, or one that someone you know has been in, the effects it has had on you, and what you did or are doing about it.
3. Pearl and other characters express what today would be seen as superstitious remarks or attitudes. Are you superstitious? Do you believe in the supernatural? Write an essay defining or illustrating your beliefs.
4. Roger Chillingworth invades Arthur Dimmesdale's privacy. Every time strangers and townspeople stare at Hester and the scarlet letter, she feels her sense of privacy is violated. Have you ever felt that your privacy was invaded? What did you do about it?
5. Many characters feel guilty about their actions in The Scarlet Letter. Explain why Hester Prynne feels guilty and what she does about it. Use specific details and information from these chapters in your explanation.

FURTHER WRITING

1. Hester Prynne faces much loneliness and disapproval for having a child out of wedlock. Do we blame women more than their partners for getting pregnant? Research the way contemporary society views and treats single mothers and the problems they face.
2. Hester Prynne lives her life as an outcast of Puritan society. Research two people in history or contemporary society who have been shunned as the objects of scandal.
3. Roger Chillingworth is obsessed with revenge, almost like an addiction. Research an addiction and the ways it can take hold of an individual, as well as avenues of treatment and rehabilitation.
4. Arthur Dimmesdale is popular with and well-loved by his congregation as a man and a minister, yet he feels tortured by the townspeople's public veneration. He reveres truth as a priest, yet feels he is sinful and cowardly for concealing his sin. Research the term *cognizant dissonance* in a psychology book or website and discuss how it might apply to Dimmesdale or another character in The Scarlet Letter.

CHAPTER 17

THE PASTOR AND HIS PARISHIONER

PRE-READING VOCABULARY
CONTEXT

Use context clues to define these words before reading. Use a dictionary as needed.

1. The tall building looked like a tower as it stood straight and *erect*. *Erect* means _____
   _____.

2. Caleb was very happy when Jasmin *consented* to become his wife. *Consent* means _____
   _____.

3. When Sallie fell in love with Anthony, she was delighted to find the feeling was *mutual*. *Mutual* means _____
   _____.

4. An *atheist* does not believe in God or organized religion. *Atheist* means
   _____.

5. Some people believe that they can *redeem* themselves from evil by prayer, penance, and good works, and that the reward will be *redemption*, the entry into heaven after death with God forever. *Redeem* means and *redemption* means
   _____.

6. To like or admire a famous celebrity or athlete is one thing, but to *idolize* someone is to show too much devotion. *Idolize* means _____
   _____.

7. Unlike rain or snow, which can be measured in inches, fog has very little *substance*. *Substance* means _____
   _____.

8. A *malevolent* person wishes you harm. *Malevolent* means _____
   _____.

9. When someone stole the bench right off the Johnson's front porch, they felt as though their space had been *violated*. *Violate* means _____.

10. Mahatma Gandhi will be *eternally* remembered by future generations for his efforts supporting human rights and peaceful protest. *Eternal* means _____

11. When the doctor suggested surgery for his back pain, Marcus asked if there were *alternative* treatments like drugs or physical therapy instead. *Alternative* means _____.

12. Lying about a car's mileage or accident record is, unfortunately, a common form of *deception*. *Deception* means _____.

13. Martha's smile turned to a *frown* when she saw that her new car had been dented in the parking lot. *Frown* means _____.

14. Lorraine *recoiled* in horror when a spider dropped onto the desk in front of her. *Recoil* means _____.

15. Arthur Dimmesdale was such a great speaker that his listeners hung on to his every *utterance*. *Utterance* means _____.

16. The terrible earthquake caused an *abyss*, an opening in the ground large enough to swallow a huge truck and several cars. *Abyss* means _____.

17. Mother firmly *clasped* the child's hand as they crossed the busy city street. *Clasp* means _____.

18. Larry hates to go shopping, so Leah was very surprised to *encounter* him at the mall. *Encounter* means _____.

19. Even though things may look hopeless at times, we must not give in to *despair* and give up. *Despair* means _____.

20. Janet *hesitated* on the doorstep, trying to decide if she wanted to go outside in the rain. *Hesitate* means _____

_____.

PRE-READING VOCABULARY
STRUCTURAL ATTACK

Define these words by solving the parts. Use the Glossary or a dictionary as needed.

1. hoarsely	11. fervently	21. ruined
2. indistinct	12. buoyed	22. incapable
3. spectre	13. summoned	23. crisis
4. conquered	14. relieve	24. misanthropy
5. invigorate	15. actually	25. alienation
6. temporary	16. estrange	26. consecration
7. extremity	17. pollute	27. vestiges
8. satiate	18. unfaithful	28. devoid
9. journeyed	19. sentinel	29. coarsely
10. bondage	20. wrecked	30. brutally

PRE-READING QUESTIONS

Try answering these questions as you read.

How and why does Hester reveal her secret to Arthur Dimmesdale?
How comfortable are Hester and Arthur with each other?
What decision do they make?

CHAPTER 17

THE PASTOR AND HIS PARISHIONER

1 Slowly as the minister walked, he had almost gone by, before Hester Prynne could gather voice enough to attract his observation. At length, she succeeded.

2 "Arthur Dimmesdale!" she said, faintly at first; then louder, but hoarsely. "Arthur Dimmesdale!"

3 "Who speaks?" answered the minister.

4 Gathering himself quickly up, he stood more erect, like a man taken by surprise in a mood to which he was reluctant to have witnesses. Throwing his eyes anxiously in the direction of the voice, he indistinctly beheld a form under the trees, clad in garments so sombre, and so little relieved from the gray twilight into which the

clouded sky and the heavy foliage had darkened the noontide, that he knew not whether it were a woman or a shadow. It may be, that his pathway through life was haunted thus, by a spectre that had stolen out from among his thoughts.

5   He made a step nigher, and discovered the scarlet letter.

6   "Hester! Hester Prynne!" said he. "Is it thou? Art thou in life?"

7   "Even so!" she answered. "In such life as has been mine these seven years past! And thou, Arthur Dimmesdale, dost thou yet live?"

8   It was no wonder that they thus questioned one another's actual and bodily existence, and even doubted of their own. So strangely did they meet, in the dim wood, that it was like the first encounter, in the world beyond the grave, of two spirits who had been intimately connected in their former life, but now stood coldly shuddering, in mutual dread; as not yet familiar with their state, nor wonted to the companionship of disembodied beings. Each a ghost, and awe-stricken at the other ghost. They were awe-stricken likewise at themselves; because the crisis flung back to them their consciousness, and revealed to each heart its history and experience, as life never does, except at such breathless epochs. The soul beheld its features in the mirror of the passing moment. It was with fear, and tremulously, and, as it were, by a slow, reluctant necessity, that Arthur Dimmesdale put forth his hand, chill as death, and touched the chill hand of Hester Prynne. The grasp, cold as it was, took away what was dreariest in the interview. They now felt themselves, at least, inhabitants of the same sphere.

9   Without a word more spoken,—neither he nor she assuming the guidance, but with an unexpressed consent,—they glided back into the shadow of the woods, whence Hester had emerged, and sat down on the heap of moss where she and Pearl had before been sitting. When they found voice to speak, it was, at first, only to utter remarks and inquiries such as any two acquaintance might have made, about the gloomy sky, the threatening storm, and, next, the health of each. Thus they went onward, not boldly, but step by step, into the themes that were brooding deepest in their hearts. So long estranged by fate and circum-stances, they needed something slight and casual to run before, and throw open the doors of intercourse, so that their real thoughts might be led across the threshold.

10   After a while, the minister fixed his eyes on Hester Prynne's.

11   "Hester," said he, "hast thou found peace?"

12   She smiled drearily, looking down upon her bosom.

13   "Hast thou?" she asked.

14   "None!—nothing but despair!" he answered. "What else could I look for, being what I am, and leading such a life as mine? Were I an atheist,—a man devoid of

conscience,—a wretch with coarse and brutal instincts,—I might have found peace, long ere now. Nay, I never should have lost it! But, as matters stand with my soul, whatever of good capacity there originally was in me, all of God's gifts that were the choicest have become the ministers of spiritual torment. Hester, I am most miserable!"

15   "The people reverence thee," said Hester. "And surely thou workest good among them! Doth this bring thee no comfort?"

16   "More misery, Hester!—only the more misery!" answered the clergyman, with a bitter smile. "As concerns the good which I may appear to do, I have no faith in it. It must needs be a delusion. What can a ruined soul, like mine, effect towards the redemption of other souls?—or a polluted soul, towards their purification? And as for the people's reverence, would that it were turned to scorn and hatred! Canst thou deem it, Hester, a consolation, that I must stand up in my pulpit, and meet so many eyes turned upward to my face, as if the light of heaven were beaming from it!—must see my flock hungry for the truth, and listening to my words as if a tongue of Pentecost were speaking!—and then look inward, and discern the black reality of what they idolize? I have laughed, in bitterness and agony of heart, at the contrast between what I seem and what I am! And Satan laughs at it!"

17   "You wrong yourself in this," said Hester, gently. "You have deeply and sorely repented. Your sin is left behind you, in the days long past. Your present life is not less holy, in very truth, than it seems in people's eyes. Is there no reality in the penitence thus sealed and witnessed by good works? And wherefore should it not bring you peace?"

18   "No, Hester, no!" replied the clergyman. "There is no substance in it! It is cold and dead, and can do nothing for me! Of penance I have had enough! Of penitence there has been none! Else, I should long ago have thrown off these garments of mock holiness, and have shown myself to mankind as they will see me at the judgment-seat. Happy are you, Hester, that wear the scarlet letter openly upon your bosom! Mine burns in secret! Thou little knowest what a relief it is, after the torment of a seven years' cheat, to look into an eye that recognizes me for what I am! Had I one friend,—or were it my worst enemy!—to whom, when sickened with the praises of all other men, I could daily betake myself, and be known as the vilest of all sinners, methinks my soul might keep itself alive thereby. Even thus much of truth would save me! But, now, it is all falsehood!—all emptiness!— all death!"

19   Hester Prynne looked into his face, but hesitated to speak. Yet, uttering his long-restrained emotions so vehemently as he did, his words here offered her the very point of circumstances in which to interpose what she came to say. She conquered her fears, and spoke.

20   "Such a friend as thou hast even now wished for," said she, "with whom to weep over thy sin, thou hast in me, the partner of it!"—Again she hesitated, but brought out the words with an effort.—"Thou hast long had such an enemy, and dwellest with him under the same roof!"

21   The minister started to his feet, gasping for breath, and clutching at his heart as if he would have torn it out of his bosom.

22   "Ha! What sayest thou?" cried he. "An enemy! And under mine own roof! What mean you?"

23   Hester Prynne was now fully sensible of the deep injury for which she was responsible to this unhappy man, in permitting him to lie for so many years, or, indeed, for a single moment, at the mercy of one, whose purposes could not be other than malevolent. The very contiguity of his enemy, beneath whatever mask the latter might conceal himself, was enough to disturb the magnetic sphere of a being so sensitive as Arthur Dimmesdale. There had been a period when Hester was less alive to this consideration; or, perhaps, in the misanthropy of her own trouble, she left the minister to bear what she might picture to herself as a more tolerable doom. But of late, since the night of his vigil, all her sympathies towards him had been both softened and invigorated. She now read his heart more accurately. She doubted not, that the continual presence of Roger Chillingworth,— the secret poison of his malignity, infecting all the air about him,—and his authorized interference, as a physician, with the minister's physical and spiritual infirmities,—that these bad opportunities had been turned to a cruel purpose. By means of them, the sufferer's conscience had been kept in an irritated state, the tendency of which was, not to cure by wholesome pain, but to disorganize and corrupt his spiritual being. Its result, on earth, could hardly fail to be insanity, and hereafter, that eternal alienation from the Good and True, of which madness is perhaps the earthly type.

24   Such was the ruin to which she had brought the man, once,—nay, why should we not speak it?—still so passionately loved! Hester felt that the sacrifice of the clergyman's good name, and death itself, as she had already told Roger Chillingworth, would have been infinitely preferable to the alternative which she had taken upon herself to choose. And now, rather than have had this grievous wrong to confess, she would gladly have lain down on the forest-leaves, and died there, at Arthur Dimmesdale's feet.

25   "O Arthur," cried she, "forgive me! In all things else, I have striven to be true! Truth was the one virtue which I might have held fast, and did hold fast through all extremity; save when thy good,—thy life,—thy fame,—were put in question! Then I consented to a deception. But a lie is never good, even though death threaten on the other side! Dost thou not see what I would say? That old man!— the physician!—he whom they call Roger Chillingworth!—he was my husband!"

26   The minister looked at her, for an instant, with all that violence of passion, which—intermixed, in more shapes than one, with his higher, purer, softer qualities—was, in fact, the portion of him which the Devil claimed, and through which he sought to win the rest. Never was there a blacker or a fiercer frown, than Hester now encountered. For the brief space that it lasted, it was a dark transfiguration. But his character had been so much enfeebled by suffering, that even its lower energies were incapable of more than a temporary struggle. He sank down on the ground, and buried his face in his hands.

27   "I might have known it!" murmured he. "I did know it! Was not the secret told me in the natural recoil of my heart, at the first sight of him, and as often as I have seen him since? Why did I not understand? O Hester Prynne, thou little, little knowest all the horror of this thing! And the shame!—the indelicacy!—the horrible ugliness of this exposure of a sick and guilty heart to the very eye that would gloat over it! Woman, woman, thou art accountable for this! I cannot forgive thee!"

28   "Thou shalt forgive me!" cried Hester, flinging herself on the fallen leaves beside him. "Let God punish! Thou shalt forgive!"

29   With sudden and desperate tenderness, she threw her arms around him, and pressed his head against her bosom; little caring though his cheek rested on the scarlet letter. He would have released himself, but strove in vain to do so. Hester would not set him free, lest he should look her sternly in the face. All the world had frowned on her,—for seven long years had it frowned upon this lonely woman,—and still she bore it all, nor ever once turned away her firm, sad eyes. Heaven, likewise, had frowned upon her, and she had not died. But the frown of this pale, weak, sinful, and sorrow-stricken man was what Hester could not bear, and live!

30   "Wilt thou yet forgive me?" she repeated, over and over again. "Wilt thou not frown? Wilt thou forgive?"

31   "I do forgive you, Hester," replied the minister, at length, with a deep utterance out of an abyss of sadness, but no anger. "I freely forgive you now. May God forgive us both! We are not, Hester, the worst sinners in the world. There is one worse than even the polluted priest! That old man's revenge has been blacker than my sin. He has violated, in cold blood, the sanctity of a human heart. Thou and I, Hester, never did so!"

32   "Never, never!" whispered she, "What we did had a consecration of its own. We felt it so! We said so to each other! Hast thou forgotten it?"

33   "Hush, Hester!" said Arthur Dimmesdale, rising from the ground. "No; I have not forgotten!"

34   They sat down again, side by side, and hand clasped in hand, on the mossy trunk of the fallen tree. Life had never brought them a gloomier hour; it was the point whither their pathway had so long been tending, and darkening ever, as it stole along;—and yet it inclosed a charm that made them linger upon it, and claim another, and another, and, after all, another moment. The forest was obscure around them, and creaked with a blast that was passing through it. The boughs were tossing heavily about their heads; while one solemn old tree groaned dolefully to another, as if telling the sad story of the pair that sat beneath, or constrained to forebode evil to come.

35   And yet they lingered. How dreary looked the forest-track that led backward to the settlement, where Hester Prynne must take up again the burden of her ignominy, and the minister the hollow mockery of his good name! So they lingered an instant longer. No golden light had ever been so precious as the gloom of this dark forest. Here, seen only by his eyes, the scarlet letter need not burn into the

bosom of the fallen woman! Here, seen only by her eyes, Arthur Dimmesdale, false to God and man, might be, for one moment, true!

36   He started at a thought that suddenly occurred to him.

37   "Hester," cried he, "here is a new horror! Roger Chillingworth knows your purpose to reveal his true character. Will he continue, then, to keep our secret? What will now be the course of his revenge?"

38   "There is a strange secrecy in his nature," replied Hester, thoughtfully; "and it has grown upon him by the hidden practices of his revenge. I deem it not likely that he will betray the secret. He will doubtless seek other means of satiating his dark passion."

39   "And I!—how am I to live longer, breathing the same air with this deadly enemy?" exclaimed Arthur Dimmesdale, shrinking within himself, and pressing his hand nervously against his heart,—a gesture that had grown involuntary with him. "Think for me, Hester! Thou art strong. Resolve for me!"

40   "Thou must dwell no longer with this man," said Hester, slowly and firmly. "Thy heart must be no longer under his evil eye!"

41   "It were far worse than death!" replied the minister. "But how to avoid it? What choice remains to me? Shall I lie down again on these withered leaves, where I cast myself when thou didst tell me what he was? Must I sink down there, and die at once?"

42   "Alas, what a ruin has befallen thee!" said Hester, with the tears gushing into her eyes. "Wilt thou die for very weakness? There is no other cause!"

43   "The judgment of God is on me," answered the conscience-stricken priest. "It is too mighty for me to struggle with!"

44   "Heaven would show mercy," rejoined Hester, "hadst thou but the strength to take advantage of it."

45   "Be thou strong for me!" answered he. "Advise me what to do."

46   "Is the world then so narrow?" exclaimed Hester Prynne, fixing her deep eyes on the minister's, and instinctively exercising a magnetic power over a spirit so shattered and subdued, that it could hardly hold itself erect. "Doth the universe lie within the compass of yonder town, which only a little time ago was but a leaf-strewn desert, as lonely as this around us? Whither leads yonder forest-track? Backward to the settlement, thou sayest! Yes; but onward, too! Deeper it goes, and deeper, into the wilderness, less plainly to be seen at every step; until, some few miles hence, the yellow leaves will show no vestige of the white man's tread. There thou art free! So brief a journey would bring thee from a world where thou hast been most wretched, to one where thou mayest still be happy! Is there not shade enough in all this boundless forest to hide thy heart from the gaze of Roger Chillingworth?"

47   "Yes, Hester; but only under the fallen leaves!" replied the minister, with a sad smile.

48   "Then there is the broad pathway of the sea!" continued Hester. "It brought thee hither. If thou so choose, it will bear thee back again. In our native land, whether in some remote rural village or in vast London,—or, surely, in Germany,

in France, in pleasant Italy,—thou wouldst be beyond his power and knowledge! And what hast thou to do with all these iron men, and their opinions? They have kept thy better part in bondage too long already!"

49   "It cannot be!" answered the minister, listening as if he were called upon to realize a dream. "I am powerless to go. Wretched and sinful as I am, I have had no other thought than to drag on my earthly existence in the sphere where Providence hath placed me. Lost as my own soul is, I would still do what I may for other human souls! I dare not quit my post, though an unfaithful sentinel, whose sure reward is death and dishonor, when his dreary watch shall come to an end!"

50   "Thou art crushed under this seven years' weight of misery," replied Hester, fervently resolved to buoy him up with her own energy. "But thou shalt leave it all behind thee! It shall not cumber they steps, as thou treadest along the forest-path; neither shalt thou freight the ship with it, if thou prefer to cross the sea. Leave this wreck and ruin here where it hath happened! Meddle no more with it! Begin all anew! Hast thou exhausted possibility in the failure of this one trial? Not so! The future is yet full of trial and success. There is happiness to be enjoyed! There is good to be done! Exchange this false life of thine for a true one. Be, if thy spirit summon thee to such a mission, the teacher and apostle of the red men. Or,—as is more thy nature,—be a scholar and a sage among the wisest and the most renowned of the cultivated world. Preach! Write! Act! Do any thing, save to lie down and die! Give up this name of Arthur Dimmesdale, and make thyself another, and a high one, such as thou canst wear without fear or shame. Why shouldst thou tarry so much as one other day in the torments that have so gnawed into thy life!—that have made thee feeble to will and to do!—that will leave thee powerless even to repent! Up, and away!"

51   "O Hester!" cried Arthur Dimmesdale, in whose eyes a fitful light, kindled by her enthusiasm, flashed up and died away, "thou tellest of running a race to a man whose knees are tottering beneath him. I must die here. There is not the strength or courage left me to venture into the wide, strange, difficult world, alone!"

52   It was the last expression of the despondency of a broken spirit. He lacked energy to grasp the better fortune that seemed within his reach.

53   He repeated the word.

54   "Alone, Hester!"

55   "Thou shalt not go alone!" answered she, in a deep whisper. Then, all was spoken!

CHAPTER 17

JOURNAL

1. **MLA Works Cited** *Using this model record this book.*
    Author's Last Name, First Name. The Scarlet Letter. 1850. Title of This Book.
    Ed. First Name Last Name. City: Publisher, year.

2. **Main Character(s)** *Describe each main character and explain why you think each is a main character.*

3. **Supporting Characters** *Describe each supporting character and explain why you think each is a supporting character.*

4. **Setting** *Describe the setting(s) and any relevant prop(s).*

5. **Sequence** *Outline the events in this chapter in order.*

6. **Plot** *Summarize this chapter's events in no more than two sentences.*

7. **Conflicts** *Identify and explain all conflicts involved in this chapter.*

8. **Significant Quotations** *Explain the importance of each of these quotations. Record the page number in the parentheses.*

   a. "Slowly as the minister walked, he had almost gone by, before Hester Prynne could gather voice enough to attract his observation. At length, she succeeded" (   ).

   b. "So strangely did they meet, in the dim wood, that it was like the first encounter, in the world beyond the grave, of two spirits who had been intimately connected in their former life, but now stood coldly shuddering, in mutual dread; [. . .]. Each a ghost, and awe-stricken at the other ghost" (   ).

   c. " 'None!—nothing but despair!' he answered. 'What else could I look for, being what I am, and leading such a life as mine? Were I an atheist,—a man devoid of conscience,—a wretch with coarse and brutal instincts,—I might have found peace, long ere now. [. . .] Hester, I am most miserable!' " (   ).

   d. " 'Thou hast long had such an enemy, and dwellest with him under the same roof!' " (   ).

   e. " '[. . .] I must die here. There is not the strength or courage left me to venture into the wide, strange, difficult world, alone!' " (   ).

9. **Recap** *Summarize what has happened so far, from the beginning of the book through this chapter.*

FOLLOW-UP QUESTIONS

6 SHORT QUESTIONS

Select the <u>best</u> answer for each.

____ 1. Arthur Dimmesdale feels
   a. anger.
   b. despair.
   c. peace.

____ 2. The reverence and respect he gets from his congregation makes Arthur feel
   a. proud.
   b. guilty.
   c. old.

____ 3. Doing penance has made
   a. Arthur feel even worse.
   b. Arthur a holier person.
   c. Arthur feel better.

____ 4. Hester reveals that
   a. Arthur Dimmesdale is Pearl's father.
   b. Roger Chillingworth is Pearl's father.
   c. Roger Chillingworth is her husband.

____ 5. Hester begs forgiveness for
   a. staying away from Arthur
      Dimmesdale for so many
      years.
   b. not telling Arthur
      Dimmesdale who Roger
      Chillingworth really is.
   c. committing adultery.

____ 6. Arthur Dimmesdale asks
      Hester to
   a. help him decide what to
      do.
   b. talk to Roger
      Chillingworth for him.
   c. ease his conscience.

5 SIGNIFICANT QUOTATIONS

Explain the importance of each of these quotations.

1. "'Happy are you, Hester, that wear the scarlet letter openly upon your bosom! Mine burns in secret! Thou little knowest what a relief it is, after the torment of a seven years' cheat, to look into an eye that recognizes me for what I am! [. . .].'"

2. "'O Arthur,' cried she, 'forgive me! In all things else, I have striven to be true! Truth was the one virtue which I might have held fast, and did hold fast through all extremity; save when thy good,—thy life,—thy fame,— were put in question! Then I consented to a deception. [. . .]. That old man!—the physician!—he whom they call Roger Chillingworth!—he was my husband!'"

3. "'[. . .] I freely forgive you now. May God forgive us both! We are not, Hester, the worst sinners in the world. There is one worse than even the pol-luted priest! That old man's revenge has been blacker than my sin. He has violated, in cold blood, the sanctity of a human heart. Thou and I, Hester, never did so!'"

4. "'And I!—how am I to live longer, breathing the same air with this deadly enemy?' exclaimed Arthur Dimmesdale, shrinking within himself, and pressing his hand nervously against his heart,—a gesture that had grown involuntary with him. 'Think for me, Hester! Thou art strong. Resolve for me!'"

5. "'Leave this wreck and ruin here where it hath happened! Meddle no more with it! Begin all anew! [. . .].'"

2 COMPREHENSION ESSAY QUESTIONS

Use specific details and information from the chapter to answer these ques-tions as completely as possible.

1. Why does Arthur Dimmesdale have so much trouble deciding what to do? Use specific details and information from this chapter and elsewhere in the novel in your explanation.

2. Why does Hester deliberately choose to meet Arthur Dimmesdale in a forest setting? What effect does the setting have on these two characters? Use specific details and information from the chapter in your explanation.

DISCUSSION QUESTIONS

Be prepared to discuss these questions in class.

1. Has Arthur Dimmesdale repented enough?
2. What effect has seven years of suffering had on Hester? On Arthur?

CHAPTER 18

A FLOOD OF SUNSHINE

PRE-READING VOCABULARY
CONTEXT

Use context clues to define these words before reading. Use a dictionary as needed.

1. Because of her nasty remarks, Isabel's friends feel *estranged* and are starting to avoid her. *Estrange* means _____
   _____.

2. Green plants have a *tendency* to grow towards the light and will bend in that direction if necessary. *Tendency* means _____
   _____.

3. As part of her punishment, Hester Prynne was *outlawed* from society, so people rarely spoke to her. *Outlawed* means _____
   _____.

4. Susan's *zeal* and passion for cooking new dishes inspire all who see her, even those who do not like to cook. *Zeal* means _____
   _____.

5. After a long and stressful day at the office, Pat finds *solace* by taking a long hot bubble bath surrounded by scented candles. *Solace* means _____
   _____.

6. Shirley wore an *exquisite* diamond and ruby necklace to the ball and everyone remarked on its beauty. *Exquisite* means _____
   _____.

7. When Hurricane Katrina struck New Orleans, the levees were *breached* and water flooded the city. *Breached* means _____
   _____.

8. Hundreds of people tried to *flee* the coast as the hurricane approached. *Flee* means _____
   _____.

9. "Your stupid mistake is *irrevocable*. I cannot fix it," said the mechanic when I explained that I had neglected to put oil in the engine. *Irrevocable* means _____.

10. To do well in college, students should *avail* themselves of the tutoring and advisement services offered on campus. *Avail* means _____ _____.

11. Leandro felt *exhilarated* and energized when the audience grew to hundreds and thunderously applauded his music. *Exhilarated* means _____ _____.

12. Christa pulled off the road onto the grassy *verge* next to the highway to answer the cell phone. *Verge* means _____ _____.

13. When little Tao unbuttoned his jacket for the first time, he exclaimed, "Look! I can *undo* my buttons!" *Undo* means _____ _____.

14. Lucille is very loyal to her family and loves gatherings with her *kindred*. *Kindred* means _____ _____.

15. The artist added just a drop of the color red to the white paint to create the faintest *tinge* of color. *Tinge* means _____ _____.

16. After he broke both legs in a fall, Jin was *confined* to a wheelchair until he healed. *Confined* means _____ _____.

17. Having a criminal record can be a serious *stigma* in society and can keep a person out of certain professions. *Stigma* means _____ _____.

18. Tamed animals like dogs and cats may live in people's homes; *untamed* animals like bears and snakes live in the wild. *Untamed* means _____ _____.

19. The pattern on the bracelet was so complicated and *intricate* that it was not easy to copy. *Intricate* means _____ _____.

20. By providing partial excuses, the lawyer explained the *extenuating* circumstances of the client's actions to try and lessen the seriousness of the offense.
Extenuating means _____

_____.

PRE-READING VOCABULARY
STRUCTURAL ATTACK

*Define these words by solving the parts. Use the Glossary or a dictionary as
needed.*

1. native	11. trammelled	21. methought
2. vastly	12. regulation	22. germs
3. latitude	13. prejudice	23. framework
4. speculation	14. sensitive	24. prospect
5. foreign	15. fretting	25. mystic
6. colloquy	16. pilgrim	26. token
7. calculate	17. citadel	27. alight
8. instances	18. assaulted	28. formal
9. principles	19. avowed	29. outward
10. minuteness	20. lawless	30. gazed

PRE-READING QUESTIONS

Try answering these questions as you read.

Hoes does Arthur feel about the decision that he and Hester make?
What does Hester remove?
How does Arthur feel about Pearl?

CHAPTER 18

A FLOOD OF SUNSHINE

1   Arthur Dimmesdale gazed into Hester's face with a look in which hope and joy
shone out, indeed, but with fear betwixt them, and a kind of horror at her boldness, who had spoken what he vaguely hinted at, but dared not speak.

2   But Hester Prynne, with a mind of native courage and activity, and for so
long a period not merely estranged, but outlawed, from society, had habituated
herself to such latitude of speculation as was altogether foreign to the clergyman.
She had wandered, without rule or guidance, in a moral wilderness; as vast, as
intricate and shadowy, as the untamed forest, amid the gloom of which they were
now holding a colloquy that was to decide their fate. Her intellect and heart had

their home, as it were, in desert places, where she roamed as freely as the wild Indian in his woods. For years past she had looked from this estranged point of view at human institutions, and whatever priests or legislators had established; criticizing all with hardly more reverence than the Indian would feel for the clerical band, the judicial robe, the pillory, the gallows, the fireside, or the church. The tendency of her fate and fortunes had been to set her free. The scarlet letter was her passport into regions where other women dared not tread. Shame, Despair, Solitude! These had been her teachers,—stern and wild ones,—and they had made her strong, but taught her much amiss.

3   The minister, on the other hand, had never gone through an experience calculated to lead him beyond the scope of generally received laws; although, in a single instance, he had so fearfully transgressed one of the most sacred of them. But this had been a sin of passion, not of principle, nor even purpose. Since that wretched epoch, he had watched, with morbid zeal and minuteness, not his acts,—for those it was easy to arrange,—but each breath of emotion, and his every thought. At the head of the social system, as the clergymen of that day stood, he was only the more trammelled by its regulations, its principles, and even its prejudices. As a priest, the framework of his order inevitably hemmed him in. As a man who had once sinned, but who kept his conscience all alive and painfully sensitive by the fretting of an unhealed wound, he might have been supposed safer within the line of virtue, than if he had never sinned at all.

4   Thus, we seem to see that, as regarded Hester Prynne, the whole seven years of outlaw and ignominy had been little other than a preparation for this very hour. But Arthur Dimmesdale! Were such a man once more to fall, what plea could be urged in extenuation of his crime? None; unless it avail him somewhat, that he was broken down by long and exquisite suffering; that his mind was darkened and confused by the very remorse which harrowed it; that, between fleeing as an avowed criminal, and remaining as a hypocrite, conscience might find it hard to strike the balance; that it was human to avoid the peril of death and infamy, and the inscrutable machinations of an enemy; that, finally, to this poor pilgrim, on his dreary and desert path, faint, sick, miserable, there appeared a glimpse of human affection and sympathy, a new life, and a true one, in exchange for the heavy doom which he was now expiating. And be the stern and sad truth spoken, that the breach which guilt has once made into the human soul is never, in this mortal state, repaired. It may be watched and guarded; so that the enemy shall not force his way again into the citadel, and might even, in his subsequent assaults, select some other avenue, in preference to that where he had formerly succeeded. But there is still the ruined wall, and, near it, the stealthy tread of the foe that would win over again his unforgotten triumph.

5   The struggle, if there were one, need not be described. Let it suffice, that the clergyman resolved to flee, and not alone.

6   "If, in all these past seven years," thought he, "I could recall one instant of peace or hope, I would yet endure, for the sake of that earnest of Heaven's mercy. But now,—since I am irrevocably doomed,—wherefore should I not snatch the

solace allowed to the condemned culprit before his execution? Or, if this be the path to a better life, as Hester would persuade me, I surely give up no fairer prospect by pursuing it! Neither can I any longer live without her companionship; so powerful is she to sustain,—so tender to soothe! O Thou to whom I dare not lift mine eyes, wilt Thou yet pardon me!"

7   "Thou wilt go!" said Hester calmly, as he met her glance.

8   The decision once made, a glow of strange enjoyment threw its flickering brightness over the trouble of his breast. It was the exhilarating effect—upon a prisoner just escaped from the dungeon of his own heart—of breathing the wild, free atmosphere of an unredeemed, unchristianized, lawless region. His spirit rose, as it were, with a bound, and attained a nearer prospect of the sky, than throughout all the misery which had kept him grovelling on the earth. Of a deeply religious temperament, there was inevitably a tinge of the devotional in his mood.

9   "Do I feel joy again?" cried he, wondering at himself. "Me-thought the germ of it was dead in me! O Hester, thou art my better angel! I seem to have flung myself—sick, sin-stained, and sorrow-blackened—down upon these forest-leaves, and to have risen up all made anew, and with new powers to glorify Him that hath been merciful! This is already the better life! Why did we not find it sooner?"

10   "Let us not look back," answered Hester Prynne. "The past is gone! Wherefore should we linger upon it now? See! With this symbol, I undo it all, and make it as it had never been!"

11   So speaking, she undid the clasp that fastened the scarlet letter, and, taking it from her bosom, threw it to a distance among the withered leaves. The mystic token alighted on the hither verge of the stream. With a hand's breadth farther flight it would have fallen into the water, and have given the little brook another woe to carry onward, besides the unintelligible tale which it still kept murmuring about. But there lay the embroidered letter, glittering like a lost jewel, which some ill-fated wanderer might pick up, and thenceforth be haunted by strange phantoms of guilt, sinkings of the heart, and unaccountable misfortune.

12   The stigma gone, Hester heaved a long, deep sigh, in which the burden of shame and anguish departed from her spirit. O exquisite relief! She had not known the weight, until she felt the freedom! By another impulse, she took off the formal cap that confined her hair; and down it fell upon her shoulders, dark and rich, with at once a shadow and a light in its abundance, and imparting the charm of softness to her features. There played around her mouth, and beamed out of her eyes, a radiant and tender smile, that seemed gushing from the very heart of womanhood. A crimson flush was glowing on her cheek, that had been long so pale. Her sex, her youth, and the whole richness of her beauty, came back from what men call the irrevocable past, and clustered themselves, with her maiden hope, and a happiness before unknown, within the magic circle of this hour. And, as if the gloom of the earth and sky had been but the effluence of these two mortal hearts, it vanished with their sorrow. All at once, as with a sudden

smile of heaven, forth burst the sunshine, pouring a very flood into the obscure forest, gladdening each green leaf, transmuting the yellow fallen ones to gold, and gleaming adown the gray trunks of the solemn trees. The objects that had made a shadow hitherto, embodied the brightness now. The course of the little brook might be traced by its merry gleam afar into the wood's heart of mystery, which had become a mystery of joy.

13 Such was the sympathy of Nature—that wild, heathen Nature of the forest, never subjugated by human law, nor illumined by higher truth—with the bliss of these two spirits! Love, whether newly born, or aroused from a deathlike slumber, must always create a sunshine, filling the heart so full of radiance, that it overflows upon the outward world. Had the forest still kept its gloom, it would have been bright in Hester's eyes, and bright in Arthur Dimmesdale's!

14 Hester looked at him with the thrill of another joy.

15 "Thou must know Pearl!" said she. "Our little Pearl! Thou hast seen her,— yes, I know it!—but thou wilt see her now with other eyes. She is a strange child! I hardly comprehend her! But thou wilt love her dearly, as I do, and wilt advise me how to deal with her."

16 "Dost thou think the child will be glad to know me?" asked the minister, somewhat uneasily. "I have long shrunk from children, because they often show a distrust,—a backwardness to be familiar with me. I have even been afraid of little Pearl!"

17 "Ah, that was sad!" answered the mother. "But she will love thee dearly, and thou her. She is not far off. I will call her! Pearl! Pearl!"

18 "I see the child," observed the minister. "Yonder she is, standing in a streak of sunshine, a good way off, on the other side of the brook. So thou thinkest the child will love me?"

19 Hester smiled, and again called to Pearl, who was visible, at some distance, as the minister had described her, like a bright-apparelled vision, in a sunbeam, which fell down upon her through an arch of boughs. The ray quivered to and fro, making her figure dim or distinct,—now like a real child, now like a child's spirit,—as the splendor went and came again. She heard her mother's voice, and approached slowly through the forest.

20 Pearl had not found the hour pass wearisomely, while her mother sat talking with the clergyman. The great black forest—stern as it showed itself to those who brought the guilt and troubles of the world into its bosom—became the playmate of the lonely infant, as well as it knew how. Sombre as it was, it put on the kindest of its moods to welcome her. It offered her the partridge-berries, the growth of the preceding autumn, but ripening only in the spring, and now red as drops of blood upon the withered leaves. These Pearl gathered, and was pleased with their wild flavor. The small denizens of the wilderness hardly took pains to move out of her path. A partridge, indeed, with a brood of ten behind her, ran forward threateningly, but soon repented of her fierceness, and clucked to her young ones not to be afraid. A pigeon, alone on a low branch, allowed Pearl to come beneath, and uttered a sound as much of greeting as alarm. A squirrel, from

the lofty depths of his domestic tree, chattered either in anger or merriment,—
for a squirrel is such a choleric and humorous little personage that it is hard to
distinguish between his moods,—so he chattered at the child, and flung down a
nut upon her head. It was a last year's nut, and already gnawed by his sharp
tooth. A fox, startled from his sleep by her light footstep on the leaves, looked
inquisitively at Pearl, as doubting whether it were better to steal off, or renew his
nap on the same spot. A wolf, it is said,—but here the tale has surely lapsed into
the improbable,—came up, and smelt of Pearl's robe, and offered his savage head
to be patted by her hand. The truth seems to be, however, that the mother-forest,
and these wild things which it nourished, all recognized a kindred wildness in
the human child.

21   And she was gentler here than in the grassy-margined streets of the settlement,
or in her mother's cottage. The flowers appeared to know it; and one and another
whispered, as she passed, "Adorn thyself with me, thou beautiful child, adorn
thyself with me!"—and, to please them, Pearl gathered the violets, and anemones,
and columbines, and some twigs of the freshest green, which the old trees held
down before her eyes. With these she decorated her hair, and her young waist, and
became a nymph-child, or an infant dryad, or whatever else was in closest sympathy with the antique wood. In such guise had Pearl adorned herself, when she heard
her mother's voice, and came slowly back.

22   Slowly; for she saw the clergyman!

CHAPTER 18

JOURNAL

1. **MLA Works Cited** *Using this model, record this book.*
   Author's Last Name, First Name. The Scarlet Letter. 1850. Title of This Book.
   Ed. First Name Last Name. City: Publisher, year.
2. **Main Character(s)** *Describe each main character and explain why you think each
   is a main character.*
3. **Supporting Characters** *Describe each supporting character and explain why you
   think each is a supporting character.*
4. **Setting** *Describe the setting(s) and any relevant prop(s).*
5. **Sequence** *Outline the events in this chapter in order.*
6. **Plot** *Summarize this chapter's events in no more than two sentences.*
7. **Conflicts** *Identify and explain all conflicts involved in this chapter.*
8. **Significant Quotations** *Explain the importance of each of these quotations.
   Record the page number in the parentheses.*
   a. "She had wandered, without rule or guidance, in a moral wilderness; as vast,
      as intricate and shadowy as the untamed forest, amid the gloom of which
      they were now holding a colloquy that was to decide their fate [. . .]" (   ).
   b. "As a priest, the framework of his order inevitably hemmed him in. As a
      man who had once sinned, but who kept his conscience all alive and

painfully sensitive by the fretting of an unhealed wound, he might have been supposed safer within the line of virtue, than if he had never sinned at all" ( ).

   c. "Let it suffice, that the clergyman resolved to flee, and not alone" ( ).

   d. " 'Do I feel joy again?' cried he, wondering at himself. 'Methought the germ of it was dead in me! [. . .]' " ( ).

   e. " 'The past is gone! Wherefore should we linger upon it now? See! With this symbol, I undo it all, and make it as it had never been!' " ( ).

9. **Recap** *Summarize what has happened so far, from the beginning of the book through this chapter.*

FOLLOW-UP QUESTIONS

6 SHORT QUESTIONS

Select the __best__ answer for each.

_____ 1. Arthur Dimmesdale sees Hester Prynne as
   a. uncertain.
   b. feeble.
   c. bold.

_____ 2. Arthur Dimmesdale decides to
   a. leave Boston with Hester and Pearl.
   b. face his sentence after all.
   c. confront Roger Chillingworth.

_____ 3. For the first time in many years, Arthur Dimmesdale feels
   a. despair.
   b. joy.
   c. nothing.

_____ 4. Hester removes
   a. the scarlet letter.
   b. her shoes and the scarlet letter.
   c. her cap and the scarlet letter.

_____ 5. Arthur Dimmesdale indicates that
   a. he will be a good father to Pearl.
   b. he is afraid of Pearl.
   c. he will help discipline Pearl.

_____ 6. When Hester calls her, Pearl
   a. walks very slowly.
   b. runs to her mother.
   c. does not hear her mother.

5 SIGNIFICANT QUOTATIONS

Explain the importance of each of these quotations.

1. "Arthur Dimmesdale gazed into Hester's face with a look in which hope and joy shone out, indeed, but with fear betwixt them, and a kind of horror at her boldness, who had spoken what he vaguely hinted at, but dared not speak."

2. "O exquisite relief! She had not known the weight, until she felt the freedom! By another impulse, she took off the formal cap that confined her hair; and

down it fell upon her shoulders, dark and rich, [. . .] imparting the charm of softness to her features [. . .]."

3. "Love, whether newly born, or aroused from a deathlike slumber, must always create a sunshine, filling the heart so full of radiance, that it overflows upon the outward world. Had the forest still kept its gloom, it would have been bright in Hester's eyes, and bright in Arthur Dimmesdale's!"

4. " 'Thou must know Pearl!' said she. 'Our little Pearl! Thou hast seen her,— yes, I know it!—but thou wilt see her now with other eyes. She is a strange child! I hardly comprehend her! But thou wilt love her dearly, as I do, and wilt advise me how to deal with her.' "

5. " 'I see the child,' observed the minister. 'Yonder she is, standing in a streak of sunshine, a good way off, on the other side of the brook. So thou thinkest the child will love me?' "

2 COMPREHENSION ESSAY QUESTIONS

Use specific details and information from the chapter to answer these questions as completely as possible.

1. After all that Hester has endured in the story so far, she feels much relief during her meeting with Arthur Dimmesdale. How do you explain Hester's relief? Use specific details and information from the chapter in your explanation.

2. Arthur Dimmesdale experiences opposing emotions during his meeting with Hester Prynne. How do you explain Arthur's emotional conflict? Use specific details and information from the chapter in your explanation.

DISCUSSION QUESTIONS

Be prepared to discuss these questions in class.

1. How does Arthur Dimmesdale feel about getting to know Pearl? Do you think he will be a good father?

2. How does Hester change? How do you feel about her in this chapter?

CHAPTER 19

THE CHILD AT THE BROOK-SIDE

PRE-READING VOCABULARY
CONTEXT

Use context clues to define these words before reading. Use a dictionary as needed.

1. Mirabel *yearns* for grandchildren and hopes that at least one of her children will soon have a baby. *Yearns* means _____ _____.

2. The aromas coming from the restaurant were so *tantalizing* that I had to follow them inside and order a meal. *Tantalizing* means _____ _____.

3. Children sometimes say silly things and *prattle* on about nonsense. *Prattle* means _____ _____.

4. The professor wrote many notes in the *margin* next to the student's essay. *Margin* means _____ _____.

5. Things that can only be understood as ideas but cannot be touched or held are said to be *intangible*. *Intangible* means _____ _____.

6. PAUL *modified* his diet to include more fruits and vegetables when he learned that he had heart disease. *Modified* means _____ _____.

7. Ian stood and *gazed* at the picture in the museum, looking at it intently for a long time. *Gazed* means _____ _____.

8. Because he hates to drive in the snow, Joseph *hastens* to get home before the snow even starts. *Hasten* means _____ _____.

9. I knew that the drain was clogging because the water in the sink was *sluggish* and wouldn't drain quickly. *Sluggish* means _____
_____.

10. The conceited celebrity gestured *imperiously* to the waiter to bring him some food immediately. *Imperiously* means _____
_____.

11. Even though Anna was disappointed when she did not win first place, she was somewhat *mollified* when she found out that she had won second place. *Mollified* means _____
_____.

12. One becomes so *inured* to the everyday noises of life that one barely hears them. *Inured* means _____
_____.

13. Jessica cannot *abide* the taste of onions and was distressed that the pizza was made with onions on top. *Abide* means _____
_____.

14. The baby *grimaces* and makes funny faces when she tastes sour things like lemons. *Grimace* means _____
_____.

15. Amy's *pallor*, or lack of color, comes from spending so much time indoors. *Pallor* means _____
_____.

16. Because he was *accustomed* to sleeping in a large bed at home, Hamid had to get used to sleeping in a narrow, small bed at college. *Accustomed* means _____
_____.

17. Yoga instructors are so flexible that they can *contort* and stretch their limbs into many different positions. *Contort* means _____
_____.

18. Mateo could not believe his eyes when he *beheld* his beautiful bride. *Beheld* means _____
_____.

19. When Niki became tired of having long hair, she cut off her *tresses* and donated them to charity. *Tresses* means _____

_____.

20. The summer was so hot and dry that many trees and flowers *withered* and died. *Wither* means _____

_____.

PRE-READING VOCABULARY
STRUCTURAL ATTACK

Define these words by solving the parts. Use the Glossary or a dictionary as needed.

1. splendid	11. steadfast	21. gesticulate
2. visible	12. glorify	22. unreasonable
3. hieroglyphic	13. fancy	23. shrieked
4. oneness	14. departed	24. infinite
5. prophet	15. talisman	25. subdued
6. magician	16. extravagant	26. tenderness
7. destiny	17. strays	27. fireside
8. tolerant	18. fatal	28. brows
9. comprehend	19. awesome	29. bounds
10. rambled	20. leapt	30. spurned

PRE-READING QUESTIONS

Try answering these questions as you read.

How does Arthur react to his meeting with Pearl?
How does Pearl act towards Arthur Dimmesdale?
Why does Pearl refuse to obey her mother?

CHAPTER 19

THE CHILD AT THE BROOK-SIDE

1 "Thou wilt love her dearly," repeated Hester Prynne, as she and the minister sat watching little Pearl. "Dost thou not think her beautiful? And see with what natural skill she has made those simple flowers adorn her! Had she gathered pearls, and diamonds, and rubies, in the wood, they could not have become her better. She is a splendid child! But I know whose brow she has!"

2 "Dost thou know, Hester," said Arthur Dimmesdale, with an unquiet smile, "that this dear child, tripping about always at thy side, hast caused me many an

alarm. Methought—O Hester, what a thought is that, and how terrible to dread it!—that my own features were partly repeated in her face, and so strikingly that the world might see them! But she is mostly thine!"

3   "No, no! Not mostly!" answered the mother with a tender smile. "A little longer, and thou needest not to be afraid to trace whose child she is. But how strangely beautiful she looks, with those wild flowers in her hair! It is as if one of the fairies, whom we left in our dear old England, had decked her out to meet us."

4   It was with a feeling which neither of them had ever before experienced, that they sat and watched Pearl's slow advance. In her was visible the tie that united them. She had been offered to the world, these seven years past, as the living hieroglyphic, in which was revealed the secret they so darkly sought to hide,— all written in this symbol,—all plainly manifest,—had there been a prophet or magician skilled to read the character of flame! And Pearl was the oneness of their being. Be the foregone evil what it might, how could they doubt that their earthly lives and future destinies were conjoined, when they beheld at once the material union, and the spiritual idea, in whom they met, and were to dwell immortally together? Thoughts like these—and perhaps other thoughts, which they did not acknowledge or define—threw an awe about the child, as she came onward.

5   "Let her see nothing strange—no passion nor eagerness—in thy way of accosting her," whispered Hester. "Our Pearl is a fitful and fantastic little elf, sometimes. Especially, she is seldom tolerant of emotion, when she does not fully comprehend the why and wherefore. But the child hath strong affections! She loves me, and will love thee!"

6   "Thou canst not think," said the minister, glancing aside at Hester Prynne, "how my heart dreads this interview, and yearns for it! But, in truth, as I already told thee, children are not readily won to be familiar with me. They will not climb my knee, nor prattle in my ear, nor answer to my smile; but stand apart, and eye me strangely. Even little babes, when I take them in my arms, weep bitterly. Yet Pearl, twice in her little lifetime, hath been kind to me! The first time,—thou knowest it well! The last was when thou ledst her with thee to the house of yonder stern old Governor."

7   "And thou didst plead so bravely in her behalf and mine!" answered the mother. "I remember it; and so shall little Pearl. Fear nothing! She may be strange and shy at first, but will soon learn to love thee!"

8   By this time Pearl had reached the margin of the brook, and stood on the farther side, gazing silently at Hester and the clergyman, who still sat together on the mossy tree-trunk, waiting to receive her. Just where she had paused the brook chanced to form a pool, so smooth and quiet that it reflected a perfect image of her little figure, with all the brilliant picturesqueness of her beauty, in its adornment of flowers and wreathed foliage, but more refined and spiritualized than the reality. This image, so nearly identical with the living Pearl, seemed to communicate somewhat of its own shadowy and intangible quality to the child herself. It was strange, the way in which Pearl stood, looking so stedfastly at

them through the dim medium of the forest-gloom; herself, meanwhile, all glo-rified with a ray of sunshine, that was attracted thitherward as by a certain sym-pathy. In the brook beneath stood another child,—another and the same,—with likewise its ray of golden light. Hester felt herself, in some indistinct and tanta-lizing manner, estranged from Pearl; as if the child, in her lonely ramble through the forest, had strayed out of the sphere in which she and her mother dwelt together, and was now vainly seeking to return to it.

9   There was both truth and error in the impression; the child and mother were estranged, but through Hester's fault, not Pearl's. Since the latter rambled from her side, another inmate had been admitted within the circle of the mother's feel-ings, and so modified the aspect of them all, that Pearl, the returning wanderer, could not find her wonted place, and hardly knew where she was.

10   "I have a strange fancy," observed the sensitive minister, "that this brook is the boundary between two worlds, and that thou canst never meet thy Pearl again. Or is she an elfish spirit, who, as the legends of our childhood taught us, is forbidden to cross a running stream? Pray hasten her; for this delay has already imparted a tremor to my nerves."

11   "Come, dearest child!" said Hester encouragingly, and stretching out both her arms. "How slow thou art! When hast thou been so sluggish before now? Here is a friend of mine, who must be thy friend also. Thou wilt have twice as much love, henceforward, as thy mother alone could give thee! Leap across the brook and come to us. Thou canst leap like a young deer!"

12   Pearl, without responding in any manner to these honeysweet expressions, remained on the other side of the brook. Now she fixed her bright, wild eyes on her mother, now on the minister, and now included them both in the same glance; as if to detect and explain to herself the relation which they bore to one another. For some unaccountable reason, as Arthur Dimmesdale felt the child's eyes upon him-self, his hand—with that gesture so habitual as to have become involuntary—stole over his heart. At length, assuming a singular air of authority, Pearl stretched out her hand, with the small forefinger extended, and pointing evidently towards her mother's breast. And beneath, in the mirror of the brook, there was the flower-girdled and sunny image of little Pearl, pointing her small forefinger too.

13   "Thou strange child, why dost thou not come to me?" exclaimed Hester.

14   Pearl still pointed with her forefinger; and a frown gathered on her brow; the more impressive from the childish, the almost baby-like aspect of the features that conveyed it. As her mother still kept beckoning to her, and arraying her face in a holiday suit of unaccustomed smiles, the child stamped her foot with a yet more imperious look and gesture. In the brook, again, was the fantastic beauty of the image, with its reflected frown, its pointed finger, and imperious gesture, giving emphasis to the aspect of little Pearl.

15   "Hasten, Pearl; or I shall be angry with thee!" cried Hester Prynne, who, however inured to such behaviour on the elf-child's part at other seasons, was naturally anxious for a more seemly deportment now. "Leap across the brook, naughty child, and run hither! Else I must come to thee!"

16 But Pearl, not a whit startled at her mother's threats, any more than mollified by her entreaties, now suddenly burst into a fit of passion, gesticulating violently, and throwing her small figure into the most extravagant contortions. She accompanied this wild outbreak with piercing shrieks, which the woods reverberated on all sides; so that, alone as she was in her childish and unreasonable wrath, it seemed as if a hidden multitude were lending her their sympathy and encouragement. Seen in the brook, once more, was the shadowy wrath of Pearl's image, crowned and girdled with flowers, but stamping its foot, wildly gesticulating, and, in the midst of all, still pointing its small forefinger at Hester's bosom!

17 "I see what ails the child," whispered Hester to the clergyman, and turning pale in spite of a strong effort to conceal her trouble and annoyance. "Children will not abide any, the slightest, change in the accustomed aspect of things that are daily before their eyes. Pearl misses something which she has always seen me wear!"

18 "I pray you," answered the minister, "if thou hast any means of pacifying the child, do it forthwith! Save it were the cankered wrath of an old witch, like Mistress Hibbins," added he, attempting to smile, "I know nothing that I would not sooner encounter than this passion in a child. In Pearl's young beauty, as in the wrinkled witch, it has a preternatural effect. Pacify her, if thou lovest me!"

19 Hester turned again towards Pearl, with a crimson blush upon her cheek, a conscious glance aside at the clergyman, and then a heavy sigh; while, even before she had time to speak, the blush yielded to a deadly pallor.

20 "Pearl," said she, sadly, "look down at thy feet! There!—before thee!—on the hither side of the brook!"

21 The child turned her eyes to the point indicated; and there lay the scarlet letter, so close upon the margin of the stream, that the gold embroidery was reflected in it.

22 "Bring it hither!" said Hester.

23 "Come thou and take it up!" answered Pearl.

24 "Was ever such a child!" observed Hester aside to the minister. "O, I have much to tell thee about her. But, in very truth, she is right as regards this hateful token. I must bear its torture yet a little longer,—only a few days longer,—until we shall have left this region, and look back hither as to a land which we have dreamed of. The forest cannot hide it! The mid-ocean shall take it from my hand, and swallow it up for ever!"

25 With these words, she advanced to the margin of the brook, took up the scarlet letter, and fastened it again into her bosom. Hopefully, but a moment ago, as Hester had spoken of drowning it in the deep sea, there was a sense of inevitable doom upon her, as she thus received back this deadly symbol from the hand of fate. She had flung it into infinite space!—she had drawn an hour's free breath!—and here again was the scarlet misery, glittering on the old spot! So it ever is, whether thus typified or no, that an evil deed invests itself with the character of doom. Hester next gathered up the heavy tresses of her hair, and confined them

beneath her cap. As if there were a withering spell in the sad letter, her beauty, the warmth and richness of her womanhood, departed, like fading sunshine; and a gray shadow seemed to fall across her.

26   When the dreary change was wrought, she extended her hand to Pearl.

27   "Dost thou know thy mother now, child?" asked she, reproachfully, but with a subdued tone. "Wilt thou come across the brook, and own thy mother, now that she has her shame upon her,—now that she is sad?"

28   "Yes: now I will!" answered the child, bounding across the brook, and clasping Hester in her arms. "Now thou art my mother indeed! And I am thy little Pearl!"

29   In a mood of tenderness that was not usual with her, she drew down her mother's head, and kissed her brow and both her cheeks. But then—by a kind of necessity that always impelled this child to alloy whatever comfort she might chance to give with a throb of anguish—Pearl put up her mouth, and kissed the scarlet letter too!

30   "That was not kind!" said Hester. "When thou hast shown me a little love, thou mockest me!"

31   "Why doth the minister sit yonder?" asked Pearl.

32   "He waits to welcome thee," replied her mother. "Come thou, and entreat his blessing! He loves thee, my little Pearl, and loves thy mother too. Wilt thou not love him? Come! he longs to greet thee!"

33   "Doth he love us?" said Pearl, looking up with acute intelligence into her mother's face. "Will he go back with us, hand in hand, we three together, into the town?"

34   "Not now, dear child," answered Hester. "But in days to come he will walk hand in hand with us. We will have a home and fireside of our own; and thou shalt sit upon his knee; and he will teach thee many things, and love thee dearly. Thou wilt love him; wilt thou not?"

35   "And will he always keep his hand over his heart?" inquired Pearl.

36   "Foolish child, what a question is that!" exclaimed her mother. "Come and ask his blessing!"

37   But, whether influenced by the jealousy that seems instinctive with every petted child towards a dangerous rival, or from whatever caprice of her freakish nature, Pearl would show no favor to the clergyman. It was only by an exertion of force that her mother brought her up to him, hanging back, and manifesting her reluctance by odd grimaces; of which, ever since her babyhood, she had possessed a singular variety, and could transform her mobile physiognomy into a series of different aspects, with a new mischief in them, each and all. The minister— painfully embarrassed, but hoping that a kiss might prove a talisman to admit him into the child's kindlier regards—bent forward, and impressed one on her brow. Hereupon, Pearl broke away from her mother, and, running to the brook, stooped over it, and bathed her forehead, until the unwelcome kiss was quite washed off, and diffused through a long lapse of the gliding water. She then remained apart, silently watching Hester and the clergyman; while they talked

together, and made such arrangements as were suggested by their new position, and the purposes soon to be fulfilled.

38   And now this fateful interview had come to a close. The dell was to be left a solitude among its dark, old trees, which, with their multitudinous tongues, would whisper long of what had passed there, and no mortal be the wiser. And the melancholy brook would add this other tale to the mystery with which its little heart was already overburdened, and whereof it still kept up a murmuring babble, with not a whit more cheerfulness of tone than for ages heretofore.

CHAPTER 19

JOURNAL

1. **MLA Works Cited** *Using this model, record this book.*
   Author's Last Name, First Name. The Scarlet Letter. *1850.* Title of This Book.
   Ed. First Name Last Name. City: Publisher, year.
2. **Main Character(s)** *Describe each main character and explain why you think each is a main character.*
3. **Supporting Characters** *Describe each supporting character and explain why you think each is a supporting character.*
4. **Setting** *Describe the setting(s) and any relevant prop(s).*
5. **Sequence** *Outline the events in this chapter in order.*
6. **Plot** *Summarize this chapter's events in no more than two sentences.*
7. **Conflicts** *Identify and explain all conflicts involved in this chapter.*
8. **Significant Quotations** *Explain the importance of each of these quotations. Record the page number in the parentheses.*
   a. " 'Thou wilt love her dearly,' repeated Hester Prynne, as she and the minister sat watching little Pearl. 'Dost thou not think her beautiful? [. . .]' " (   ).
   b. " 'Thou canst not think,' said the minister, glancing aside at Hester Prynne, 'how my heart dreads this interview, and yearns for it! [. . .]' " (   ).
   c. "[T]he child and mother were estranged, but through Hester's fault, not Pearl's. Since the latter had rambled from her side, another inmate had been admitted within the circle of her mother's feelings, and so modified the aspect of them all, that Pearl, the returning wanderer, could not find her wonted place, and hardly knew where she was" (   ).
   d. " 'Yes; now I will!' answered the child, bounding across the brook, and clasping Hester in her arms. 'Now thou art my mother indeed! And I am thy little Pearl!' " (   ).
   e. "The minister—painfully embarrassed, but hoping that a kiss might prove a talisman to admit him into the child's kindlier regards—bent forward, and impressed one on her brow. Hereupon, Pearl broke away from her mother, and running to the brook, stooped over it, and bathed her forehead, until the unwelcome kiss was quite washed off [. . .]" (   ).

9. **Recap** *Summarize what has happened so far, from the beginning of the book through this chapter.*

FOLLOW-UP QUESTIONS

6 SHORT QUESTIONS

Select the __best__ answer for each.

____ 1. Arthur Dimmesdale is
      a. ready to be a father.
      b. popular with the children of the church.
      c. afraid to be a father.

____ 2. Pearl refuses to
      a. pick flowers.
      b. cross the brook.
      c. look at her mother.

____ 3. Pearl wants her mother to
      a. wear the scarlet letter.
      b. let down her hair.
      c. give her a kiss.

____ 4. To get her way, Pearl
      a. begs Hester and Arthur.
      b. throws a tantrum.
      c. stands still.

____ 5. Pearl would like her father to
      a. kiss her.
      b. walk into town together with her and Hester.
      c. sit in the sunshine.

____ 6. When Arthur Dimmesdale kisses Pearl, she
      a. washes her face.
      b. kisses him back.
      c. smiles happily.

5 SIGNIFICANT QUOTATIONS

Explain the importance of each of these quotations.

1. " 'How slow thou art! When hast thou been so sluggish before now? Here is a friend of mine, who must be thy friend also. Thou wilt have twice as much love, henceforward, as thy mother alone could give thee! Leap across the brook and come to us. Thou canst leap like a young deer!' "

2. "But Pearl [. . .] now suddenly burst into a fit of passion, gesticulating violently, and throwing her small figure into the most extravagant contortions. She accompanied this wild outbreak with piercing shrieks, which the woods reverberated on all sides [. . .]."

3. " 'I see what ails the child,' whispered Hester [. . .]. 'Children will not abide any, the slightest, change in the accustomed aspect of things that are daily before their eyes. Pearl misses something which she has always seen me wear!' "

4. "Hester next gathered up the heavy tresses of her hair, and confined them beneath her cap. As if there were a withering spell in the sad letter, her beauty, the warmth and richness of her womanhood, departed, like fading sunshine; and a gray shadow seemed to fall across her."

5. "'Doth he love us?' said Pearl, looking up with acute intelligence into her mother's face. 'Will he go back with us, hand in hand, we three together, into the town?'"

2 COMPREHENSION ESSAY QUESTIONS

Use specific details and information from the chapter to answer these questions as completely as possible.

1. Children respond to changes in accustomed routines in unexpected ways. How does Pearl respond to change in this chapter? Use specific details and information from this chapter and other parts of the novel to support your explanation.
2. What is the role of the scarlet letter in this chapter? Use specific details and information from this chapter and other parts of the novel to support your explanation.

DISCUSSION QUESTIONS

Be prepared to discuss these questions in class.

1. With which character(s) do you identify the most?
2. Was Pearl's response to Arthur and her mother a surprise? Why or why not?

CHAPTER 20

THE MINISTER IN A MAZE

PRE-READING VOCABULARY
CONTEXT

Use context clues to define these words before reading. Use a dictionary as needed.

1. When Maritza became lost in a *maze* of one-way and dead-end streets in an unknown neighborhood, she had to ask for directions to find her way out. *Maze* means _____
   _____.

2. We have all experienced the ups and downs of life and we simply have to face these *vicissitudes* as they happen. *Vicissitudes* means _____
   _____.

3. The loud music from the neighbor's apartment *intruded* into our peace and quiet. *Intruded* means _____
   _____.

4. Jasper told lies to get people to admire him, and these acts of *duplicity* misled people about his true nature. *Duplicity* means _____
   _____.

5. The children experienced *disquietude* when they heard their parents arguing every night. *Disquietude* means _____
   _____.

6. Jody was quite *vexed* when the children tracked mud all over her clean floor. *Vexed* means _____
   _____.

7. Once Maryam completes 120 credits, she will be *eligible* for graduation. *Eligible* means _____
   _____.

8. The two-lane roadway was *inadequate* to handle the increased traffic of the growing township. *Inadequate* means _____
   _____.

9. Although Linda was on a diet to lose weight, she was very *tempted* to eat the chocolate pie with whipped cream. *Tempted* means _____.

10. Michael hurried to catch the plane before it *departed* for Seattle. *Departed* means _____.

11. The generous donor wanted no one to know the source of the gift, so her name was kept in *secrecy*. *Secrecy* means _____.

12. These days, both parents work to *sustain* an adequate income to provide for their children and pay their mortgage. *Sustain* means _____.

13. Trains from Florida to northern cities will *terminate* in New York City and you must switch trains if you want to go further. *Terminate* means _____.

14. The sounds from the noisy classroom *ceased* when the instructor entered the room. *Cease* means _____.

15. In the 1600s, the Puritans, Pilgrims, and other immigrants left the *Old World*, or Europe, and traveled to the *New World*, settling in various colonies in America. *Old World* means and *New World* means _____.

16. The farmer *toiled* all day, turning over the soil and planting new seed. *Toil* means _____.

17. In philosophy class we discuss such *profound* ideas as life and death, ethics and morality, and our own sense of identity. *Profound* means _____.

18. It would be *blasphemous* for a minister or priest to deny the existence of God. *Blasphemous* means _____.

19. Not saying "Thank you" or "Excuse me" when in the company of others, and burping at the table are considered *uncouth* acts. *Uncouth* means _____.

20. Everyone at the party laughed when Barbara tried to prove she knew more jokes and *jests* than anyone else. *Jests* means _____
_____ .

PRE-READING VOCABULARY
STRUCTURAL ATTACK

Define these words by solving the parts. Use the Glossary or a dictionary as needed.

1. backward	13. fragrantly	25. commune
2. overthrown	14. pithy	26. deliberate
3. wigwam	15. maiden	27. gratuitous
4. impulsive	16. bartered	28. eccentricity
5. rudely	17. gilded	29. formerly
6. vibrate	18. ransack	30. unperformed
7. requite	19. ludicrous	31. tracts
8. patriarchal	20. valiantly	32. steeds
9. entitle	21. professional	33. sheltered
10. bewilder	22. improper	34. seaboard
11. incite	23. recompense	
12. reminiscence	24. decorum	

PRE-READING QUESTIONS

Try answering these questions as you read.

Where does Arthur Dimmesdale plan to go?
At what big event will Arthur Dimmesdale give a speech?
How does Arthur Dimmesdale act towards the townspeople?
What are Arthur Dimmesdale's inner feelings?

CHAPTER 20

THE MINISTER IN A MAZE

1 As the minister departed, in advance of Hester Prynne and little Pearl, he threw a backward glance; half expecting that he should discover only some faintly traced features or outline of the mother and the child, slowly fading into the twilight of the woods. So great a vicissitude in his life could not at once be received as real. But there was Hester, clad in her gray robe, still standing beside the tree-trunk, which some blast had overthrown a long antiquity ago, and which time had ever since been covering with moss, so that these two fated ones, with earth's heaviest burden on them, might there sit down together, and find a single hour's

rest and solace. And there was Pearl, too, lightly dancing from the margin of the brook,—now that the intrusive third person was gone,—and taking her old place by her mother's side. So the minister had not fallen asleep, and dreamed!

2   In order to free his mind from this indistinctness and duplicity of impression, which vexed it with a strange disquietude, he recalled and more thoroughly defined the plans which Hester and himself had sketched for their departure. It had been determined between them, that the Old World, with its crowds and cities, offered them a more eligible shelter and concealment than the wilds of New England, or all America, with its alternatives of an Indian wigwam, or the few settlements of Europeans, scattered thinly along the seaboard. Not to speak of the clergyman's health, so inadequate to sustain the hardships of a forest life, his native gifts, his culture, and his entire development would secure him a home only in the midst of civilization and refinement; the higher the state, the more delicately adapted to it the man. In furtherance of this choice, it so happened that a ship lay in the harbour; one of those questionable cruisers, frequent at that day, which, without being absolutely outlaws of the deep, yet roamed over its surface with a remarkable irresponsibility of character. This vessel had recently arrived from the Spanish Main, and, within three days' time, would sail for Bristol. Hester Prynne—whose vocation, as a self-enlisted Sister of Charity, had brought her acquainted with the captain and crew—could take upon herself to secure the passage of two individuals and a child, with all the secrecy which circumstances rendered more than desirable.

3   The minister had inquired of Hester, with no little interest, the precise time at which the vessel might be expected to depart. It would probably be on the fourth day from the present. "That is most fortunate!" he had then said to himself. Now, why the Reverend Mr. Dimmesdale considered it so very fortunate, we hesitate to reveal. Nevertheless,—to hold nothing back from the reader,—it was because, on the third day from the present, he was to preach the Election Sermon, and, as such an occasion formed an honorable epoch in the life of a New England clergyman, he could not have chanced upon a more suitable mode and time of terminating his professional career. "At least, they shall say of me," thought this exemplary man, "that I leave no public duty unperformed, nor ill performed!" Sad, indeed, that an introspection so profound and acute as this poor minister's should be so miserably deceived! We have had, and may still have, worse things to tell of him; but none, we apprehend, so pitiably weak; no evidence, at once so slight and irrefragable, of a subtle disease, that had long since begun to eat into the real substance of his character. No man, for any considerable period, can wear one face to himself, and another to the multitude, without finally getting bewildered as to which may be the true.

4   The excitement of Mr. Dimmesdale's feelings, as he returned from his interview with Hester, lent him unaccustomed physical energy, and hurried him townward at a rapid pace. The pathway among the woods seemed wilder, more uncouth with its rude natural obstacles, and less trodden by the foot of man, than he remembered it on his outward journey. But he leaped across the plashy places,

thrust himself through the clinging underbrush, climbed the ascent, plunged into the hollow, and overcame, in short, all the difficulties of the track, with an unweariable activity that astonished him. He could not but recall how feebly, and with what frequent pauses for breath, he had toiled over the same ground only two days before. As he drew near the town, he took an impression of change from the series of familiar objects that presented themselves. It seemed not yesterday, not one, nor two, but many days, or even years ago, since he had quitted them. There, indeed, was each former trace of the street, as he remembered it, and all the peculiarities of the houses, with the due multitude of gable-peaks, and a weathercock at every point where his memory suggested one. Not the less, however, came this importunately obtrusive sense of change. The same was true as regarded the acquaintances whom he met, and all the well-known shapes of human life, about the little town. They looked neither older nor younger, now; the beards of the aged were no whiter, nor could the creeping babe of yesterday walk on his feet to-day; it was impossible to describe in what respect they differed from the individuals on whom he had so recently bestowed a parting glance; and yet the minister's deepest sense seemed to inform him of their mutability. A similar impression struck him most remarkably, as he passed under the walls of his own church. The edifice had so very strange, and yet so familiar, an aspect, that Mr. Dimmesdale's mind vibrated between two ideas; either that he had seen it only in a dream hitherto, or that he was merely dreaming about it now.

5   This phenomenon, in the various shapes which it assumed, indicated no external change, but so sudden and important a change in the spectator of the familiar scene, that the intervening space of a single day had operated on his consciousness like the lapse of years. The minister's own will, and Hester's will, and the fate that grew between them, had wrought this transformation. It was the same town as heretofore; but the same minister returned not from the forest. He might have said to the friends who greeted him,—"I am not the man for whom you take me! I left him yonder in the forest, withdrawn into a secret dell, by a mossy tree-trunk, and near a melancholy brook! Go, seek your minister, and see if his emaciated figure, his thin cheek, his white, heavy, pain-wrinkled brow, be not flung down there like a cast-off garment!" His friends, no doubt, will still have insisted with him,—"Thou art thyself the man!"—but the error would have been their own, not his.

6   Before Mr. Dimmesdale reached home, his inner man gave him other evidences of a revolution in the sphere of thought and feeling. In truth, nothing short of a total change of dynasty and moral code, in that interior kingdom, was adequate to account for the impulses now communicated to the unfortunate and startled minister. At every step he was incited to do some strange, wild, wicked thing or other, with a sense that it would be at once involuntary and intentional; in spite of himself, yet growing out of a profounder self than that which opposed the impulse. For instance, he met one of his own deacons. The good old man addressed him with the paternal affection and patriarchal privilege, which his

venerable age, his upright and holy character, and his station in the Church, entitled him to use; and, conjoined with this, the deep, almost worshipping respect, which the minister's professional and private claims alike demanded. Never was there a more beautiful example of how the majesty of age and wisdom may comport with the obeisance and respect enjoined upon it, as from a lower social rank and inferior order of endowment, towards a higher. Now, during a conversation of some two or three moments between the Reverend Mr. Dimmesdale and this excellent and hoary-bearded deacon, it was only by the most careful self-control that the former could refrain from uttering certain blasphemous suggestions that rose into his mind, respecting the communion-supper. He absolutely trembled and turned pale as ashes, lest his tongue should wag itself, in utterance of these horrible matters, and plead his own consent for so doing, without his having fairly given it. And, even with this terror in his heart, he could hardly avoid laughing to imagine how the sanctified old patriarchal deacon would have been petrified by his minister's impiety!

7   Again, another incident of the same nature. Hurrying along the street, the Reverend Mr. Dimmesdale encountered the eldest female member of his church; a most pious and exemplary old dame; poor, widowed, lonely, and with a heart as full of reminiscences about her dead husband and children, and her dead friends of long ago, as a burial-ground is full of storied gravestones. Yet all this, which would else have been such heavy sorrow, was made almost a solemn joy to her devout old soul by religious consolations and the truths of Scripture, wherewith she had fed herself continually for more than thirty years. And, since Mr. Dimmesdale had taken her in charge, the good grandam's chief earthly comfort—which, unless it had been likewise a heavenly comfort, could have been none at all—was to meet her pastor, whether casually, or of set purpose, and be refreshed with a word of warm, fragrant, heaven-breathing Gospel truth from his beloved lips into her dulled, but rapturously attentive ear. But, on this occasion, up to the moment of putting his lips to the old woman's ear, Mr. Dimmesdale, as the great enemy of souls would have it, could recall no text of Scripture, nor aught else, except a brief, pithy, and, as it then appeared to him, unanswerable argument against the immortality of the human soul. The instilment thereof into her mind would probably have caused this aged sister to drop down dead, at once, as by the effect of an intensely poisonous infusion. What he really did whisper, the minister could never afterwards recollect. There was, perhaps, a fortunate disorder in his utterance, which failed to impart any distinct idea to the good widow's comprehension, or which Providence interpreted after a method of its own. Assuredly, as the minister looked back, he beheld an expression of divine gratitude and ecstasy that seemed like the shine of the celestial city on her face, so wrinkled and ashy pale.

8   Again, a third instance. After parting from the old church-member, he met the youngest sister of them all. It was a maiden newly won—and won by the Reverend Mr. Dimmesdale's own sermon, on the Sabbath after his vigil—to barter the transitory pleasures of the world for the heavenly hope, that was to

assume brighter substance as life grew dark around her, and which would gild the utter gloom with final glory. She was fair and pure as a lily that had bloomed in Paradise. The minister knew well that he was himself enshrined within the stainless sanctity of her heart, which hung its snowy curtains about his image, imparting to religion the warmth of love, and to love a religious purity. Satan, that afternoon, had surely led the poor young girl away from her mother's side, and thrown her into the pathway of this sorely tempted, or—shall we not rather say?—this lost and desperate man. As she drew nigh, the arch-fiend whispered him to condense into small compass and drop into her tender bosom a germ of evil that would be sure to blossom darkly soon, and bear black fruit betimes. Such was his sense of power over this virgin soul, trusting him as she did, that the minister felt potent to blight all the field of innocence with but one wicked look, and develop all its opposite with but a word. So—with a mightier struggle than he had yet sustained—he held his Geneva cloak before his face, and hurried onward, making no sign of recognition, and leaving the young sister to digest his rudeness as she might. She ransacked her conscience,—which was full of harmless little matters, like her pocket or her work-bag,—and took herself to task, poor thing, for a thousand imaginary faults; and went about her household duties with swollen eyelids the next morning.

9   Before the minister had time to celebrate his victory over this last temptation, he was conscious of another impulse, more ludicrous, and almost as horrible. It was,—we blush to tell it,—it was to stop short in the road, and teach some very wicked words to a knot of little Puritan children who were playing there, and had but just begun to talk. Denying himself this freak, as unworthy of his cloth, he met a drunken seaman, one of the ship's crew from the Spanish Main. And, here, since he had so valiantly forborne all other wickedness, poor Mr. Dimmesdale longed, at least, to shake hands with the tarry blackguard, and recreate himself with a few improper jests, such as dissolute sailors so abound with, and a volley of good, round, solid, satisfactory, and heaven-defying oaths! It was not so much a better principle, as partly his natural good-taste, and still more his buckramed habit of clerical decorum, that carried him safely through the latter crisis.

10   "What is it that haunts and tempts me thus?' cried the minister to himself, at length, pausing in the street, and striking his hand against his forehead. "Am I mad? or am I given over utterly to the fiend? Did I make a contract with him in the forest, and sign it with my blood? And does he now summon me to its fulfilment, by suggesting the performance of every wickedness which his most foul imagination can conceive?"

11   At the moment when the Reverend Mr. Dimmesdale thus communed with himself, and struck his forehead with his hand, old Mistress Hibbins, the reputed witch-lady, is said to have been passing by. She made a very grand appearance; having on a high head-dress, a rich gown of velvet, and a ruff done up with the famous yellow starch, of which Ann Turner, her especial friend, had taught her the secret, before this last good lady had been hanged for Sir Thomas Overbury's

murder. Whether the witch had read the minister's thoughts, or no, she came to a full stop, looked shrewdly into his face, smiled craftily, and—though little given to converse with clergymen—began a conversation.

12   "So, reverend Sir, you have made a visit into the forest," observed the witch-lady, nodding her high head-dress at him. "The next time, I pray you to allow me only a fair warning, and I shall be proud to bear you company. Without taking overmuch upon myself, my good word will go far towards gaining any strange gentleman a fair reception from yonder potentate you wot of!"

13   "I profess, madam," answered the clergyman, with a grave obeisance, such as the lady's rank demanded, and his own good-breeding made imperative,—"I profess, on my conscience and character, that I am utterly bewildered as touching the purport of your words! I went not into the forest to seek a potentate; neither do I, at any future time, design a visit thither, with a view to gaining the favor of such personage. My one sufficient object was to greet that pious friend of mine, the Apostle Eliot, and rejoice with him over the many precious souls he hath won from heathendom!"

14   "Ha, ha, ha!" cackled the old witch-lady, still nodding her high head-dress at the minister. "Well, well, we must needs talk thus in the daytime! You carry it off like an old hand! But at midnight, and in the forest, we shall have other talk together!"

15   She passed on with her aged stateliness, but often turning back her head and smiling at him, like one willing to recognize a secret intimacy of connection.

16   "Have I then sold myself," thought the minister, "to the fiend whom, if men say true, this yellow-starched and velveted old hag has chosen for her prince and master!"

17   The wretched minister! He had made a bargain very like it! Tempted by a dream of happiness, he had yielded himself with deliberate choice, as he had never done before, to what he knew was deadly sin. And the infectious poison of that sin had been thus rapidly diffused throughout his moral system. It had stupefied all blessed impulses, and awakened into vivid life the whole brotherhood of bad ones. Scorn, bitterness, unprovoked malignity, gratuitous desire of ill, ridicule of whatever was good and holy, all awoke, to tempt, even while they frightened him. And his encounter with old Mistress Hibbins, if it were a real incident, did but show his sympathy and fellowship with wicked mortals and the world of perverted spirits.

18   He had by this time reached his dwelling, on the edge of the burial-ground, and, hastening up the stairs, took refuge in his study. The minister was glad to have reached this shelter, without first betraying himself to the world by any of those strange and wicked eccentricities to which he had been continually impelled while passing through the streets. He entered the accustomed room, and looked around him on its books, its windows, its fireplace, and the tapestried comfort of the walls, with the same perception of strangeness that had haunted him throughout his walk from the forest-dell into the town, and thitherward. Here he had studied and written; here, gone through fast and vigil, and come

forth half alive; here, striven to pray; here, borne a hundred thousand agonies! There was the Bible, in its rich old Hebrew, with Moses and the Prophets speaking to him, and God's voice through all! There, on the table, with the inky pen beside it, was an unfinished sermon, with a sentence broken in the midst, where his thoughts had ceased to gush out upon the page two days before. He knew that it was himself, the thin and white-cheeked minister, who had done and suffered these things, and written thus far into the Election Sermon! But he seemed to stand apart, and eye this former self with scornful, pitying, but half-envious curiosity. That self was gone! Another man had returned out of the forest; a wiser one; with a knowledge of hidden mysteries which the simplicity of the former never could have reached. A bitter kind of knowledge that!

19   While occupied with these reflections, a knock came at the door of the study, and the minister said, "Come in!"—not wholly devoid of an idea that he might behold an evil spirit. And so he did! It was old Roger Chillingworth that entered. The minister stood, white and speechless, with one hand on the Hebrew Scriptures, and the other spread upon his breast.

20   "Welcome home, reverend Sir!" said the physician. "And how found you that godly man, the Apostle Eliot? But methinks, dear Sir, you look pale; as if the travel through the wilderness had been too sore for you. Will not my aid be requisite to put you in heart and strength to preach your Election Sermon?"

21   "Nay, I think not so," rejoined the Reverend Mr. Dimmesdale. "My journey, and the sight of the holy Apostle yonder, and the free air which I have breathed, have done me good, after so long confinement in my study. I think to need no more of your drugs, my kind physician, good though they be, and administered by a friendly hand."

22   All this time, Roger Chillingworth was looking at the minister with the grave and intent regard of a physician towards his patient. But, in spite of this outward show, the latter was almost convinced of the old man's knowledge, or, at least, his confident suspicion, with respect to his own interview with Hester Prynne. The physician knew then, that, in the minister's regard, he was no longer a trusted friend, but his bitterest enemy. So much being known, it would appear natural that a part of it should be expressed. It is singular however, how long a time often passes before words embody things; and with what security two persons, who choose to avoid a certain subject, may approach its very verge, and retire without disturbing it. Thus, the minister felt no apprehension that Roger Chillingworth would touch, in express words, upon the real position which they sustained towards one another. Yet did the physician, in his dark way, creep frightfully near the secret.

23   "Were it not better," said he, "that you use my poor skill to night? Verily, dear Sir, we must take pains to make you strong and vigorous for this occasion of the Election discourse. The people look for great things from you; apprehending that another year may come about, and find their pastor gone."

24   "Yea, to another world," replied the minister, with pious resignation. "Heaven grant it be a better one; for, in good sooth, I hardly think to tarry with

my flock through the flitting seasons of another year! But, touching your medicine, kind Sir, in my present frame of body I need it not."

25   "I joy to hear it," answered the physician. "It may be that my remedies, so long administered in vain, begin now to take due effect. Happy man were I, and well deserving of New England's gratitude, could I achieve this cure!"

26   "I thank you from my heart, most watchful friend," said the Reverend Mr. Dimmesdale, with a solemn smile. "I thank you, and can but requite your good deeds with my prayers."

27   "A good man's prayers are golden recompense!" rejoined old Roger Chillingworth, as he took his leave. "Yea, they are the current gold coin of the New Jerusalem, with the King's own mint-mark on them!"

28   Left alone, the minister summoned a servant of the house, and requested food, which, being set before him, he ate with ravenous appetite. Then, flinging the already written pages of the Election Sermon into the fire, he forthwith began another, which he wrote with such an impulsive flow of thought and emotion, that he fancied himself inspired; and only wondered that Heaven should see fit to transmit the grand and solemn music of its oracles through so foul an organ-pipe as he. However, leaving that mystery to solve itself, or go unsolved for ever, he drove his task onward, with earnest haste and ecstasy. Thus the night fled away, as if it were a winged steed, and he careering on it; morning came, and peeped blushing through the curtains; and at last sunrise threw a golden beam into the study, and laid it right across the minister's bedazzled eyes. There he was, with the pen still between his fingers, and a vast, immeasurable tract of written space behind him!

CHAPTER 20

JOURNAL

1. **MLA Works Cited** *Using this model, record this book.*
   Author's Last Name, First Name. The Scarlet Letter. 1850. Title of This Book.
   Ed. First Name Last Name. City: Publisher, year.
2. **Main Character(s)** *Describe each main character and explain why you think each is a main character.*
3. **Supporting Characters** *Describe each supporting character and explain why you think each is a supporting character.*
4. **Setting** *Describe the setting(s) and any relevant prop(s).*
5. **Sequence** *Outline the events in this chapter in order.*
6. **Plot** *Summarize this chapter's events in no more than two sentences.*
7. **Conflicts** *Identify and explain all conflicts involved in this chapter.*
8. **Significant Quotations** *Explain the importance of each of these quotations. Record the page number in the parentheses.*
   a. "'At least, they shall say of me,' thought this exemplary man, 'that I leave no public duty unperformed, nor ill performed! [. . .]'" (   ).

    b. "No man, for any considerable period, can wear one face to himself, and another to the multitude, without finally getting bewildered as to which may be the true [. . .]" (   ).

    c. "But he leaped across the plashy places, thrust himself through the clinging underbrush, climbed the ascent, plunged into the hollow, and overcame, in short, all the difficulties of the track, with an unweariable activity that astonished him. He could not but recall how feebly, and with what frequent pauses for breath, he had toiled over the same ground only two days before [. . .]" (   ).

    d. "At every step he was incited to do some strange, wild, wicked thing or other, with a sense that it would be at once involuntary and intentional [. . .]" (   ).

    e. "The physician knew then, that, in the minister's regard, he was no longer a trusted friend, but his bitterest enemy [. . .]" (   ).

9. **Recap** *Summarize what has happened so far, from the beginning of the book through this chapter.*

FOLLOW-UP QUESTIONS

6 SHORT QUESTIONS

Select the <u>best</u> answer for each.

____ 1. Arthur Dimmesdale and Hester Prynne plan to
    a. move to a different part of New England.
    b. explore the wilderness.
    c. return to Europe.

____ 2. Arthur Dimmesdale and Hester Prynne plan to leave
    a. in less than a week.
    b. after a week.
    c. in a month.

____ 3. Arthur Dimmesdale will give an important speech
    a. within the next few days.
    b. one week later.
    c. one month later.

____ 4. The one person who recognizes Arthur's new feelings is
    a. Apostle Eliot.
    b. Mistress Hibbins.
    c. a maiden from his church.

____ 5. Arthur Dimmesdale refuses to
    a. hold Pearl's hand.
    b. take drugs from the physician.
    c. meet Mistress Hibbins.

____ 6. Roger Chillingworth knows that
    a. Arthur Dimmesdale sees him as a friend.
    b. Arthur Dimmesdale recognizes him as an enemy.
    c. Hester Prynne has kept their secret.

5 SIGNIFICANT QUOTATIONS

Explain the importance of each of these quotations.

1. "It had been determined between them, that the Old World, with its crowds and cities, offered them a more eligible shelter and concealment than the wilds of New England, or all America, with its alternatives of an Indian wigwam, or the few settlements of Europeans, scattered thinly along the seaboard [. . .]."
2. "[O]n the third day from the present, he was to preach the Election Sermon; and, as such an occasion formed an honorable epoch in the life of a New England clergyman, he could not have chanced upon a more suitable mode and time of terminating his professional career."
3. " 'What is it that haunts and tempts me thus?' cried the minister to himself, at length, pausing in the street, and striking his hand against his forehead. 'Am I mad? or am I given over utterly to the fiend? Did I make a contract with him in the forest, and sign it with my blood? [. . .].' "
4. " 'Were it not better,' said he, 'that you use my poor skill tonight? Verily, dear Sir, we must take pains to make you strong and vigorous for this occasion of the Election discourse. The people look for great things from you; apprehending that another year may come about, and find their pastor gone.' "
5. " 'I thank you from my heart, most watchful friend,' said the Reverend Mr. Dimmesdale, with a solemn smile. 'I thank you, and can but requite your good deeds with my prayers.' "

2 COMPREHENSION ESSAY QUESTIONS

Use specific details and information from the chapter to answer these questions as completely as possible.

1. Arthur Dimmesdale and Hester Prynne have made a major decision and Arthur has many new feelings as a result. What Arthur is going through? Use specific details and information from this chapter and the novel to explain.
2. What are the ironies in this chapter? Use specific details and information from the chapter in your explanation.

DISCUSSION QUESTIONS

Be prepared to discuss these questions in class.

1. The Reverend Arthur Dimmesdale has always been a model of good, moral behavior. How do you feel about his actions in this chapter?
2. How does the relationship between Arthur Dimmesdale and Roger Chillingworth change?

CHAPTERS 17–20

1. **MLA Works Cited** *Using this model, record this book.*
   Author's Last Name, First Name. The Scarlet Letter. 1850. Title of This Book.
   Ed. First Name Last Name. City: Publisher, year.
2. **Main Character(s)** *Describe each main character and explain why you think each is a main character.*
3. **Supporting Characters** *Describe each supporting character and explain why you think each is a supporting character.*
4. **Setting** *Describe the setting(s) and any relevant prop(s).*
5. **Sequence** *Outline the events in these chapters in order.*
6. **Plot** *Summarize these chapter's events in no more than five sentences.*
7. **Conflicts** *Identify and explain all conflicts involved in these chapters.*
8. **Significant Quotations** *Explain the importance of each of these quotations. Record the page number in the parentheses.*
   a. "'Had I but one friend,—or were it my worst enemy!—to whom, when sickened with the praises of all other men, I could daily betake myself, and be known as the vilest of sinners, methinks my soul might keep itself alive thereby. Even thus much of truth would save me! But, now, it is all falsehood!—all emptiness!—all death!'" ( ).
   b. "All the world had frowned on her,—for seven long years had it frowned upon this lonely woman,—and still she bore it all, nor ever once turned away her firm, sad eyes. Heaven, likewise, had frowned upon her, and she had not died. But the frown of this pale, weak, sinful, and sorrow-stricken man was what Hester could not bear, and live!" ( ).
   c. "'Thou shalt not go alone!' answered she, in a deep whisper.
      Then, all was spoken!" ( ).
   d. "So speaking, she undid the clasp that fastened the scarlet letter, and, taking it from her bosom, threw it to a distance among the withered leaves. [. . .]. The stigma gone, Hester heaved a long, deep sigh, in which the burden of shame and anguish departed from her spirit" ( ).
   e. "'Methought—O Hester, what a thought is that, and how terrible to dread it!—that my own features were partly repeated in her face, and so strikingly that the world might see them! But she is mostly thine!'" ( ).
   f. "With these words, she advanced to the margin of the brook, took up the scarlet letter, and fastened it again into her bosom. Hopefully, but a moment ago, as Hester had spoken of drowning it in the deep sea, there was a sense of inevitable doom upon her, as she thus received back this deadly symbol from the hand of fate [. . .]" ( ).
   g. "'Doth he love us?' said Pearl, looking up with acute intelligence into her mother's face. 'Will he go back with us, hand in hand, we three together, into the town?'" ( ).

h. "No man, for any considerable period, can wear one face to himself, and another to the multitude, without finally getting bewildered as to which may be the true [. . .]" (   ).

i. "Before the minister had time to celebrate his victory over this last temptation, he was conscious of another impulse, more ludicrous, and almost as horrible. It was,—we blush to tell it,—it was to stop short in the road, and teach some very wicked words to a knot of little Puritan children who were playing there, and had but just begun to talk [. . .]" (   ).

j. " 'But, touching your medicine, kind Sir, in my present frame of body I need it not' " (   ).

9. **Recap** *Summarize what has happened so far, from the beginning of the novel through these chapters.*

FOLLOW-UP QUESTIONS

20 SHORT QUESTIONS

Select the <u>best</u> answer for each.

____ 1. The members of his church
   a. revere Arthur Dimmesdale.
   b. barely tolerate Arthur Dimmesdale.
   c. scorn Arthur Dimmesdale.

____ 2. Regarding the way the church members feel about him, Arthur feels
   a. pride and happiness.
   b. guilt and despair.
   c. wisdom and experience.

____ 3. Years of good works and secret penance have
   a. helped ease Arthur's conscience.
   b. made Arthur a very holy man.
   c. made Arthur feel like a sinner.

____ 4. Hester reveals to Arthur that
   a. Roger Chillingworth is Pearl's father.
   b. Roger Chillingworth was her husband.
   c. Arthur is Pearl's father.

____ 5. When he hears this revelation, Arthur
   a. feels strengthened.
   b. frowns at Hester.
   c. laughs out loud.

____ 6. Arthur asks Hester
   a. to help him decide what to do.
   b. to confront Roger Chillingworth for him.
   c. to send Pearl away.

____ 7. Hester asks Arthur
   a. for money.
   b. to remove the scarlet letter.
   c. for forgiveness.

____ 8. Hester and Arthur decide
   a. not to tell Pearl about her father.
   b. to leave Boston.
   c. to confront the physician.

____ 9. When Hester removes the scarlet letter,
   a. the sun shines on her.
   b. Pearl is happy.
   c. Arthur gets up and leaves.

____ 10. Hester removes
    a. Arthur's hand from his heart.
    b. the flowers from Pearl's hair.
    c. her cap.

____ 11. While Arthur and Hester are talking, Pearl is
    a. sitting with them.
    b. heading into town.
    c. on the other side of the brook.

____ 12. Pearl is around
    a. three years old.
    b. seven years old.
    c. eleven years old.

____ 13. Arthur feels that Roger Chillingworth's sin is
    a. worse than theirs.
    b. less than theirs.
    c. similar to theirs.

____ 14. Hester and Arthur meet
    a. in the forest.
    b. at the beach.
    c. on the scaffold.

____ 15. Pearl refuses to
    a. leave her mother's side.
    b. play in the forest.
    c. come to Hester and Arthur.

____ 16. When Arthur Dimmesdale kisses her, Pearl
    a. is very happy.
    b. kisses him back.
    c. washes her face.

____ 17. As Arthur walks through town, he
    a. behaves as he usually does.
    b. is tempted to behave improperly.
    c. has no energy.

____ 18. After his visit with Hester, Arthur Dimmesdale spends the night
    a. dreaming of Hester.
    b. doing penance.
    c. rewriting a sermon.

____ 19. Roger Chillingworth knows that
    a. Arthur Dimmesdale sees him as an enemy.
    b. Arthur Dimmesdale sees him as a friend.
    c. Hester Prynne has kept her secret.

____ 20. Arthur Dimmesdale refuses to
    a. meet with Mistress Hibbins.
    b. take advice or medicine from Roger Chillingworth.
    c. give the Election Sermon.

10 SIGNIFICANT QUOTATIONS

Explain the importance of each of these quotations.

1. " 'You wrong yourself in this,' said Hester, gently. 'You have deeply and sorely repented. Your sin is left behind you, in the days long past. Your present life is not less holy, in very truth, than it seems in people's eyes. Is there no reality in the penitence thus sealed and witnessed by good works? And wherefore should it not bring you peace?' "

2. " 'O Arthur,' cried she, 'forgive me! [. . .] I consented to a deception. But a lie is never good, even though death threaten on the other side! Dost thou

not see what I would say? That old man!—the physician!—he whom they call Roger Chillingworth!—he was my husband!'"

3. "'Be thou strong for me!' answered he. 'Advise me what to do.'"

4. "'Let us not look back,' answered Hester Prynne. 'The past is gone! Wherefore should we linger upon it now? See! With this symbol, I undo it all, and make it as it had never been!'

   So speaking, she undid the clasp that fastened the scarlet letter, and [. . .] threw it to a distance among the withered leaves [. . .]."

5. "All at once, as with a sudden smile of heaven, forth burst the sunshine, pouring a very flood into the obscure forest, gladdening each green leaf, transmuting the yellow fallen ones to gold, and gleaming adown the gray trunks of the solemn trees [. . .]."

6. "It was with a feeling which neither of them had ever before experienced, that they sat and watched Pearl's slow advance. In her was visible the tie that united them [. . .]."

7. "Hester felt herself, in some indistinct and tantalizing manner, estranged from Pearl; as if the child, in her lonely ramble through the forest, had strayed out of the sphere in which she and her mother dwelt together, and was now vainly seeking to return to it."

8. "'Dost thou know thy mother now, child?' asked she, reproachfully, but with a subdued tone. 'Wilt thou come across the brook, and own thy mother, now that she has her shame upon her,—now that she is sad?'"

9. "The minister had inquired of Hester, with no little interest, the precise time at which the vessel might be expected to depart. It would probably be on the fourth day from the present. 'That is most fortunate!' he had then said to himself [. . .]."

10. "The wretched minister! He had made a bargain very like it! Tempted by a dream of happiness, he had yielded himself with deliberate choice, as he had never done before, to what he knew was deadly sin. And the infectious poison of that sin had been thus rapidly diffused throughout his moral system [. . .]."

2 COMPREHENSION ESSAY QUESTIONS

Use specific details and information from these chapters to answer these questions as completely as possible.

1. Which characters do you feel are most important in the story? Choose two characters that you feel you know the best. Describe the relationship between these two characters as well as their personalities and actions.

2. Betrayal from a trusted friend or associate can be difficult to face. Which characters are guilty of betrayal? Discuss their actions and the reasons for their actions.

DISCUSSION QUESTIONS

Be prepared to discuss these questions in class.

1. Which actors would you choose to play Hester Prynne, Roger Chillingworth, Arthur Dimmesdale, and little Pearl in a movie version of The Scarlet Letter?
2. How well does the meeting between Hester and Arthur go? Between Arthur and Pearl? Were you surprised by any of their actions or reactions?

WRITING

Use each of these ideas to write an essay.

1. Decisions can have far-reaching effects, as Hester Prynne, Roger Chillingworth, and Arthur Dimmesdale are finding out in The Scarlet Letter. Write about a decision that you have made—or that someone you know has made—and the effects it has had on your life.
2. Hester Prynne, Roger Chillingworth, and Arthur Dimmesdale have each, in some way, engaged in the deception of another character. Is deception ever justified? Justify your argument with examples from The Scarlet Letter or from real life.
3. We can see that the Puritans in The Scarlet Letter consider themselves to be very religious people. Do you consider yourself a religious person? Why or why not?
4. Hester chooses deliberately to meet Arthur Dimmesdale in a forest setting. Why? What effect does the setting have on these two characters? Use specific details and information from these chapters and the novel in your explanation.

FURTHER WRITING

1. Roger Chillingworth seems fixated on revenge. In fact, revenge has become the focus of his entire life. Does this make him psychopathic? Research characteristics of the psychopathic mind.
2. Much of the land surrounding Boston in this tale was wilderness. Today, much of that wilderness has disappeared. What efforts has your state or community made to preserve woods or parks? Research what has been saved or lost in your area.
3. Many medicinal remedies in the story come from plants. Research medicine in seventeenth century New England for common and uncommon ailments. Are any of these remedies still used in contemporary society?
4. While there are some dark or strange qualities to these characters and the colony, there are also some good qualities. Select a quality that you like about your family, community, or culture. Using specific examples, explain that quality to someone who knows nothing about your community, family, or culture.

CHAPTER 21

THE NEW ENGLAND HOLIDAY

PRE-READING VOCABULARY
CONTEXT

Use context clues to define these words before reading. Use a dictionary as needed.

1. Trains, buses, and automobiles all *convey* workers back and forth from home to work every day. *Convey* means _____
   _____.

2. Three small companies *incorporated* to form one large group. *Incorporate* means
   _____.

3. When Ellen's checkbook did not balance, she spent hours looking for the *inconsistency* until she found the error. *Inconsistency* means _____
   _____.

4. The women were all talking about the *apparel* they would wear to Tori's wedding on Saturday. *Apparel* means _____
   _____.

5. After running off the road, Marco was in extreme *peril* when his truck hung over the edge of a cliff. *Peril* means _____
   _____.

6. Overcome with emotion at the funeral, the grieving parents were *inarticulate*, unable to speak. *Inarticulate* means _____
   _____.

7. After drinking five cups of coffee, Adam was *restless* and could not sit still. *Restless* means _____
   _____.

8. At the Memorial Day parade, the mayor, leading the *procession*, was followed by the marching band and then the war veterans. *Procession* means _____
   _____.

9. After the *desperadoes* robbed the bank and shot up the town, the police and FBI were looking for them in seven states. *Desperadoes* means _____ _____.

10. Boston started as a small town, but eventually grew into a large *metropolis*, where thousands of people live and work. *Metropolis* means _____ _____.

11. Bees are noted for their great *industry* and hard work—they pollinate flowers, bring nectar back to the hive, and make large quantities of honey. *Industry* means _____ _____.

12. Alison's dream was so *vivid* that she thought about it all day. *Vivid* means _____.

13. After the hurricane, the *ferocity* of the waves scared even the bravest swimmers. *Ferocity* means _____ _____.

14. To pay for all of her purchases, Jacqueline *tendered* her credit card to the cashier. *Tendered* means _____ _____.

15. Many restaurants by the seashore adopt a *nautical* look to entice customers to eat there, decorating with plastic fish, diving equipment, and sailors' nets. *Nautical* means _____ _____.

16. The small child loved his teddy bear and would not *relinquish* it to anyone, so we had to wait until he fell asleep to wash it off. *Relinquish* means _____ _____.

17. Debbie and Wilson planned a trip to the Caribbean Islands, but, to their *consternation*, a hurricane canceled their plans. *Consternation* means _____ _____.

18. Paul loves the ocean and has always wanted to sail the seas as a *mariner*. *Mariner* means _____ _____.

19. When the soccer teams came out on the field, there was a great *stir and bustle* in the crowd and the eager fans grew excited as the game began. *Stir and bustle* means _____ _____.

20. When planning their wedding, Michael and Kim spent much time writing the words for the official *ceremony*. *Ceremony* means _____
_____.

PRE-READING VOCABULARY
STRUCTURAL ATTACK

Define these words by solving the parts. Use the Glossary or a dictionary as needed

1. betimes	12. improbable	23. bonfire
2. craftsman	13. weary	24. banquet
3. plebeian	14. languor	25. pageantry
4. marble	15. cordials	26. relaxed
5. inflexible	16. shimmer	27. posterity
6. miens	17. sparkle	28. exception
7. seer	18. domestic	29. gallantly
8. necessity	19. effervescence	30. apothecary
9. convert	20. cheery	31. vacant
10. triumph	21. exaggerate	32. scurvy
11. quenched	22. hereditary	

PRE-READING QUESTIONS

Try answering these questions as you read.

How has Boston changed over the years?
What kinds of people attend the celebration?
How do people treat Hester and Pearl?
What news does Hester learn?

CHAPTER 21

THE NEW ENGLAND HOLIDAY

1 Betimes in the morning of the day on which the new Governor was to receive his office at the hands of the people, Hester Prynne and little Pearl came into the marketplace. It was already thronged with the craftsmen and other plebeian

inhabitants of the town, in considerable numbers; among whom, likewise, were many rough figures, whose attire of deer-skins marked them as belonging to some of the forest settlements, which surrounded the little metropolis of the colony.

2   On this public holiday, as on all other occasions, for seven years past, Hester was clad in a garment of coarse gray cloth. Not more by its hue than by some indescribable peculiarity in its fashion, it had the effect of making her fade personally out of sight and outline; while, again, the scarlet letter brought her back from this twilight indistinctness, and revealed her under the moral aspect of its own illumination. Her face, so long familiar to the townspeople, showed the marble quietude which they were accustomed to behold there. It was like a mask; or rather, like the frozen calmness of a dead woman's features; owing this dreary resemblance to the fact that Hester was actually dead, in respect to any claim of sympathy, and had departed out of the world with which she still seemed to mingle.

3   It might be, on this one day that there was an expression unseen before, nor, indeed, vivid enough to be detected now; unless some preternaturally gifted observer should have first read the heart, and have afterwards sought a corresponding development in the countenance and mien. Such a spiritual seer might have conceived, that, after sustaining the gaze of the multitude through seven miserable years as a necessity, a penance, and something which it was a stern religion to endure, she now, for one last time more, encountered it freely and voluntarily, in order to convert what had so long been agony into a kind of triumph. "Look your last on the scarlet letter and its wearer!"—the people's victim and life-long bond-slave, as they fancied her, might say to them. "Yet a little while, and she will be beyond your reach! A few hours longer, and the deep, mysterious ocean will quench and hide for ever the symbol which ye have caused to burn upon her bosom!" Nor were it an inconsistency too improbable to be assigned to human nature, should we suppose a feeling of regret in Hester's mind, at the moment when she was about to win her freedom from the pain which had been thus deeply incorporated with her being. Might there not be an irresistible desire to quaff a last, long, breathless draught of the cup of wormwood and aloes, with which nearly all her years of womanhood had been perpetually flavored? The wine of life henceforth to be presented to her lips, must be indeed rich, delicious, and exhilarating, in its chased and golden beaker; or else leave an inevitable and weary languor, after the lees of bitterness wherewith she had been drugged, as with a cordial of intensest potency.

4   Pearl was decked out with airy gayety. It would have been impossible to guess that this bright and sunny apparition owed its existence to the shape of gloomy gray; or that a fancy, at once so gorgeous and so delicate as must have been requisite to contrive the child's apparel, was the same that had achieved a task perhaps more difficult, in imparting so distinct a peculiarity to Hester's simple robe. The dress, so proper was it to little Pearl, seemed an effluence, or inevitable development and outward manifestation of her character, no more to be separated from her than the many-hued brilliancy from a butterfly's wing, or the painted glory from the leaf of a bright flower. As with these, so with the child; her garb was all

of one idea with her nature. On this eventful day, moreover, there was a certain singular inquietude and excitement in her mood, resembling nothing so much as the shimmer of a diamond, that sparkles and flashes with the varied throbbings of the breast on which it is displayed. Children have always a sympathy in the agitations of those connected with them; always, especially, a sense of any trouble or impending revolution, of whatever kind, in domestic circumstances; and therefore Pearl, who was the gem on her mother's unquiet bosom, betrayed, by the very dance of her spirits, the emotions which none could detect in the marble passiveness of Hester's brow.

5   This effervescence made her flit with a bird-like movement, rather than walk by her mother's side. She broke continually into shouts of a wild, inarticulate, and sometimes piercing music. When they reached the market-place, she became still more restless, on perceiving the stir and bustle that enlivened the spot; for it was usually more like the broad and lonesome green before a village meeting-house, than the centre of a town's business.

6   "Why, what is this, mother?" cried she. "Wherefore have all the people left their work to-day? Is it a play-day for the whole world? See, there is the blacksmith! He has washed his sooty face, and put on his Sabbath-day clothes, and looks as if he would gladly be merry, if any kind body would only teach him how! And there is Master Brackett, the old jailer, nodding and smiling at me. Why does he do so, mother?"

7   "He remembers thee a little babe, my child," answered Hester.

8   "He should not nod and smile at me, for all that,—the black, grim, ugly-eyed old man!" said Pearl. "He may nod at thee if he will; for thou art clad in gray, and wearest the scarlet letter. But, see, mother, how many faces of strange people, and Indians among them, and sailors! What have they all come to do here in the market-place?"

9   "They wait to see the procession pass," said Hester. "For the Governor and the magistrates are to go by, and the ministers, and all the great people and good people, with the music, and the soldiers marching before them."

10   "And will the minister be there?" asked Pearl. "And will he hold out both his hands to me, as when thou ledst me to him from the brook-side?"

11   "He will be there, child," answered her mother. "But he will not greet thee to-day; nor must thou greet him."

12   "What a strange, sad man is he!" said the child, as if speaking partly to herself. "In the dark night-time, he calls us to him, and holds thy hand and mine, as when we stood with him on the scaffold yonder! And in the deep forest, where only the old trees can hear, and the strip of sky see it, he talks with thee, sitting on a heap of moss! And he kisses my forehead, too, so that the little brook would hardly wash it off! But here in the sunny day, and among all the people, he knows us not; nor must we know him! A strange, sad man is he, with his hand always over his heart!"

13   "Be quiet, Pearl! Thou understandest not these things," said her mother. "Think not now of the minister, but look about thee, and see how cheery is every

body's face to-day. The children have come from their schools, and the grown people from their workshops and their fields, on purpose to be happy. For, to-day, a new man is beginning to rule over them; and so—as has been the custom of mankind ever since a nation was first gathered—they make merry and rejoice; as if a good and golden year were at length to pass over the poor old world!"

14 It was as Hester said, in regard to the unwonted jollity that brightened the faces of the people. Into this festal season of the year—as it already was, and continued to be during the greater part of two centuries—the Puritans compressed whatever mirth and public joy they deemed allowable to human infirmity; thereby so far dispelling the customary cloud, that, for the space of a single holiday, they appeared scarcely more grave than most other communities at a period of general affliction.

15 But we perhaps exaggerate the gray or sable tinge, which undoubtedly characterized the mood and manners of the age. The persons now in the market-place of Boston had not been born to an inheritance of Puritanic gloom. They were native Englishmen, whose fathers had lived in the sunny richness of the Elizabethan epoch; a time when the life of England, viewed as one great mass, would appear to have been as stately, magnificent, and joyous, as the world has ever witnessed. Had they followed their hereditary taste, the New England settlers would have illustrated all events of public importance by bonfires, banquets, pageantries, and processions. Nor would it have been impracticable, in the observance of majestic ceremonies, to combine mirthful recreation with solemnity, and give, as it were, a grotesque and brilliant embroidery to the great robe of state, which a nation, at such festivals, puts on. There was some shadow of an attempt of this kind in the mode of celebrating the day on which the political year of the colony commenced. The dim reflection of a remembered splendor, a colorless and manifold diluted repetition of what they had beheld in proud old London,—we will not say at a royal coronation, but at a Lord Mayor's show,—might be traced in the customs which our forefathers instituted, with reference to the annual installation of magistrates. The fathers and founders of the commonwealth—the statesman, the priest, and the soldier—deemed it a duty then to assume the outward state and majesty, which, in accordance with antique style, was looked upon as the proper garb of public or social eminence. All came forth, to move in procession before the people's eye, and thus impart a needed dignity to the simple framework of a government so newly constructed.

16 Then, too, the people were countenanced, if not encouraged, in relaxing the severe and close application to their various modes of rugged industry, which, at all other times, seemed of the same piece and material with their religion. Here, it is true, were none of the appliances which popular merriment would so readily have found in the England of Elizabeth's time, or that of James;—no rude shows of a theatrical kind; no minstrel with his harp and legendary ballad, nor glee-man, with an ape dancing to his music; no juggler, with his tricks of mimic witchcraft; no Merry Andrew, to stir up the multitude with jests, perhaps hundreds of years old, but still effective, by their appeals to the very broadest sources

of mirthful sympathy. All such professors of the several branches of jocularity would have been sternly repressed, not only by the rigid discipline of law, but by the general sentiment which gives law its vitality. Not the less, however, the great, honest face of the people smiled, grimly, perhaps, but widely too. Nor were sports wanting, such as the colonists had witnessed, and shared in, long ago, at the country fairs and on the village-greens of England; and which it was thought well to keep alive on this new soil, for the sake of the courage and manliness that were essential in them. Wrestling-matches, in the differing fashions of Cornwall and Devonshire, were seen here and there about the market-place; in one corner, there was a friendly bout at quarterstaff; and—what attracted most interest of all—on the platform of the pillory, already so noted in our pages, two masters of defence were commencing an exhibition with the buckler and broadsword. But, much to the disappointment of the crowd, this latter business was broken off by the interposition of the town beadle, who had no idea of permitting the majesty of the law to be violated by such an abuse of one of its consecrated places.

17   It may not be too much to affirm, on the whole, (the people being then in the first stages of joyless deportment, and the offspring of sires who had known how to be-merry, in their day,) that they would compare favorably, in point of holiday keeping, with their descendants, even at so long an interval as ourselves. Their immediate posterity, the generation next to the early emigrants, wore the blackest shade of Puritanism, and so darkened the national visage with it, that all the subsequent years have not sufficed to clear it up. We have yet to learn again the forgotten art of gayety.

18   The picture of human life in the market-place, though its general tint was the sad gray, brown, or black of the English emigrants, was yet enlivened by some diversity of hue. A party of Indians—in their savage finery of curiously embroidered deerskin robes, wampum-belts, red and yellow ochre, and feathers, and armed with the bow and arrow and stone headed spear—stood apart, with countenances of inflexible gravity, beyond what even the Puritan aspect could attain. Nor, wild as were these painted barbarians, were they the wildest feature of the scene. This distinction could more justly be claimed by some mariners,— a part of the crew of the vessel from the Spanish Main,—who had come ashore to see the humors of Election Day. They were rough-looking desperadoes, with sun-blackened faces, and an immensity of beard; their wide, short trousers were confined about the waist by belts, often clasped with a rough plate of gold, and sustaining always a long knife, and, in some instances, a sword. From beneath their broad-brimmed hats of palm-leaf, gleamed eyes which, even in good nature and merriment, had a kind of animal ferocity. They transgressed, without fear or scruple, the rules of behaviour that were binding on all others; smoking tobacco under the beadle's very nose, although each whiff would have cost a townsman a shilling; and quaffing, at their pleasure, draughts of wine or aqua-vitæ from pocket-flasks, which they freely tendered to the gaping crowd around them. It remarkably characterized the incomplete morality of the age, rigid as we call it,

that a license was allowed the seafaring class, not merely for their freaks on shore, but for far more desperate deeds on their proper element. The sailor of that day would go near to be arraigned as a pirate in our own. There could be little doubt, for instance, that this very ship's crew, though no unfavorable specimens of the nautical brotherhood, had been guilty, as we should phrase it, of depredations on the Spanish commerce, such as would have perilled all their necks in a modern court of justice.

19   But the sea, in those old times, heaved, swelled, and foamed very much at its own will, or subject only to the tempestuous wind, with hardly any attempts at regulation by human law. The buccaneer on the wave might relinquish his calling, and become at once, if he chose, a man of probity and piety on land; nor, even in the full career of his reckless life, was he regarded as a personage with whom it was disreputable to traffic, or casually associate. Thus, the Puritan elders, in their black cloaks, starched bands, and steeple-crowned hats, smiled not unbenignantly at the clamor and rude deportment of these jolly seafaring men; and it excited neither surprise nor animadversion when so reputable a citizen as old Roger Chillingworth, the physician, was seen to enter the market-place, in close and familiar talk with the commander of the questionable vessel.

20   The latter was by far the most showy and gallant figure, so far as apparel went, anywhere to be seen among the multitude. He wore a profusion of ribbons on his garment, and gold lace on his hat, which was also encircled by a gold chain, and surmounted with a feather. There was a sword at his side, and a sword-cut on his forehead, which, by the arrangement of his hair, he seemed anxious rather to display than hide. A landsman could hardly have worn this garb and shown this face, and worn and shown them both with such a galliard air, without undergoing stern question before a magistrate, and probably incurring fine or imprisonment, or perhaps an exhibition in the stocks. As regarded the shipmaster, however, all was looked upon as pertaining to the character, as to a fish his glistening scales.

21   After parting from the physician, the commander of the Bristol ship strolled idly through the market-place; until, happening to approach the spot where Hester Prynne was standing, he appeared to recognize, and did not hesitate to address her. As was usually the case wherever Hester stood, a small, vacant area—a sort of magic circle—had formed itself about her into which, though the people were elbowing one another at a little distance, none ventured, or felt disposed to intrude. It was a forcible type of the moral solitude in which the scarlet letter enveloped its fated wearer; partly by her own reserve, and partly by the instinctive, though no longer so unkindly, withdrawal of her fellow-creatures. Now, if never before, it answered a good purpose, by enabling Hester and the seaman to speak together without risk of being overheard; and so changed was Hester Prynne's repute before the public, that the matron in town most eminent for rigid morality could not have held such intercourse with less result of scandal than herself.

22   "So, mistress," said the mariner, "I must bid the steward make ready one more berth than you bargained for! No fear of scurvy or ship-fever, this voyage!

What with the ship's surgeon and this other doctor, our only danger will be from drug or pill; more by token, as there is a lot of apothecary's stuff aboard, which I traded for with a Spanish vessel."

23   "What mean you?" inquired Hester, startled more than she permitted to appear. "Have you another passenger?"

24   "Why, know you not," cried the shipmaster, "that this physician here—Chillingworth, he calls himself—is minded to try my cabin-fare with you? Ay, ay, you must have known it; for he tells me he is of your party, and a close friend to the gentleman you spoke of,—he that is in peril from these sour old Puritan rulers!"

25   "They know each other well, indeed," replied Hester, with a mien of calmness, though in the utmost consternation. "They have long dwelt together."

26   Nothing further passed between the mariner and Hester Prynne. But, at that instant, she beheld old Roger Chillingworth himself, standing in the remotest corner of the market-place, and smiling on her; a smile which—across the wide and bustling square, and through all the talk and laughter, and various thoughts, moods, and interests of the crowd—conveyed secret and fearful meaning.

CHAPTER 21

JOURNAL

1. **MLA Works Cited** *Using this model, record this book.*
   Author's Last Name, First Name. The Scarlet Letter. *1850.* Title of This Book.
   Ed. First Name Last Name. City: Publisher, year.
2. **Main Character(s)** *Describe each main character and explain why you think each is a main character.*
3. **Supporting Characters** *Describe each supporting character and explain why you think each is a supporting character.*
4. **Setting** *Describe the setting(s) and any relevant prop(s).*
5. **Sequence** *Outline the events in this chapter in order.*
6. **Plot** *Summarize this chapter's events in no more than two sentences.*
7. **Conflicts** *Identify and explain all conflicts involved in this chapter.*
8. **Significant Quotations** *Explain the importance of each of these quotations. Record the page number in the parentheses.*
   a. "On this public holiday, as on all other occasions, for seven years past, Hester was clad in a garment of coarse gray cloth [. . .]" (   ).
   b. "Her face, so long familiar to the townspeople, showed the marble quietude which they were accustomed to behold there. It was like a mask; or rather, like the frozen calmness of a dead woman's features [. . .]" (   ).
   c. "'Why, what is this, mother?' cried she. 'Wherefore have all the people left their work to-day? Is it a play-day for the whole world? [. . .]'" (   ).
   d. "'What a strange, sad man is he!' said the child, as if speaking partly to herself. 'In the dark night-time, he calls us to him, and holds thy hand and

mine [. . .]. But here in the sunny day, and among all the people, he
knows us not; nor must we know him! A strange, sad man is he, with his
hand always over his heart!' " (   ).

   e. " 'So, mistress,' said the mariner, 'I must bid the steward make ready one
more berth than you bargained for! No fear of scurvy or ship-fever, this voyage! What with the ship's surgeon and this other doctor [. . .]' " (   ).

  9. **Recap** *Summarize what has happened so far, from the beginning of the book through
this chapter.*

FOLLOW-UP QUESTIONS

6 SHORT QUESTIONS

Select the <u>best</u> answer for each.

_____ 1. At the Election Day
celebration,
   a. only Puritans can attend.
   b. Hester and Pearl are not
allowed.
   c. the town is full of many
different types of people.

_____ 2. Hester wears
   a. bright clothing and the
scarlet letter.
   b. coarse gray clothing and
the scarlet letter.
   c. new clothes for the
occasion.

_____ 3. Roger Chillingworth talks
with
   a. the Puritan elders.
   b. a ship's captain.
   c. sailors from a ship.

_____ 4. The mariner's news
   a. surprises Hester.
   b. pleases Hester.
   c. does not matter to
Hester.

_____ 5. Roger Chillingworth smiles at
   a. Pearl.
   b. Arthur Dimmesdale.
   c. Hester.

_____ 6. Hester Prynne finds out that
Roger Chillingworth
   a. plans to travel with them
on the ship.
   b. wants to reveal
Arthur's sin.
   c. will give a speech
at the Election Day
celebration.

5 SIGNIFICANT QUOTATIONS

Explain the importance of each of these quotations.

  1. "Betimes in the morning of the day on which the new Governor was to
receive his office at the hands of the people, Hester Prynne and little Pearl
came into the marketplace. It was already thronged with the craftsmen and
other plebeian inhabitants of the town, in considerable numbers [. . .]."

2. "'And will the minister be there?' asked Pearl. 'And will he hold out both his hands to me, as when thou ledst me to him from the brook-side?'"

3. "'For, to-day, a new man is beginning to rule over them; and so—as has been the custom of mankind ever since a nation was first gathered—they make merry and rejoice; as if a good and golden year were at length to pass over the poor old world!'"

4. "As was usually the case wherever Hester stood, a small, vacant area—a sort of magic circle—had formed itself about her into which, though the people were elbowing one another at a little distance, none ventured, or felt disposed to intrude [. . .]."

5. "'Why, know you not,' cried the shipmaster, 'that this physician here—Chillingworth, he calls himself—is minded to try my cabin-fare with you? Ay, ay, you must have known it; for he tells me he is of your party, and a close friend to the gentleman you spoke of,—he that is in peril from these sour old Puritan rulers!'"

2 COMPREHENSION ESSAY QUESTIONS

Use specific details and information from the chapter to answer these questions as completely as possible.

1. The colony of Boston is no longer such a small town. How has it changed? Use specific details and information from this chapter and other parts of the book in your explanation.

2. We can make plans in life, but, sometimes, circumstances occur to change those plans. Whose plans have changed and what does this mean for the main characters? Use specific details and information from this chapter and other parts of the book in your explanation.

DISCUSSION QUESTIONS

Be prepared to discuss these questions in class.

1. What is the importance of the Election Day celebration? How does it figure into the lives of the main characters?

2. What plans have Hester and Arthur made and what happens to those plans?

CHAPTER 22

THE PROCESSION

Use context clues to define these words before reading. Use a dictionary as needed.

1. Traffic police often pull over *erratic* drivers, those who veer from lane to lane without using turn signals or who drive too close to other drivers at inconsistent speeds. *Erratic* means _____
_____.

2. Some marathon runners are *indefatigable*, able to run ten or twenty miles without getting tired. *Indefatigable* means _____
_____.

3. Poor Cinderella had to serve and wait on her *haughty* stepsisters, who thought they were better than she. *Haughty* means _____
_____.

4. The writer Nathaniel Hawthorne was a *descendant* of the Puritans who had settled in New England two hundred years earlier. *Descendant* means _____
_____.

5. The piles of snow left by the blizzard began to *diminish* as the weather became warmer. *Diminish* means _____
_____.

6. Students gain more knowledge and earn more credits as they *advance* towards their degrees. *Advance* means _____
_____.

7. Citizens expect those in positions of authority to have *integrity*, or a sense of moral soundness. *Integrity* means _____
_____.

8. After giving Jerry a hard time about riding on all the roller coasters, Jessica had the *audacity* to jump out of a plane and go sky-diving on her twenty-first birthday. *Audacity* means _____
_____.

9. During solemn occasions like funerals or memorials, it is appropriate to maintain a sense of *sobriety*. *Sobriety* means _____
_____.

10. Hester Prynne has the strength and *fortitude* to face her punishment while Arthur Dimmesdale does not. *Fortitude* means _____
_____.

11. Eagles and hawks build their nests in *lofty* tree tops, high above the landscape. *Lofty* means _____
_____.

12. After working on the project for two weeks straight, Jonathan began to *exhibit* signs of stress and fatigue. *Exhibit* means _____
_____.

13. The professor *scowled* as the student's cell phone went off and disrupted his lecture. *Scowl* means _____
_____.

14. In some cultures, brides wear *garlands* of flowers in their hair. *Garlands* means _____
_____.

15. On hot days, when Angela feels sweaty and tired, she jumps into the pool to cool off and comes out feeling *invigorated*. *Invigorated* means _____
_____.

16. After he had a fight with his girlfriend, Justin was cold and *remote* towards her. *Remote* means _____
_____.

17. Shirley and Helena's friendship constitutes a powerful *bond* between them. *Bond* means _____
_____.

18. Mark wanted to sit outside but the mosquitoes *harassed* him so much that he came into the house. *Harass* means _____
_____.

19. The test was so hard and confusing that Kathy was in a state of *perplexity*. *Perplexity* means _____
_____.

20. When Jared considered joining the *military*, he called the Army, the Navy, the Air Force, and the Marines. *Military* means _____

_____ .

PRE-READING VOCABULARY
STRUCTURAL ATTACK

Define these words by solving the parts. Use the Glossary or a dictionary as needed.

1. irreverent	9. vulgarity	17. zigzag
2. contiguous	10. absurd	18. powwow
3. denote	11. stability	19. trifled
4. soldiery	12. self-reliance	20. pathos
5. mercenary	13. inducement	21. preliminary
6. martial	14. exhibit	22. boorish
7. shrillness	15. necromancy	23. abstracted
8. eminence	16. confidentially	24. trampled

PRE-READING QUESTIONS

Try answering these questions as you read.

Who takes part in the procession?
Does Arthur Dimmesdale acknowledge Hester and Pearl?
What does Mistress Hibbins say to Hester and Pearl?

CHAPTER 22

THE PROCESSION

1 Before Hester Prynne could call together her thoughts, and consider what was practicable to be done in this new and startling aspect of affairs, the sound of military music was heard approaching along a contiguous street. It denoted the advance of the procession of magistrates and citizens, on its way towards the meeting-house; where, in compliance with a custom thus early established, and ever since observed, the Reverend Mr. Dimmesdale was to deliver an Election Sermon.

2 Soon the head of the procession showed itself, with a slow and stately march, turning a corner, and making its way across the market-place. First came the music. It comprised a variety of instruments, perhaps imperfectly adapted to one another, and played with no great skill, but yet attaining the great object for which the harmony of drum and clarion addresses itself to the multitude,—that

of imparting a higher and more heroic air to the scene of life than passes before
the eye. Little Pearl at first clapped her hands, but then lost, for an instant, the
restless agitation that had kept her in a continual effervescence throughout
the morning; she gazed silently, and seemed to be borne upward, like a floating
sea-bird, on the long heaves and swells of sound. But she was brought back to
her former mood by the shimmer of the sunshine on the weapons and bright
armour of the military company, which followed after the music, and formed the
honorary escort of the procession. This body of soldiery—which still sustains a
corporate existence, and marches down from past ages with an ancient and honorable fame—was composed of no mercenary materials. Its ranks were filled with
gentlemen, who felt the stirrings of martial impulse, and sought to establish a
kind of College of Arms, where, as in an association of Knights Templars, they
might learn the science, and, so far as peaceful exercise would teach them, the
practices of war. The high estimation then placed upon the military character
might be seen in the lofty port of each individual member of the company. Some
of them, indeed, by their services in the Low Countries and on other fields of
European warfare, had fairly won their title to assume the name and pomp of sol-
diership. The entire array, moreover, clad in burnished steel, and with plumage
nodding over their bright morions, had a brilliancy of effect which no modern
display can aspire to equal.

3   And yet the men of civil eminence, who came immediately behind the military escort, were better worth a thoughtful observer's eye. Even in outward
demeanour they showed a stamp of majesty that made the warrior's haughty
stride look vulgar, if not absurd. It was an age when what we call talent had far
less consideration than now, but the massive materials which produce stability
and dignity of character a great deal more. The people possessed, by hereditary
right, the quality of reverence; which, in their descendants, if it survive at all,
exists in smaller proportion, and with a vastly diminished force in the selection
and estimate of public men. The change may be for good or ill, and is partly, perhaps, for both. In that old day, the English settler on these rude shores,—having
left king, nobles, and all degrees of awful rank behind, while still the faculty and
necessity of reverence were strong in him,—bestowed it on the white hair and
venerable brow of age; on long-tried integrity; on solid wisdom and sad-colored
experience; on endowments of that grave and weighty order, which gives the idea
of permanence, and comes under the general definition of respectability. These
primitive statesmen, therefore,—Bradstreet, Endicott, Dudley, Bellingham, and
their compeers,—who were elevated to power by the early choice of the people,
seem to have been not often brilliant, but distinguished by a ponderous sobriety,
rather than activity of intellect. They had fortitude and self-reliance, and, in time
of difficulty or peril, stood up for the welfare of the state like a line of cliffs
against a tempestuous tide. The traits of character here indicated were well represented in the square cast of countenance and large physical development of the
new colonial magistrates. So far as a demeanour of natural authority was concerned, the mother country need not have been ashamed to see these foremost

men of an actual democracy adopted into the House of Peers, or made the Privy Council of the sovereign.

4   Next in order to the magistrates came the young and eminently distinguished divine, from whose lips the religious discourse of the anniversary was expected. His was the profession, at that era, in which intellectual ability displayed itself far more than in political life; for—leaving a higher motive out of the question—it offered inducements powerful enough, in the almost worshipping respect of the community, to win the most aspiring ambition into its service. Even political power—as in the case of Increase Mather—was within the grasp of a successful priest.

5   It was the observation of those who beheld him now, that never, since Mr. Dimmesdale first set his foot on the New England shore, had he exhibited such energy as was seen in the gait and air with which he kept his pace in the procession. There was no feebleness of step, as at other times; his frame was not bent; nor did his hand rest ominously upon his heart. Yet, if the clergyman were rightly viewed, his strength seemed not of the body. It might be spiritual, and imparted to him by angelic ministrations. It might be the exhilaration of that potent cordial, which is distilled only in the furnace-glow of earnest and long-continued thought. Or, perchance, his sensitive temperament was invigorated by the loud and piercing music, that swelled heavenward, and uplifted him on its ascending wave, Nevertheless, so abstracted was his look, it might be questioned whether Mr. Dimmesdale even heard the music. There was his body, moving onward, and with an unaccustomed force. But where was his mind? Far and deep in its own region, busying itself, with preternatural activity, to marshal a procession of stately thoughts that were soon to issue thence, and so he saw nothing, heard nothing, knew nothing, of what was around him; but the spiritual element took up the feeble frame, and carried it along, unconscious of the burden, and converting it to spirit like itself. Men of uncommon intellect, who have grown morbid, possess this occasional power of mighty effort, into which they throw the life of many days, and then are lifeless for as many more.

6   Hester Prynne, gazing stedfastly at the clergyman, felt a dreary influence come over her, but wherefore or whence she knew not; unless that he seemed so remote from her own sphere, and utterly beyond her reach. One glance of recognition, she had imagined, must needs pass between them. She thought of the dim forest, with its little dell of solitude, and love, and anguish, and the mossy tree-trunk, where, sitting hand in hand, they had mingled their sad and passionate talk with the melancholy murmur of the brook. How deeply had they known each other then! And was this the man? She hardly knew him now! He, moving proudly past, enveloped, as it were, in the rich music, with the procession of majestic and venerable fathers; he, so unattainable in his worldly position, and still more so in that far vista of his unsympathizing thoughts, through which she now beheld him! Her spirit sank with the idea that all must have been a delusion, and that, vividly as she had dreamed it, there could be no real bond betwixt the clergyman and herself. And thus much of woman was there in Hester, that

she could scarcely forgive him,—least of all now, when the heavy footstep of their approaching Fate might be heard, nearer, nearer, nearer!—for being able so completely to withdraw himself from their mutual world; while she groped darkly, and stretched forth her cold hands, and found him not.

7   Pearl either saw and responded to her mother's feelings, or herself felt the remoteness and intangibility that had fallen around the minister. While the procession passed, the child was uneasy, fluttering up and down, like a bird on the point of taking flight. When the whole had gone by, she looked up into Hester's face.

8   "Mother," said she, "was that the same minister that kissed me by the brook?"

9   "Hold thy peace, dear little Pearl!" whispered her mother. "We must not always talk in the market-place of what happens to us in the forest."

10   "I could not be sure that it was he; so strange he looked," continued the child. "Else I would have run to him, and bid him kiss me now, before all the people; even as he did yonder among the dark old trees. What would the minister have said, mother? Would he have clapped his hand over his heart, and scowled on me, and bid me begone?"

11   "What should he say, Pearl," answered Hester, "save that it was no time to kiss, and that kisses are not to be given in the market-place? Well for thee, foolish child, that thou didst not speak to him!"

12   Another shade of the same sentiment, in reference to Mr. Dimmesdale, was expressed by a person whose eccentricities—or insanity, as we should term it—led her to do what few of the townspeople would have ventured on; to begin a conversation with the wearer of the scarlet letter, in public. It was Mistress Hibbins, who, arrayed in great magnificence, with a triple ruff, a broidered stomacher, a gown of rich velvet, and a gold-headed cane, had come forth to see the procession. As this ancient lady had the renown (which subsequently cost her no less a price than her life) of being a principal actor in all the works of necromancy that were continually going forward, the crowd gave way before her, and seemed to fear the touch of her garment, as if it carried the plague among its gorgeous folds. Seen in conjunction with Hester Prynne,—kindly as so many now felt towards the latter,—the dread inspired by Mistress Hibbins was doubled, and caused a general movement from that part of the market-place in which the two women stood.

13   "Now, what mortal imagination could conceive it!" whispered the old lady confidentially to Hester. "Yonder divine man! That saint on earth, as the people uphold him to be, and as—I must needs say—he really looks! Who, now, that saw him pass in the procession, would think how little while it is since he went forth out of his study,—chewing a Hebrew text of Scripture in his mouth, I warrant,—to take an airing in the forest! Aha! we know what that means, Hester Prynne! But, truly, forsooth, I find it hard to believe him the same man. Many a church-member saw I, walking behind the music, that has danced in the same measure with me, when Somebody was fiddler, and it might be, an Indian powwow or a Lapland wizard changing hands with us! That is but a trifle, when a woman

knows the world. But this minister! Couldst thou surely tell, Hester, whether he was the same man that encountered thee on the forest path!"

14 "Madam, I know not of what you speak," answered Hester Prynne, feeling Mistress Hibbins to be of infirm mind; yet strangely startled and awe-stricken by the confidence with which she affirmed a personal connection between so many persons (herself among them) and the Evil One. "It is not for me to talk lightly of a learned and pious minister of the Word, like the Reverend Mr. Dimmesdale!"

15 "Fie, woman, fie!" cried the old lady, shaking her finger at Hester. "Dost thou think I have been to the forest so many times, and have yet no skill to judge who else has been there? Yea; though no leaf of the wild garlands, which they wore while they danced, be left in their hair! I know thee, Hester; for I behold the token. We may all see it in the sunshine; and it glows like a red flame in the dark. Thou wearest it openly; so there need be no question about that. But this minister! Let me tell thee in thine ear! When the Black Man sees one of his own servants, signed and sealed, so shy of owning to the bond as is the Reverend Mr. Dimmesdale, he hath a way of ordering matters so that the mark shall be disclosed in open daylight to the eyes of all the world! What is it that the minister seeks to hide, with his hand always over his heart? Ha, Hester Prynne!"

16 "What is it, good Mistress Hibbins?" eagerly asked little Pearl. "Hast thou seen it?"

17 "No matter, darling!" responded Mistress Hibbins, making Pearl a profound reverence. "Thou thyself wilt see it, one time or another. They say, child, thou art of the lineage of the Prince of the Air! Wilt thou ride with me, some fine night, to see thy father? Then thou shalt know wherefore the minister keeps his hand over his heart!"

18 Laughing so shrilly that all the market-place could hear her, the weird old gentlewoman took her departure.

19 By this time the preliminary prayer had been offered in the meeting-house, and the accents of the Reverend Mr. Dimmesdale were heard commencing his discourse. An irresistible feeling kept Hester near the spot. As the sacred edifice was too much thronged to admit another auditor, she took up her position close beside the scaffold of the pillory. It was in sufficient proximity to bring the whole sermon to her ears, in the shape of an indistinct, but varied, murmur and flow of the minister's very peculiar voice.

20 This vocal organ was in itself a rich endowment; insomuch that a listener, comprehending nothing of the language in which the preacher spoke, might still have been swayed to and fro by the mere tone and cadence. Like all other music, it breathed passion and pathos, and emotions high or tender, in a tongue native to the human heart, wherever educated. Muffled as the sound was by its passage through the church-walls, Hester Prynne listened with such intentness, and sympathized so intimately, that the sermon had throughout a meaning for her, entirely apart from its indistinguishable words. These, perhaps, if more distinctly heard, might have been only a grosser medium, and have clogged the spiritual sense. Now she caught the low undertone, as of the wind sinking down

to repose itself; then ascended with it, as it rose through progressive gradations of sweetness and power, until its volume seemed to envelop her with an atmosphere of awe and solemn grandeur. And yet, majestic as the voice sometimes became, there was for ever in it an essential character of plaintiveness. A loud or low expression of anguish,—the whisper, or the shriek, as it might be conceived, of suffering humanity, that touched a sensibility in every bosom! At times this deep strain of pathos was all that could be heard, and scarcely heard, sighing amid a desolate silence. But even when the minister's voice grew high and commanding,—when it gushed irrepressibly upward,—when it assumed its utmost breadth and power, so overfilling the church as to burst its way through the solid walls, and diffuse itself in the open air,—still, if the auditor listened intently, and for the purpose, he could detect the same cry of pain. What was it? The complaint of a human heart, sorrow-laden, perchance guilty, telling its secret, whether of guilt or sorrow, to the great heart of mankind; beseeching its sympathy or forgiveness,—at every moment,—in each accent,—and never in vain! It was this profound and continual undertone that gave the clergyman his most appropriate power.

21   During all this time Hester stood, statue-like, at the foot of the scaffold. If the minister's voice had not kept her there, there would nevertheless have been an inevitable magnetism in that spot, whence she dated the first hour of her life of ignominy. There was a sense within her,—too ill-defined to be made a thought, but weighing heavily on her mind,—that her whole orb of life, both before and after, was connected with this spot, as with the one point that gave it unity.

22   Little Pearl, meanwhile, had quitted her mother's side, and was playing at her own will about the market-place. She made the sombre crowd cheerful by her erratic and glistening ray; even as a bird of bright plumage illuminates a whole tree of dusky foliage by darting to and fro, half seen and half concealed, amid the twilight of the clustering leaves. She had an undulating, but, oftentimes, a sharp and irregular movement. It indicated the restless vivacity of her spirit, which to-day was doubly indefatigable in its tiptoe dance, because it was played upon and vibrated with her mother's disquietude. Whenever Pearl saw any thing to excite her ever active and wandering curiosity, she flew thitherward, and, as we might say, seized upon that man or thing as her own property, so far as she desired it; but without yielding the minutest degree of control over her motions in requital. The Puritans looked on, and, if they smiled, were none the less inclined to pronounce the child a demon offspring, from the indescribable charm of beauty and eccentricity that shone through her little figure, and sparkled with its activity. She ran and looked the wild Indian in the face; and he grew conscious of a nature wilder than his own. Thence, with native audacity, but still with a reserve as characteristic, she flew into the midst of a group of mariners, the swarthy-cheeked wild men of the ocean, as the Indians were of the land; and they gazed wonderingly and admiringly at Pearl, as if a flake of the sea-foam had taken the shape of a little maid, and were gifted with a soul of the sea-fire, that flashes beneath the prow in the night-time.

23   One of these seafaring men—the shipmaster, indeed, who had spoken to Hester Prynne—was so smitten with Pearl's aspect, that he attempted to lay hands upon her, with purpose to snatch a kiss. Finding it as impossible to touch her as to catch a humming-bird in the air, he took from his hat the gold chain that was twisted about it, and threw it to the child. Pearl immediately twined it around her neck and waist, with such happy skill, that, once seen there, it became a part of her, and it was difficult to imagine her without it.

24   "Thy mother is yonder woman with the scarlet letter," said the seaman. "Wilt thou carry her a message from me?"

25   "If the message pleases me I will," answered Pearl.

26   "Then tell her," rejoined he, "that I spake again with the black-a-visaged, hump-shouldered old doctor, and he engages to bring his friend, the gentleman she wots of, aboard with him. So let thy mother take no thought, save for herself and thee. Wilt thou tell her this, thou witch-baby?"

27   "Mistress Hibbins says my father is the Prince of the Air!" cried Pearl, with her naughty smile. "If thou callest me that ill name, I shall tell him of thee; and he will chase thy ship with a tempest!"

28   Pursuing a zigzag course across the market-place, the child returned to her mother, and communicated what the mariner had said. Hester's strong, calm, stedfastly enduring spirit almost sank, at last, on beholding this dark and grim countenance of an inevitable doom, which—at the moment when a passage seemed to open for the minister and herself out of their labyrinth of misery— showed itself, with an unrelenting smile, right in the midst of their path.

29   With her mind harassed by the terrible perplexity in which the shipmaster's intelligence involved her, she was also subjected to another trial. There were many people present, from the country roundabout, who had often heard of the scarlet letter, and to whom it had been made terrific by a hundred false or exaggerated rumors, but who had never beheld it with their own bodily eyes. These, after exhausting other modes of amusement, now thronged about Hester Prynne with rude and boorish intrusiveness. Unscrupulous as it was, however, it could not bring them nearer than a circuit of several yards. At that distance they accordingly stood, fixed there by the centrifugal force of the repugnance which the mystic symbol inspired. The whole gang of sailors, likewise, observing the press of spectators, and learning the purport of the scarlet letter, came and thrust their sunburnt and desperado-looking faces into the ring. Even the Indians were affected by a sort of cold shadow of the white man's curiosity, and, gliding through the crowd, fastened their snake-like black eyes on Hester's bosom; con- ceiving, perhaps, that the wearer of this brilliantly embroidered badge must needs be a personage of high dignity among her people. Lastly, the inhabitants of the town (their own interest in this worn-out subject languidly reviving itself, by sympathy with what they saw others feel) lounged idly to the same quarter, and tormented Hester Prynne, perhaps more than all the rest, with their cool, well- acquainted gaze at her familiar shame. Hester saw and recognized the self-same faces of that group of matrons, who had awaited her forthcoming from the

prison-door, seven years ago; all save one, the youngest and only compassionate among them, whose burial-robe she had since made. At the final hour, when she was so soon to fling aside the burning letter, it had strangely become the centre of more remark and excitement, and was thus made to sear her breast more painfully, than at any time since the first day she put it on.

30   While Hester stood in that magic circle of ignominy, where the cunning cruelty of her sentence seemed to have fixed her for ever, the admirable preacher was looking down from the sacred pulpit upon an audience, whose very inmost spirits had yielded to his control. The sainted minister in the church! The woman of the scarlet letter in the market-place! What imagination would have been irreverent enough to surmise that the same scorching stigma was on them both?

CHAPTER 22

JOURNAL

1. **MLA Works Cited** *Using this model, record this book.*
   Author's Last Name, First Name. The Scarlet Letter. *1850.* Title of This Book.
   Ed. First Name Last Name. City: Publisher, year.
2. **Main Character(s)** *Describe each main character and explain why you think each is a main character.*
3. **Supporting Characters** *Describe each supporting character and explain why you think each is a supporting character.*
4. **Setting** *Describe the setting(s) and any relevant prop(s).*
5. **Sequence** *Outline the events in this chapter in order.*
6. **Plot** *Summarize this chapter's events in no more than two sentences.*
7. **Conflicts** *Identify and explain all conflicts involved in this chapter.*
8. **Significant Quotations** *Explain the importance of each of these quotations. Record the page number in the parentheses.*
   a. "Before Hester Prynne could call together her thoughts, and consider what was practicable to be done in this new and startling aspect of affairs, the sound of military music was heard approaching along a contiguous street. It denoted the advance of the procession of magistrates and citizens, on its way towards the meeting-house; where [. . .] the Reverend Mr. Dimmesdale was to deliver an Election Sermon" (   ).
   b. "It was the observation of those who beheld him now, that never, since Mr. Dimmesdale first set his foot on the New England shore, had he exhibited such energy as was seen in the gait and air with which he kept his pace in the procession. There was no feebleness of step, as at other times; his frame was not bent; nor did his hand rest ominously upon his heart [. . .]" (   ).
   c. "Hester Prynne, gazing stedfastly at the clergyman, felt a dreary influence come over her, but wherefore or whence she knew not; unless that he

seemed so remote from her own sphere, and utterly beyond her reach. One glance of recognition, she had imagined, must needs pass between them [. . .]" (   ).

d. " 'Hold thy peace, dear little Pearl!' whispered her mother. 'We must not always talk in the market-place of what happens to us in the forest' " (   ).

e. " 'But this minister! Couldst thou surely tell, Hester, whether he was the same man that encountered thee on the forest-path!' " (   ).

9. **Recap** *Summarize what has happened so far, from the beginning of the book through this chapter.*

FOLLOW-UP QUESTIONS

6 SHORT QUESTIONS

Select the __best__ answer for each.

____ 1. Walking in the procession, Arthur Dimmesdale's gait is
   a. feeble.
   b. out of step with the others.
   c. energetic.

____ 2. Others in the procession include
   a. sailors.
   b. magistrates.
   c. Indians.

____ 3. Arthur Dimmesdale
   a. looks at Hester.
   b. does not look at Hester.
   c. stumbles as he walks.

____ 4. Hester talks with
   a. Roger Chillingworth.
   b. the ship's captain.
   c. Mistress Hibbins.

____ 5. Mistress Hibbins asks Pearl
   a. who her father is.
   b. to ride with her some night.
   c. to take a message to the sea captain.

____ 6. Mistress Hibbins says she is good friends with
   a. the devil.
   b. Arthur Dimmesdale.
   c. Hester Prynne.

5 SIGNIFICANT QUOTATIONS

Explain the importance of each of these quotations.

1. "Nevertheless, so abstracted was his look, it might be questioned whether Mr. Dimmesdale even heard the music. There was his body, moving onward, and with an unaccustomed force. But where was his mind? Far and deep in its own region [. . .] and so he saw nothing, heard nothing, knew nothing, of what was around him [. . .]."

2. "She thought of the dim forest, with its little dell of solitude, and love, and anguish, and the mossy tree-trunk, where, sitting hand in hand, they had

mingled their sad and passionate talk with the melancholy murmur of the brook. How deeply had they known each other then! [. . .]."

3. " 'Fie, woman, fie!' cried the old lady, shaking her finger at Hester. 'Dost thou think I have been to the forest so many times, and have yet no skill to judge who else has been there? [. . .].' "

4. " 'They say, child, thou art of the lineage of the Prince of the Air! Wilt thou ride with me, some fine night, to see thy father? Then thou shalt know wherefore the minister keeps his hand over his heart!' "

5. "The sainted minister in the church! The woman of the scarlet letter in the market-place! What imagination would have been irreverent enough to surmise that the same scorching stigma was on them both?"

2 COMPREHENSION ESSAY QUESTIONS

Use specific details and information from the chapter to answer these questions as completely as possible.

1. Mistress Hibbins is a minor character but shows up regularly in the story. What is her role in this chapter? Use specific details and information from the chapter in your explanation.
2. With the Election Day celebration, a sense of change is in the air. What changes are going on in the lives of the main characters? Use specific details and information from the chapter in your explanation.

DISCUSSION QUESTIONS

Be prepared to discuss these questions in class.

1. What do you think of Arthur Dimmesdale? Does he acknowledge Hester and Pearl?
2. What kind of person is Mistress Hibbins? Can we trust her?

CHAPTER 23

THE REVELATION OF THE SCARLET LETTER

PRE-READING VOCABULARY
CONTEXT

Use context clues to define these words before reading. Use a dictionary as needed.

1. The *revelation* scene occurs at the end of a murder mystery when the detective reveals the name of the murderer. *Revelation* means _____
   _____.

2. Francis wanted his speech to be *eloquent*, so he practiced and made sure that his delivery was smooth and convincing. *Eloquent* means _____
   _____.

3. Debbie *murmured* so quietly that I could not hear or understand her. *Murmur* means _____
   _____.

4. Emanuel was struck with *awe* as he viewed the astonishing depth of the Grand Canyon. *Awe* means _____
   _____.

5. Listening to the choir sing in the ancient cathedral put Louise into a perfect state of *rapture*. *Rapture* means _____
   _____.

6. The witness gave his *testimony* in court under oath, and the court reporter took down his every word. *Testimony* means _____
   _____.

7. The fortuneteller *prophesied* Lorraine's wedding, telling her that she would marry in one year. *Prophesied* means _____
   _____.

8. Because she likes to argue and interpret law, Addison believes it is her *destiny* to become a lawyer. *Destiny* means _____
   _____.

9. The house stands high upon an *eminence* looking out at the sea below. *Eminence* means _____ _____.

10. We were all saddened by the young man's *untimely* death at such an early age. *Untimely* means _____ _____.

11. Childhood is only a *transitory* state because, in a relatively short time, it gives way to adulthood. *Transitory* means _____ _____.

12. Having a party to celebrate a marriage or good fortune seems to be a *universal occurrence* in cultures around the world. *Universal* means _____ _____.

13. Before she went to bed, Lena *extinguished* all the candles by blowing them out. *Extinguished* means _____ _____.

14. The horrors of *war* bring *woe* and misery to many people. *Woe* means _____ _____.

15. By the end of the night, the campfire had burned down to just a few *embers*. *Embers* means _____ _____.

16. Out of respect, when a flag becomes *tattered* and torn, it is time to replace it. *Tattered* means _____ _____.

17. After becoming a minister, Martin preached to the *brethren* in the church every Sunday morning. *Brethren* means _____ _____.

18. As the accident victim grew weaker, he *lapsed* into a coma. *Lapsed* means _____.

19. The king ruled the land, holding the most *exalted* position in the realm. *Exalted* means _____ _____.

20. Aaron was dismayed to see how much money was *withheld* from his paycheck for taxes. *Withheld* means _____ _____.

PRE-READING VOCABULARY
STRUCTURAL ATTACK

Define these words by solving the parts. Use the Glossary or a dictionary as needed.

1. aloft	8. escorted	15. imperceptible
2. oracles	9. majestic	16. appalled
3. transport	10. kindled	17. cunning
4. relapse	11. hasten	18. sportive
5. constrain	12. triumph	19. farewell
6. superiority	13. totter	20. mercy
7. clangor	14. wavered	21. expired

PRE-READING QUESTIONS

Try answering these questions as you read.

Where and what does Arthur Dimmesdale reveal to the townspeople?
Does Arthur Dimmesdale escape from Roger Chillingworth?
Will Pearl kiss Arthur Dimmesdale?
What does Hester Prynne do?

CHAPTER 23

THE REVELATION OF THE SCARLET LETTER

1 The eloquent voice, on which the souls of the listening audience had been borne aloft, as on the swelling waves of the sea, at length came to a pause. There was a momentary silence, profound as what should follow the utterance of oracles. Then ensued a murmur and half-hushed tumult; as if the auditors, released from the high spell that had transported them into the region of another's mind, were returning into themselves, with all their awe and wonder still heavy on them. In a moment more, the crowd began to gush forth from the doors of the church. Now that there was an end, they needed other breath, more fit to support the gross and earthly life into which they relapsed, than that atmosphere which the preacher had converted into words of flame, and had burdened with the rich fragrance of his thought.

2 In the open air their rapture broke into speech. The street and the market-place absolutely babbled, from side to side, with applauses of the minister. His hearers could not rest until they had told one another of what each knew better than he could tell or hear. According to their united testimony, never had man spoken in so wise, so high, and so holy a spirit, as he that spake this day; nor had inspiration ever breathed through mortal lips more evidently than it did through

his. Its influence could be seen, as it were, descending upon him, and possessing him, and continually lifting him out of the written discourse that lay before him, and filling him with ideas that must have been as marvellous to himself as to his audience. His subject, it appeared, had been the relation between the Deity and the communities of mankind, with a special reference to the New England which they were here planting in the wilderness. And, as he drew towards the close, a spirit as of prophecy had come upon him, constraining him to its purpose as mightily as the old prophets of Israel were constrained; only with this difference, that, whereas the Jewish seers had denounced judgments and ruin on their country, it was his mission to foretell a high and glorious destiny for the newly gathered people of the Lord. But, throughout it all, and through the whole discourse, there had been a certain deep, sad undertone of pathos, which could not be interpreted otherwise than as the natural regret of one soon to pass away. Yes; their minister whom they so loved—and who so loved them all, that he could not depart heavenward without a sigh—had the foreboding of untimely death upon him, and would soon leave them in their tears! This idea of his transitory stay on earth gave the last emphasis to the effect which the preacher had produced; it was as if an angel, in his passage to the skies, had shaken his bright wings over the people for an instant,—at once a shadow and a splendor,—and had shed down a shower of golden truths upon them.

3   Thus, there had come to the Reverend Mr. Dimmesdale—as to most men, in their various spheres, though seldom recognized until they see it far behind them—an epoch of life more brilliant and full of triumph than any previous one, or than any which could hereafter be. He stood, at this moment, on the very proudest eminence of superiority, to which the gifts of intellect, rich lore, prevailing eloquence, and a reputation of whitest sanctity, could exalt a clergyman in New England's earliest days, when the professional character was of itself a lofty pedestal. Such was the position which the minister occupied, as he bowed his head forward on the cushions of the pulpit, at the close of his Election Sermon. Meanwhile, Hester Prynne was standing beside the scaffold of the pillory, with the scarlet letter still burning on her breast!

4   Now was heard again the clangor of the music, and the measured tramp of the military escort, issuing from the church-door. The procession was to be marshalled thence to the town-hall, where a solemn banquet would complete the ceremonies of the day.

5   Once more, therefore, the train of venerable and majestic fathers was seen moving through a broad pathway of the people, who drew back reverently, on either side, as the Governor and magistrates, the old and wise men, the holy ministers, and all that were eminent and renowned, advanced into the midst of them. When they were fairly in the market-place, their presence was greeted by a shout. This—though doubtless it might acquire additional force and volume from the childlike loyalty which the age awarded to its rulers—was felt to be an irrepressible outburst of the enthusiasm kindled in the auditors by that high strain of eloquence which was yet reverberating in their ears. Each felt the

impulse in himself, and, in the same breath, caught it from his neighbour. Within the church, it had hardly been kept down; beneath the sky, it pealed upward to the zenith. There were human beings enough, and enough of highly wrought and symphonious feeling, to produce that more impressive sound than the organ-tones of the blast, or the thunder, or the roar of the sea; even that mighty swell of many voices, blended into one great voice by the universal impulse which makes likewise one vast heart out of the many. Never, from the soil of New England, had gone up such a shout! Never, on New England soil, had stood the man so honored by his mortal brethren as the preacher!

6   How fared it with him then? Were there not the brilliant particles of a halo in the air about his head? So etherealized by spirit as he was, and so apotheosized by worshipping admirers, did his footsteps in the procession really tread upon the dust of earth?

7   As the ranks of military men and civil fathers moved onward, all eyes were turned towards the point where the minister was seen to approach among them. The shout died into a murmur, as one portion of the crowd after another obtained a glimpse of him. How feeble and pale he looked amid all his triumph! The energy—or say rather, the inspiration which had held him up, until he should have delivered the sacred message that brought its own strength along with it from heaven—was withdrawn, now that it had so faithfully performed its office. The glow, which they had just before beheld burning on his cheek, was extinguished, like a flame that sinks down hopelessly among the late-decaying embers. It seemed hardly the face of a man alive, with such a deathlike hue; it was hardly a man with life in him, that tottered on his path so nervelessly, yet tottered, and did not fall!

8   One of his clerical brethren,—it was the venerable John Wilson,—observing the state in which Mr. Dimmesdale was left by the retiring wave of intellect and sensibility, stepped forward hastily to offer his support. The minister tremulously, but decidedly, repelled the old man's arm. He still walked onward, if that movement could be so described, which rather resembled the wavering effort of an infant, with its mother's arms in view, outstretched to tempt him forward. And now, almost imperceptible as were the latter steps of his progress, he had come opposite the well-remembered and weather-darkened scaffold, where, long since, with all that dreary lapse of time between, Hester Prynne had encountered the world's ignominious stare. There stood Hester, holding little Pearl by the hand! And there was the scarlet letter on her breast! The minister here made a pause; although the music still played the stately and rejoicing march to which the procession moved. It summoned him onward,—onward to the festival!—but here he made a pause.

9   Bellingham, for the last few moments, had kept an anxious eye upon him. He now left his own place in the procession, and advanced to give assistance; judging from Mr. Dimmesdale's aspect that he must otherwise inevitably fall. But there was something in the latter's expression that warned back the magistrate, although a man not readily obeying the vague intimations that pass from one

spirit to another. The crowd, meanwhile, looked on with awe and wonder. This earthly faintness was, in their view, only another phase of the minister's celestial strength; nor would it have seemed a miracle too high to be wrought for one so holy, had he ascended before their eyes, waxing dimmer and brighter, and fading at last into the light of heaven!

10   He turned towards the scaffold, and stretched forth his arms.

11   "Hester," said he, "come hither! Come, my little Pearl!"

12   It was a ghastly look with which he regarded them; but there was something at once tender and strangely triumphant in it. The child, with the bird-like motion which was one of her characteristics, flew to him, and clasped her arms about his knees. Hester Prynne—slowly, as if impelled by inevitable fate, and against her strongest will—likewise drew near, but paused before she reached him. At this instant old Roger Chillingworth thrust himself through the crowd,—or, perhaps, so dark, disturbed, and evil was his look, he rose up out of some nether region,—to snatch back his victim from what he sought to do! Be that as it might, the old man rushed forward and caught the minister by the arm.

13   "Madman, hold! What is your purpose?" whispered he. "Wave back that woman! Cast off this child! All shall be well! Do not blacken your fame and perish in dishonor! I can yet save you! Would you bring infamy on your sacred profession?"

14   "Ha, tempter! Methinks thou art too late!" answered the minister, encountering his eye, fearfully, but firmly. "Thy power is not what is was! With God's help, I shall escape thee now!"

15   He again extended his hand to the woman of the scarlet letter.

16   "Hester Prynne," cried he, with a piercing earnestness, "in the name of Him, so terrible and so merciful, who gives me grace, at this last moment, to do what—for my own heavy sin and miserable agony—I withheld myself from doing seven years ago, come hither now, and twine thy strength about me. Thy strength, Hester; but let it be guided by the will which God hath granted me! This wretched and wronged old man is opposing it with all his might!—with all his own might and the fiend's! Come, Hester, come! Support me up yonder scaffold!"

17   The crowd was in a tumult. The men of rank and dignity, who stood more immediately around the clergyman, were so taken by surprise, and so perplexed as to the purport of what they saw,—unable to receive the explanation which most readily presented itself, or to imagine any other,—that they remained silent and inactive spectators of the judgment which Providence seemed about to work. They beheld the minister, leaning on Hester's shoulder and supported by her arm around him, approach the scaffold, and ascend its steps; while still the little hand of the sin-born child was clasped in his. Old Roger Chillingworth followed, as one intimately connected with the drama of guilt and sorrow in which they had all been actors, and well entitled, therefore, to be present at its closing scene.

18   "Hadst thou sought the whole earth over," said he, looking darkly at the clergyman, "there was no place so secret,—no high place nor lowly place, where thou couldst have escaped me,—save on this very scaffold!"

19   "Thanks be to Him who hath led me hither!" answered the minister.

20   Yet he trembled, and turned to Hester with an expression of doubt and anxiety in his eyes, not the less evidently betrayed, that there was a feeble smile upon his lips.

21   "Is not this better," murmured he; "than what we dreamed of in the forest?"

22   "I know not! I know not!" she hurriedly replied. "Better? Yea; so we may both die, and little Pearl die with us!"

23   "For thee and Pearl, be it as God shall order," said the minister; "and God is merciful! Let me now do the will which he hath made plain before my sight. For, Hester, I am a dying man. So let me make haste to take my shame upon me."

24   Partly supported by Hester Prynne, and holding one hand of little Pearl's, the Reverend Mr. Dimmesdale turned to the dignified and venerable rulers; to the holy ministers, who were his brethren; to the people, whose great heart was thoroughly appalled, yet overflowing with tearful sympathy, as knowing that some deep life-matter—which, if full of sin, was full of anguish and repentance likewise—was now to be laid open to them. The sun, but little past its meridian, shone down upon the clergyman, and gave a distinctness to his figure, as he stood out from all the earth to put in his plea of guilty at the bar of Eternal Justice.

25   "People of New England!" cried he, with a voice, that rose over them, high, solemn, and majestic,—yet had always a tremor through it, and sometimes a shriek, struggling up out of a fathomless depth of remorse and woe,—"ye, that have loved me!—ye, that have deemed me holy!—behold me here, the one sinner of the world! At last!—at last!—I stand upon the spot where, seven years since, I should have stood; here, with this woman, whose arm, more than the little strength wherewith I have crept hitherward, sustains me, at this dreadful moment, from grovelling down upon my face! Lo, the scarlet letter which Hester wears! Ye have all shuddered at it! Wherever her walk hath been,—wherever, so miserably burdened, she may have hoped to find repose,—it hath cast a lurid gleam of awe and horrible repugnance roundabout her. But there stood one in the midst of you, at whose brand of sin and infamy ye have not shuddered!"

26   It seemed, at this point, as if the minister must leave the remainder of his secret undisclosed. But he fought back the bodily weakness,—and, still more, the faintness of heart,—that was striving for the mastery with him. He threw off all assistance, and stepped passionately forward a pace before the woman and the child.

27   "It was on him!" he continued, with a kind of fierceness; so determined was he to speak out the whole. "God's eye beheld it! The angels were for ever pointing at it! The Devil knew it well, and fretted it continually with the touch of his burning finger! But he hid it cunningly from men, and walked among you with the mien of a spirit, mournful, because so pure in a sinful world!—and sad, because he missed his heavenly kindred! Now, at the death-hour, he stands up before you! He bids you look again at Hester's scarlet letter! He tells you, that, with all its mysterious horror, it is but the shadow of what he bears on his own breast, and that even this, his own red stigma, is no more than the type of what

has seared his inmost heart! Stand any here that question God's judgement on a sinner? Behold! Behold a dreadful witness of it!"

28   With a convulsive motion he tore away the ministerial band from before his breast. It was revealed! But it were irreverent to describe that revelation. For an instant the gaze of the horror-stricken multitude was concentrated on the ghastly miracle; while the minister stood with a flush of triumph in his face, as one who, in the crisis of acutest pain, had won a victory. Then, down he sank upon the scaffold! Hester partly raised him, and supported his head against her bosom. Old Roger Chillingworth knelt down beside him, with a blank, dull countenance, out of which the life seemed to have departed.

29   "Thou hast escaped me!" he repeated more than once. "Thou hast escaped me!"

30   "My God forgive thee!" said the minister. "Thou, too, hast deeply sinned!"

31   He withdrew his dying eyes from the old man, and fixed them on the woman and the child.

32   "My little Pearl," said he feebly,—and there was a sweet and gentle smile over his face, as of a spirit sinking into deep repose; nay, now that the burden was removed, it seemed almost as if he would be sportive with the child,—"dear little Pearl, wilt thou kiss me now? Thou wouldst not yonder, in the forest! But now thou wilt?"

33   Pearl kissed his lips. A spell was broken. The great scene of grief, in which the wild infant bore a part, had developed all her sympathies; and as her tears fell upon her father's cheek, they were the pledge that she would grow up amid human joy and sorrow, nor for ever do battle with the world, but be a woman in it. Towards her mother, too, Pearl's errand as a messenger of anguish was all fulfilled.

34   "Hester," said the clergyman, "farewell!"

35   "Shall we not meet again?" whispered she, bending her face down close to his. "Shall we not spend our immortal life together? Surely, surely, we have ransomed one another, with all this woe! Thou lookest far into eternity, with those bright dying eyes! Then tell me what thou seest?"

36   "Hush, Hester, hush!" said he, with tremulous solemnity. "The law we broke!—the sin here so awfully revealed!—let these alone be in thy thoughts! I fear! I fear! It may be, that, when we forgot our God,—when we violated our reverence each for the other's soul,—it was thenceforth vain to hope that we could meet hereafter, in an everlasting and pure reunion. God knows; and He is merciful! He hath proved his mercy, most of all, in my afflictions. By giving me this burning torture to bear upon my breast! By sending yonder dark and terrible old man, to keep the torture always at red-heat! By bringing me hither, to die this death of triumphant ignominy before the people! Had either of these agonies been wanting, I had been lost for ever! Praised be his name! His will be done! Farewell!"

37   That final word came forth with the minister's expiring breath. The multitude, silent till then, broke out in a strange, deep voice of awe and wonder, which could not as yet find utterance, save in this murmur that rolled so heavily after the departed spirit.

CHAPTER 23

JOURNAL

1. **MLA Works Cited** *Using this model, record this book.*
   Author's Last Name, First Name. The Scarlet Letter. 1850. Title of This Book.
   Ed. First Name Last Name. City: Publisher, year.
2. **Main Character(s)** *Describe each main character and explain why you think each is a main character.*
3. **Supporting Characters** *Describe each supporting character and explain why you think each is a supporting character.*
4. **Setting** *Describe the setting(s) and any relevant prop(s).*
5. **Sequence** *Outline the events in this chapter in order.*
6. **Plot** *Summarize this chapter's events in no more than two sentences.*
7. **Conflicts** *Identify and explain all conflicts involved in this chapter.*
8. **Significant Quotations** *Explain the importance of each of these quotations. Record the page number in the parentheses.*
   a. "The street and the market-place absolutely babbled, from side to side, with applauses of the minister. His hearers could not rest until they had told one another of what each knew better than he could tell or hear [. . .]" (   ).
   b. "Never, from the soil of New England, had gone up such a shout! Never, on the New England soil, had stood the man so honored by his mortal brethren as the preacher!" (   ).
   c. " 'Hester,' said he, 'come hither! Come, my little Pearl!' " (   ).
   d. " 'Madman, hold! What is your purpose?' whispered he. 'Wave back that woman! Cast off this child! All shall be well! Do not blacken your fame, and perish in dishonor! I can yet save you! [. . .]' " (   ).
   e. " '[. . .] [D]ear little Pearl, wilt thou kiss me now? Thou wouldst not yonder, in the forest! But now thou wilt?' " (   ).
9. **Recap** *Summarize what has happened so far, from the beginning of the book through this chapter.*

FOLLOW-UP QUESTIONS

6 SHORT QUESTIONS

Select the best answer for each.

____ 1. The townspeople
    a. love Arthur Dimmesdale's speech.
    b. are disappointed in Arthur Dimmesdale's speech.
    c. can barely hear Arthur Dimmesdale's voice.

____ 2. Arthur asks Hester and Pearl
    a. to leave the market-place.
    b. to come up onto the scaffold with him.
    c. to find Roger Chillingworth.

____ 3. Roger Chillingworth
    a. supports Arthur
       Dimmesdale with
       his arms.
    b. tries to stop Arthur
       Dimmesdale from
       climbing the scaffold.
    c. walks away in disgust
       from the scaffold.

____ 4. The crowd and magistrates are
    so taken by surprise that they
    a. push and shove their way
       to Arthur Dimmesdale.
    b. call out and shout to each
       other.
    c. stand and watch in silence.

____ 5. Arthur Dimmesdale
    a. praises the devil.
    b. does not mention Roger
       Chillingworth.
    c. reveals his guilt.

____ 6. Pearl kisses
    a. Hester.
    b. her father.
    c. Roger Chillingworth.

5 SIGNIFICANT QUOTATIONS

Explain the importance of each of these quotations.

1. "According to their united testimony, never had man spoken in so wise, so high, and so holy a spirit, as he that spake this day; nor had inspiration ever breathed through mortal lips more evidently than it did through his [. . .]."
2. "'Hester Prynne,' cried he, with piercing earnestness, 'in the name of Him, so terrible and so merciful, who gives me grace, at this last moment, to do what—for my own heavy sin and miserable agony—I withheld myself from doing seven years ago, come hither now, and twine thy strength about me! [. . .].'"
3. "'Hadst thou sought the whole earth over,' said he, looking darkly at the clergyman, 'there was no place so secret,—no high place nor lowly place, where thou couldst have escaped me,—save on this very scaffold!'"
4. "'For, Hester, I am a dying man. So let me make haste to take my shame upon me.'"
5. "'With a convulsive motion he tore away the ministerial band from before his breast. It was revealed! [. . .].'"

2 COMPREHENSION ESSAY QUESTIONS

Use specific details and information from the chapter to answer these questions as completely as possible.

1. What effect does Pearl have on Arthur Dimmesdale? Use specific details and information from the chapter and the rest of the novel in your explanation.

2. For seven years, Arthur Dimmesdale has kept his secret. How and why does he finally reveal it? Use specific details and information from the novel in your explanation.

DISCUSSION QUESTIONS

Be prepared to discuss these questions in class.

1. For which character do you feel the most sympathy? The least? Why?
2. Do you respect Arthur Dimmesdale for the way he chooses to reveal his secret?

CHAPTER 24

CONCLUSION

PRE-READING VOCABULARY
CONTEXT

Use context clues to define these words before reading. Use a dictionary as needed.

1. We expect our lawmakers and government to *uphold* the laws as an example to others. *Uphold* means _____
   _____.

2. Because she was a witness to the crime, Marta had to *testify* in court and relate what she saw. *Testify* means _____
   _____.

3. There were many people at the free concert but the organizers worked hard at maintaining a *semblance* of order so that future events would be allowed. *Semblance* means _____
   _____.

4. When Mike and Ann were married for fifty years, they *affirmed* their wedding vows in a special ceremony. *Affirm* means _____
   _____.

5. Once a glass has shattered, it is *futile* to try to glue it back together again. *Futile* means _____
   _____.

6. After the hurricane, the survivors had to *contend* with cleaning up the mess and building new lives. *Contend* means _____
   _____.

7. Planning her will, Aunt Veronica *bequeathed* all her jewelry to her daughters so that it would stay in the family. *Bequeath* means _____
   _____.

8. After he told a lie, Rafael's guilt *gnawed* at him until he confessed the truth. *Gnaw* means _____
   _____.

9. When a couple gets married, they *profess* their vows to love and protect each other. *Profess* means _____
   _____.

10. A *parable* is a simple story used to teach a lesson or a moral. *Parable* means
    _____
    _____.

11. After her co-workers admitted to stealing from the bank, Dee *repudiated* their friendship and found a new place to work. *Repudiate* means _____
    _____.

12. When he decided to drop the atomic bomb on Japan to end World War II, President Truman made a *momentous* decision. *Momentous* means _____
    _____.

13. The empty and windswept landscape was so *desolate* that no one wanted to live there. *Desolate* means _____
    _____.

14. A *recluse* lives a solitary life away from people. *Recluse* means _____
    _____.

15. The balloon *shriveled* up after Charles poked it with a pin and let the air out of it. *Shrivel* means _____
    _____.

16. A good friend shows *fidelity* by keeping secrets and being faithful in promises. *Fidelity* means _____
    _____.

17. When we walked barefoot on the beach, we left *imprints* of our feet in the sand. *Imprint* means _____
    _____.

18. When Rebecca missed her flight to London, she was lucky enough to get a ticket for the *subsequent* flight that was leaving three hours later. *Subsequent* means _____
    _____.

19. The dog had such *antipathy* for cats that he growled and chased every one that entered the yard. *Antipathy* means _____
    _____.

20. When Roberta inherited a large amount of money from her grandmother, she became a rich *heiress*. *Heiress* means _____

_____.

PRE-READING VOCABULARY
STRUCTURAL ATTACK

Define these words by solving the parts. Use the Glossary or a dictionary as needed.

1. fleshy	7. nugatory	13. decease
2. infinite	8. lavished	14. marriageable
3. contemporary	9. recurs	15. persisted
4. heraldry	10. ethereal	16. counsel
5. wilting	11. slabs	17. sable
6. consummation	12. consisted	18. gules

PRE-READING QUESTIONS

Try answering these questions as you read.

How do the townspeople react to Arthur's revelation?
What happens to Pearl and Hester?
What happens to Roger Chillingworth?

CHAPTER 24

CONCLUSION

1   After many days, when time sufficed for the people to arrange their thoughts in reference to the foregoing scene, there was more than one account of what had been witnessed on the scaffold.

2   Most of the spectators testified to having seen, on the breast of the unhappy minister, a SCARLET LETTER—the very semblance of that worn by Hester Prynne—imprinted in the flesh. As regarded its origin, there were various explanations, all of which must necessarily have been conjectural. Some affirmed that the Reverend Mr. Dimmesdale, on the very day when Hester Prynne first wore her ignominious badge, had begun a course of penance,—which he afterwards, in so many futile methods, followed out,—by inflicting a hideous torture on himself. Others contended that the stigma had not been produced until a long time subsequent, when old Roger Chillingworth, being a potent necromancer, had caused it to appear, through the agency of magic and poisonous drugs. Others, again,—and those best able to appreciate the minister's peculiar sensibility, and the wonderful

operation of his spirit upon the body,—whispered their belief, that the awful symbol was the effect of the ever active tooth of remorse, gnawing from the inmost heart outwardly, and at last manifesting Heaven's dreadful judgment by the visible presence of the letter. The reader may choose among these theories. We have thrown all the light we could acquire upon the portent, and would gladly, now that it has done its office, erase its deep print out of our own brain; where long meditation has fixed it in very undesirable distinctness.

3   It is singular, nevertheless, that certain persons, who were spectators of the whole scene, and professed never once to have removed their eyes from the Reverend Mr. Dimmesdale, denied that there was any mark whatever on his breast, more than on a new-born infant's. Neither, by their report, had his dying words acknowledged, nor even remotely implied, any, the slightest connection, on his part, with the guilt for which Hester Prynne had so long worn the scarlet letter. According to these highly respectable witnesses, the minister, conscious that he was dying,—conscious, also, that the reverence of the multitude placed him already among saints and angels,—had desired, by yielding up his breath in the arms of that fallen woman, to express to the world how utterly nugatory is the choicest of man's own righteousness. After exhausting life in his efforts for mankind's spiritual good, he had made the manner of his death a parable, in order to impress on his admirers the mighty and mournful lesson, that, in the view of Infinite Purity, we are sinners all alike. It was to teach them, that the holiest among us has but attained so far above his fellows as to discern more clearly the Mercy which looks down, and repudiate more utterly the phantom of human merit, which would look aspiringly upward. Without disputing a truth so momentous, we must be allowed to consider this version of Mr. Dimmesdale's story as only an instance of that stubborn fidelity with which a man's friends— and especially a clergyman's—will sometimes uphold his character; when proofs, clear as the mid-day sunshine on the scarlet letter, establish him a false and sin-stained creature of the dust.

4   The authority which we have chiefly followed—a manuscript of old date, drawn up from the verbal testimony of individuals, some of whom had known Hester Prynne, while others had heard the tale from contemporary witnesses— fully confirms the view taken in the foregoing pages. Among many morals which press upon us from the poor minister's miserable experience, we put only this into a sentence:—"Be true! Be true! Be true! Show freely to the world, if not your worst, yet some trait whereby the worst may be inferred!"

5   Nothing was more remarkable than the change which took place, almost immediately after Mr. Dimmesdale's death, in the appearance and demeanour of the old man known as Roger Chillingworth. All his strength and energy—all his vital and intellectual force—seemed at once to desert him; insomuch that he positively withered up, shrivelled away, and almost vanished from mortal sight, like an uprooted weed that lies wilting in the sun. This unhappy man had made the very principle of his life to consist in the pursuit and systematic exercise of revenge; and when, by its completest triumph and consummation, that evil

principle was left with no further material to support it,—when, in short, there was no more devil's work on earth for him to do, it only remained for the unhumanized mortal to betake himself whither his Master would find him tasks enough, and pay him his wages duly. But, to all these shadowy beings, so long our near acquaintances,—as well Roger Chillingworth as his companions,—we would fain be merciful. It is a curious subject of observation and inquiry, whether hatred and love be not the same thing at bottom. Each, in its utmost development, supposes a high degree of intimacy and heart-knowledge, each renders one individual dependent for the food of his affections and spiritual life upon another; each leaves the passionate lover, or the no less passionate hater, forlorn and desolate by the withdrawal of his object. Philosophically considered, therefore, the two passions seem essentially the same, except that one happens to be seen in a celestial radiance, and the other in a dusky and lurid glow. In the spiritual world, the old physician and the minister—mutual victims as they have been—may, unawares, have found their earthly stock of hatred and antipathy transmuted into golden love.

6   Leaving this discussion apart we have a matter of business to communicate to the reader. At old Roger Chillingworth's decease (which took place within the year), and by his last will and testament of which Governor Bellingham and the Reverend Mr. Wilson were executors, he bequeathed a very considerable amount of property, both here and in England, to little Pearl, the daughter of Hester Prynne.

7   So Pearl—the elf-child,—the demon offspring, as some people, up to that epoch, persisted in considering her—became the richest heiress of her day, in the New World. Not improbably, this circumstance wrought a very material change in the public estimation, and, had the mother and child remained here, little Pearl, at a marriageable period of life, might have mingled her wild blood with the lineage of the devoutest Puritan among them all. But, in no long time after the physician's death, the wearer of the scarlet letter disappeared, and Pearl along with her. For many years, though a vague report would now and then find its way across the sea,—like a shapeless piece of driftwood tost ashore, with the initials of a name upon it,—yet no tidings of them unquestionably authentic were received. The story of the scarlet letter grew into a legend. Its spell, however, was still potent, and kept the scaffold awful where the poor minister had died, and likewise the cottage by the sea-shore, where Hester Prynne had dwelt. Near this latter spot, one afternoon, some children were at play, when they beheld a tall woman, in a gray robe, approach the cottage-door. In all those years it had never once been opened; but either she unlocked it, or the decaying wood and iron yielded to her hand, or she glided shadow-like through these impediments,— and, at all events, went in.

8   On the threshold she paused,—turned partly round,—for, perchance, the idea of entering, all alone, and all so changed, the home of so intense a former life, was more dreary and desolate than even she could bear. But her hesitation was only for an instant, though long enough to display a scarlet letter on her breast.

9   And Hester Prynne had returned, and taken up her long-forsaken shame. But where was little Pearl? If still alive, she must now have been in the flush and bloom of early womanhood. None knew—nor ever learned, with the fulness of perfect certainty—whether the elf-child had gone thus untimely to a maiden grave; or whether her wild, rich nature had been softened and subdued, and made capable of a woman's gentle happiness. But, through the remainder of Hester's life, there were indications that the recluse of the scarlet letter was the object of love and interest with some inhabitant of another land. Letters came, with armorial seals upon them, though of bearings unknown to English heraldry. In the cottage there were articles of comfort and luxury, such as Hester never cared to use, but which only wealth could have purchased, and affection have imagined for her. There were trifles, too, little ornaments, beautiful tokens of a continual remembrance, that must have been wrought by delicate fingers, at the impulse of a fond heart. And, once, Hester was seen embroidering a baby-garment, with such a lavish richness of golden fancy as would have raised a public tumult, had any infant, thus apparelled, been shown to our sombre-hued community.

10   In fine, the gossips of that day believed,—and Mr. Surveyor Pue, who made investigations a century later, believed,—and one of his recent successors in office, moreover, faithfully believes,—that Pearl was not only alive, but married, and happy, and mindful of her mother; and that she would most joyfully have entertained that sad and lonely mother at her fireside.

11   But there was a more real life for Hester Prynne, here, in New England, than in that unknown region where Pearl had found a home. Here had been her sin; here, her sorrow; and here was yet to be her penitence. She had returned, there-fore, and resumed,—of her own free will, for not the sternest magistrate of that iron period would have imposed it,—resumed the symbol of which we have related so dark a tale. Never afterwards did it quit her bosom. But, in the lapse of the toilsome, thoughtful, and self-devoted years that made up Hester's life, the scarlet letter ceased to be a stigma which attracted the world's scorn and bitter-ness, and became a type of something to be sorrowed over, and looked upon with awe, yet with reverence too. And, as Hester Prynne had no selfish ends, nor lived in any measure for her own profit and enjoyment, people brought all their sor-rows and perplexities, and besought her counsel, as one who had herself gone through a mighty trouble. Women, more especially,—in the continually recurring trials of wounded, wasted, wronged, misplaced, or erring and sinful passion,—or with the dreary burden of a heart unyielded, because unvalued and unsought,— came to Hester's cottage, demanding why they were so wretched, and what the remedy! Hester comforted and counselled them, as best she might. She assured them, too, of her firm belief, that, at some brighter period, when the world should have grown ripe for it, in Heaven's own time, a new truth would be revealed, in order to establish the whole relation between man and woman on a surer ground of mutual happiness. Earlier in life, Hester had vainly imagined that she herself might be the destined prophetess, but had long since recognized the impossibility that any mission of divine and mysterious truth should be

confided to a woman stained with sin, bowed down with shame, or even burdened with a life-long sorrow. The angel and apostle of the coming revelation
must be a woman, indeed, but lofty, pure, and beautiful; and wise, moreover, not
through dusky grief, but the ethereal medium of joy; and showing how sacred
love should make us happy, by the truest test of a life successful to such an end!

12   So said Hester Prynne, and glanced her sad eyes downward at the scarlet letter. And, after many, many years, a new grave was delved, near an old and sunken
one, in that burial-ground beside which King's Chapel has since been built. It
was near that old and sunken grave, yet with a space between, as if the dust of the
two sleepers had no right to mingle. Yet one tombstone served for both. All
around, there were monuments carved with armorial bearings; and on this
simple slab of slate—as the curious investigator may still discern, and perplex
himself with the purport—there appeared the semblance of an engraved
escutcheon. It bore a device, a herald's wording of which might serve for a motto
and brief description of our now concluded legend; so sombre is it, and relieved
only by one ever-glowing point of light gloomier than the shadow:—

"On a field, sable, the letter A. gules"

CHAPTER 24

JOURNAL

1. **MLA Works Cited** *Using this model, record this book.*
   *Author's Last Name, First Name. The Scarlet Letter. 1850. Title of This Book.
   Ed. First Name Last Name. City: Publisher, year.*
2. **Main Character(s)** *Describe each main character and explain why you think each
   is a main character.*
3. **Supporting Characters** *Describe each supporting character and explain why you
   think each is a supporting character.*
4. **Setting** *Describe the setting(s) and any relevant prop(s).*
5. **Sequence** *Outline the events in this chapter in order.*
6. **Plot** *Summarize this chapter's events in no more than two sentences.*
7. **Conflicts** *Identify and explain all conflicts involved in this chapter.*
8. **Significant Quotations** *Explain the importance of each of these quotations. Record
   the page number in the parentheses.*
   a. "Most of the spectators testified to having seen, on the breast of the
      unhappy minister, a SCARLET LETTER—the very semblance of that worn by
      Hester Prynne—imprinted in the flesh [. . .]" (   ).
   b. "Nothing was more remarkable than the change which took place,
      almost immediately after Mr. Dimmesdale's death, in the appearance and
      demeanor of the old man known as Roger Chillingworth. All his strength
      and energy—all his vital and intellectual force—seemed at once to desert
      him; insomuch that he positively withered up, shrivelled away, and almost

vanished from mortal sight, like an uprooted weed that lies wilting in the sun [. . .]" (   ).

c. "So Pearl—the elf-child,—, the demon offspring, as some people, up to that epoch, persisted in considering her,—became the richest heiress of her day, in the New World [. . .]" (   ).

d. "[P]eople brought all their sorrows and perplexities, and besought her counsel, as one who had herself gone through a mighty trouble" (   ).

e. "And, after many, many years, a new grave was delved, near an old and sunken one [. . .] yet with a space between, as if the dust of the two sleepers had no right to mingle" (   ).

9. **Recap** *Summarize what has happened so far, from the beginning of the book through this chapter.*

FOLLOW-UP QUESTIONS

6 SHORT QUESTIONS

Select the <u>best</u> answer for each.

_____ 1. Roger Chillingworth dies
   a. immediately after Arthur Dimmesdale's death.
   b. within a year of Arthur Dimmesdale's death.
   c. when he returns to England.

_____ 2. Pearl inherits property from
   a. Mistress Hibbins.
   b. Arthur Dimmesdale.
   c. Roger Chillingworth.

_____ 3. Hester and Pearl
   a. leave Boston.
   b. never return to Boston.
   c. move into Arthur Dimmesdale's old rooms.

_____ 4. Hester Prynne returns
   a. with Pearl.
   b. with a grandchild.
   c. without Pearl.

_____ 5. People come to Hester
   a. with their personal problems.
   b. to learn embroidery.
   c. to talk about Arthur Dimmesdale.

_____ 6. Hester Prynne is buried next to
   a. Pearl.
   b. Arthur Dimmesdale.
   c. Roger Chillingworth.

5 SIGNIFICANT QUOTATIONS

Explain the importance of each of these quotations.

1. "Some affirmed that the Reverend Mr. Dimmesdale, on the very day when Hester Prynne first wore her ignominious badge, had begun a course of penance,—which he afterwards, in so many futile methods, followed out,—by inflicting a hideous torture on himself [. . .]."

2. "This unhappy man had made the very principle of his life to consist in the pursuit and systematic exercise of revenge; and [. . .] by its completest triumph and consummation, that evil principle was left with no further material to support it [. . .]."

3. "At old Roger Chillingworth's decease (which took place within the year), and by his last will and testament of which Governor Bellingham and the Reverend Mr. Wilson were executors, he bequeathed a very considerable amount of property, both here and in England, to little Pearl, the daughter of Hester Prynne."

4. "Women, more especially,—in the continually recurring trials of wounded, wasted, wronged, misplaced, or erring and sinful passion,—or with the dreary burden of a heart unyielded, because unvalued and unsought,—came to Hester's cottage, demanding why they were so wretched, and what the remedy! [. . .]."

5. "Yet one tombstone served for both."

2 COMPREHENSION ESSAY QUESTIONS

Use specific details and information from the chapter to answer these questions as completely as possible.

1. How and why does Roger Chillingworth change after Arthur Dimmesdale's death? Use specific details and information from the entire novel in your explanation.

2. Why does Hester Prynne come back to her cottage on the peninsula? How does she spend the rest of her life? Use specific details and information from the entire novel in your explanation.

DISCUSSION QUESTIONS

Be prepared to discuss these questions in class.

1. What do you think happens to Pearl?

2. Why does Hester return to Boston? Why does she continue to wear the scarlet letter?

1. **MLA Works Cited** *Using this model, record this book.*
   Author's Last Name, First Name. The Scarlet Letter. *1850.* Title of This Book.
   Ed. First Name Last Name. City: Publisher, year.
2. **Main Character(s)** *Describe each main character and explain why you think each is a main character.*
3. **Supporting Characters** *Describe each supporting character and explain why you think each is a supporting character.*
4. **Setting** *Describe the setting(s) and any relevant prop(s).*
5. **Sequence** *Outline the events in these chapter in order.*
6. **Plot** *Summarize these chapter's events in no more than five sentences.*
7. **Conflicts** *Identify and explain all conflicts involved in this chapter.*
8. **Significant Quotations** *Explain the importance of each of these quotations. Record the page number in the parentheses.*

   a. "Children have always a sympathy in the agitations of those connected with them; always, especially, a sense of any trouble or impending revolution, of whatever kind, in domestic circumstances; and therefore Pearl, who was the gem on her mother's unquiet bosom, betrayed, by the very dance of her spirits, the emotions which none could detect in the marble passiveness of Hester's brow" (   ).

   b. "Nothing further passed between the mariner and Hester Prynne. But, at that instant, she beheld old Roger Chillingworth himself, standing in the remotest corner of the market-place, and smiling on her; a smile which—across the wide and bustling square, and through all the talk and laughter, and various thoughts, moods, and interests of the crowd—conveyed secret and fearful meaning" (   ).

   c. "Hester Prynne, gazing stedfastly at the clergyman, felt a dreary influence come over her, but wherefore or whence she knew not; unless that he seemed so remote from her own sphere, and utterly beyond her reach. One glance of recognition, she had imagined, must needs pass between them [. . .]" (   ).

   d. "'Fie, woman, fie!' cried the old lady, shaking her finger at Hester. 'Dost thou think I have been to the forest so many times, and yet have no skill to judge who else has been there? Yea; though no leaf of the wild garlands, which they wore while they danced, be left in their hair! [. . .]'" (   ).

   e. "An irresistible feeling kept Hester near the spot. As the sacred edifice was too much thronged to admit another auditor, she took up her position close beside the scaffold of the pillory [. . .]" (   ).

   f. "The child, with the bird-like motion which was one of her characteristics, flew to him, and clasped her arms about his knees. Hester Prynne—slowly, as if impelled by inevitable fate, and against her strongest will—likewise drew near, but paused before she reached him. At this instant old Roger Chillingworth thrust himself through the crowd [. . .]" (   ).

g. "'Hadst thou sought the whole earth over,' said he, looking darkly at the clergyman, 'there was no place so secret,—no high place nor lowly place, where thou couldst have escaped me,—save on this very scaffold!'" (   ).

h. "Pearl kissed his lips. A spell was broken. The great scene of grief, in which the wild infant bore a part, had developed all her sympathies; and as her tears fell upon her father's cheek, they were the pledge that she would grow up amid human joy and sorrow, not for ever do battle with it, but be a woman in it. Towards her mother, too, Pearl's errand as a messenger of anguish was all fulfilled" (   ).

i. "'Hester,' said the clergyman, 'farewell!'" (   ).

j. "Here had been her sin; here, her sorrow; and here was yet to be her penitence [. . .]" (   ).

9. **Recap** *Summarize what has happened so far, from the beginning of the novel through these chapters.*

FOLLOW-UP QUESTIONS

20 SHORT QUESTIONS

Select the <u>best</u> answer for each.

____ 1. The Puritans are celebrating
a. a religious holiday.
b. the election of a new governor.
c. a market-place festival.

____ 2. Walking in the procession, Arthur Dimmesdale
a. does not look at Hester Prynne.
b. is weak and feeble.
c. exchanges a look with Hester Prynne.

____ 3. Waiting for the speech, Hester has a conversation with
a. Master Brackett.
b. Roger Chillingworth.
c. Mistress Hibbins.

____ 4. The procession begins with
a. music and soldiers.
b. magistrates and ministers.
c. mariners and matrons.

____ 5. Pearl is invited to ride some night with
a. Mistress Hibbins.
b. Roger Chillingworth.
c. Arthur Dimmesdale.

____ 6. Hester Prynne is wearing
a. new clothes.
b. her usual attire.
c. her hair down.

____ 7. Roger Chillingworth is seen talking to
a. Mistress Hibbins.
b. Hester Prynne.
c. the sea captain.

____ 8. The mariner tells Hester that
a. Arthur Dimmesdale has changed his mind.
b. Roger Chillingworth is joining the voyage.
c. the ship is not ready to sail.

____ 9. During Arthur's speech, Hester stands near the
   a. prison.
   b. rose-bush.
   c. scaffold.

____ 10. The townspeople think that Arthur Dimmesdale's sermon
   a. is the best they have ever heard.
   b. is unclear and uneven.
   c. is long and boring.

____ 11. On the procession from the church, when Arthur Dimmesdale sees Hester and Pearl,
   a. he keeps going.
   b. he smiles gently.
   c. he pauses and stops the procession.

____ 12. Roger Chillingworth
   a. helps Arthur up the stairs.
   b. rushes from the crowd to keep Arthur from ascending the scaffold.
   c. gives Arthur some medicine.

____ 13. Arthur Dimmesdale invites Hester and Pearl
   a. to pray with him.
   b. to help him up the scaffold.
   c. to take him back to his room.

____ 14. Arthur asks for a kiss from
   a. Hester.
   b. Pearl.
   c. Hester and Pearl.

____ 15. Arthur Dimmesdale
   a. finally reveals his secret.
   b. dies before he can reveal his secret.
   c. does not talk to Roger Chillingworth.

____ 16. Roger Chillingworth dies
   a. the same day as Arthur Dimmesdale.
   b. when he returns to England.
   c. within a year of Arthur Dimmesdale's death.

____ 17. Roger Chillingworth bequeaths money and property to
   a. Mistress Hibbins.
   b. Hester Prynne.
   c. Pearl.

____ 18. Hester and Pearl
   a. leave the colony for England.
   b. move to a different part of New England.
   c. move in with Mistress Hibbins.

____ 19. After many years Hester returns to Boston and
   a. becomes a minister.
   b. counsels many women.
   c. refuses to wear the scarlet letter.

____ 20. Hester is buried next to
   a. Roger Chillingworth.
   b. Arthur Dimmesdale.
   c. Pearl.

10 SIGNIFICANT QUOTATIONS

Explain the importance of each of these quotations.

1. "'But, see, mother, how many faces of strange people, and Indians among them, and sailors! What have they all come to do here in the market-place?'"

2. "'They wait to see the procession pass,' said Hester. 'For the Governor and the magistrates are to go by, and the ministers, and all the great people and good people, with the music, and the soldiers marching before them.'"

3. "'What a strange, sad man is he!' said the child, as if speaking partly to herself. 'In the dark night-time, he calls us to him, and holds thy hand and mine, as when we stood with him on the scaffold yonder! And in the deep forest, where only the old trees can hear, and the strip of sky see it, he talks with thee, sitting on a heap of moss! And he kisses my forehead, too, so that the little brook would hardly wash it off! But here in the sunny day, and among all the people, he knows us not; nor must we know him! A strange, sad man is he, with his hand always over his heart!'"

4. "'Hold thy peace, dear little Pearl!' whispered her mother. 'We must not always talk in the market-place of what happens to us in the forest.'"

5. "'Yonder divine man! That saint on earth, as the people uphold him to be, and as—I must needs say—he really looks! Who, now, that saw him pass in the procession, would think how little while it is since he went forth out of his study [. . .] to take an airing in the forest!'"

6. "But even when the minister's voice grew high and commanding,—when it gushed irrepressibly upward,—when it assumed its utmost breadth and power, so overfilling the church as to burst its way through the solid walls, and diffuse itself in the open air,—still, if the auditor listened intently, and for the purpose, he could detect the same cry of pain [. . .]."

7. "'Ha, tempter! Methinks thou art too late!' answered the minister, encountering his eye, fearfully, but firmly. 'Thy power is not what it was! With God's help, I shall escape thee now!'"

8. "'Thy strength, Hester; but let it be guided by the will which God hath granted me! This wretched and wronged old man is opposing it with all his might!—with all his own might and the fiend's! Come, Hester, come! Support me up yonder scaffold!'"

9. "'Thou hast escaped me!' he repeated more than once. 'Thou hast escaped me!'"

10. "So Pearl—the elf-child,—the demon offspring, as some people, up to that epoch, persisted in considering her—became the richest heiress of her day, in the New World."

2 COMPREHENSION ESSAY QUESTIONS

Use specific details and information from these chapters to answer these questions as completely as possible.

1. Consider the character of Arthur Dimmesdale. He privately punishes himself and carries a heavy burden of guilt, yet he does not have the courage to confess until the very end of his life. Do you see him as a strong or weak character? Use specific details and information from these chapters in your explanation.

2. Arthur Dimmesdale makes the decision to leave Boston with Hester and Pearl, or, rather, allows Hester to make the decision. Consider his actions in these chapters. Would Arthur Dimmesdale really have been able to leave his life and position in this New England colony?

DISCUSSION QUESTIONS

Be prepared to discuss these questions in class.

1. What effect does Arthur's public confession have on Pearl? On Hester? Are you surprised by these events?
2. What happens to Chillingworth after Arthur confesses and dies on the scaffold? Where do Pearl and Hester end up?

WRITING

Use each of these ideas to write an essay.

1. After Arthur Dimmesdale tears open his shirt and collapses on the scaffold, witnesses give differing accounts of what they have seen and what has happened to Arthur Dimmesdale. Have you ever seen or experienced something with other people only to find that your account of the incident differed from theirs? Write an essay in which you describe the incident from your point of view. Then tell how other people's accounts differed from yours.
2. Hester Prynne and Arthur Dimmesdale experience much shame in the novel as a result of the Puritan code of punishment. To what extent do people experience shame for punishment in contemporary American culture?
3. The ending of a novel may not resolve all questions that we have as readers. What questions does the narrator of The Scarlet Letter leave unanswered? Are you satisfied with this ending?
4. The Puritans outlawed witchcraft, fearing and prosecuting witches. Using examples from television, movies, the Internet, and popular books that feature witches and witchcraft, discuss how contemporary society views the practice of witchcraft, compared to Puritan New England.

FURTHER WRITING

1. The leaders of Transcendentalism, a nineteenth-century movement, included Hawthorne's contemporaries, Henry David Thoreau and Ralph Waldo Emerson. Hawthorne was partly influenced by the Transcendentalists, who emphasized intuition over empirical science. Read an essay by each of these authors and discuss how they looked at life.
2. Watch one of the several movie versions of The Scarlet Letter and report on it in an essay. What scenes were added or cut? How well does the movie portray

the characters and the setting? Compared to the book, for which character(s) do you feel the most sympathy in the movie? For which characters do you feel the least sympathy?

3. By the end of the novel, Pearl is living in Europe. From the clues in Chapter 24 and Pearl's actions throughout the novel, explain what you think she does with the rest of her life. Does she marry and have children? Does she learn to control her emotions?

4. The narrator exhorts, "Be true! Be true! Be true!" Which character in The Scarlet Letter has shown the most integrity?

5. Hawthorne has several interview scenes between characters who ask and answer questions. Interview a classmate to create a portrait of a contemporary student living in your area.

THE NOVEL

JOURNAL

1. **MLA Works Cited** *Using this model, record this book.*
   Author's Last Name, First Name *The Scarlet Letter.* 1850. *Title of This Book.*
   Ed. First Name Last Name. City: Publisher, year.
2. **Main Character(s)** *Describe each main character and explain why you think each is a main character.*
3. **Supporting Characters** *Describe each supporting character and explain why you think each is a supporting character.*
4. **Setting** *Describe the setting(s) and any relevant prop(s).*
5. **Sequence** *Outline the events in the novel in order.*
6. **Plot** *Summarize the novel's events in no more than five sentences.*
7. **Conflicts** *Identify and explain all conflicts involved in the novel.*
8. **Significant Quotations** *Explain the importance of these quotations. Record the page number in the parentheses.*
   a. "A throng of bearded men, in sad-colored garments and gray, steeple-crowned hats, intermixed with women, some wearing hoods, and others bareheaded, was assembled in front of a wooden edifice, the door of which was heavily timbered with oak, and studded with iron spikes" (   ).
   b. "'This woman has brought shame upon us all, and ought to die. Is there not law for it? Truly there is, both in the Scripture and the statute-book. Then let the magistrates who have made it of no effect, thank themselves if their own wives and daughters go astray'" (   ).
   c. "'Thus she will be a living sermon against sin, until the ignominious letter be engraved upon her tombstone. It irks me, nevertheless, that the partner of her iniquity should not, at least, stand on the scaffold by her side. But he will be known!—he will be known!—he will be known!'" (   ).
   d. "'Good Master Dimmesdale,' said he, 'the responsibility of this woman's soul lies greatly with you. It behooves you, therefore, to exhort her to repentance, and to confession [. . .]'" (   ).
   e. "'Foolish woman!' responded the physician, half coldly and half soothingly. 'What should ail me to harm this misbegotten and miserable babe? The medicine is potent for good; and were it my child,—yea, mine own, as well as thine!—I could do no better for it'" (   ).
   f. "'Wilt thou go with us to-night? There will be a merry company in the forest; and I wellnigh promised the Black Man that comely Hester Prynne should make one'" (   ).
   g. "In this manner, the mysterious old Roger Chillingworth became the medical advisor of the Reverend Mr. Dimmesdale. As not only the disease interested the physician, but he was strongly moved to look into the character and qualities of the patient, these two men, so different in age, came gradually to spend much time together [. . .]" (   ).
   h. "But with what a wild look of wonder, joy, and horror! [. . .]. Had a man seen old Roger Chillingworth, at that moment of his ecstasy, he would

have had no need to ask how Satan comports himself, when a precious human soul is lost to heaven, and won into his kingdom" (   ).

i. "To the untrue man, the whole universe is false,—it is impalpable,—it shrinks to nothing within his grasp. And he himself, in so far as he shows himself in a false light, becomes a shadow, or, indeed, ceases to exist [. . .]" (   ).

j. "'Who is that man, Hester?' gasped Mr. Dimmesdale, overcome with terror. 'I shiver at him! Dost thou know the man? I hate him, Hester!'" (   ).

k. "'Since that day, no man is so near to him as you. You tread behind his every footstep. You are beside him, sleeping and waking. You search his thoughts. You burrow and rankle in his heart! Your clutch is on his life, and you cause him to die daily a living death; and still he knows you not [. . .]'" (   ).

l. "'Wilt thou yet purge [this hatred] out of thee, and be once more human? If not for his sake, then doubly for thine own! Forgive, and leave his further retribution to the Power that claims it! [. . .]'" (   ).

m. "She marvelled how she could ever have been wrought upon to marry him! She deemed it her crime most to be repented of, that she had ever endured, and reciprocated, the lukewarm grasp of his hand, and had suffered the smile of her lips and eyes to mingle and melt into his own [. . .]" (   ).

n. "'What does the letter mean, mother?—and why dost thou wear it?—and why does the minister keep his hand over his heart?'" (   ).

o. "'What we did had a consecration of its own. We felt it so! We said so to each other! Hast thou forgotten it?'" (   ).

p. "'Thou shalt not go alone!' answered she, in a deep whisper.
Then, all was spoken!" (   ).

q. "'Doth he love us?' said Pearl, looking up with acute intelligence into her mother's face. 'Will he go back with us, hand in hand, we three together, into the town?'" (   ).

r. "'Why, know you not,' cried the shipmaster, 'that this physician here—Chillingworth, he calls himself—is minded to try my cabin-fare with you? Ay, Ay, you must have known it; for he tells me he is of your party, and a close friend to the gentleman you spoke of,—he that is in peril from these sour old Puritan rulers!'" (   ).

s. "'Hester Prynne,' cried he, with a piercing earnestness, 'in the name of Him, so terrible and so merciful, who gives me grace, at this last moment, to do what—for my own heavy sin and miserable agony—I withheld myself from doing seven years ago, come hither now, and twine thy strength about me! [. . .]'" (   ).

t. "Here had been her sin; here, her sorrow; and here was yet to be her penitence. She had returned, therefore, and resumed,—of her own free will, for not the sternest magistrate of that iron period would have imposed it,—resumed the symbol of which we have related so dark a tale. Never afterwards did it quit her bosom [. . .]" (   ).

9. **Recap** *Summarize what has happened throughout the novel.*

FOLLOW-UP QUESTIONS

50 SHORT QUESTIONS

Select the <u>best</u> answer for each.

____ 1. Imprisoned at the beginning
of the novel is
  a. Mistress Hibbins.
  b. Roger Chillingworth.
  c. Hester Prynne.

____ 2. Next to the prison door is a
  a. stand of oak trees.
  b. stand of pine trees.
  c. rosebush.

____ 3. The name of this Puritan
colony is
  a. Salem.
  b. Boston.
  c. Utopia.

____ 4. The prisoner's crime is
  a. adultery.
  b. witchcraft.
  c. murder.

____ 5. Standing on the scaffold, Hester Prynne holds
  a. a Bible.
  b. a baby.
  c. a sword.

____ 6. On the scaffold, Hester
Prynne
  a. begs for mercy.
  b. cries to be let down.
  c. recalls her earlier life.

____ 7. From the scaffold, Hester
recognizes
  a. her husband.
  b. no one.
  c. the Black Man.

____ 8. The punishment includes
  a. wearing the red letter A
  and standing on the
  scaffold.
  b. wearing the red letter A
  and a public whipping.
  c. wearing the red letter A
  and naming the baby's
  father.

____ 9. The stranger at the edge of
the crowd
  a. is handsome and
  well-built.
  b. is the baby's father.
  c. pretends not to know
  Hester Prynne.

____ 10. Hester Prynne does not
receive the death penalty
because
  a. her husband is missing
  and presumed dead.
  b. the ministers can not
  agree on the penalty.
  c. she reveals the name of
  the baby's father.

____ 11. Arthur Dimmesdale is
  a. young and deformed.
  b. old and feeble.
  c. young and handsome.

____ 12. Hester Prynne is a member of
the church led by
  a. Governor Winthrop.
  b. Arthur Dimmesdale.
  c. John Wilson.

____ 13. Roger Chillingworth is
  a. the baby's father.
  b. Hester's husband.
  c. a Puritan magistrate.

____ 14. At their meeting in the jail, Roger asks Hester
a. to reveal his identity.
b. to return to England with him.
c. the name of the baby's father.

____ 15. The new physician in town is
a. Roger Chillingworth.
b. Master Brackett.
c. John Wilson.

____ 16. In the crowd, the matrons
a. sympathize with Hester Prynne.
b. call for harsher punishment.
c. say nothing at all.

____ 17. Hester Prynne makes a living by
a. nursing the sick.
b. collecting plants and roots.
c. sewing and embroidery.

____ 18. Hester does not leave the colony because
a. she loves the baby's father.
b. her punishment forbids it.
c. she does not have enough money.

____ 19. After her release from prison, Hester lives
a. within the town of Boston.
b. on the outskirts of Boston.
c. with Roger Chillingworth.

____ 20. Pearl is
a. quiet and obedient.
b. a model Puritan child.
c. impulsive and wilful.

____ 21. Hester embroiders all manner of Puritan garments except
a. baby linens.
b. funeral clothing.
c. bridal veils.

____ 22. Governor Bellingham wants
a. to take Pearl away from Hester.
b. Hester to leave the colony.
c. Pearl to wear a scarlet letter like her mother.

____ 23. The governor's mansion is
a. bare and gloomy.
b. full of rare and poisonous plants.
c. decorated with portraits and armor.

____ 24. When Reverend John Wilson asks Pearl who her maker is, she answers
a. that Hester and Arthur Dimmesdale made her.
b. that God made her.
c. that she was plucked from a rose-bush.

____ 25. At the governor's mansion, Arthur Dimmesdale
a. argues that Hester should be allowed to keep Pearl.
b. agrees that Hester has no control over Pearl.
c. suggests that Pearl be dressed more somberly.

____ 26. The leech in the tale is
a. Mistress Hibbins.
b. Roger Chillingworth.
c. Pearl.

____ 27. Roger Chillingworth
a. is old and handsome.
b. is old and deformed.
c. is young and handsome.

____ 28. Hester Prynne promises
Roger Chillingworth
   a. that she will keep his
      secret.
   b. to reveal the name of her
      husband.
   c. to reveal the name of the
      baby's father to the
      magistrates.

____ 29. With the passage of time,
Roger Chillingworth's face
grows
   a. more handsome.
   b. more pale.
   c. more ugly.

____ 30. Roger Chillingworth moves
into the same house as
   a. Arthur Dimmesdale.
   b. John Wilson.
   c. Hester Prynne.

____ 31. Arthur Dimmesdale's health
over time
   a. stays the same.
   b. improves.
   c. deteriorates.

____ 32. What gesture does Arthur
Dimmesdale make through-
out the story?
   a. He raises his eyes to
      heaven.
   b. He puts his hand over his
      heart.
   c. He strokes his chin.

____ 33. While Arthur Dimmesdale is
asleep one day, Roger Chillingworth looks inside
   a. Arthur's books.
   b. Arthur's closet.
   c. Arthur's shirt.

____ 34. Roger Chillingworth becomes
obsessed with
   a. medicine.
   b. revenge.
   c. religion.

____ 35. Mistress Hibbins is the sister
of
   a. Arthur Dimmesdale.
   b. Governor Bellingham.
   c. Master Brackett.

____ 36. Eventually executed for witchcraft is
   a. John Wilson.
   b. Roger Chillingworth.
   c. Mistress Hibbins.

____ 37. Roger Chillingworth eventually finds out
   a. the name of Hester's
      husband.
   b. the name of Pearl's father.
   c. the names of those who
      dance in the woods with
      the devil.

____ 38. Hester confronts Roger
Chillingworth about Arthur
Dimmesdale's condition
   a. in the forest.
   b. on the beach.
   c. in the prison.

____ 39. The love and admiration of
the church members makes
Arthur feel
   a. proud and happy.
   b. wise and experienced.
   c. guilty and ashamed.

____ 40. Arthur finds out that Roger
Chillingworth has been Hester's husband because
   a. Hester tells him.
   b. Chillingworth tells him.
   c. Mistress Hibbins tells
      him.

____ 41. By the brook with Arthur,
Hester removes
   a. her shoes.
   b. her cap.
   c. Arthur's hand from his
      heart.

____ 42. When Pearl first sees her
mother without the scarlet
letter, she
a. runs to hug her mother.
b. will not cross the brook.
c. kisses Arthur Dimmesdale.

____ 43. Hester and Arthur's plans are
ruined by
a. Roger Chillingworth.
b. Mistress Hibbins.
c. Pearl.

____ 44. After the Election Day sermon, Arthur Dimmesdale
a. leaves town with Hester
and Pearl.
b. goes home with Roger
Chillingworth.
c. acknowledges Pearl as his
daughter.

____ 45. Arthur Dimmesdale dies
a. on the scaffold.
b. at the pulpit.
c. in the Old World.

____ 46. Hester and Pearl
a. return to England.
b. live with Roger
Chillingworth until
he dies.
c. stay in seclusion on the
peninsula.

____ 47. At the end of the story, Roger
Chillingworth leaves his
money to
a. Arthur Dimmesdale.
b. Pearl.
c. the Puritan Church.

____ 48. According to the narrator,
the greatest sin committed
by the characters is
a. adultery.
b. witchcraft.
c. violation of a human
heart.

____ 49. The story takes place in the
a. sixteenth century.
b. seventeenth century.
c. eighteenth century.

____ 50. Hawthorne completed The
Scarlet Letter in
a. 1650.
b. 1850.
c. 1950.

20 SIGNIFICANT QUOTATIONS

Explain the importance of each of these quotations.

1. "But, on one side of the portal, and rooted almost at the threshold, was a
wild rose-bush, covered, in this month of June, with its delicate gems,
which might be imagined to offer their fragrance and fragile beauty to the
prisoner as he went in, and to the condemned criminal as he came forth to
his doom, in token that the deep heart of Nature could pity and be kind
to him."

2. "'At the very least, they should have put the brand of a hot iron on Hester
Prynne's forehead. Madam Hester would have winced at that, I warrant me.
But she,—the naughty baggage,—little will she care what they put upon

the bodice of her gown! Why, look you, she may cover it with a brooch, or such like heathenish adornment, and so walk the streets as brave as ever!'"

3. "[A]t the first instant of perceiving that thin visage, and the slight deformity of the figure, she pressed her infant to her bosom, with so convulsive a force that the poor babe uttered another cry of pain [. . .]."

4. "'She will not speak!' murmured Mr. Dimmesdale, who, leaning over the balcony, with his hand upon his heart, had awaited the result of his appeal. He now drew back, with a long respiration. 'Wondrous strength and generosity of a woman's heart! She will not speak!'"

5. "'I have thought of death,' she said,—'have wished for it,—would even have prayed for it, were it fit that such as I should pray for any thing. Yet, if death be in this cup, I bid thee think again, ere thou beholdest me quaff it. See! It is even now at my lips.'"

6. "She possessed an art that sufficed, even in a land that afforded comparatively little scope for its exercise, to supply food for her thriving infant and herself. It was the art—then, as now, almost the only one within a woman's grasp—of needlework [. . .]."

7. "'Woman, it is thy badge of shame!' replied the stern magistrate. 'It is because of the stain which that letter indicates, that we would transfer thy child to other hands.'"

8. "'Speak thou for me!' cried she. 'Thou wast my pastor, and hadst charge of my soul, and knowest me better than these men can. I will not lose the child! [. . .].'"

9. "'Therefore it is good for this poor, sinful woman that she hath an infant immortality, a being capable of eternal joy or sorrow, confided to her care,— to be trained up by her to righteousness,—to remind her, at every moment, of her fall,—but yet to teach her, as it were by the Creator's sacred pledge, that, if she bring the child to heaven, the child will also bring its parent thither! Herein is the sinful mother happier than the sinful father [. . .].'"

10. "'Make my excuse to him, so please you!' answered Hester, with a triumphant smile. 'I must tarry at home, and keep watch over my little Pearl. Had they taken her from me, I would willingly have gone with thee into the forest, and signed my name in the Black Man's book too, and that with mine own blood!'"

11. "Few secrets can escape an investigator, who has opportunity and license to undertake such a quest, and skill to follow it up. A man burdened with a secret should especially avoid the intimacy of his physician [. . .]."

12. "[. . .] 'Come away, mother! Come away, or yonder old Black Man will catch you! He hath got hold of the minister already. Come away, mother, or he will catch you! But he cannot catch little Pearl!'"

13. "Calm, gentle, passionless, as he appeared, there was yet, we fear, a quiet depth of malice, hitherto latent, but active now, in this unfortunate old man, which led him to imagine a more intimate revenge than any mortal had ever wreaked upon an enemy [. . .]."

14. "It is inconceivable, the agony with which this public veneration tortured him! It was his genuine impulse to adore the truth [. . .]."
15. "'Come up hither, Hester, you and little Pearl,' said the Reverend Mr. Dimmesdale. 'Ye have both been here before, but I was not with you. Come up hither once again, and we will stand all three together!'"
16. "'Let us not look back,' answered Hester Prynne. 'The past is gone! Wherefore should we linger upon it now? See! With this symbol, I undo it all, and make it as it had never been!'"
17. "'Do not blacken your fame, and perish in dishonor! I can yet save you! Would you bring infamy on your sacred profession?'"
18. "Pearl kissed his lips. A spell was broken [. . .]."
19. "[. . .] 'Be true! Be true! Be true! Show freely to the world, if not your worst, yet some trait whereby the worst may be inferred!'"
20. "And, as Hester Prynne had no selfish ends, nor lived in any measure for her own profit and enjoyment, people brought all their sorrows and perplexities, and besought her counsel, as one who had herself gone through a mighty trouble [. . .]."

2 COMPREHENSION ESSAY QUESTIONS

Use specific details and information from the novel to answer these questions as completely as possible.

1. Hester Prynne has been on the scaffold three times in the story. What happens in each scaffold scene and why are these events important to the story?
2. How does Arthur Dimmesdale reveal his secret? Does he triumph over evil in the end? Explain using specific examples and information from the story.

DISCUSSION QUESTIONS

Be prepared to discuss these questions in class.

1. Are you surprised at the ending of the tale? Could Arthur Dimmesdale have been happy elsewhere? How do you think Hester feels?
2. What do you think happens to Pearl? Why does Hester return to Boston?

WRITING

Use each of these ideas to write an essay.

1. Is Roger Chillingworth truly evil? Do Arthur Dimmesdale's final actions save Roger from his sins?
2. We know that Hester receives mail from Pearl in Europe. Pretend that you are Pearl and write a letter to Hester telling her what you have been doing since she returned to Boston.

3. Hawthorne added "The Custom-House" to The Scarlet Letter to lighten what he thought was a dark and somber tale. "The Custom-House" was very well received, at the time, for its humorous and political insights. Read "The Custom-House" and discuss the autobiographical, political, and humorous aspects of the essay.

4. We can see that the Puritans in The Scarlet Letter consider themselves to be very religious people. Do you consider yourself a religious person? Why or why not?

5. The Puritans, though somber and stern, attend several public ceremonies in the novel. We often attend or participate in public ceremonies like weddings, graduations, funerals, inaugurations, and so on. Describe a public ceremony that you once attended. What was your role?

FURTHER WRITING

1. The Scarlet Letter was first published in 1850. Research the political, economic, social, and literary trends or events of that time period. Were Hawthorne's themes relevant to his time?

2. In his obsessive pursuit of revenge, Roger Chillingworth psychologically tortures Arthur Dimmesdale, weakening him with guilt and fear while keeping him alive with medicine. Is torture ever justified? Research contemporary attitudes toward and current uses of torture.

3. After Hester is released from prison, she hides her hair beneath a cap and represses her femininity. In many cultures, women hide their hair beneath a veil or hat. Research a culture in which women cover their hair or are restricted in clothing styles by religious or societal rules. Explain the roles of women in that society.

4. Read two of the following Hawthorne short stories, and write a paper in which you discuss recurring images or themes similar to those in The Scarlet Letter: "The Minister's Black Veil," "The Birthmark," "Young Goodman Brown," "Ethan Brand," and "My Kinsman, Major Molineux."

5. Nathaniel Hawthorne briefly joined the Transcendentalist utopian community, Brook Farm. Research utopian communities of the nineteenth and twentieth centuries in the United States, such as Brook Farm, the Shaker communities, and the Oneida Community. What were their ideals? What challenges did they face?

6. Nathaniel Hawthorne added a "w" to his name to distance himself from his harsh Puritan ancestors, particularly Judge John Hathorne, who sentenced many people to death during the Salem witchcraft trials of 1692. Research the Salem witchcraft trials and explain why Nathaniel Hawthorne felt as he did. Is The Scarlet Letter an accurate portrayal of the Puritan colony?

7. Hawthorne was friends with Ralph Waldo Emerson and Henry David Thoreau and lived near them in Concord for many years. Read some of their nature journals and discuss their Transcendentalist beliefs about nature and humanity's purpose on earth.

8. The Puritans used civil laws to reinforce religious behavior within the colony. Who should decide what the rules are in society? Who should determine the level of separation between church and state? Consider such issues as religion and science, religion and business, prayer in school and at sports events, and/or other relevant examples.

GLOSSARY OF PREFIXES
AND SUFFIXES

Some words in the **Pre-Reading Vocabulary—Structural Attack** are simple words that have been combined or have extra syllables, which make these words look strange or difficult. When you take these words apart, they are usually quite simple to define.

When two or more words are combined to form a new word, the new word is called a **compound word**. By combining the meaning of each of the words, you can define the new word. Look at the word *everyday*. Here, two simple words— *every* and *day*—combine to mean "all the time." Look at the word *worn-whiskered*. *Worn* means "tired" or "old," and *whiskered* implies "old man" or "mature man." Thus, *worn-whiskered* is a word used to describe an old man.

Another way to build a new word is to add a prefix or suffix to a **root** word, or a core word. A **prefix** is a syllable added to the front of the root word that often changes the meaning of the word. A **suffix** is a syllable added to the end of the root word that may alter the use or the meaning of the word. Prefixes and suffixes are called **affixes**. As you define the words in the Pre-reading Vocabulary— Structural Attack exercises, look for and define the root word, and then define the affixes added onto the root word.

For instance, look at the word *provider*. *Provide* is the root word and is a verb that means "to supply." The suffix *-er* at the end means "one who." Thus, the verb *provide* becomes a person, and the noun *provider* means "a person who supplies something." Now, look at the word *nonprovider*. The prefix *non-* at the beginning means "not" and greatly changes the meaning of the word. *Nonprovider* means "a person who does *not* supply something."

To define the words in **Pre-Reading Vocabulary—Structural Attack**, you need to know the prefixes and suffixes that are listed in Tables G–1 and G–2. Prefixes are defined and are listed in alphabetical order. Suffixes are arranged alphabetically in definition groups. Use the lists to help you in defining these words.

Prefixes

A **prefix** is added to the beginning of a root word. A prefix usually changes the meaning of the root word. *Be especially aware of prefixes because they can greatly change the meaning of a word.* Note that some prefixes have more than one meaning and these meanings may be different.

TABLE G–1
Prefixes

Prefix	Meaning	Application
a-	full of	*Acrawl* means "creeping or spreading everywhere." The town was *acrawl* with gossip when people learned the mayor was arrested.
a-	total absence	*Amoral* means "totally unable to tell right from wrong." When a shark kills, it is *amoral* because a shark does not know right from wrong.
be-	full of	*Belov*ed means "very much loved." The solider dearly missed his *beloved* wife.
counter-	against	*Counterplot* means "a plan to work against another plan." The police developed a *counterplot* to ruin the criminals' robbery plan.
de-	against, wrong	*Deform* means "badly or wrongly formed." The fire *deformed* the house and left it twisted and falling down.
de-	out of	*Deplane* means "to get off the airplane." The team claimed their luggage after they *deplaned.*
dis-	not, against	*Distrust* means "not to trust." Fatima felt *distrust* toward the salesman who lied to her.
en-	within, into	*Encircle* means "to place in the middle" or "to surround." The floodwaters *encircled* the house.
il-	not	*Illegal* means "not legal." Many laws state that stealing is *illegal* and will put you in jail.
il-	more so	*Illuminate* means "to light up brightly." The fireworks *illuminated* the night sky so brightly that it looked like daylight.
im-	not	*Immeasurable* means "not able to be measured." The joy Teddy felt when he won the championship was *immeasurable.*
im-	more so	*Impoverished* means "very poor." The *impoverished* family did not even have enough money for food.
in-	not	*Incurable* means "not able to be healed." Doug caught an *incurable* disease, which he will have for the rest of his life.
in-	in, into	*Inside* means "to go in the side" or "to enter through the side." Michelle walked through the door to get *inside* the room.
inter-	between, among	*Intercollegiate* means "between two or more colleges." Michigan defeated Alabama in *intercollegiate* football.
kin-	relative	*Kinfolk* means "the people you are related to or your family." All my *kinfolk* will gather together at Thanksgiving for a family reunion.

non-	not	*Nonaccompanied* means "no company or alone." Will preferred to attend the party alone, *nonaccompanied* by others.
pre-	before	*Predictable* means "able to tell beforehand." Tom's speeding ticket was *predictable* because he always drives too fast.
re-	again	*Refamiliarize* means "become familiar with again." To pass the test, Sue will *refamiliarize* herself with her notes.
self-	alone, one's own	*Self-satisfied* means "satisfied with oneself." After passing the test, Robert felt good about himself and was quite *self-satisfied*.
semi-	half	*Semiconscious* means "only half or partly aware." With all the noise at the concert, Rich was only *semiconscious* of the sirens outside.
sub-	under	*Subway* means "a road that goes underground." When there is too much traffic on the city roads, it is easier to take the *subway*.
super-	larger, above	*Superman* means "a man larger or better than other men." Bravely running into a burning building to help others is the act of a *superman*.
trans-	across	*Transoceanic* means "across the ocean." Steve will catch a *transoceanic* flight from New York to Paris.
un-	not	*Unperceived* means "not noticed." Geri usually notices everything, but this time the dirty room went *unperceived*.
under-	below	*Underbrush* means "low bushes and shrubs that grow under the trees." Tony decided to weed out the *underbrush* that was growing under his garden plants.

Suffixes

A **suffix** is added to the end of a root word. A suffix may have very little effect on the meaning of a word, but a suffix will often change the part of speech of a root word.

What is the part of speech of a word? The part of speech of a word is, very simply, the function or use of the word. For instance, look at the word *ski*. In the sentence "Sue's *ski* was damaged," *ski* is a noun—the thing Sue had that was damaged. In "Sue and Bill *ski* downhill," *ski* is a verb—the action Sue and Bill do. In "Sue took *ski* lessons," *ski* is an adjective that describes the kind of lessons that Sue took. The word *ski* remains the same three letters, but the function it serves and the information it communicates change slightly depending on the part of speech it demonstrates. Note that although the use changes—from thing to action to description—the basic idea of a downhill sport remains the same.

In the same way, a suffix may often change the part of speech of a root word while leaving the root word's basic meaning largely unchanged. For instance, if we add *-ed* to the noun and say, "Sue *skied* down the hill," the noun becomes a verb, and the action is in the past. Thus, Sue is still involved with skiing, but now she has done it in the past.

In Table G–2, suffixes you will need to know are listed alphabetically within definition groups and with the relevant parts of speech noted. You will see several words from Pre-Reading Vocabulary—Structural Attack.

TABLE G–2
Suffixes

Suffix	Application

The following suffixes mean "one who" or "that which." Each turns a root word into a noun because the root word becomes the person or the thing that does something.

-ant	A *servant* is "one who serves." The *servants* cleaned the mansion before the guests arrived.
-ary	A *visionary* is "one who sees clearly or into the future." Einstein was a *visionary* and saw the future uses of nuclear energy.
-ee	A *payee* is "one to whom things are paid." When Dodee owed her brother money, she wrote a check to him and made him the *payee*.
-ent	A *student* is "one who studies." College students are usually serious about their studies and work for good grades.
-er	A *fancier* is "one who fancies or likes something." Jen is a proven cat *fancier* and currently has four cats that she loves living in her home.
-ess	A *princess* is "a female who acts like a prince." The *princess* sat on the throne next to her husband, the prince.
-folk	*Townsfolk* are "people of the town." The *Townsfolk* held a general meeting so that they could all welcome the new mayor.
-ian	A *musician* is "one who plays music." Jessica hired several *musicians* so that people would be able to dance at her party.
-ist	A *futurist* is "one who predicts the future on the basis of current trends." *Futurists* advise those in the government in Washington about issues on which they may someday need to enact laws.
-man	A *horseman* is "a person who is skilled at riding and driving horses." Dave is a fine *horseman* who often rides his horse around the park.
-or	A *survivor* is "one who survives or lasts." Rich lasted the longest on the deserted island and was named the *survivor*.

The following suffixes make a root word an adjective, and each changes the meaning of the root word.

-able   *Distinguishable* means "able to tell apart or distinguish." The greasy spots
             made the dirty clothes *distinguishable* from the clean clothes.

-er   *Lovelier* means, by comparison, "more lovely than another."
             Carmen's garden, filled with blooms, is *lovelier* than Margaret's weed patch.

-est   *Kindliest* means, by comparison, "the most kind of all." The mother's
             gentle pat was the *kindliest* touch of all.

-ful   *Frightful* means "full of fright or awful." With all its costumes and noisy
             bell-ringing, Halloween is a *frightful* night.

-less   *Hapless* means "without happiness or luck" or "unfortunate." The *hapless*
             student had two flat tires and got a headache on his way to school.

-most   *Uppermost* means "most high" or "important." With a record of no
             accidents for two years, safety is the company's *uppermost* concern.

-ous   *Nervous* means "full of nerves" or "tense." Kirk was so *nervous* before his
             test that his hands were shaking.

The following suffixes mean "related to," "like," or "having the quality of" and generally change the meaning of a root word very little. Mostly, they change the parts of speech of the root word.

-al   The noun *cone* means "a form that comes to a circular point" and becomes
             the adjective *conical*. The tip of the space shuttle is rounded and *conical*.

-ance   The verb *repent* means "to feel sorry about" and becomes the noun
             repentance. After he broke his Mom's favorite vase, John felt awful and was
             filled with *repentance*.

-ant   The verb *observe* means "to see" and becomes the adjective *observant*.
             Lydia watches everything closely and is very *observant*.

-ed   The noun *candy* means "something sweet" and becomes the adjective
             candied. Mom used lots of sugar to sweetly coat the *candied* apples.

-ed   The noun *ink* means "writing fluid" and becomes the past-tense verb
             inked. Jefferson took pen and *inked* his signature on the declaration
             he wrote.

-en   The verb *choose* means "select" and becomes the adjective *chosen*.
             He had joined the Marines and became one of the *chosen* few.

-ence   The verb *depend* means "to rely on" and becomes the noun *dependence*.
             When Jill paid her own bills, she knew her *dependence* on her parents
             would end.

-ic   The noun *metal* means "shiny element" and becomes the adjective *metallic*.
             Laura's silvery dress had a *metallic* shine.

-ing   The verb *terrify* means "to scare" and becomes the adjective *terrifying*.
             The *terrifying* thunder scared all of us as it seemed to shake the
             whole house.

(Continued)

TABLE G–2   Continued

Suffix	Application
-ish	The noun *fever* means "internal heat" and becomes the adjective *feverish*. Joel felt *feverish* from the heat of his sunburn.
-ism	The adjective *ideal* means "perfect" and becomes the noun *idealism*, which means "belief in perfection." George's *idealism* often leaves him disappointed because things are not always perfect.
-ity	The adjective *stupid* means "unthinking" and becomes the noun *stupidity*. Alice could not believe her *stupidity* when she locked her keys in the car.
-ive	The noun *feast* means "cheerful meal" and becomes the adjective *festive*. The wedding, with all its foods and colorful flowers, was a most *festive* affair.
-ly, -ily	The adjective *stealthy* means "moving quietly" and becomes the adverb *stealthily*. Ken crept so *stealthily* in the back door that no one knew he had entered the house.
-ment	The verb *confine* means "to restrain" and becomes the noun *confinement*. When the children misbehaved, Dad sent them to their rooms for silent *confinement*.
-ness	The adjective *nervous* means "tense" and becomes the noun *nervousness*. It was very hard for the groom to overcome his *nervousness* on his wedding day.
-tation	The adjective *ornamental* means "decorated" and becomes the noun *ornamentation*. Her diamond rings and pearl necklaces created *ornamentation* fit for a queen.
-ty	The adjective *frail* means "delicate" and becomes the noun *frailty*. At Aunt Alice's ninetieth birthday, we were all concerned about her *frailty*.
-y	The noun *stone* means "hard item" and becomes the adjective *stony*. The policeman had a *stony* look when the boy who was driving did not have a license.

Yvonne Collioud Sisko

INDEX